Janet Gleeson was born in Sri Lanka, where her father was a tea planter. After taking a degree in History of Art and English she worked for Sotheby's, and later Bonham's Auctioneers. In 1991 she joined Reed Books, where she was responsible for devising and writing *Miller's Antiques and Collectibles*. She is the bestselling author of two works of non-fiction, *The Arcanum* and *The Moneymaker*, and three novels, *The Grenadillo Box*, *The Serpent in the Garden* and *The Thief-Taker*.

*Also by Janet Gleeson*

*Fiction*
THE GRENADILLO BOX
THE THIEF-TAKER

*Non-fiction*
THE ARCANUM
THE MONEYMAKER

# THE SERPENT
# IN THE GARDEN

## Janet Gleeson

**BANTAM BOOKS**

LONDON • TORONTO • SYDNEY • AUCKLAND • JOHANNESBURG

THE SERPENT IN THE GARDEN
A BANTAM BOOK: 0 553 81524 5

Originally published in Great Britain by Bantam Press,
a division of Transworld Publishers

PRINTING HISTORY
Bantam Press edition published 2003
Bantam edition published 2004

1 3 5 7 9 10 8 6 4 2

Set in 11/13pt Goudy by
Falcon Oast Graphic Art Ltd.

Bantam Books are published by Transworld Publishers,
61–63 Uxbridge Road, London W5 5SA,
a division of The Random House Group Ltd,
in Australia by Random House Australia (Pty) Ltd,
20 Alfred Street, Milsons Point, Sydney, NSW 2061, Australia,
in New Zealand by Random House New Zealand Ltd,
18 Poland Road, Glenfield, Auckland 10, New Zealand
and in South Africa by Random House (Pty) Ltd,
Endulini, 5a Jubilee Road, Parktown 2193, South Africa.

Printed and bound in Great Britain by
Cox & Wyman Ltd, Reading, Berkshire.

Papers used by Transworld Publishers are natural, recyclable products
made from wood grown in sustainable forests. The manufacturing
processes conform to the environmental regulations of the
country of origin.

*To Sarah, George and Olivia from your godmother with love*

# Author's Note

Pineapples have long fascinated British gardeners. According to John Evelyn the first pineapple seen in this country was given to Oliver Cromwell in 1657. Among the earliest gardens where pineapples were successfully grown was Matthew Decker's at Richmond. The eighteenth-century fascination with growing pineapples is documented in many publications including A *general Treatise of Husbandry and Gardening* by Richard Bradley, which was published in 1721, and *Ananas: or, a Treatise on the Pine-apple* by John Giles (1767). Many of these publications include designs for pineapple frames or pits as well as tips on heating. Pineapples were widely grown in Britain by the middle of the century. The gardens at Heligan, Cornwall, include an eighteenth-century pineapple pit which, since the restorations, is once again in production. By the middle of the century extravagant pinerys containing a hundred plants or more were not unusual.

Apart from eighteenth-century accounts detailed above I am indebted to *Charleston Kedding, A History of Kitchen Gardening* by Susan Campbell (1996); *The Lost Gardens of Heligan* by Tim Smit (1997); and *Early Nurserymen* by John Harvey (1974). The role played in this story by Capability Brown is entirely fictitious but his career and lively character is well described in *Capability Brown and the Late 18th Century Landscape* by Roger Turner (1985).

Joshua Pope is a fictitious character but his working techniques and practices are those of portraitists of the age, which are well documented. I am grateful to Rica Jones from the restoration department at the Tate Gallery, London, for her help in my research into this subject. I have also relied upon *The Portrait in Britain and America*, Robin Simon (1987), *Paint and Purpose*, ed. Stephen Hackney *et al* (1999); *George Romney*, Alex Kidson (2002); *The Artist's Craft*, James Ayres (1985); and *The Art of Thomas Gainsborough*, Michael Rosenthal (1999).

Finally, special thanks are due to my agent Christopher Little; to Sally Gaminara, Patrick Janson-Smith, Simon Taylor and Simon Thorogood at Transworld for their encouragement, criticism and support; and my family Paul, Lucy, Annabel and James for their forbearance when the fridge was empty and supper late.

# Chapter One

Joshua Pope was not expecting a visitor to call. It was an October evening in the year 1786, and, as was his habit when circumstances permitted, he intended to pass the evening at his easel. He had donned his morocco slippers and Indian nightgown, and taken a light supper – a slab of cold pie and a bottle of claret – to his parlour in St Peter's Court.

Outside, an autumn tempest had got up. A keen east wind howled through St Martin's Lane and the surrounding alleys and streets. Rain flailed roofs with such insistence as to drown the cries of streetwalkers, scavengers and watchmen in this vicinity of London. The wind creaked the signboards on Slaughter's Coffee House, the Coach and Horses Inn and the gilded showrooms of cabinetmakers Thomas Chippendale. No respector of status, the tempest picked debris from the gutter and tossed it ferociously against the windows of the house once occupied by the eminent painter Francis Hayman; it dislodged slates from the roofs of the great architect James Paine and the great tenor John Beard, as easily as those on a hovel. It penetrated to the very fabric of Joshua Pope's rooms, rattling doors and panes, guttering candles, blowing his papers about.

Thanking God for the comforts of a good supper and a plentiful supply of fuel, Joshua Pope rubbed his hands together contentedly, threw another log on the fire and sat, with feet outstretched to the flames, to consume his repast. Half an hour later, feeling as lively as a bubble in a glass of champagne, he loosened the silk sash about his girth and strode to the back of the parlour, where he threw open the double doors that led to his painting room. Utterly satisfied at the prospect of passing a few uninterrupted nocturnal hours at what he enjoyed best, he put on his smock, selected a hog's-hair brush and three medium-sized sable brushes from a pot and picked up his palette, upon which paint had already been charged. He turned to his canvas – a delightful composition, undoubtedly one of his best (but he always told himself this) – and smiled contentedly. He was about to embark upon the sweetening – the final stages of painting when highlights and deepened shadows bring the composition to life. The prospect was enjoyable and he painted with a passion, filling in the background with broad sweeps, pencilling detail, scratching, hatching, rubbing in oil, until he had achieved the desired effect.

He was still at his easel at about eleven o'clock, when above the gale he heard the sound of tapping at his parlour door. 'Who's there?' he cried, dropping his sable brush in surprise. He had thought he was alone. He was expecting no one. As far as he knew, his household were abed. How, then, had a stranger gained entry and come to his painting-room door?

A clear female voice replied. 'I come in search of Mr Joshua Pope, the renowned painter of portraits. I believe you are that gentleman.'

Joshua was both irked and intrigued by this announcement. If she wished to commission a portrait, could she not make an appointment like anyone else? If viewing his work was what she desired, she should visit on a Sunday and join the mob that, knowing of his fashionable status, arrived every week to gawp and pass nonsensical comment upon his latest masterpiece. And what other reason could there be for a stranger to call on him?

But then he couldn't help wondering how she had got here

10

and why she had come at this time of night. Surely the matter must be grave to bring her out in such inclement weather. In any event, he could not leave an interloper to wander his house. He would have to attend to her.

With no premonition of danger, Joshua put down his palette, picked up a candlestick and went to the parlour door. His visitor stood in the gloom of the landing: a lady of medium build, dressed from head to toe in black. Her clothes though dull were of fine quality – kid gloves, skirts of sarcenet silk, cuffs of Brussels lace, all surmounted by a heavy velvet cloak. Being fastidious in his own dress, Joshua approved of fine costume, and his visitor's made him feel more kindly disposed towards her. He raised his candle to peer at her face. Light glanced on the very tip of her chin and nose, but he was able to discern little else. Her features were hidden from his scrutiny by the shadow cast by the hood of her cloak.

He waited for her to introduce herself, but when she said nothing the flicker of annoyance he had felt earlier now returned. 'I do not know how you have arrived here, and I am not in the habit of receiving unsolicited calls at this late hour. But since you are here, you may as well come in and tell me who you are and what you want,' Joshua said, gruffly signalling towards a chair positioned by a candelabrum in which half a dozen candles burned.

But the caller wanted none of it. She would not approach the light. She stood on the threshold, clutching her cloak as if Joshua might wrench it from her. Her eyes flitted about with the speed of a butterfly, scanning the walls as if she were looking for something she hoped would be there, or had heard of this room many times before, and wished to reassure herself of the accuracy of every detail. Then, without so much as a by-your-leave, she walked through the parlour to the easel in the painting room and examined the work upon it. But although the portrait was one of which Joshua was exceedingly proud, her face signalled disappointment. She uttered no word of praise; nor did she offer any opinion.

Riled by her reticence and what he deemed a complacent air, Joshua's temper — usually mild — wore thin. He was accustomed to compliments upon the excellence of his work. If his eminent contemporaries Sir Joshua Reynolds and Thomas Gainsborough could discern the merit in his brush-strokes, the subtlety in the gradation of tone, the deftness of his detail, why did she not show admiration? He did his best to suppress his disappointment, addressing her with the utmost correctness, but the speed with which he spoke belied his frustration. 'Forgive me for not knowing whom I have the honour of receiving. May I repeat my earlier request. Perhaps, madam, you would be kind enough to make yourself known and explain your purpose.'

She seemed to flinch a little at his directness. 'I have heard you are a portrait painter of distinction,' she ventured. 'You have painted several of my acquaintances.' Here she mentioned two or three names, some he dimly remembered from a decade or more ago. 'I was curious to see your work — perhaps with a view to a commission — and to discover a little about the profession. I should like to see more. Tell me, what talent is needed to be a successful painter of faces? Do you observe more clearly than others? Are you more sensitive to character or better at perceiving what is true and what is sham?'

Joshua was an adept when it came to recognizing dis-simulation. He often said that a portraitist's skill lay as much in reading faces as representing them. The lameness of her excuse was thus immediately apparent and, since the hour was late, he saw no reason to play along with her. 'Why, madam,' he said, 'this is scarcely the hour for an exhibition. As to the second part of your question, the painter of faces doesn't see more clearly than any other man — or woman, for that matter. Far from it. To become successful, as some say I have, the portrait painter must be expert at telling untruths. And now, forgive me, madam. I don't know by whose leave you have ventured here at this time of night, but since you refuse to intro-duce yourself or reveal your purpose I must ask you to depart.'

She gave a mirthless laugh and threw down her hood to reveal her face. 'That is a fine way to treat a visitor. There, does this satisfy you?' she said.

He saw now that she was a woman in her middle years, somewhat younger than he was. Her hair was streaked with grey and elegantly coiffed in a ringlet coiled over one shoulder. From an artist's perspective her countenance had many of the elements that constitute perfection. Her face was oval, her lips were full, her nose small and straight, her eyes wide-set and almond-shaped in form. But the configuration was marred by a cross-hatching of lines on her skin, haggard cheeks, dark circles beneath her eyes, all of which bespoke years of tribulation. Undoubtedly her life had not been an easy one; she had suffered reversals of fortune. There was, too, a certain inflexibility in the set of her mouth and the unblinking stare of her eyes.

He peered harder at those eyes. Surely he remembered their unusual form. Was she familiar? Had he met her before? He was certain now that he had; yet he could not place her. He shook his head, fearing that if he strained himself his brain might start to throb, as it so often did these days. He had looked on so many faces it was little wonder that, at this time of night, with three glasses of claret inside him, his recollections became confused.

'So you believe a painter of faces should be a liar? Is that what you mean?' she pressed, laughing again in a sharper tone. 'Why, you must think me a fool to say so.'

'Far from it, madam. I meant it with all my heart,' he fairly barked at her. He was unaccustomed to being challenged, still less by a woman. Should he eject her now or wait to hear her out?

She recoiled, as if his harsh tone offended her. 'If that was so, every charlatan and trickster would be as famous as your namesake, Sir Joshua Reynolds, the President of the Royal Academy,' she murmured.

Joshua composed himself and managed to reply more

13

civilly. 'Ah, but there are other qualities required that most vagabonds do not possess. I term myself a "phizmonger" – a pedlar of faces – and do so with good reason.'

'What reason is that?'

'Why, to be a phizmonger one must mirror fact, read souls, not to mention master one's medium – oil or pastel or whatever one chooses. What I mean, dear lady, is that the painter of likenesses represents what he sees and yet does more. He encourages confidence, he is sympathetic, he interprets, softens. He shows his subjects what they are and what they would be.'

As Joshua spoke these words, the absurdity of the situation in which he found himself struck him. It was nearly midnight. How ridiculous to be conversing with an uninvited stranger who refused to give her name or state her business. No sooner had this thought occurred than the woman approached directly, settling her penetrating gaze upon him, as if she sought to plunge to the depths of his soul. Her eyes, caught in the candlelight, were bluish-grey, hard as gunmetal, yet swimming with an intensity that forced him to look away. As he did so he caught sight of the shadow thrown by her features on the wall. Her profile there had become monstrously distorted – a brooding gargoyle's silhouette of misshapen features and wild, wiry hair, a form such as a nightmare might conjure.

The feeling of mild irritation Joshua had experienced earlier now shifted to a less comfortable one. He blanched; a hollow sensation invaded the pit of his stomach; his mouth grew parched. He forced himself to meet the woman's eye. In her glare he now saw an almost tangible hunger, but for what he did not know. Dreadful thoughts flashed through his brain. What manner of person comes calling in the dead of night but one of evil intent? He had willingly let this unknown woman into his sanctum. He had enabled her to perpetrate any dreadful deed she chose.

Joshua shuddered and turned away to the window. Not a light showed. The sky was dense and starless, the storm within it audible yet invisible. Pressing his nails deep into the palms of his hands, he told himself he was foolish to have taken fright. What reason had he to fear a mere woman? Not even the woman herself, but merely her shadow. He had allowed himself to be alarmed by no more than a chimera.

Yet even as he did so a talon of pain gripped his temples. The truth was that something in that distorted profile brought to mind another shadow, one he had seen two decades ago, one that had nearly blighted his life, although until that moment he believed it forgotten. It was that memory more than the woman herself that had set trepidation coursing through his veins like a swig of brandy.

'And was "softening the truth" what you did when you painted the marriage portrait?' she said quietly.

There was something in her urgent tone that surprised Joshua. He turned slowly back and raised his eyes to hers. 'I am in my fifty-fourth year. I have been a painter for thirty of them and during that time painted many a marriage portrait. Of which one do you speak?' he asked, though he feared he already knew the answer.

'Herbert Bentnick's.' Her voice had dropped now to a mere whisper – so quiet that when at first she said this name Joshua hoped he might have misheard. But there was no mistake for she repeated it again, more defiantly. 'That is right: I said Herbert Bentnick.'

He had expected this, yet still her confirmation set his heart racing. His temples began to pound with such intensity he felt they might explode at any moment. He looked at her closer now. He must recognize her. Why else was she here? 'I know I should remember you. Perhaps you are a relative of that family. Is that why you have come?'

She said nothing. The hunger he had earlier observed seemed to soften, yet still she regarded him with an air of expectancy. But then, just as she seemed on the brink of answering, she wheeled wordlessly away.

Silence settled between them; a taut hush that seemed to

Joshua infinitely more unsettling than any demanding look or menacing gesture. He longed for her to break it; he craved a speech or tirade, something that would explain her intention no matter how dreadful it was.

But the only sounds were the creaks and sighs of the storm-buffeted building. Inside, silence, interminable silence, dragged on. Joshua stared at his visitor's immobile back, willing her to turn round. He wanted to shout out, 'Speak openly or for God's sake go now and leave me in peace!' But some instinct held him back and made him mute. He knew that unless he waited she would gain an advantage and he might never discover what had brought her.

At length, after what seemed an eternity had passed, she did turn back to address him. 'The reason I have come, Mr Pope, is to show you something.' She rummaged in the folds of her cloak.

Joshua started at the sudden movement. Was she about to extract a weapon and assault him? For safety's sake he edged towards the fire and positioned himself close to the poker. But his fears were groundless, for the article she took out was nothing more fearsome than a shagreen box.

Joshua watched with fascination as she opened it. Inside, couched in grey silk, gleamed an emerald necklace, one he had not seen for twenty years. The stones were just as he recalled them: a dozen or more, baguette-cut and set in gold links, with a single ruby at the centre. Flashes of verdigris, orpiment and Prussian blue sparkled in the candlelight. He felt sick to the heart to see it. The form of this necklace was as disturbing as ever. It had been the cause of more distress than he cared to recall. It had nearly cost him his life.

'I have come, Mr Pope, to offer this in return for your co-operation.'

Joshua did not regard himself as an avaricious man, yet in that instant he forgot his earlier unease and gasped at the offer. The jewel must be worth close on a thousand guineas –

more, perhaps. What could he tell her that made his information so valuable? Plainly his fears were unfounded; she did not intend to harm him after all. On the contrary, there was something she wanted. 'Does the jewel belong to you?' he said coolly.

'As you see, it is in my possession. I offer it to you as proof of my intimate involvement in these matters, as well as a generous form of payment.'

'That is not the same. How do I know you are entitled to the jewel? You might have stolen it. After all, it wouldn't be the first time it has been misappropriated.'

'I will prove to you I am no thief once you have told me what I wish to know.'

'What can I say to you that is so precious as to warrant a jewel of this calibre in payment?'

'I wish to hear your version of the events surrounding the painting of the portrait. What happened then has had a profound impact upon my life. Moreover, I want to know what became of the portrait. No one has seen it in the last twenty years.'

By now Joshua's earlier fear had dissipated to be eclipsed by curiosity. Believing the threat was all in his mind and he had nothing to fear, he spoke frankly. 'During the course of my career I have of necessity stayed in many homes, and unwittingly become involved with numerous surprising and strange adventures. Of all these the Bentnick affair is one that still troubles me the most to remember. I have never spoken of it to anyone, although I confess that often when I lie awake in my bed and hear the rain flogging at the window, or when I walk in a beautiful garden and pass a cascade or a hothouse or a grotto, I remember those sad and singular events.'

'Then you accept my proposal, Mr Pope?'

He pondered a while. 'Yes and no. I will not *tell* you what I know, for the tale is too long and involved and my memory is not good at this time of night. I will write you an objective account, allowing my imagination to furnish what my certain

17

knowledge does not. Return to my rooms one month from today and I will hand it to you.' He paused for a moment before adding: 'One more condition: I do not desire the necklace in payment. With all I know of its history, nothing on earth would induce me to take it.'

She scowled. 'What, then, do you require?'

'Merely to know who you are and how you came by the jewel and why you require this information.'

Her eyes half closed, her mouth contracted to a thin line. She stepped forward until she was no more than a couple of paces from Joshua. Displeasure emanated from every fibre of her being. He half expected her to scream or fly at him like some demented creature in the madhouse. And yet now that he knew the nature of her requirements, he had no difficulty in facing her.

Perhaps she realized this change, for she dropped her head, as if conceding to his will, and he fancied that, through the thin fabric of her dress, he saw her shoulders shake. 'Very well,' she said, in a voice so low he had to strain to hear it. 'If those are your terms, and you have not discovered the answer when I return, then I can do little but agree to them.'

Joshua bowed, maintaining a solemn expression. 'I shall expect you thirty days from this evening. Until then, madam, I bid you goodnight.'

With this, he ushered her down the stairs to his front door, where her carriage was waiting. He watched her step into the vehicle, which immediately sped away into the gloom. Joshua bolted the door, returned to his painting room and stood before his easel, thoughtfully stroking his chin. He had no more appetite for work. The visitor had disturbed his concentration; he couldn't bring himself to pick up a brush, let alone paint with it. He snuffed the candles and made his way to his bedchamber. But even there, with the rhythmic breath of his sleeping wife to soothe him, he found no peace. His mind was awhirl with reminiscence and he passed a fitful night.

# Chapter Two

It was late in May, in the year 1766, over a breakfast of ham in jelly, sponge cakes and tea, that Sabine Mercier told Joshua Pope she intended to go for a promenade in the gardens of Astley.

Sabine was a handsome woman in her middle years, lively of movement, yet serene of countenance. She had been married and widowed twice before her engagement to Herbert Bentnick, yet dual bereavement had not withered her. A bewitching woman, she was full of face, tawny of complexion, with rich-brown eyes, black arched brows, a small, flower-like mouth and hair so dark and glossy it might have been made from polished wood.

Sabine was to be one of the subjects of the Bentnick marriage portrait that Joshua had been commissioned to paint. In the interests of his art, therefore, Joshua observed her as she picked at a sponge cake while describing her excursion – the same one she took every day. He remarked how the very anticipation of the visit was enough to transform her eyes, and make them gleam bright and lustrous as a Bristol decanter. It intrigued Joshua that a face could be so altered by the thought of plants. Could any leaf or fruit merit such attention? A person might have the capacity to inspire or move a fellow being; even a painting of a person on occasion could arouse a certain sentiment, but a *plant*? Was there any such thing as what Sabine termed 'a plant of great significance'? But then, Joshua smiled condescendingly to himself, it was no surprise Sabine Mercier's tastes were a little particular. She had lived all her life until recently in the West Indies. In such a place she could have learned little of society and less of art. Plants were a substitute for civilization.

Sabine's abiding passion was for growing pineapples. The so-called pinery at Astley was largely her creation, although the structure itself had been built fifty years earlier by Herbert's grandfather, Horace Bentnick, who had been inspired by the nearby orangery at Ham, which was, he considered, the acme of such edifices. The Astley orangery, originally intended as a conservatory for growing pomegranates and myrtles as well as oranges, was a grandiose structure, cruciform in shape, measuring a hundred feet long, with columns and large marble urns planted with vast specimen orange trees. In the centre, set beneath a cupola, was a circular atrium, featuring an ornamental fountain, where on fine spring days it was pleasant to sit and take refreshment. It was, in short, a veritable cathedral of glass in which exotic plants of scented bloom took the place of stained glass and statuary.

Herbert had always had a particular fondness for this legacy from his grandfather and it was a measure of his infatuation with Sabine that he had allowed her to take over one half of the building, replace many of the plants nurtured by himself and his grandfather with pineapples, and rename the building 'the pinery'. It was here she intended to go for her walk.

At their first encounter Joshua had innocently asked Sabine what had drawn her to such an unusual pastime as horti-culture. The question astonished her. Her eyes widened so that the white was visible all round the sable iris, yet there was something distant in her gaze. 'What is so unusual about it, Mr Pope? To me it seems extraordinary that you need even to ask. Do you question that gardening is a prerequisite of civilized society? Or that plants are essential to man's wellbeing? Can you deny that the introduction of foreign species has contributed immensely to the richness of our landscape? And quite apart from their visual attractions . . . well, man could not exist without plants: he needs them to furnish his home, feed him, heal him. Imagine a table without fruit or vegetables! Why, even the table itself would not exist. The cultivation of plants is far more than a mere hobby; it is an occupation of the greatest moment. Civilization depends upon it.'

Joshua mentally raised his eyes to heaven and outwardly nodded politely. Having never given the subject of gardening much thought, the vehemence of her arguments was faintly amusing, but his artistic faculties were roused. There was a glow in her eye that he wanted to store in his memory and reproduce on canvas. He wanted to see more of her passion, to draw her out. For this reason, although the subject held no fascination for him, he feigned interest and pressed her further. 'Why have you settled upon pineapples in particular?'

Again he saw the flash of fervour, although her tone now turned withering rather than zealous. 'Anyone who knows anything of the subject understands that, among culinary plants, this fruit surpasses all others. It is the most succulent and esteemed of foreign species. For any gardener to grow a ripened fruit for the table is the pinnacle of achievement.'

After that she went on, in similar tones, to describe how she had been asked by Herbert to supervise the growing of pineapples at Astley. She had relished the challenge and, even though it was more usual in this country to cultivate pineapples in purpose-built frames and pits, she had confidently overseen the alterations to the vast glass and wood conservatory. The entire structure was warmed by charcoal-fuelled stoves, but since pineapples required hotter conditions than oranges and myrtles she had augmented the heat in her portion of the building by installing channels under the floor to contain tanner's bark – crushed oak, used by the local leather tannery to soften animal hides. The decaying process of this matter could be relied on to produce considerable heat, and by carefully stirring and modulating the bark the correct temperature to coax the plants to grow would be reached. Sabine had supervised the potting and bedding of plants brought from Barbados in fine sandy loam and compost. She had ordered more plants from local nurserymen and potted them up likewise. She viewed the pinery as a great achievement and took inordinate pride in it.

Joshua stifled a yawn and declared it would be an honour if one day she would consent to show the pinery to him. Sabine had scarcely acknowledged his request at the time, but that morning at breakfast she had suggested he accompany her to the pinery. 'Madam,' he had replied, silently thanking God for his appointment with Herbert, 'you are very kind, and as you know I am all eagerness to admire the pinery. However, this morning circumstances forbid me. I have arranged a sitting . . .'

'Some other time then, Mr Pope,' she had said, smiling as she rose from the table.

Sabine entered the conservatory alone. She reached the central atrium, then turned left as she always did towards the beds where her pineapples were planted. At the beginning of the row, she sniffed, and then sniffed again, this time more cautiously. Something jarred; some new strange odour permeated the familiar, well-loved warmth: a foreign scent that was on the one hand sickly sweet, yet on the other had an acrid taint that was unsettling, poisonous, intrusive.

She cast about to find its source. At first, all seemed in perfect order. The air was warmed by rotting bark and dung. Her pineapple plants, many of them rooted in Barbados and transported to Astley under her supervision, had been re-potted in larger containers only last week. They stood as she had directed, ranged in tiered beds, so that no more than the circle of the upper rims were visible. From the centre of these halos spoked leaves emerged erect, silvery grey, like the long, pointed shafts of spears.

Sabine walked along the narrow path, examining each pot for signs of interference, pausing to note and admire several plants that were a little larger and more developed than the rest. In the heart of several crowns small green fruits, no larger than an infant's fist, had formed. In others were larger fruits ready to ripen during the next few months. Sabine walked towards them; these were the plants she treasured most, the plants she had personally tended on the long journey from Barbados. Perspiration rose on her lip and forehead as she entered further into the pinery and the unfamiliar smell became more potent.

Halfway along the path the stench was so pungent as to be overwhelming. Sabine tried to breathe shallowly. She held a kerchief to her mouth. Yet nothing diminished the invasion in her nostrils and mouth. She could taste as well as smell it. Her stomach heaved, yet at no point did she consider withdrawing to call for assistance. She was a newcomer to Astley but the pinery was already her domain. If something untoward had taken place here it was imperative she should witness the extent of it.

It was not until Sabine reached the end of the path that her probing was rewarded. A cluster of the precious containers in which half a dozen or more of the largest plants were rooted had apparently been removed from their protective bed and carelessly discarded. Several plants were strewn over the path, like so many unwanted weeds; others lay heaped against the wall. Their removal had caused earth to spill out of most of the containers and several of the pots to shatter, leaving a tangle of plump white roots helplessly exposed to the air.

She stared in disbelief. Her cheeks burned, her palms grew clammy. She turned towards the portion of bed from which the pineapples had been extracted. Where a row of plants had formerly stood lay the source of the foul smell – an interloper.

The man was stretched on his back in the bed of bark and

dung. A wall of plants and pots concealed his head, yet Sabine did not move towards his face to examine him. Transfixed, she gazed at what lay before her.

At first she assumed the man had fallen comatose asleep. She didn't think to be afraid. She could see enough of the body to know that this was not one of the under gardeners. The hands were clean, the nails manicured, the clothes of middling quality, too fine to belong to a labourer. She shivered, a mixture of apprehension and annoyance written on her face. He should not be here. Why had he deemed it necessary to destroy her precious pines? Could he not have collapsed on the path?

She pressed the kerchief closer to her mouth. Then, shaking her head as if chastising herself for her weakness, she stooped down and tugged at the foot to rouse him. 'Wake up, man,' she commanded.

The foot felt warm but limp. The man's cotton stocking separated from his breeches, exposing a hairy, mud-streaked calf. Still he remained obstinately immobile. Sabine tugged more insistently and then when there was still no sign of movement inched between the pots towards his head. She could now see the man's tousled brown hair, the underside of his chin, shadowed with stubble. A small beetle, roused by her interference, scurried over his lips and into a cavernous nostril. She swallowed uncomfortably and looked away.

Sabine's hands were now clammy from touching his leg; her breath came fast and shallow – revulsion and fury intermingled. She resisted the instinct to wipe her palms on her skirts. She could no longer wholly convince herself that the man was merely in a stupor, but nor did she wish to contemplate the alternative. Steeling herself, unable to confront the possibility there was something seriously amiss, she placed her hand on the man's torso and shook him. 'Did you hear me, sir? I said wake up! This instant!'

He lay there, insolently unconscious, oblivious to her presence and the destruction he had wrought. Sabine grew more uneasy by the minute. She grabbed at the fabric of his collar and yanked upwards, intending to bring him to a seated position. The man was compact of stature, yet broad-chested, and surprisingly heavy to lift. It took her some time and several attempts to raise him. Nevertheless, at length, from out of the sea of bark and earth and dung his floppy head, shoulders and entire torso rose up like some ghastly apparition.

As soon as she lifted him up, there was no longer any doubt in her mind about his true condition. Far from having fallen comatose into sleep, the man was dead. He was still youthful of appearance, no more than thirty years of age, she guessed. His eyes were open, yet dull. Wisps of brown detritus clung to his lashes and brows. Pooled inside the mouth cavity, staining the tongue and teeth, was a brownish, soupy liquid in which pieces of fibrous matter were suspended. The smell of this substance was sweet yet acrid and had apparently been vomited prior to death. In so doing it had coursed down his chin and the front of his torso, subsequently drying to a paste in which morsels of bark lay set like glue. The reek was only partly identifiable. The acrid smell of vomit had mingled in the humid air with a certain heavy sweetness. She feared that sweetness might be the stench of death.

# Chapter Three

It was the same fine May morning, not fifty yards distant from this distressing scene, that Joshua Pope took up his long-handled sable brush and a palette on which blobs of lead white, red ochre, vermilion and yellow ochre had been mixed to produce various flesh tones. When he began to paint, he abandoned his usual composure, his expression of calm curiosity, and adopted instead a brisk yet flamboyant manner that matched the extravagant garb concealed beneath his paint-stained linen smock.

Although only three and thirty years of age, within his profession Joshua Pope was already regarded as the equal of any portraitist in the land. He had recently triumphed over Reynolds and Gainsborough in a masterly conversation-piece, depicting the royal princes George and Frederick at play, that had been exhibited at the Society of Arts. Critics had deemed his works a little warmer and more profound than Romney's, and, being youthful and agreeable and immaculate in his dress, he was more in vogue with polite society than Hudson, Hayman and Ramsay.

For some years now his popularity had been such that patrons usually visited him in his rooms for sittings. Exceptional circumstances had altered his routine and taken him to Astley. The previous summer Joshua's wife Rachel had died in a tragic boating accident on the river Thames. Their only child, Benjamin, had perished with her. Joshua felt himself culpable for their deaths. A slight touch of influenza had prevented him from accompanying them on their outing. He couldn't forgive himself for his lapse. Since then, to distract himself from the agonies of bereavement, he had moved to new lodgings, thrown himself into his work, purchased a dozen new items of dress – waistcoats, breeches, coats – each more elaborate than the last. But none of these measures succeeded in shifting the bouts of melancholy to which he had grown increasingly prone. The blackness was often unbearable. Every object in his new rooms only served to remind him of his darling Rachel and sweet Benjamin. Every item in his closet, no matter how vivid and newly acquired, seemed dull and worn. He developed a morbid fear of water. He took a mistress, a comely widow by the name of Meg Dunn, but although he slept a little more soundly after their meetings, still the shadow of melancholy remained.

As the anniversary of Rachel and Benjamin's deaths approached, Joshua yearned to leave London. Thus, when Herbert Bentnick had offered a commission to paint his marriage portrait, Joshua had suggested he come to stay at Astley House in Richmond, to carry this out. Herbert had hurried to accept this proposal (as far as he knew, it was unheard of for Joshua Pope to agree to leave his premises) and declared he would gladly pay a fee of twenty guineas. All parties were thus very well satisfied.

Joshua steadfastly believed that painting a portrait should involve more than just executing a representation; the mental part was all. He wanted to discover in his subject's physiognomy something no one else had seen. He invested extraordinary energies in this pursuit, and although he painted in a traditional manner he had developed a somewhat singular technique. Positioning himself so close to the canvas that his nose threatened to wipe the wet paint straight off it again, he made a few small hatchings; then, leaning back, holding his brush at the very tip of its handle, he would apply a thin line of paint in a broad sweeping stroke. He was presently engaged in the early stages of his portrait: yesterday on a primed canvas he had briskly sketched in the outline of his figures in thin grey paint. Today he had begun the first painting – laying in dead colouring, a range of low-key pigments to position everything in its correct place, and starting to build the likeness. Several minutes of this frenetic activity ensued, before he deposited his palette on the side table, wiped his nose on his sleeve and stepped back almost to the doorway.

This stage of portraiture always struck Joshua as if he were seeing the composition through a veil or a dense fog that flattened and dulled everything. The tones were monochrome, the strokes spontaneous and thinly laid; richness, shadow, highlight, detail, all would come later. Nevertheless, from the artist's point of view, there was immense satisfaction to be derived from seeing the shape and pattern each figure created on the canvas.

His sitter meanwhile was captivated by his antics. Joshua was aware of Herbert Bentnick's eyes watching every portion of his physiognomy that creased and crumpled and puckered with countless capricious expressions. Joshua smiled to himself. Sometimes it was politic to feign a little oddity. If he had the air of a blockhead, what of it? Jigging about held Herbert's attention, made him forget his self-consciousness; his character became visible. Faces were like maps: you had to unfurl them to make sense of them.

With his head to one side Joshua squinted at the canvas. His lips distorted in a grimace, signalling moderate satisfaction in his work thus far. Herbert began to mirror his apparently dispirited look. Joshua charged his brush with lead white and vermilion, sucking in his cheeks so that they became triangular cavities and his eyes no more than small slashes in his narrowed face. He looked up again, throwing a lengthy, almost accusing glance in the direction of Herbert, at some foible of his physiognomy that eluded him thus far. At length, having pondered his handiwork sufficiently at a distance, he approached until he was no more than two feet from his sitter's face. Joshua peered intently at Herbert's profile. From the turn of his mouth, the slope of his brow, the crease of his chin, Joshua was aware his scrutiny was uncivil and made Herbert profoundly uncomfortable. Irritation, as much as Herbert ever experienced such a sentiment – he was a man of equable humour – began to niggle within him. Joshua discerned it tightening up his warming-pan face, darkening his complexion to the colour of rubies, contracting the pupils of his pale-blue eyes.

For more than an hour Herbert uttered no word of complaint, partly because he had, after all, been warned. It was Joshua's habit to explain something of his methods to his patrons, reasoning that it would help them tolerate his methods and, more importantly, make them properly appreciate the finished work. Last night in the salon, dressed in his best coat of pale-blue satin trimmed with silver frogging and matching breeches and waistcoat, he had held forth. 'Transverse illumination is essential,' he had declared, studying the air-twist stem of the glass that held his claret. 'It provides depth of shadow, which in turn enhances the beauty and character of the sitter. In the same way that beauty seems more radiant when juxtaposed with ugliness, without extremes of darkness and light a subject would seem devoid of contour and therefore much less compelling, d'you see?'

'Indeed,' said Herbert, who was intrigued, as he always was, with any new insight into a world with which he was unfamiliar. 'I had never considered it, but now I see that it must of course be so.'

'Every good rival of mine believes it to be so. They say Mr Gainsborough paints only by candlelight.'

Joshua proceeded then to explain that the pose and background were equally crucial elements of the composition.

'They too should add to the momentousness of the portrait, conveying to the viewer something of the character and achievements and interests of the subject. Why, you can have no idea, sir, of the eloquence of a pair of hands. They may impart stern authority, graciousness, candour – myriad traits – depending on the positioning.'

'Quite so,' said Herbert, who was as thirsty for Joshua's knowledge as Joshua for his wine.

'Thus the composition will be transformed from a mere likeness into a work of significance, something truly deserving to be called a "work of art". As for the sketchy backdrops of my rivals – those who use parsley and sheep's wool and mirror and coal for woodland, cloud, water and rocks – is it not an outrage that such men should call themselves "portraitists", when they are no better than the daubers of stage scenery?'

'Come, come, Mr Pope,' said Herbert, laughing. 'Surely the visage is most crucial? Is not the background merely a distraction from that?'

'I beg to disagree with you, sir,' said Joshua, smiling smoothly, for he greatly enjoyed discussions of this nature. 'In any portrait worth the name, the setting should be as identifiable and as individual and as carefully executed as the subject. It is an intrinsic part of the whole. Do not believe anyone who tells you otherwise.'

'Then I am fortunate indeed to have commissioned you. And I confess myself eager to see the finished work,' replied Herbert with a bow, before turning, as politeness demanded, to attend to the ladies.

But whereas the previous night Joshua's explanations were politely delivered, now, with a palette and several brushes in his hand, his manner had perceptibly changed. He became an observer of life, not a participant in it. Decorum was lost. Herbert Bentnick was no different from the jug on the plinth beside him, an object to represent. Joshua was possessed by paint.

Herbert Bentnick had commissioned this portrait to mark

his forthcoming nuptials with Sabine Mercier, who would become his second wife in three months' time. Since a fondness for gardens had brought the pair together, Joshua had settled on the famously verdant grounds of Astley as a setting for the portrait. Thus he had arranged the composition and sketched it in grey paint on his canvas. Herbert stood, one hand on the back of a seat in which Sabine would recline like an exotic Venus. To one side stood a small plinth, over which an assortment of fruits and flowers from the garden would be artfully strewn. Bearing in mind Sabine's particular passion, Joshua decided – with the happy couple's concurrence – that a pineapple would be the centrepiece of this arrangement. Sabine was turned towards him. In one outstretched hand she tendered him a ripened fruit; the other hand was behind her head, as if she were offering herself. Beyond would be a prospect of the gardens of Astley: the grottoes, lakes, the aviaries, the temples, and, of course, the pinery.

Joshua was presently working on Herbert's hands and face in tandem, progressing from light to dark tints, following the structure of the face with his strokes, making no attempt to soften the patches of different hue. Herbert tried not to flinch as he felt himself once again coming under Joshua's dissecting gaze. He raised his head a trifle and held his eye steady, his fingers contracted on the back of the chair. The clock on the wall behind ticked languidly.

Herbert was a large man of heavy torso, yet his limbs appeared rather fragile, birdlike, seemingly inadequate for the burden of the body they supported. Like most men in their middle years he had the face he deserved. An even temper and a benign disposition were written in the smoothness of his complexion; vivacity and brio in his plump, upturned lips. Herbert loved to dabble in many subjects. His library bore testimony to his various interests: the shelves held not only a vast number of books, but also, *inter alia*, a collection of bird eggs, a case of shells, a cherry stone he believed to be carved

31

with a hundred faces, folios of engravings of fauna discovered on foreign expeditions, and portfolios of investments in a ragbag of businesses including fish farms and strangely adventurous pumps. Few of these enterprises had yielded the financial fruit he had hoped for, but Herbert measured remuneration not just in monetary terms but also by the diversion they afforded. In this respect he thought himself very rich indeed.

Since Herbert's recent return from Barbados, several of his acquaintances had remarked to Joshua that his sitter had grown perhaps a little less placid, a little more taciturn, a little quicker to growl. Now was one such occasion. Joshua observed Herbert's legs twitch, his arms flinch; his belly rumbled audibly. The effort of remaining standing in this position was evidently uncomfortable. Joshua sensed that he longed to stamp and shuffle, to sneeze, or yawn, or scratch his nose, but he had been obliged to stand for an hour without respite. Herbert had already pointedly remarked that the last time he sat it had been to Sir Joshua Reynolds, who painted him with only a trio of half-hour sittings.

When this oblique request for a curtailment failed to achieve the desired result, Herbert approached the subject more directly. 'Upon my word, Mr Pope, I find my legs grow uncommonly heavy. I will pause for a few minutes, sir, before resuming.'

Joshua pretended not to have heard him; he was just then at a delicate stage, concentrating on Herbert's chin. With his head leaning close to the canvas, he painted on without pause.

Herbert spoke again, this time more fiercely, 'I say, Pope, sir, did you not hear me? I said I must halt this instant. I am grown extremely uncomfortable.' With this he began to rotate his stiffened jaw and stamp his boots upon the platform, as much to attract Joshua's attention as to relieve the tingling discomfort in his feet.

It was only when the sound of Herbert's feet grew into a

thumping crescendo that Joshua acknowledged it had penetrated his consciousness. He shook his head and flickered his eyelids as if rousing himself from a trance. He cast a rueful look at the canvas before glancing at the clock.

'Forgive me, Mr Bentnick,' he said with a preoccupied smile. 'I had quite forgot the time. We should have ceased half an hour ago; I ought to have given you some intermission from the discomfort of standing. My profound apologies, sir. How could I be so thoughtless? How have you endured it so long and so patiently? Do sit down, I beg of you.'

Herbert sat down slowly, holding his palm aloft to indicate Joshua was to chastise himself no further. Still Joshua felt himself blush, for in truth he saw now he shouldn't have made Herbert stand so long. He was ashamed at his self-centredness.

Joshua unbuttoned his smock, removed it and smoothed his embroidered waistcoat and adjusted his cravat. He turned in silence to the window. He pulled back the curtain – it was a habit of his to work with a curtain partially drawn to give the half-light he required. Sun streamed into the room, so much light after the gloom that they blinked at the prospect before them. And what a prospect it was!

Astley House, Richmond, the seat of the Bentnick family, was a wide red-bricked and flat-fronted mansion, with porticoed entrance and eight large sash windows in both of its main façades. It had been built a half-century earlier by Herbert's grandfather, Horace Bentnick, a seafaring merchant who had prospered spectacularly from sugar plantations acquired thanks to a lucky hand at whist.

As a memorial to mankind's enduring desire for sweetness, and the wisdom of occasionally throwing caution to the wind and putting everything on a pair of queens, Horace had razed the earlier, medieval Astley of his ancestors and replaced it with a new-style grander version complete with splendid glasshouse, which afforded a magnificent prospect of the river

Thames and the purple undulations of the royal park and countryside of Surrey beyond.

When Herbert Bentnick inherited the property, he had been determined to set his own stamp upon the place. His interest in horticulture had been nurtured by a handful of orange pips given to him by his grandfather after dinner with the instruction to go and see what happened if he planted them. Some of the seeds grew and bore fruit. Herbert had become a compulsive collector of exotic plants and trees, with a weakness for buying all manner of foreign novelties from local nurserymen.

He had spent a considerable sum of money and much of his time making Astley's gardens and parklands among the most alluring in the region. He had commissioned the master of all landscape-gardeners, Mr Lancelot Brown, to enhance Astley's natural beauties. Brown had triumphed, forming a serpentine lake, with an island in its midst and cascades and a grotto at one end, where once only swampy fields and rocky wastes had been. Dotted about parkland of nine miles compass were ponds of carp, enclosures for fowl, walks of lime and elm. Lawns had been cleared and scythed, copses of native trees planted, vistas opened up and punctuated with a scattering of architectural delights – a Palladian bridge, a fountain of Neptune, a temple to Diana, a Gothic ruin, an octagonal pump room and an obelisk. Of his grandfather's gardens, only the parterres surrounding the house remained untouched – those and the conservatory, for what improvement could any man make to such a palace of plants?

Herbert and Joshua thus surveyed an Arcadian prospect: the green parklands, the lakes, the temples and vistas of Astley. Beneath, to one side, lay the kitchen gardens. Against high brick walls fans of espaliered apricot, peach, quince, medlar and other fruit trees were presently in bloom. In the centre, parterres laid out in a complex geometrical design were filled with flowers interspersed with fruit and vegetables. Beyond rose the cupola roof of the pinery, one half of which had lately been given over to the growing of Sabine Mercier's pineapples.

'The scene is as fine today as I have ever seen it,' said Herbert, amiable once more now he was no longer standing still.

Joshua nodded, eager to appease now he had torn himself from his work. 'Is not nature prodigal? What a legacy you have here, sir. More splendid gardens I have never seen. Now that we are finished here, and since the day is so remarkably clement, I intend to take my pocket book and begin my sketches outdoors,' he declared with gravitas.

'An excellent plan, Mr Pope! And if I were any use with a crayon I would join you on such a delightful day. Perhaps I might assist by pointing out some of the choicest places?'

Joshua welcomed this offer and Herbert began describing their whereabouts. He was just getting into his stride, when Sabine appeared in the vista before them and Herbert fell abruptly silent.

They watched her emerge from the side gate and stride along the gravel path in the direction of the hothouses and the pinery at the far end. From this distance she was a tiny figure shrouded in a billowing cloak, yet poised and elegant still.

An instant later Sabine disappeared from view. Herbert swiftly resumed his drift. There was a sunken garden with a sundial that Joshua should not ignore; beyond it, in the middle of a rose garden, lay a delightful fountain in the form of a cupid, which many found most enchanting. Scarcely had he begun to give Joshua his directions to these attractions, when the discourse was once more interrupted.

Minutes after she had disappeared into the pinery, Sabine rushed out again. Judging by the speed of her exit, all the monsters of Hades might have been snapping at her heels. Herbert again fell silent, although this time it appeared, from the ridges in his brow, it was concern rather than ardour that beat in his breast. Even at this distance Sabine's strange gestures and demeanour told them something was dreadfully amiss. Together they watched in astonishment as she threw back her head, like a soul in torment, and let out a fearful scream.

# Chapter Four

The singular circumstances of Herbert Bentnick and Sabine Mercier's betrothal had become the subject for much tittle-tattle among the polite circles of Richmond.

Until she arrived in England three months earlier, Sabine had lived most of her life on the West Indian island of Barbados. Her fascination with plants was inherited from her father, a naval physician of Huguenot descent, who, drawn by the medicinal properties of foreign species, had gathered seeds and saplings throughout his working career and settled in Antigua to nurture them. He married a coffee-complexioned girl who spawned two children to play among his plants. The elder child, a son, followed his father into the navy, rising to become the master of a frigate. Sabine, the younger child, inherited her mother's sable eyes, honey-coloured skin and pleasant demeanour, and, it later transpired, her father's fascination with the world of botany.

Sabine's passion for horticulture (one cannot call it a hobby, for it was more absorbing than that) flourished after the death of her second husband, Charles Mercier. She had inherited a comfortable house on an agreeable hillside overlooking the port of Bridgetown, and with it came ten hectares of land. Charles Mercier had been a shipping clerk, a man of good sense and frugal habits, who wanted no more than to provide for his family's modest comfort and, in order to do so, invested every spare penny of income in order to make more. During his lifetime the garden had been a narrow strip leading to the door within which a few necessary culinary plants and trees were grown to supply the table. The remaining land was planted up with sugar canes that provided useful additional income. After her husband's death, Sabine removed the cane and invested most of Charles's savings and her energies into cultivating the ground. She employed an Irish dockworker and trained him as her gardener; she bought several slaves to work under him. She practised the art of propagation and cultivation of every tropical plant she could find, searching her memory for the knowledge she had gleaned from her father. She learned how to multiply and increase her plants; how to grow cuttings and slips in moist shaded places; how to make layers by cutting through a joint and bowing a branch into the soil with a peg; how to collect seeds from the lustiest and most vigorous stems.

Thus the brilliance and beauty of Sabine's gardens were increased. Frangipani, banana, lemon and orange trees and jacaranda replaced the canes and flourished in her care. Orchids bloomed for her as nowhere else on the island; arums and cannas burgeoned in unparalleled abundance. In an island famed for the profuseness of its vegetation, Sabine's garden became renowned as the most verdant and luxuriant, and she became a fêted connoisseur on the subject.

It was occasionally the habit of conscientious and intrepid British plantation owners to visit their lands, in order to satisfy themselves of the efficiency with which they were managed. For many of these gentlemen visitors this was the first journey to such foreign parts. When the boat drew close to shore and they viewed the terrain, they were frequently overwhelmed. The climate affected them most forcibly. It was rarely temperate; indeed, it was often excessively rainy or searingly hot. Either they were drenched to the skin by downpours, or their fine woollen dress coats were soaked by sweat; or, if a hurricane happened to blow, their wigs and hats were tossed into the air, at some cost to their dignity.

They were struck by the richness of the views around them. Such luxuriance, such abundance, such handsome buildings! There was scarcely a foot of land on Barbados that was not cultivated. Frequently they remarked their interest to the host at their lodging house, whereupon Sabine Mercier's name might be mentioned. Anyone drawn by the natural curiosities and wonders of the island could not miss a visit to her garden. Replete with the finest specimens, it was a wonder of the island.

Visitors with the right introduction Sabine gladly permitted entry to her domain. Her gardener was a willing and informative escort. Moreover, during the tour visitors might encounter the chatelaine herself. They had only to express admiration for her achievements, and reveal a passable knowledge in the subject of horticulture, whereupon she would talk energetically on the most worthwhile way to grow custard apples, avocado pears, ginger, pawpaw, calabash, pineapples – in short, any tropical horticultural subject that the visitor cared to name.

For gentlemen plantation owners so far from the comforts of home and hearth, to be tutored in a fascinating subject by a lady of bewitching eyes and generous disposition held understandable appeal. Not only did she welcome visitors in her garden, when they returned home she bestowed farewell gifts of leaves and branches and seeds, and instructions on their cultivation. Thus beguiled, they took up correspondence with her, and from these exchanges more introductions were made, more callers came, and her reputation burgeoned like an extravagant tropical bloom.

So it was that the horticulturally enthusiastic Herbert Bentnick, visiting Barbados to view the sugar plantations that were the source of his inherited wealth, made the acquaintance of Sabine Mercier. And she, with customary hospitality, invited him to view her gardens. Unusually for those times,

Herbert's wife Jane had accompanied him on his voyage. She was a woman of bright intellect who was also curious to view the gardens that were, it was deemed, as near to being an earthly paradise as anywhere on this globe, and to meet their illustrious creator.

Herbert and Jane Bentnick were thus treated to Sabine's generous ministrations. She ushered them through ravishing walks and fragrant groves. Afterwards she provided refreshments – fruits and cordials – and she charmed them, as she charmed every visitor, with her formidable knowledge, her pleasant manners, her solicitude.

As misfortune would have it, Sabine's acquaintance with Jane was brief. Tropical diseases were rife in the Indies and it was not uncommon for those unaccustomed to the climate to fall prey to all manner of ailment. A week after their first visit to Sabine's garden, Jane Bentnick was taken ill and retired to her bed. Soon after she succumbed to a virulent fever, followed by a delirium from which she never recovered. She died a fortnight later.

Herbert, who had loved his wife deeply, was shaken by the suddenness of her demise. Jane had been strong and loyal, a companion as well as wife for twenty years and the mother of his two children. Throughout their marriage she had never been prone to the complaints that bedevilled other ladies of his acquaintance. He had believed her more robust than any other woman, as invincible as he himself; had he not, he would never have agreed to let her accompany him on his journey.

Amid his torment, which seemed worse in a distant land of strange customs and foreign climate, Sabine became his solace. Throughout Jane's illness Sabine was kindness personified, nursing Jane through climaxes of fever, providing balms and tinctures to ease her pain, bathing her forehead through her final death throes, and, afterwards, aiding Herbert with every detail of the formalities of death.

Some weeks after the funeral, when a decent interval had

elapsed, Sabine invited Herbert to dine. Having referred, sensitively, to his recent bereavement and made mention of her own sorrow at the death of her husband Charles, Sabine endeavoured to turn the conversation to easier, less painful matters. Among other things, the subject of the pineapple was raised.

The pineapple's taste of honey and perfume needed no commendation, since she had served it to him on his first visit with Jane and presented it now for dessert. Herbert was grateful to be so distracted. 'Perhaps you are not aware of it,' he said, savouring the succulent flesh, 'but in Europe the fruit has become quite the rage. So much so that it has inspired every form of art, from architecture to silver and ceramics. They sprout upon gateposts, sugar bowls and teapots with unparalleled profusion.'

Here Herbert paused, observing to himself how handsome Sabine looked in a dress of golden silk, an unusual emerald necklace gleaming darkly about her neck. He warmed to his theme. 'And yet, dear lady, I must confess that no artist, however clever he may be, could capture the greatest quality of this fruit you have given me – the succulence of its taste.'

'I am delighted the fruit gives you pleasure,' replied Sabine, lowering her eyes modestly.

'It is not merely my pleasure that it arouses, dear lady, but my admiration. Why, in England your knowledge would be most coveted. It is the greatest triumph of a gardener to produce such a fruit. There is scarcely a gentleman of my acquaintance who does not desire pineapples on his table, or possess images of them about his house.'

Sabine smiled, filled his glass and thought, as she had since their first meeting, how pleasant Herbert was. She could not say he was strikingly good-looking; nonetheless, the solidity of his jaw (even though it was a trifle heavily jowled) and his steady-eyed gaze bore testimony to his upright character; the readiness with which he conversed, kissed her hand and paid compliments was highly agreeable.

During the weeks that passed, more engagements followed. Herbert described his own gardens at Astley, and as they exchanged tips in a horticultural vein fondness grew between them. At length came the week of Herbert's departure. Sabine held a farewell dinner. During this last repast, Herbert felt uncommonly downhearted. He couldn't prevent feelings of regret every time he looked at her. He shuddered at the thought of returning to Astley alone, to an empty bed.

It was during the dessert – which naturally included the pineapple that had now become a tradition with them – that Sabine demurely looked at her plate and drew breath.

'I am sorry indeed to see you leave, Mr Bentnick,' she said, 'but I have a parting gift that I hope will serve as a memento of the warmth of our recent friendship. It is something I have prepared for you over the past weeks, bearing in mind our conversations on the subject of growing pineapples: a dozen of the finest cuttings – all crated ready for the journey back to Astley. I know such plants may be bought from nurseries in England, but these are mature plants with fruit already set, that will be ready for the table within three months.'

'But, my dear lady, what would you have me do with them?'

'I propose that you introduce the latest horticultural novelty to your own gardens. You have told me of your immense conservatory. Do what you have so often told me is all the rage. Install a pinery within it. Once the plants have fruited it is a simple matter to root further cuttings from them, and I warrant the fruit they yield will be sweeter and more succulent than any your local nursery can supply. You could fill the whole structure if you desired.'

Herbert gazed at her unhappily. He didn't know what to say. He felt bereft and lonely. His shoulders sagged as he twirled his glass. The thought of returning to Astley made him gloomy. How he ached for his dead wife! How his solitary bed filled him with despondency! Was he capable of running his mansion without Jane's assistance, let alone an ambitious new project in his garden? Why, it was enough to pitch any man into despair.

Seeing his consternation, Sabine crimsoned. 'Forgive me, sir. I am too presumptuous. I see I have offended you. Believe me when I say I did not intend to do so. It is only that, after you told me of the fashion for pineapples in England, I thought the plants would please you. As for me, why, nothing gives me more pleasure than the thought that you will enjoy my fruit in your own home. And perhaps, on occasion, you might remember me fondly?'

Herbert surveyed Sabine's golden flesh and felt gloomier than ever. And it was at this nadir of despondency that a flicker of light began to shine through the darkness. A solution surfaced in his consciousness. It was impulsive, but spur-of-the-moment action had always been his forte. If he didn't act now it would be too late.

'My dear Mrs Mercier . . . Sabine . . . it is you who should forgive me for my rudeness. Your proposal has not offended me. Quite the contrary. I am deeply touched by it. Indeed, never before has the subject of cuttings stirred such a passion in me.

'I, in turn, have a proposal to make to you. Return with me to Astley. Instigate the alterations necessary for the pinery. Plant its first crop – these cuttings you have carefully prepared for me. And then, if you will, since I have no great appetite for living alone . . . become my second wife.'

Sabine lowered her eyes most becomingly. She had scarcely dared hope for a proposal. There was no doubt in her mind that this was what she wanted, but it wouldn't do to say so instantly. She paused, wafting her fan in front of her face. At length she lifted her gaze to meet his. Herbert, overwhelmed with the emotions of the moment, riven with uncertainty, reached out his large hand to take her small one in his. She felt the warmth of his squeeze on her wrist, she sensed his desire in his grip; smilingly she acquiesced.

*   *   *

Thus Sabine had quit her home and its blooming vegetation, leaving its care to the ministrations of her gardener and his wife. She followed on behind Herbert within a month, accompanied by her daughter Violet, a radiant girl of nearly one and twenty years. They arrived at Astley in the New Year. The wedding was set for the following summer. The reason for the delay was evident. Pineapples had brought them together. She was quite determined that a vast display of these succulent fruits grown at Astley would adorn the table at their wedding breakfast.

Meanwhile, she voraciously read every treatise on the subject of pineapple cultivation in England by experts in the field. She employed and instructed the new head gardener, Granger, and a dozen under gardeners in the cultivation of pineapples, not a day passing without her visiting her plants to monitor their progress. For in some strange way she had convinced herself that if the pineapples thrived, so too would she with Herbert.

# Chapter Five

It was little wonder that the discovery of a body in the pinery and the damage it had wrought rocked Sabine's composure. Alarmed by her cry, Herbert and Joshua hurried to her side in a matter of minutes. Granger, the head gardener, who had been closer to hand in the gardens, had reached her more quickly. As soon as they arrived Granger took Herbert to one side and muttered something before handing some papers to him.

Joshua observed this exchange from the corner of his eye, while he turned his attentions to Sabine. Her skin was unnaturally pallid, her manner listless and withdrawn, as if she saw them through a fog. Joshua ushered her to a nearby seat, and tried to ask her a few simple questions, but her responses were whispered so faintly as to be unintelligible. Fearing she might fall at any minute into a swoon, he delved into his pocket for his salts and wafted them near her face. After a minute or two, she seemed to revive well enough to relate more coherently something of her unpleasant discovery. A man was dead in the pinery. She didn't know who he was, but he had caused considerable damage to her plants.

When Herbert attempted to press her further she seemed to sway slightly in her seat. She repeated that she didn't know the man's identity, but she was as certain as she could be that he was dead. He seemed to be a man of some means –

certainly not a labourer. More than that she could not say.

Realizing that she was in a severe state of shock, Herbert took Sabine's arm and, with Joshua's aid, escorted her back to the house. Once in the drawing room, they settled her on a daybed and Herbert offered her brandy or wine or whatever she desired. She took nothing. She was, she declared, unaccountably exhausted by the distress of it all. All she needed was to sit and reflect for a moment in peace.

Herbert appeared most disconcerted. He regarded Sabine for some time, quite still and silent, as if musing what more he might do. Then he walked to the far end of the room, sat down at his writing desk and took out two letters from his pocket. Joshua supposed that these were the papers he had been handed by Granger, though he couldn't be certain of it. He watched as Herbert unfolded and read each of the letters in turn. His expression remained implacable, giving no sense of whether or not their contents surprised him. If anything, he seemed to grow a little morose, but that, reflected Joshua, was only natural bearing in mind the dead body that had just been found in his pinery.

Having read the letters, Herbert tore one into shreds and threw it into the unlit grate, then he stored the other in his writing desk. After this, looking no less miserable than before, he poured himself a brandy and sat down on a wing chair some distance from Sabine to drink it.

Lost in her thoughts, Sabine seemed oblivious to what Herbert had done. Or if she did remark it, she passed no comment. For his part, Joshua began to feel extremely uncomfortable. The atmosphere in the room struck him as most oppressive. There was a sense of strain between Sabine and Herbert that he didn't comprehend. Not wishing to add to the awkwardness, he rose, intending to leave them and return to his work.

Before he reached the threshold Sabine called after him. 'Mr Pope, one moment, if you please.' She beckoned him close and spoke in a voice so low it would have been difficult for Herbert to hear it. 'I intend to retire to my sitting room upstairs shortly. Kindly attend me there in ten minutes. There is a small matter I wish to discuss with you.'

Joshua raised one eyebrow. 'Certainly, madam,' he said.

Ten minutes later, Joshua knocked on the door of Sabine Mercier's room. Her voice instructed him to enter. The room was large and comfortably furnished and decorated in oriental style, with wallpaper featuring a bamboo pattern and elaborate japanned furniture. There were watercolours of exotic birds and flowers on the walls and a thick-piled Chinese rug patterned with roses and ribbons on the floor. Although the day was warm and sunny and the room faced south, the windows were closed and the curtains drawn. The room was stifling hot and the air was strangely scented with a cloying perfume which Joshua didn't find entirely pleasant.

Sabine sat at her dressing table – an elaborate piece of furniture draped in moiré silk with hinged mirrors and numerous drawers. She said nothing to Joshua after bidding him wait a moment. He hovered awkwardly by the door, watching her back. Over her shoulder he could see the surface of the dressing table was strewn with various expensive-looking objects: combs and brushes of tortoiseshell, pots for powder and pomade with heavily wrought silver lids, enamelled boxes for patches and dishes for pins, an ivory necessaire. The top drawer of the table was half opened; she had apparently extracted a shagreen box from it and placed it before her. The box was open; inside, nestling in a bed of oyster silk, lay an emerald necklace.

Joshua had seen this piece of jewellery several times before. Sabine had worn it on both evenings since his arrival and when she sat for her portrait. As on every previous occasion he had seen it, Joshua found himself both drawn and repelled. It was composed of a dozen stones graduated in size, the largest the size of his thumbnail. Each stone was set in gold and joined to the next by a heavy gold link. What made the piece so peculiarly unsettling was its curious design. It was fashioned as a serpent, with the mouth clasping the tail, the head, formed from the largest stone, the eye, a single ruby.

Sabine picked the necklace up and held it in front of the looking glass. A sliver of sunlight penetrating between the drawn curtains like a blade glanced from the emeralds' facets. Shades of ultramarine, orpiment, verdigris, green earth and bone black were juxtaposed with Sabine's own reflection, which seemed somehow faded by the faceted brilliance of stone. Points of brilliant green glittered with such vibrancy, it seemed as if the serpent were somehow alive.

What could possess a woman to wear with impunity so disturbing an object about her neck? Joshua found himself appalled; the very sight of it made his flesh crawl.

Some minutes passed as Sabine remained silent, appearing to be utterly transfixed by her jewel. He waited, aware all the time of the stuffy heat and the sweet scent, which seemed to grow stronger by the minute. At length, without turning, Sabine spoke. 'It is beautiful, is it not, Mr Pope?' she said, gazing at her reflection in the glass.

He nodded uncomfortably, looking at his hands and wondering at the purpose of all of this. He felt as uneasy now as he had been in the drawing room earlier. For one so used to hobnobbing with gentry he was unsure how he should comport himself in a lady's boudoir. He felt sympathy for her, for the shock she had suffered; he didn't want to cause offence, but neither did he want to encourage her to keep him there. For what purpose had she summoned him? Ever courteous, he attempted to draw it out of her.

'Indeed, madam, it is a most remarkable object. Did Mr Bentnick give it to you?'

'Whatever gave you such an idea? The necklace doesn't belong to Bentnick. It is mine. I brought it with me when I came.'

'You mentioned you had some service to ask of me, madam.

Does it concern your next sitting? Perhaps you would rather postpone it?'

She gave her head a little shake, as if Joshua had awakened her from some secret reverie. 'Indeed I have a request to make, Mr Pope, and I thank you for reminding me of it. I would like you to go to the head gardener, Granger. See if he has disposed of the body. I believe I heard Mr Bentnick instruct him to do so. Ask if he has found out anything of note about the man. Was there anything in his pockets, for instance? I cannot help feeling curious as to his identity. You may tell me what you find at our next sitting. Oh, and one more thing, Mr Pope . . .'

'Yes, madam?' said Joshua, with a polite smile and a sinking heart.

'You will do me a great service if you say none of this to the other members of this household. Mr Bentnick has recently suffered the loss of his wife. I wish to spare him any unnecessary disturbance. It is no concern of anyone else's.'

# Chapter Six

Dinner at Astley always took place at the fashionable time of three in the afternoon, and the day of Sabine's discovery of the body in the pinery was no different from any other. There were only four at table, Herbert, his two children, Francis and Caroline, and Joshua.

Having retired to her room, Sabine remained there. Violet, her daughter, had gone to London early the previous day for an appointment with her dressmaker and was not expected to return until the following afternoon.

They ate in the morning room, an annex to the drawing room, decorated on a classical theme with swags of acanthus and friezes in *faux* marble depicting wrestling gods enjoying the pleasures of the senses. Below the frieze the walls were painted a vibrant shade of yellow and pasted with engravings. Scenes of the Parthenon and Mount Olympus and the Temples of Zeus and Diana were interspersed with figures of sundry classical gods – Apollo, Poseidon, Athena and Bacchus – who seemed to survey disapprovingly those assembled about the circular mahogany table to devour, in place of nectar and ambrosia, a collation of cold ham, boiled fowl and brawn.

Up until that moment Joshua had believed that Herbert Bentnick was as happy as any man could be, given the recent loss of his wife. He had compared his own situation with Herbert's, and found them entirely dissimilar. For several

50

months after his dear wife Rachel and their son Benjamin had been drowned, Joshua could scarcely bring himself to contemplate intimacy with another woman. Then, two months ago, believing he would go mad with melancholy, he had found himself his mistress, Meg Dunn. Warm and willing though she was, Meg was never a substitute for Rachel. He still longed for a second wife, yet despite various attempts at finding one none had been forthcoming. He had fruitlessly strolled about the gardens at Vauxhall, attended assemblies at Ranelagh and Sunday Matins in St Paul's Covent Garden – generally considered the best places to come across eligible young women. Yet all to no avail.

Herbert, by contrast, had no sooner lost Jane than he had found and captured Sabine, and clearly he was besotted with her. Herbert, moreover, had two children; his house contained numerous treasures; exquisite grounds surrounded it. Herbert was possessed of everything a gentleman could possibly desire. Fate had dealt him a generous hand. How could Joshua not feel a little envious? Not until after this dinner did he begin to see the situation differently.

Caroline and Francis were already seated at the table when Joshua entered the room. He bade them good day and was greeted with a bold stare and the curtest of nods. He took his seat, pretending to look with rapt interest at an engraving of Europa propelled away on the back of a bull. Had he imagined the absence of civility? Had he offended them in some way? Was something amiss in his dress? He was wearing a coat of puce-coloured silk, fine black breeches and a shirt trimmed with Brussels lace; he looked down surreptitiously. All was as it should be. Why did Herbert not remark their singular behaviour? He was presently carving a fowl, apparently oblivious to the strain.

A lesser man than Joshua might perhaps have felt mortified, or at the very least chastened, by their coolness. But Joshua's self-possession was in no sense diminished. Though modestly inclined, he knew he was at the peak of his profession. He was a visitor to this distinguished household; he had been commissioned to perform a service. But he did not view himself as subservient. Instead, like a spectator in a theatre who observes a play, Joshua believed he belonged to a separate order entirely.

Confronted by this unnatural atmosphere, once he had overcome his initial shock his artistic zest was inflamed. He sat up at table, alert, watching. As a surveyor of mankind, the unusual was what most intrigued him. Caroline and Francis's insolence was fascinating. How does a face contort when it is annoyed but cannot express it? How do eyes alter when they hold some grievance suppressed within? What inner resentment lurks behind a twitching lip? Here was fertile ground to observe. The only frustration was that he could not take out his pencil and draw as well as witness it.

Herbert's son Francis was heir to the Astley estate and fortune. Twenty-three years of age, Francis had a straight, high-bridged nose, brows that met in the middle and a rather small mouth. He had the physique of a young Hercules; well-muscled shoulders bulged beneath his coat, and strong thighs shaped his breeches. He must have stood at six foot three in his stockinged feet, and towered half a head taller than Joshua's five foot nine inches.

Francis's sister Caroline was two years his senior and an altogether different confection of parts. Her face was narrow and angular, her nose straight but rather long, her mouth wide and surprisingly voluptuous. They were features that might have held a certain allure had some spark of animation enlivened them; but at present, with dissatisfaction reflected in the downturn of her lip and eyes that seemed flat and cold as a pewter dish, there was nothing whatsoever to recommend them.

What struck Joshua most forcefully was the contrast between their father's habitual joviality and his children's incontrovertible gloom. How curious, thought he, that such an amiable fellow as Herbert Bentnick should spawn such dreary, ill-tempered offspring. What in heaven's name made them behave so badly? Thus, from merely observing the outward manifestations of their bad temper, he began idly to wonder what the reason for their downcast spirits might be. So curiosity swelled like a pimple that if scratched develops to a contagion. Having begun to question Caroline and Francis's behaviour he found himself dwelling on the subject.

Meanwhile, Herbert made valiant attempts to sustain the conversation. He discussed the progress of the portrait with Joshua, trying all the while to entice Caroline's interest in the exchange. 'It seems to be going along splendidly, does it not, Pope? You must come and admire it, Caroline, and show Mr Pope your own album while you're about it.'

Caroline's face looked blacker than a chimney-sweep's coat; she said nothing.

'Does Miss Bentnick draw?' Joshua enquired, watching her intently.

Caroline regarded her plate in silence.

Herbert, with no trace of awkwardness, addressed Joshua. 'I dare say, Pope, you believe, as most men do, that no woman can draw like a man, for they have inferior powers of concentration. I believed as much myself till I saw my daughter's work. I warrant when you see it you will change your view too and declare it as accomplished as any you have seen.'

Joshua waved his napkin with an extravagant flourish to show he disagreed entirely with Herbert's presumption. 'Indeed,' he drawled, 'I pride myself on my lack of prejudice. A woman may concentrate as avidly as a man if the subject is agreeable to her. I should be honoured to view your work, Miss Bentnick.'

This entreaty was to no avail. Caroline's eyes flashed at her father. She ignored Joshua's comment.

'You have only to regard the profiles by the chimney piece, for they are works by my daughter,' said Herbert hastily, pointing to three watercolours. 'Two I'm sure you recognize – they are of my son and myself. The person in the centre is a neighbour of ours, Lizzie Manning. She is Caroline's great friend and the daughter of the local justice.'

Joshua murmured some half-hearted compliment about the quality of the drawing and then an uncomfortable silence descended. He gamely tried to alleviate matters by turning the conversation to the dead man in the pinery. Had anything been discovered as to the man's identity? Herbert's expression suggested he found the subject an unsavoury one to bring up over dinner. He chewed his meat slowly before answering: he had learned that the corpse was that of a man who had recently arrived from Barbados.

'How do you know?' asked Joshua with interest. He had yet to comply with Sabine's request and question Granger; perhaps Herbert would save him the trouble.

'There were two letters in his pocket. Granger found them and passed them to me. One mentioned the fact of his recent arrival from Bridgetown.'

Joshua recalled the letters he had seen Herbert read in the drawing room. 'Did the letters not reveal more? His name perhaps? Have you reached any conclusion about how the unfortunate fellow died?'

Herbert laughed and scratched his wig. He seemed far less interested in the subject than Joshua, and almost embarrassed to be talking about the incident. He didn't recall the man's name, 'though I suppose it must have been written on the documents, which I have put somewhere or other. As to the cause of death – choking, I presume. The reason for his coming to Astley remains a mystery. None of the gardeners or servants appear to know anything about him.'

'If he came from Barbados, perhaps he was an acquaintance of Mrs Mercier's?' Joshua suggested.

'I fancy not, for she would have mentioned as much when she found him. You heard her as well as I declare she didn't know him.' Herbert's tone had sharpened. He wanted the subject dropped, but Joshua was afire with interest.

'Then perhaps word of Mrs Mercier's project circulated the

54

island of Barbados and, hearing of Astley's pinery, he came in search of employ?' Joshua said, in a voice that was soft yet laden with irony. Then, in case Herbert thought him rude, he added, 'What do the physician and justice make of the death?'

'Physician?' said Herbert. 'Justice? The fellow's dead. No one can help him now. I have given orders to have him interred as swiftly as possible. Furthermore, Pope, I can't see the purpose in picking over the matter at dinner. It's damaging to my appetite.' He took a forkful of boiled fowl and examined it closely before putting it in his mouth.

'Forgive me, sir,' said Joshua. 'I didn't mean to give offence.' But after a short pause, while Herbert was busy ordering the manservant to bring more wine, he turned to Francis and Caroline. 'What d'you think on it?' he said, addressing them quietly. 'D'you recall seeing the fellow at all?'

To judge from the blankness of Caroline's expression, she was not in the least interested in the mysterious death. Francis's response was more intriguing. He blinked rapidly several times and scratched an ear lobe, yet he too affected ignorance. He had neither seen nor spoken to the dead man, he declared, before once more falling back into sullen silence.

Herbert was by now showing signs of disquiet. His children's glumness, his own efforts to coax them out of it, coupled with Joshua's stubbornness in the matter of the corpse, had ripened his face from its usual placid rosiness to a less comfortable shade of plum. His chair creaked as he rocked back and forth and racked his brains for some more suitable subject to divert them. Moreover, as he himself had remarked, his usually robust appetite had dwindled. He ate his food half-heartedly, pushing a wedge of liver pudding round his plate with scarcely a taste.

As a last, desperate resort, Herbert turned to a topic that any normal young person would have found impossible to resist. There was to be a ball held at Astley, within a fortnight, on the sixth of June. The entertainment had been arranged in order that the local gentry might make the acquaintance of

Sabine, the future mistress of Astley, and her daughter Violet. One hundred guests were expected to attend.

Discussion of this forthcoming event did not, however, succeed in its aim. Francis and Caroline remained unwavering in their incivility. They volunteered nothing, responding to questions only with a mumbled 'yes', or 'no', or 'fancy that', or 'whatever you chose, father'.

Joshua found it remarkable that not once in all this did Herbert resort to anger. On the contrary, he looked curiously sad, like a chastened schoolboy who knows he has made some misdemeanour that he cannot redress. He made no attempt to remonstrate with either of his children. Never did he raise his voice, or even an eyebrow, at their challenging rudeness. It was, Joshua observed, as if he knew the reason, comprehended there was nothing to be done to alter it, and believed himself to be in some way culpable.

'Will Lizzie Manning attend the ball with her brother, or will her father chaperone her?' asked Herbert patiently of his stony-faced son.

'I do not recall Lizzie's arrangements, father.'

'Is her brother returned from overseas?' persisted Herbert.

'As far as I know he remains in Florence.'

'Well, then, if he remains in Italy he cannot very well escort Lizzie, can he?'

'As you say, father.'

'Perhaps, in that case, you might ask Lizzie if she wishes to stay here for the night?'

'Will Sabine permit it?'

As if he had been struck in the belly, Herbert flinched. 'What possible objection could Sabine have to Lizzie staying here?'

'I merely thought that, as mistress of the house, she should be consulted.'

'Am I not master here?' replied his father.

Francis shrugged his shoulders and pushed a spoonful of jelly into his mouth.

Herbert forced a smile and in desperation turned to his daughter. 'Have you settled upon your costume for the ball, Caroline?'

She shook her head. 'No, father, I have not.'

'Then is it not time you did so? The entertainment is only a fortnight away, dear girl. Do you not wish to look your best for it?'

'I have not given the matter much thought.'

Costume was a source of endless concern to Joshua Pope. 'What colour will you chose for your gown, Miss Bentnick?' he enquired with genuine interest. He pictured her in a dark jewel hue – deep red or blue, or green perhaps – that would bring out the warmth of her complexion and the richness of her eyes.

She flushed at his intrusion, but ignored him, declaring only, 'Indeed, I misled you, father. The reason I have not ordered a gown is that I thought I might wear one of my mother's. The crimson brocade that she wore on the last occasion we dined together, before you took her to Barbados and her death, becomes me particularly well, I think. And perhaps it will serve as a reminder to us all, while we celebrate your new union, that she is scarcely cold in her grave.'

A hush fell over the room. Herbert's eyes glistened, as if tears welled in them. The muscles in his jaw contracted and twitched, but he didn't appear surprised in the least. It was as if he had known all along what was coming and now wrestled to decide on a response.

'Caroline! Dearest child! I beg you, restrain yourself. Surely you do not blame me for your dear mother's death?' he managed to say at length. 'She accompanied me to Barbados at her own request. I loved her as much as you did and I mourn her as much as you do now. Her death from fever was a tragedy, but we cannot rewrite history any more than we may see into the future.'

Caroline's fine cold eyes were now lit up with passion. 'For someone who loved and mourns her so sincerely, it did not take you long to replace her!'

As Joshua observed Herbert's reaction to this retort he was again reminded of a child that had been hurt to the quick. Herbert quivered with helpless emotion. His face gleamed with sweat and the edge of his wig grew damp. His fingers played with his cutlery, as if he were tongue-tied by the knowledge he had to say something to his daughter's challenge, but that whatever he said would only make matters worse.

'It was fate that brought Sabine and me together. She was kindness itself to your mother when she grew ill. Is it any wonder that afterwards I visited her, warmed to her and found her sympathetic?'

Caroline scowled. 'How good of dear Sabine to be so solicitous to my poor sick mother, as she schemed all the while to steal her husband away from her!' she shouted. 'Why, she is so clever it wouldn't surprise me to learn she'd poisoned my poor mother!' With this, she threw down her napkin in a ferment of fury, whipped up her skirts and rushed from the room. Herbert was left gaping and speechless.

Gazing intently into Caroline's empty chair Joshua pondered on this astonishing outburst. He glanced up and caught Francis's eye. The earlier cool hostility had disappeared and the expression on Francis's face was now one of unmistakable sadness. A similar emotion was etched upon Herbert's face. Seeing this brought a sense of profound melancholy upon Joshua Pope. He had hoped that coming to Astley would rid him of his sense of gloomy, lonely despair. In Herbert's betrothal to Sabine he had seen hope, light, the belief that his own sad plight might also one day be similarly happily resolved. Witnessing the discord at the dinner table made him comprehend that all was not as blissful as he believed. Despite his longing to escape it, the cloud of despondency he had intended to leave in London had followed him to Astley.

# Chapter Seven

After Caroline Bentnick's outburst, dinner concluded swiftly and in awkward silence. Joshua rose from the table. The late-afternoon weather was still fine and bright. Still oppressed by the atmosphere at dinner, Joshua decided to follow his earlier determination. He would take advantage of the dwindling sunshine and spend an hour or two outdoors. He would make some sketches first and then seek out the gardener as Mrs Mercier had asked. After donning a broad-brimmed velvet hat garnished with an extravagant plume and a woollen frock coat lined in purple silk – fine dress sometimes helped lift his spirits – Joshua took up his sketchbook, placed a box of watercolours under his arm and went out.

He walked in search of a view and tranquillity, some respite from the taint of malevolence and wrath. Dinner had intrigued him more than a little, but it had also been profoundly fatiguing. Before Rachel died, Joshua had always been of sociable disposition. On occasion, after a bottle or two of claret, he might even appear rather too full of *bonhomie*. Since her death his appetite for company had lessened. Furthermore, Joshua's marriage, though brief, had been a contented one. Now, confronted by such an excess of discord he felt unsettled and unsteady and ill equipped to cope. He felt a twinge in his temple and a slight rise in the rate of his pulse. Immediately he began to fret a headache might be poised to smite him. A walk in solitude was what he needed.

For some time Joshua patrolled the walled garden at Astley in search of a suitable position, somewhere that would afford both the requisite view and shelter from the breeze and a sanctuary from human distraction. At length he came upon a possible spot – a row of sunken terraces filled with formal parterres; each resembled a small verdant room, with its own arched entrance, clipped privet walls and stone furnishings. In the second terrace, a sundial supported on the back of a plump Cupid was set amid urns of crimson auriculas and shell-coloured pinks. The beds were filled with tangled roses and campanulas in hues of crimson and deep blue. The place would suit his purpose very well. Settling himself on a stone bench, beneath a pergola over which clematis clambered in wild profusion, he took out his charcoal and began to draw.

Some minutes later, he heard the crunch of footsteps approaching on the gravel path behind the hedge. Whoever the promenader might be, he or she was invisible, hidden behind a wall of privet. Joshua wondered whether he should call out and make himself known. Before he could decide, a second set of steps approached and a conversation began.

Joshua's heart plummeted. The voices were those of Francis and Caroline Bentnick. He sat there, taut and silent, sketching quietly as he waited for them to pass by. But then it dawned upon him that the brother and sister had arranged this meeting. Caroline had emerged from wherever it was she had hidden herself after fleeing the dinner table and come to this spot expressly in order to converse with her brother unobserved. Joshua remembered also Francis's agitation at the mention of the dead man. He recalled Caroline's animosity towards Sabine, and curiosity – that brief niggling itch that had earlier emerged – became a burning rash. He was overwhelmed with a desire to know what would be said.

'That was a creditable display you provided,' said Francis to his sister.

'I could not help myself. How can our father believe we

could be as callous as he? Does he expect us to forget our mother and take Sabine to our hearts at the drop of a hat?'

'His gullibility is quite beyond me,' agreed her brother. 'We will do him a great service if we persuade him to view her more critically, or more prudently at least.'

'How to achieve it, though, when he is so much in her thrall?'

From his listening post behind the hedge, Joshua noted that Francis and Caroline had abandoned their earlier dismal tones. Their voices were tinged with bitterness and unmistakable fervour.

'Perhaps we have the means already,' continued Francis. 'The corpse that Sabine found in the pinery: it was no coincidence. The man *was* acquainted with the Merciers.'

'How do you know? Did you see him? Did you speak to him?'

'I believe I did. When I was walking with Violet, we met a man recently arrived from Barbados.'

There was a sharp intake of breath. Caroline's voice rose an octave. 'You went walking with Violet Mercier! I might ask you what do you think you were about? What sort of conversation did you have? Did you discuss the benefits of satin over silk as an underskirt, or whether the latest musical entertainment at Ranelagh is as ravishing as at Vauxhall?'

'You are very cynical. Violet's outward attractions don't make her a fool. I'm not convinced she's any happier with her mother's betrothal than we are. There's more to her than we know. But to return to the dead man. The conversation I refer to was not between Violet and myself but between Violet and him. What I meant was that I was present when she spoke to him. And the exchange was most intriguing.'

'Violet smiled prettily at you and now she has you snared. Is that what you mean? Then you are no better than our father,' said Caroline, still apparently so distracted at the news of her brother's promenade she didn't pay full attention to what he said concerning the dead youth.

'Caroline, for pity's sake, listen to what I say. What

happened was this. I had just returned from a ride when Violet approached me and insisted that I accompany her on a turn about the gardens. I tried to excuse myself, but she wouldn't give way. I fancy she has grown quite fond of me.'

'As you seem to be of her.'

'You know my agreement with Lizzie. We hope to marry.'

'Indeed? I thought perhaps you had cooled since the alteration in her circumstances.'

'Her fortune or lack of it makes no difference. Besides, it was no fault of hers.'

'And does Violet know of your situation?'

'I believe she does, though I hazard it doesn't please her.'

There was a lengthy, uncomfortable silence, during which Joshua, perched behind the hedge, clutching his sketchbook on his knee, imagined the two glowering at each other. Goose pimples of anticipation rose on his spine and he scarcely dared breathe.

'At any rate, as I said, Violet insisted I go with her. Short of downright rudeness, she left me no choice but to comply. I consented to a short stroll, thinking I would make some excuse to escape as soon as the opportunity arose. We set off towards the pinery, and almost at once came upon a strange young fellow walking in the garden. He was personable, dressed fairly well – at any rate, not as a labourer. Violet seemed surprised to see him. She stopped and asked what he was doing. She didn't introduce me, but I had the strong impression she knew him. I thought he seemed shocked at my presence, yet not at all displeased to see her. He replied that he had recently arrived from the Indies and had come here seeking employment.'

'And how did Violet respond?'

'She said that she could be of no assistance, that this was a private garden and he should leave at once.'

'Did she ask anything else?'

'Nothing. The conversation was very brief and, I would say, moreover, very stilted.'

'What do you mean by that?'

'I mean that as soon as she saw this stranger, I felt that I was an embarrassment and she was eager to be rid of me. I had the feeling that what was said was for my benefit, a sham. She wanted to say more, but would not do so in my presence. She ushered me away and back to the house as speedily as she was able, saying she was grown tired. Once indoors, I asked how she knew the fellow and what his name was, but she was reluctant to disclose anything at all. She said she wanted to lie down, but I suspect she intended to go back to the garden and find him, for she kept peering out of the window, as if to catch a glimpse of him.'

'She must have given some further word of explanation?'

'Only that she had thought when she saw him first he was a servant of her mother's, but that she was mistaken.'

'And you said nothing of this to our father?'

'I was on the point of doing so at dinner today. But that wretched man Pope was there – probing in the matter, which is no concern of his. And then I thought, why speak when holding back may yield us the fruit we desire? When Violet returns I intend to discuss the matter with her, in the light of the fellow's death. If she knew him it is likely that her mother did too. His death may be a sign of some subterfuge or complicity between them – it is even possible Sabine was responsible for it. In which case, perhaps your suspicions concerning our mother's death are not as far-fetched as I first thought. In any case, whatever Violet's business with the man, there can be no doubt there is something she's holding back. Our task is to unearth it.'

# Chapter Eight

Once Caroline and Francis Bentnick had gone, Joshua sat for some time musing on all he had overheard. Until this moment he had been curious about the death in a detached way, as if the whole affair were a passing scene viewed from a carriage window. Now, however, he began to find himself drawn in. It seemed to him singularly strange that Herbert Bentnick, whose house this was, and who was usually consumed with curiosity by all manner of subjects, should manifest so little interest in the demise of a man in his pinery. Only Sabine Mercier had asked after the corpse. Surely, he thought, there was something devilishly wrong if a man could arrive mysteriously from Barbados, die in a pinery in a private garden, and be buried so precipitously with barely a question being asked. Could any life be worth so little?

Equally intriguing were the questions raised by Francis and Caroline's conversation. They suspected Sabine might be responsible for the death and implied she might also have done away with their mother. Having heard Francis's account of his meeting in the garden with the victim, Joshua agreed there was more to the matter, some concealment. Yet it was also clear to him that if Sabine had been responsible for the man's death, she would not have invited Joshua to probe into it. She would want the matter forgotten as quickly as possible. But then, recalling Sabine's emphatic command that he should tell no one what he found, he felt less sure again. Perhaps she was guilty in some way and was merely using him to discover what was generally known.

The more Joshua considered these conflicting points, the more, in some curious manner, he felt a charge upon him to act for the dead man. He too was a stranger here. He too was unfamiliar with these surroundings. Death was no stranger to him. He knew the torment it brings to those left behind. Suppose this dead man had a wife, children, parents, who as yet were ignorant of his demise. The thought of some poor woman fretting over her husband's whereabouts troubled him profoundly. Joshua was not a busybody by nature. Never before had he been disposed to meddle in the affairs of others, yet now he felt a sense of duty to probe a little into the circumstances of this unfortunate fellow's death.

All this while in the garden he had worked with his customary precision. An hour later his sketch was complete. He emerged from his sanctuary in the sunken terrace and made his way towards the pinery. A gravel path led past a knot garden, a pond filled with a galaxy of fish in shades of red and gold, and a border of rose bushes, to the gate leading to the kitchen garden. Sheltered from the wind by high brick walls, the air here reeked of dung. In several beds under gardeners, ranging from mere lads to elderly men, were busy planting, lifting, digging and hoeing. One spindly lad was occupied in planting out hairy-leaved cucumbers and melons in forcing frames; another was cutting pink-tipped asparagus that reared like spears through mounds of manure.

Beyond, in the furthest corner of the garden, three small lean-to glasshouses hugged the wall. In contrast to the monumental pinery in which Sabine Mercier had discovered the body, these were modest structures, used for raising melons for the kitchens or for bringing on ornamental blooms.

Joshua recognized the head gardener from his previous encounter that morning. Granger was standing at a bench, chewing on a long-stemmed clay pipe of tobacco, while he planted up large silver-leaved pineapple plants on a bench strewn with shards of broken pot. Smoke billowed about his head as he worked. His hands were large and calloused and ingrained with dirt, yet his fingers were surprisingly slender and he handled the plants with great delicacy, like a child lifting eggs from a bird's nest. As Joshua approached, Granger looked up and grunted an acknowledgement without breaking off what he was doing or removing his pipe. He cut a striking figure, thought Joshua, appraising him with an artist's eye. His hair had the colour and shine of ancient polished oak. His face was long and leathery of complexion. A scar on the left side of his face stretched from his chin to the top of his cheek, dragging down the eye to give him a curious lopsided appearance.

'Good day to you, Mr Granger,' said Joshua. He nodded briefly towards the plants that Granger was tending. 'I suppose pineapples must present a challenge to your skills.'

'I've seen them grown before in a small way, but never on such a scale.' His voice was gravelly, well spoken and assured.

'At Astley?'

'No. At a previous estate, Beechwood. We tried them with some success.'

'Mrs Mercier was fortunate to find a man of your expertise. You are only lately arrived here, I gather?'

'That's right, sir. '

'And how do you find it, compared with other places?'

'As good as any, better than some,' said Granger, 'though as for pineapples it seems to me, from all she has shown me, there's enough written on the subject to fill a library and turn the most inexperienced grower to an expert.'

'Must you always break the pots to replant them?'

'Not as a rule, sir. Nor in this instance either.'

'Then what are you doing now?'

'In dying where he did the man's proved uncommonly troublesome.' He grinned, revealing surprisingly white teeth.

'In what way?'

'Before he died he removed these pots from their beds and broke them,' Granger said flatly. 'Lord knows why he did it. But Mrs Mercier was most agitated on account of it and gave orders to put them to rights before the plants perished from a want of moisture. So here you see me doing the same as was done already not a week since.'

With that he took up a plant, placed it in a new pot and tucked compost around it. The task was accomplished swiftly but with great gentleness.

'I gather the dead man was a stranger to these parts. Perhaps he came in search of work?'

This question prompted Granger to remove his pipe and place it upon the bench, alongside the shards of broken terracotta. He gave Joshua a level gaze, as if waiting for something. 'You are a stranger here yourself, are you not, sir?' he said.

Joshua threw his travelling cloak back over his shoulder, allowing the gardener a flash of his brilliant waistcoat. 'Indeed I am,' he declared, fanning himself with his hat, before banging his head with his fist at his own stupidity. 'Forgive me, Mr Granger, I haven't told you who I am. I must introduce myself: Joshua Pope, come to Astley on commission to paint the marriage portrait of Mr Bentnick and his future bride.'

Granger nodded his head slowly, looking Joshua up and down, taking in his strangely plumed hat, the extravagant cravat about his neck, the sketchbook under his arm, as if weighing up this information carefully to see if it tallied with what he had just been told. 'An artist, is it?' he said slowly. 'And what would an artist be wanting with a gardener? Fancy painting some of my flowers, do you?'

'No. Yes. In a manner of speaking, I suppose I do.' Joshua replied frankly. Despite his disfigurement Granger had a pleasing face, strong bones beneath a skin coloured by weather and life's vicissitudes. Joshua imagined him dressed as a buccaneer or a brigand waving his curved sword aloft. He found himself itching to take out his chalks and sketch him.

'But it wasn't that which brought me here. I came because Mrs Mercier asked me to.'

'And why did she do that?'

'She bade me ask you if you'd found anything about him.'

'No more than she already knows, for I told her before what I knew of him.'

'You met him before, then?'

'He came walking in the garden two days ago. I accosted him and he said it was work he was after, and that he was expert in the cultivation of pineapples. It was my opinion he'd not done much in this line before so I sent him packing.'

'On what did you base your judgement?'

'In part his shifty look. But mostly because of his hands, sir. They were more carefully manicured than your own.'

Joshua looked down at his fingers, which seemed oddly feeble by comparison with Granger's long, earthy digits.

'Forgive me, sir. But I can't see what all this is to you,' added Granger with unexpected curtness.

Joshua met his gaze. 'People intrigue me, Mr Granger. Just as I presume you take note when you encounter a strange plant, so do I when I encounter some human idiosyncrasy. I heard Francis Bentnick say Miss Violet recognized the fellow. Yet Herbert Bentnick believed him to be a stranger to Sabine and her daughter. And now you tell me he claimed to know about pineapples and that his hands were not those of a gardener. That strikes me as a rare and curious fact. And it is a rare coincidence too that he should turn up here at Astley, at the very moment you turn the conservatory into a pinery.'

'What gives you the impression any of it was a rare coincidence? It was nothing of the kind. He said it was Mrs Mercier who wrote and urged him to come on account of it. I didn't believe him, but there's no doubt in my mind that he knew her.'

'What else did you learn of him?'

'He was a destructive man.'

'In what way?'

'Is this not proof enough?' Here Granger waved at the broken pots before him.

'Is that all? You can't be sure this damage wasn't accidental. He might have staggered about in his last moments and broken the pots unwittingly.'

'The pots were half-buried, sir. I think not. The damage was certainly deliberate. And there's more. When he came here two days ago he cut one of the most advanced fruits without my noticing, and took it away.'

'How do you know he did it?'

'Who else would have done it?'

'And what did you make of such an action?'

'I thought that I was correct to label him a rascal and that he can't have known a jot about pineapples. He should have known you cannot eat a green fruit: it's the bitterest thing you ever tasted.'

'Did you not go after him and chastise him?'

Granger shrugged his shoulders. 'What would be the purpose? The damage was done.'

'I take it you spoke of this to Mrs Mercier?'

Granger nodded.

'And how did she respond?'

Granger paused a moment. 'Not as I expected. I believe I caught her off guard, for she seemed startled. She stared, asked me to repeat myself, shook her head. Then she said, "I do not know this man; nor have I written to anyone and asked him to come here. I am glad you sent him away. You did well to do so, Granger."'

Here the gardener paused again, while his earthy fingers pressed compost round a plant to secure it. Then he looked away into the far distance. 'She never mentioned his name, yet I suspected she knew exactly who he was and that he wasn't at all welcome. Why else would she have been so pleased I acted as I did?'

Joshua ignored his question, pursuing his own train doggedly. 'Did you discover his name?'

'Only this morning. I searched his pockets; there were two letters in one of them, both addressed to a man called John Cobb.'

'What became of the letters?'

'I gave them to Mr Bentnick, when you and he arrived to assist this morning.'

'And what were your impressions when you found Mrs Mercier?'

'All in all her behaviour this morning was singular.'

Granger confided then that not only had he been first on the scene, he had nearly witnessed the discovery. He had been standing by, waiting for Sabine's arrival; it was her custom to stop and speak to him every morning on her way to the pinery. More often than not she required that he accompany her on her rounds of the building so that she could instruct him on new tasks to undertake.

'This morning, when I saw Mrs Mercier enter the walled garden, I expected her to come towards me or at very least acknowledge my presence. She did neither. She seemed preoccupied. Her eye was set on the pinery – she didn't look for me at all. I followed her into the pinery because I had several matters of business to discuss: more young pines to pot on, cuttings to be rooted, a question of tan bark to discuss. I entered the pinery just behind her and in no time came across her crouched on the path, cradling the dead man.'

'How did she seem?'

Granger screwed up his eyes as if searching for the right words. 'She wasn't sobbing or screaming. Her eyes were wide open, her brow knotted. I would say she looked surprised rather than fearful. It was only when I called out and offered to help her that the horror of the situation seemed to strike her. She let go her hold on the body, which flopped back, then placed a kerchief over his face, as if she couldn't bear to look at him. When she stood up she shuddered visibly, as if frozen to the core. I was not four feet distant from her, yet I might

70

have been ten miles away for all the heed she paid me. She pushed past and fled to the door. Once outside, she filled her lungs then let out a piercing cry. I dare say that was what brought you and Mr Bentnick running.'

Joshua nodded. 'What then?'

'I offered her my assistance again. This time she registered the offer and ordered me to go at once and examine the body. I did as she instructed and retrieved the letters. I intended to give them to her, but by the time I returned, you and Mr Bentnick had arrived and Mrs Mercier's condition seemed worse. I thought it more appropriate to hand them to Mr Bentnick.'

'Did you read them? Did you see who wrote them?' Joshua demanded.

'No, there was no time. Besides, it wasn't my place to do so. I saw only the name. John Cobb.'

# Chapter Nine

In those days Joshua always noticed paintings of people, though landscapes left him cold. He had already remarked the miniature of Elizabeth Manning, or 'Lizzie', as she was affectionately termed by the Bentnick family. It had been painted by her friend Caroline Bentnick, who had framed it in ebony and hung it on a ribbon in the morning room at Astley, between miniatures of her father and brother. Herbert had pointed it out to Joshua during that awkward dinner after John Cobb was found dead.

When Joshua met Miss Manning on the following day, his first impression was that she was quite as insipid in the flesh as the wan portrait her friend had drawn. She had arrived in the same carriage as Violet Mercier, who was just returned from London. He caught sight of her from an upstairs window – a slight figure clad in her travelling dress: a black bonnet, a coat of dull mouse brown, a plain grey skirt beneath.

In the drawing room that evening Joshua began to temper his view. Miss Manning was less nondescript than at first he supposed – no beauty, perhaps, but not entirely without charm all the same. Her face was small and rather birdlike, with a pointed chin, a well-defined nose, and lustrous grey eyes set wide apart in a complexion unblemished by pox. Her lips were compactly drawn and playful. She had small, perfectly white teeth that showed whenever she smiled, which was often.

That evening she wore a black bodice garnished with oyster ribbons from bosom to waist. Her hair, a thick mass of chestnut tresses, had been dressed with a single white-silk rose. About her neck, another white rose was attached to an oyster ribbon. However, none of this would have altered his impression of her ordinariness had he not made another discovery. Her outward appearance was a shell. Her attraction lay within.

Conversation was Lizzie Manning's lifeblood. She was born with an insatiable desire to discuss her thoughts, to eke out confidences. Silence was anathema to her. Though it was often said that she had learned to talk before she walked, the truth was that when Lizzie was only five her mother had died in childbirth, leaving her daughter and infant son to be raised by a nurse with a fortunate capacity for chatter. This was why to be left in solitude by her father (who was in the north on business) and her brother (whose whereabouts she didn't mention) had been like purgatory. The discovery that her dear friend Francis Bentnick had arranged for Violet to collect her on her return from London and spirit her to Astley for the evening had thus delighted her beyond words.

New acquaintances were trophies to Lizzie Manning; she collected them as others collect sea shells or coins or buttons. Until that day she had never met Violet Mercier. From the moment she stepped into the carriage she had bombarded her with words of welcome and questions and confidences. The interrogation continued unabated throughout the afternoon and early evening.

'Tell me, dear Violet, what was Barbados like?'

'Most verdant and most pleasant, Miss Manning.'

'Not Miss Manning – I am Lizzie to everyone. How I long to see it. Tell me about your mother's garden. I have heard it was like Eden.'

'It is difficult to describe, Lizzie. It was lush, lavish, abundant . . .'

'It can't be easy for you and your mother in such a strange

73

environment so far from home? Do you have acquaintances, friends?

'None, but we have each other.'

'And tell me of the ball. What an event it will be! Have you decided what you will wear?'

'I have a gown nearly finished; it is pale-blue silk with flowers and seed-pearl embroidery.'

'What an unusual necklace your mother is wearing. I don't believe I have ever set eyes on such stones. Nor such a design.'

'It came from her second husband, Charles Mercier, my former stepfather.'

'What is its history?'

'It is a curious one. The necklace dates from medieval times. Apparently it was made in Nuremberg – a city famous for the excellence of its craftsmen – as a love token. It was commissioned by a German princeling for a lady he wished to marry.'

Lizzie's eyes were illuminated with interest. 'But is not the serpent a most unusual love token for a besotted prince?'

'Perhaps,' replied Violet with a smile, 'though it is often used as a symbol of fertility.'

'And did the prince win his lady?'

'Yes, though the story was not entirely happy. Soon after the pair married, the jewel was stolen by a jealous sister, who was apprehended and later burned as a witch. This gave rise to the superstition that the necklace would bring happiness if given in love, but ill fortune if it changed ownership for any material reason.'

'What an intriguing and poignant history,' said Lizzie, smiling. 'It only adds to the allure of the jewel – if that is possible.'

'You should say so to my mother,' declared Violet, rising to bring her mother to speak to Lizzie, 'for ever since she set eyes on the necklace she has taken inordinate pride in wearing it, and does so at every opportunity.'

Joshua watched Violet drift across the room to bring her mother over.

74

He had met her only fleetingly prior to her departure for London, on the morning after his arrival. Already he had remarked the perfect symmetry of her face and the elegance of her bearing. She was a remarkably handsome young woman: as tall as Juno, finely boned with plentiful hair dark gold in hue, blue-grey eyes fringed with dark lashes, and the same honey-coloured complexion as her mother. Her dress, he noted with great pleasure, was as immaculate as her face: she wore a bodice and skirt of lilac silk embroidered with flowers and trimmed with a tulle pleated frill about the neck and cuffs. The skirt was pinned back to reveal a petticoat of rich purple brocade.

Her face and garb were like those of an angel, that much was clear to Joshua, but he had found unravelling her character less simple. At their first meeting she had avoided light conversation whenever possible, speaking only in response to direct questions. On several occasions he had caught sight of her gazing into the distance, or out of the window, seemingly oblivious to her immediate surroundings, as if some pressing matter preoccupied her. Now, however, he began to suspect that it was Caroline's animosity towards Violet that had made her reticent and withdrawn. This evening, with Lizzie Manning to encourage her, she presented an altogether different side. She conversed easily with Lizzie, and by the time supper was finished and the assembled party had moved to the drawing room, Lizzie Manning and Violet Mercier threaded their arms together and appeared to be on the most cordial terms.

The drawing room was long and narrow with an ornate moulded ceiling and walls lined with pea-green damask silk studded with landscapes and portraits of various Bentnick forebears. In the centre of one wall, above a grand chimney-piece, hung a full-length portrait of Jane Bentnick painted by Thomas Gainsborough at Bath only a year or two earlier. As Joshua joined Herbert and Francis Bentnick at a table by a window for a hand of cards his eyes were riveted upon the portrait. Few artists, in Joshua's opinion, gave the viewer pleasure with such ease as Gainsborough. There was depth yet enviable naturalness to his style. Jane wore a fashionable Van Dyck costume of sky-blue silk with a pointed lace collar and a lavishly plumed hat. She looked the ideal of graceful womanhood and yet, in the turn of her head, the set of her mouth and in those heavy-lidded brown eyes, there was wit, determination, character in abundance. Such was the spell Gainsborough wove that for some time Joshua paid little attention to the cards he was dealt, pondering instead what kind of woman Jane Bentnick had been. What would she have made of her husband's choice of new bride? What would she have thought of her children's suspicions? Was Herbert's hurried engagement a sign that his union with Jane had been blissfully contented or unhappy?

Joshua shifted his gaze to regard the ladies, who had settled themselves on gilded chairs around the fire. Caroline Bentnick took up her embroidery and put it down again. Then she began to plead with Lizzie Manning to divert them by playing something on the piano. 'And I shall sing,' declared Violet Mercier, her glowing face now looking more radiant than ever. Lizzie Manning agreed and the two moved to the piano, just as Herbert gave a loud cough and urged Joshua to concentrate on the cards on the table. From the corner of his eye Joshua saw Sabine move closer to Caroline, and he dimly heard the beginnings of their conversation.

'Your father tells me you intend to wear a dress that belonged to your mother at our engagement ball,' said Sabine without preamble. 'I think that is a delightful notion. Now, tell me, what jewellery will you wear with it? Did your mother leave you anything?'

'My mother cared little for jewels. I have a small locket that will serve admirably,' said Caroline warily.

Stroking the jewel at her throat, Sabine smiled benevolently. 'Never mind the locket, dear Caroline, you may wear my necklace with your mother's dress. I don't offer it lightly. But I believe it will be appropriate – after all, I will soon become your stepmother.'

Joshua heard no more of this curious conversation, for, sensing disapproval beneath Herbert's fidgeting and coughing, he turned his attentions to play. As it turned out, his cards were lucky, and he was so diverted by victory that only after winning several hands did he turn his head back.

What he saw immediately caught his attention. Caroline was now sitting, motionless and silent, some distance away from Sabine. Joshua saw her gaze transfixed on the emerald necklace about Sabine's neck. The expression on her face seemed to suggest she believed it the foulest object she ever set eyes on (a sentiment with which Joshua heartily concurred). Joshua saw her turn wildly to her brother for assistance, but Francis was immersed in his hand of cards. She looked back at the necklace about Mrs Mercier's neck, then down at her hands. She pressed her palms to her neck as if she burned with embarrassment and could not think what to do.

Some minutes passed, during which not a word was uttered, and Sabine stared at Caroline with an odd, fierce expression. Eventually Sabine broke the silence. 'Then you accept my offer,' Joshua heard her say clearly, just as the piano struck up and Violet began to sing a tuneful accompaniment to Lizzie's playing.

Later, when the gentlemen left the card table to rejoin the ladies by the fire, Francis Bentnick went immediately to Lizzie's side. She began to recount a yarn that involved her taking on the voice and character of at least half a dozen personalities. Herbert, whom Joshua had vanquished modestly enough for him to remain in genial humour, drew up a chair beside Sabine and Violet. Joshua stood by the fire, his hand in his pocket, chinking the two sovereigns he had won. His attention was all on Caroline, whose peculiar expression still intrigued him. Her eyes were bright with unshed tears. Her long narrow jaw twitched with tension and her cheeks were unnaturally flushed. Her face seemed . . . what exactly? For an instant he was unsure – not anger, not embarrassment – then it flashed upon him: she looked *terrified*.

What had Sabine Mercier said to bring about such a transformation? Clearly it had to do with the necklace, but what precisely? Joshua swiftly concluded that if Sabine had offered her most prized possession to someone who so plainly viewed her with ambivalence, she had some hidden purpose. Was this purely a way to ingratiate herself, or was there some other reason? Joshua was still pondering this question when Caroline seemed to sense his gaze and looked up. Catching his eyes upon her, she looked perplexed, then pale and uneasy. She took out her fan and wafted it rapidly in front of her face. Then she rose without a word and went to the far end of the room. For some time she paced about, looking nervous and pathetic like a bird battering itself on a window pane. Eventually Herbert noticed her agitation and passed some remark, wondering if she was perhaps unwell. She assured him nothing was amiss. As if to convince him of the fact, she sat down, took out her embroidery and began to work at it with a look of feigned concentration on her face.

Joshua was certain she was not quite well. Nevertheless, since there was nothing for the moment to learn, he turned his attentions to Lizzie Manning, who was still engrossed with Francis, her face aglow with animation. She was a sparrow, and yet an intriguing one. Her faintly coloured costume served as a frame, its blandness enhancing her expressiveness. Never did he recall observing a face of such mercurial fluctuations. He would have liked to ask her to pose for him, but, since they were barely acquainted, decorum forbade him from doing so. Nevertheless, he wondered what it would be like to paint her. Would she ever sit still? How would he draw her? What pose would convey her animation? Did her unpredictable expression reflect a similarly inconstant temperament?

# Chapter Ten

The Star and Garter Inn was set high upon the crest of Richmond Hill, overlooking the town. It was a tall brick-built building resembling a nobleman's mansion, with a garden behind that was famed throughout the vicinity. Honeysuckle and jasmine and roses trailed over paths, and sweeps of lawn lay between trees and avenues of lime. Joshua entered the parlour of the inn on the off chance. Having paced the main street of Richmond, asking himself where he might go were he a stranger recently arrived from Barbados in need of a bed for the night, he had already been refreshed in the Red Lyon, the Talbot, the Feathers in Water Lane, the Compasses and the Rose and Crown.

'And what can I be doing for you, sir?' said James Dunstable, the landlord, spying Joshua hovering by the counter in his front room. Joshua felt the landlord take in his satin-lined cape, his embroidered waistcoat, his lace cravat. He thought to himself that few men decked in such finery could pass through here and plainly Dunstable was flummoxed. Joshua could almost hear him wonder what manner of gentleman dressed with such extravagance to promenade the high street of Richmond at eleven o'clock of the morning. The thought pleased him no end.

Joshua placed his tricorn on the counter. 'I'll have an ale if you please, sir,' he replied. 'I have come in search of a Mr John

Cobb. He has arrived recently from overseas. I believe he might be staying here?'

Dunstable took down a pewter tankard from a high shelf and examined it for signs of dirt.

'Mr Cobb from Barbados? And what's he to you?' he said as he gave the mug a hefty shake.

'He's an acquaintance of mine. I have a proposition for him.'

Dunstable edged the tankard beneath the nozzle of the pump and began to pull slowly on its handle. 'Whatever the nature of your proposition, I regret to say you have come too late,' he said, handing over the foaming vessel.

Joshua took a moment to sip his ale, regarding Dunstable from behind the tankard's rim. 'Would you not take a drink for yourself, sir? Why am I too late?'

'He paid for his lodgings two days ago. Said he'd be back shortly for his portmanteau. I've seen and heard nothing of him since.'

'How long did he stay here?' said Joshua with scarcely a pause, for he knew Cobb had disappeared and why, though there was no reason to disclose this to the landlord.

'Three or four weeks. You may tell him when you find him that his portmanteau is still gathering dust and I'd be grateful to see the back of it.' Dunstable took up his mug and fairly gulped down the ale, as if he'd not drunk for a week.

'Did he have any visitors during that time?

'Aye, a few. But there was one that made him wait.'

'What d'you mean?'

'Cobb was forever asking if anyone had called; if any letters had arrived.'

'He never said who the person he expected was?'

'Not in so many words, but it was a lady. He said more than once, "If anyone comes, tell *her* I will not be long, and look after her well till my return." '

'Do you remember any of the callers who *did* come? Did they leave names?'

'Hold on, not so fast,' said the landlord, thumping his empty mug on the counter. 'What's all this to do with your proposition?'

'Another drink, Mr Dunstable? I need to talk to Cobb,' Joshua said, lying through his teeth without any visible qualm. 'It's a delicate family matter.' Here he winked knowingly at Dunstable and tapped the side of his nose. 'If I can trace one of his visitors, perhaps they will help me find him. I would be most grateful for your assistance.'

Dunstable shrugged his shoulders and refilled his mug to the brim. 'One was a solicitor, who worked for a London office.'

'How d'you know?'

'He left a card with a message for Mr Cobb.'

'His name?'

'Bartholomew Hoare, attorney of Gray's Inn Lane.'

'Any others?'

'Herbert Bentnick. He had a grand disagreement with your Mr Cobb.'

'*Herbert Bentnick*? Are you certain it was he?'

'As certain as I am there's paint on the end of your nose.'

Joshua dabbed at his face hastily with a handkerchief. 'And what was the argument about? Were you present when it took place? Did you overhear it?'

Dunstable looked a little peeved at this suggestion. 'The gentlemen were at the seats you see there.' He waved a broad, hairy hand in the direction of an oak settle in a dark corner of the inn. 'So I could hardly fail to, could I?'

'Quite so. I didn't mean to suggest you were intruding.'

'No, well, perhaps not. But I have to mind what happens here . . .'

'Yes, yes, Mr Dunstable, but did you hear anything?'

'Have patience; I'm telling you now, aren't I? They had scarce taken a sip of their wine when Mr Bentnick set to shouting at Mr Cobb. "I tell you she will not see you and there's an end to it," he fairly bellowed, whereupon Mr Cobb says, "I ask for no more than is rightfully mine." Then Mr

Bentnick responds, "There is only your say-so on it," and Cobb says, "No, there's more. I have letters to prove it." At that point the two stood and faced each other and I grew afraid for their safety. Mr Bentnick says he knows nothing of any papers, but he's sure they must be counterfeit if they exist. Next thing Cobb's thrown his tankard and soaked Mr Bentnick, who's told him if he stays a moment longer he'll be in danger of doing Mr Cobb some terrible injury. Then he stormed off, drenched to the skin and fuming.'

This was all most interesting; Dunstable had earned his ale and another besides. 'Were there other encounters between the two of them?' Joshua asked as he sipped.

'None that I witnessed, though 'tis my guess that the lady they spoke of and the lady he was always waiting for were one and the same. 'Tis possible she was the lady who came the very day Cobb disappeared.'

'Who was she?'

'There I cannot help you. I was occupied with the stables and the grooms; I caught a brief glimpse of her entering the inn. That is all. She wasn't known to me.'

'What variety of lady was she?'

'A fair one.'

'Her age? Manner?'

'Wigged, powdered, twenty or thereabouts, dressed in the grandest style feathers, and flowers and ribbons and lace and anything else you care to mention. As conscious of her charms as anyone with her attractions would be.'

'What makes you associate her with Mr Bentnick?'

Dunstable looked down at his half-empty mug. 'Naught in particular. Only I have heard there's ladies staying and, having heard a lady mentioned in the argument, I suppose I just assumed it.'

Three tankards of ale and one hour later, Joshua glanced at his pocket watch, and out of the window. He contemplated the short walk back to Astley without enthusiasm. The sky had grown low and heavy and a sharp north breeze had begun to blow. He left the inn, knowing that if he lingered on he would be late for Sabine Mercier's sitting, and that a downpour was imminent, but wishing he could stay. With little choice but to spoil his new leather boots, he buttoned his coat and adjusted his cravat and set out.

Half a mile down the road large gouts of rain began to drop on his hat. Within quarter of an hour the downpour had strengthened sufficiently to make inroads to his collar and seep through to his neck. He was certain now that by tomorrow at the very least he would have to take to bed with a cold. At worst there was the possibility of contracting fevers and ailments he didn't even want to speculate upon. To make matters worse, the road had now veered so close to the detestable river he fancied he could smell it. So damp and morose and uneasy was he that the creak and jangle of chassis and harness signalling a coach-and-two thundering over the summit of a hill from the direction of Astley didn't make him alter his stride; nor did he move to the verge of the road to avoid being splashed. Since he was already soaked and saturated beyond recognition, what difference would a little more mud and water make?

The carriage drew to a clattering halt in a large puddle three feet in front of him. A quart of gritty brown water slopped over his boots and began to drip down his stockings. A gloved hand pushed down the window. A dun bonnet framing a pair of sparkling grey eyes peered back. 'You have chosen a nasty day for a promenade, Mr Pope. Would you not care for a ride?' It was Lizzie Manning, dressed in her dreary outdoor garb, but wearing an expression that was a study of amusement, solicitude and curiosity.

'If it is not an inconvenience, then that is most kind indeed,' said Joshua, drawing near, 'for, as you so astutely remark, the weather has turned very dirty indeed.'

'Do not mention it, I beg of you,' answered Lizzie Manning with an airy wave. 'The carriage is Mr Bentnick's. He has sent me home in it. It will be no trouble at all for the driver to return with you, since he will be going there anyway. Besides, I am perfectly sure Mr Bentnick would not desire his latest portraitist to fall ill with a virulent fever.'

Joshua bowed low in acceptance of her offer, thinking what a miracle it was to find someone as considerate for his health as this. He opened the door and climbed in. He had scarce time to open his mouth to utter a pleasantry or even reiterate his thanks for her charity when he was assaulted by a battery of questions. Where had he been? Why had he gone there? What had he learned? To begin with, his replies were measured. Lizzie Manning was as good as a member of the Bentnick family. He assumed anything he confided to her would be relayed to them. And did he really want Herbert Bentnick to know he had been prying into Cobb's comings and goings? Or that Herbert had been witnessed in some mighty disagreement with the fellow though he claimed never to have set eyes on him?

But Lizzie Manning was not easily fobbed off. After Joshua had provided a modified account of the morning's activities, she smiled knowingly. 'That is all very well, and prettily related, but since there's another two miles till we arrive at my door you may as well speak candidly, Mr Pope. Don't you trust me? What is the secret that presses so insistently within you? What *really* engaged you this morning?'

Joshua blinked and tried to conceal the astonishment he felt. Before he married he had been fond of the female sex and enjoyed several close friendships among them. Rachel and he had enjoyed easy conversation. Even his mistress Meg was something of a chatterbox, yet he was unaccustomed to females speaking so boldly and with so little pretence at decorum, and he wasn't entirely sure how to respond.

Lizzie must have sensed his consternation; she patted his arm comfortingly. 'You will find me the very essence of discretion, Mr Pope. Why, I have heard secrets as would make your ears tingle, yet I have never spoken a word to anyone.'

Any niggle of disapproval he felt was no match for her easy candour. Why should he not explain a little – after all, there was a possibility she knew something of relevance. He began, guardedly, to speak of his discoveries. He told her he had gone in search of the truth about the recent death in the pinery, because any man deserved as much when his death was so untimely and bizarre. Furthermore, Sabine had instructed him to find what he could about the dead man from Granger. According to Granger and Francis Bentnick, the man had been seen in the garden some days before he died. He was recently arrived from Barbados. Francis suspected there was some intrigue between the dead man and Violet; and Sabine might also have been acquainted with him, or so Granger thought. His name was discovered on a letter in his pocket. It was John Cobb.

'John Cobb?' echoed Lizzie, as if she were trying it for size. 'Is that who he was?'

'Did you know him?'

'Know him? No, I didn't. But I believe you are right to be wary of Sabine Mercier and her daughter,' said Lizzie, smiling brightly. 'And your sentiments are most commendable. I agree with them wholeheartedly. How could Mr Bentnick behave so callously towards a corpse in his pinery? Does he think it flew there like a dead leaf carried on the wind? Why, the very least he should do is to make some enquiries. I should write immediately and tell him so.'

'No, no, Miss Manning,' said Joshua, swiftly adopting a purposeful tone that allowed no argument. 'I pray you will do no such thing. Why, don't you see that if there is some subterfuge here then it might be of a dangerous variety? Cobb is dead, perhaps even murdered, for what else explains the singular circumstances of his death? You might cast both of us in peril if you reveal too much to the wrong person.'

Lizzie Manning's eyes opened round as sovereigns and she begged him to explain his suspicions. He replied that he had formulated none as yet. His only other research thus far was a

85

conversation with Dunstable, the landlord of the Star and Garter, where Cobb had stayed for several weeks prior to meeting his end. Cobb had received several visitors. Bartholomew Hoare, a lawyer from London; and, more intriguingly, Herbert Bentnick, with whom he had had a violent disagreement. He had also received a lady visitor, whom he described as fair, well dressed and youthful of appearance, but her identity remained a mystery.

'Mystery be damned,' said Lizzie Manning, too caught up in his account to remember feminine propriety. 'The woman must certainly be Violet. Who else do you think would fit the description? Certainly not Caroline or I.'

Joshua reddened but remained doubtful. 'You may be right,' he conceded, 'but let us not forget there are sure to be other fair-haired beauties in the vicinity of Richmond. And there is nothing to say the visitor didn't come from further afield. Violet is not unique in respect of her colouring.'

With this, Lizzie fell uncharacteristically silent. Joshua felt a strange sensation of anxiety and pleasure stir in his heart. Yesterday evening he had seen Lizzie's sociable exterior. She had amused him, entertained him, bewildered him. Now, however, his opinion of her altered. Few women of her youth would take an interest in these events. The fact that she was concerned for the fate of the dead man – a stranger – the fact she had defended Caroline and viewed the Merciers with ambivalence, were touching testimony of her humanity, loyalty and intelligence.

Yes, thought Joshua, as the carriage lurched up the rutted drive of Barlow Court and drew to a halt, Lizzie Manning wasn't the mercurial flibbertigibbet he had suspected; she might be volatile, but that was born of youth. Beneath this external show lay a woman of discernment and surprising depths.

Barlow Court, the Mannings' residence, was a square stone Queen Anne mansion, set squarely in a small park, overlooking the river near Barnes. The view of the great swathe of grey-blue water was one many people admired, although personally Joshua found it odious, for his dislike of the river continued to disturb him. While the footman opened the carriage door and dropped the step, Joshua averted his eyes from the view. He descended from the carriage and stood in the rain, which was still falling with great persistence, to help Lizzie Manning down.

'Farewell, Miss Manning,' he said, offering her his hand. He would have liked to say something more, something that would mark his new esteem for her; moreover, he was as keen to sketch her now as he had been the previous night. Never good at conveying such delicate matters to the gentle sex, however, he found himself tongue-tied with confusion. 'And may I express my heartfelt gratitude for your stopping and letting me travel in your carriage,' he managed to murmur, though this was not at all what he wanted to say.

Lizzie looked surprised, yet she smiled sweetly at him. 'Don't mention it, Mr Pope. It was no more than anyone would have done.' Here she laughed aloud, revealing her small, perfectly even teeth. 'I confess I am much intrigued by our conversation and your enquiries, and, as I said before, I believe you are right to make them. Thus, if you will accept, I have a proposition for you.'

'What manner of proposition?'

'I offer you my assistance,' she replied. Joshua was flabbergasted and clearly showed it in his face, for her expression turned a little cross. 'You may think me useless but I have my purposes – in gaining entry where you could not, for instance, and in extracting confidences you would not. I am quite famous for wheedling out what is hidden and obscure. Ask anyone who knows me.'

Joshua wanted to say no. He was, in truth, uncertain even that *he* should be meddling in these matters. Lizzie's candid grey eyes held him captive, yet he was not so entangled as to forget to question the reason for her determination. 'You are an audacious young lady. Do you not fear putting your life in jeopardy? Consider Mr Cobb's fate,' he replied.

She tossed her head. 'You have already mentioned it. Have you no stronger argument?'

'Suppose you arouse your friends' displeasure? It may be that one of them is caught up in all of this. And since your father is the local justice, what would he say on learning of his daughter's involvement?'

Lizzie snorted disdainfully. 'Displeasure, what displeasure? I don't give a halfpenny for any such thing. Caroline and Francis are the greatest of friends to me. I have no doubt of their probity. And since they have voiced certain doubts regarding Mrs Mercier and her daughter, perhaps I may do them all a service if I aid you in discovering their involvement. As you point out, my father is the justice, so is it not appropriate that in his absence I assist you? I am sure my father would agree with me.'

'And how do you propose to proceed?' He asked this not merely to humour her, but because he would be intrigued to hear her reply.

'By speaking to Violet's maid. She might know who this Cobb was.'

Joshua drew himself back and looked at her directly. Yet again she had caught his attention. 'Have you no fear at all?'

'I could ask the very same of you, Mr Pope,' she parried. 'And while we are on the subject, may I suggest that you find some pretext to return to London and seek out Mr Hoare, the attorney, and discover the nature of his business with John Cobb?'

She said this just as Joshua had remounted into the carriage, and was preparing to slam shut the door. He leaned forward to grab the handle. He could feel a frown ruffling his brow and vexation gathering in his breast, like mustering troops on a battlefield. Her offer of assistance filled him with misgiving despite his growing regard. Now, however, he grew annoyed. A man of Joshua Pope's standing didn't expect to be treated with condescension or ordered about like a footman – especially by a girl of barely one and twenty years. Her charm was no excuse. He half wanted to tell her to take up a more suitable pastime – embroidery or watercolours, for instance – and leave him be. Yet, though it pained him to admit it, what she had said was precisely what he had already determined to do as soon as he had learned of the attorney's visit. Furthermore, her own resolve to question Violet Mercier's maid would prove extremely useful. By virtue of her sex, she would stand more chance than he would of encouraging the maid's confidence and discovering something significant. Had he not experienced her capacity for extracting confidences first-hand? There was, conceded Joshua, logic in her plans. Besides, she would never agree to sit for him unless he humoured her. And so, regardless of his reservations, he agreed.

# Chapter Eleven

He was, as he feared, late for Sabine Mercier's sitting. He found her already in his rooms, examining the unfinished canvas on his easel. He noticed she had left her travelling cloak on his chair and that she had removed the cloth with which he always covered unfinished works. When he entered she was staring at the portrait. Her eyes seemed to rest for several moments on her figure and that of Herbert, still vaguely delineated, and then scan the sketchy outline of landscape beyond. There was no telling as to her opinion of what she saw. The expression on her face wasn't one of pleasure or disapproval; rather, he judged it to be of remoteness, indifference even – as if the people in the portrait were strangers to her.

When she began to speak, however, the façade slipped and there was no doubting her displeasure. 'I confess, Mr Pope, I am a little surprised to find myself waiting for our appointment close on three-quarters of an hour. By now our sitting should be almost over and you have yet to open your paint box.'

'Madam,' said Joshua, with a remorseful droop of his eyelids, 'please accept my most profound apologies. I was caught in the rain, and Miss Manning offered me a lift. I never imagined it would take quite so long to drive there and back.' As he spoke he was already unbuttoning his sodden coat and flinging it over a chair, where the hem began to drip and form a pool on the floor. He pushed up his sleeves and donned his paint-stained smock before moving briskly to his worktable. With practised ease he took out his paint box, removed the tacks with which he stoppered bladders of paint and began to squeeze out miniature dollops onto his palette. He placed a nugget of glistening lead white next to his thumb and then, in a wide crescent, Naples yellow, orpiment, vermilion, red ochre, burnt umber, bone black, smalt and Prussian blue, like gems waiting to be strung. This done, he drew small amounts to the centre and mixed various shades, thinning the paint with linseed where necessary.

He was aware that, throughout this process, Sabine Mercier watched him closely from behind the easel. She sniffed the air, which was heavily scented with linseed, paint and spirit, and shook her head.

'I grant you were not to know it, but I intend to go to London this afternoon directly after this sitting. Let us proceed now without further delay, or I shall be late for my appointment.'

With no more fuss than that, she took up her pose reclining on the seat with her head turned slightly away from him, so that the underside of her chin was visible. She wasn't dressed as she would be in the portrait. The grand gown – stiff-bodiced, made of ivory sarcenet silk embroidered with purple and crimson flowers – presently clad a life-sized lay wooden figure which stood in one corner of Joshua's painting room. Nevertheless she wore her precious emerald necklace, and he saw that every now and again, catching the light, it burned an angry shade of green. He noticed that the box in which she stored it was open on his side table, and presumed she had brought it with her because of her intended trip. He made some small adjustments to her position. He raised her arm. He unfurled a lace sleeve to expose the flesh. He turned her head just so, as if he were arranging flowers in a vase. He tweaked the curtain half closed.

91

Then he returned to his easel and set to with aplomb. He had already completed the first stage and now he began the second, working up the composition, using glazes of colour to define the way the light fell and shadows emerged and retreated over the face and on the curve of her arm and breast. He painted in silence out of choice. Chitchat while he worked was anathema to him. In any case it was obvious that Sabine Mercier was already annoyed and to talk would only risk rousing further irritation.

After a few minutes, however, she broke the silence, still holding her head perfectly still as she spoke. 'Did you say you were out walking, Mr Pope?'

He scarcely heard her, for by now he was entirely caught up in his composition. She coughed, reminding him of his manners, and he was forced to answer. 'I went to Richmond, ma'am,' he said, applying a wash of bluish grey upon a layer of oyster.

'For what purpose?'

'None in particular, madam. Merely a desire to enjoy these beautiful environs.'

'And what did you do in Richmond?'

'There is a well-known posting inn, the Star and Garter. The gardens there are quite famous. I went for some refreshment and found it most pleasant.'

His concentration was broken now and he glanced up, curious to see her reaction to the name of the inn. Her head was still perfectly immobile; her expression betrayed no more than the mildest curiosity at this information.

'Indeed? I have never been there,' she replied, 'though if the gardens are pretty perhaps I should.'

'They cannot hold a candle to Astley, ma'am, but I hazard you might enjoy them. While I was there I fell into conversation with the landlord, a Mr Dunstable. He seemed a pleasant enough fellow. He chanced to mention that the man you discovered dead in the pinery had stayed there.'

Sabine's expression remained unchanged and she

continued to hold her position. Yet Joshua sensed a difference. She had stiffened imperceptibly. There was a new gleam in her eye and a slight change in the timbre of her voice. 'What a curious subject to "chance" upon. What did this Dunstable say about the dead man? How did he know it was the same man who was dead in the pinery? Did you show him a sketch perhaps?' Her voice was soft yet laden with irony; there was unmistakable insistence in it.

Joshua stopped painting for a moment and looked up. In the half-light her silhouetted profile was cast upon the wall. Her brow jutted forward, her nose had become a distorted beak, her chin had all but disappeared into the column of her neck; she looked half-human and strangely predatory. Joshua shivered involuntarily.

'I learned the dead man's name from Granger, after you asked me to question him on your behalf. His name was on a letter in his pocket. John Cobb.'

There was a pause while she seemed to digest this information. She turned. 'John Cobb, did you say? Are you quite certain that was the name?' she said, as neutrally as if the name was one she had never heard before.

'Indeed, ma'am, there was no doubt at all.'

'What else did you learn?' She had turned her head back to its correct position. Her tone was now one of disinterest, as if she were humouring him with her questions.

'Naught save that he stayed for a few weeks and on the day of his disappearance, early the same morning you found him, he departed saying he would be back shortly. Only he never returned.'

'Is that all? Had he no callers? Did he mention no reason for being here?

Something in the detached persistence of her questions made Joshua wary. Or perhaps it was that lowering black shadow on the wall, or his natural discretion. In any event, he thought it prudent for the time being to play his hand close and not to mention Herbert's visit.

93

'He had no callers that the landlord remembered. The trouble with such fellows is that, seeing all manner of people coming and going through their door, they forget the individual. Unless there is something wildly remarkable, faces merge into one, facts become blurred. Mr Cobb may well have divulged his reasons for coming, but Dunstable has a feeble mind and remembers things no better than lace keeps you warm. Anything he knew has escaped him days ago.'

'And what of Granger? You say you spoke to him as I asked. Had he anything further to reveal concerning the dead man? Was there anything on his person to reveal his origins or intentions?'

Joshua knew he must tell her something or she would not be satisfied, and there was nothing to be gained by arousing her suspicion or her wrath. How much should he reveal? Certainly not that Granger suspected she knew the dead man. He looked at her surreptitiously and found that, though her head remained turned away as the pose demanded, she seemed to be watching him closely from the corner of her eye. Something in her expression was curiously expectant. He was aware in that instant of a peculiar sensation creeping upon him. He remembered the look of trepidation on Caroline Bentnick's face the evening before in the drawing room. Was he being fanciful to sense an air of menace about Sabine Mercier? Caroline must have felt it and so too now did he – although it wasn't terror that she aroused in him so much as inquisitiveness. He wanted to discover what inspired her malevolent gleam. If he had any doubts before, he was certain now that she must have been involved in some subterfuge – otherwise, why ask him to discover what Granger knew, and why conceal the fact that she knew Cobb? A disturbing thought then occurred to Joshua. Given her questionable actions and reticence, did it follow that Francis and Caroline were correct in their suspicions? Was she involved in his death?

'Granger said little of interest, save that Cobb came looking for employment a few days ago, and, as I told you before, that he found two letters in his pocket, which is how he learned his name.'

'What became of the letters?'

'He handed them to Mr Bentnick.'

She seemed to consider this for a moment; she passed no remark, yet Joshua sensed she wasn't entirely pleased to hear that Herbert had the letters. 'Is that all? Did Granger read them? He said nothing of the contents?'

'Nothing at all, ma'am. He claims there was no time. He saw only the name.'

With that, mercifully, she seemed satisfied and Joshua was left to return his attentions to his canvas. He found, however, that his concentration had been shaken by their conversation. Part of him wanted to return to his work and part of him was tempted to probe her on the matter of her necklace and her curious conversation with Caroline Bentnick. In the end the professional side of him won, although, as he painted, the thought that Sabine might have killed poor Cobb continued to disturb him profoundly. He tried to banish all thoughts of this, telling himself he was jumping to conclusions, that there were countless other reasons why she might withhold the fact she knew Cobb which didn't mean she was a murderess. And in any case what concern was it of his? Nevertheless, his preoccupations with Cobb affected his ability to paint. He was oddly agitated, no longer able to achieve the same sweeping, confident strokes, instead daubing a little mixture of lead white and umber onto the canvas with unusual hesitancy.

Very soon after that the clock sounded three. Sabine rose abruptly from her seat. 'Mercy me, 'tis past the hour for me to go. I had meant to leave you half an hour ago.'

'Forgive me, madam. The fault is all mine for keeping you waiting.'

'I will not disagree with you, Mr Pope. But there's a further service you can do me if you will.'

He was curious as to what might be coming. 'You have only to name it, madam,' he said, bowing decorously.

'Look after my necklace for me. You can use it for the painting if it pleases you.' She walked to the side table where she had placed the shagreen box, unfastened the necklace and placed it reverentially on the silk lining. Her pupils were large and dilated, as though handling it brought her some secret rapture. 'I must leave directly.'

'Forgive me, madam, but would it not be better for me to summon your maid?'

'Marie has gone to Richmond on an errand for me and will only return later this afternoon.'

'I regret, madam, that I am expected by Mr Bentnick at dinner.'

'Never mind. Place it somewhere safe in the meantime. And after dinner, once you have finished painting it, pass it straight to Marie to put away. You do me a great service. I have not the time to do it myself, since I am already late in leaving for London, and nor do I want to take it with me. It is much too precious to risk losing to a highwayman.'

Joshua took the box and locked it in the drawer of his work-table. 'Very well. Please do not worry about it. After dinner I will send for Marie directly and hand it to her,' he said.

Sabine thanked him and then, with a brief word that she would not be available to sit for the portrait until three days hence, on her return from London, she left.

As soon as she had gone, he placed his palette face down in a trough of water to keep the paints soft and cleaned his hands. This done, he repaired to his bedchamber, removed his smock, donned a dry coat – sky-blue silk with grey braid – and his periwig and, having splashed a little rosewater about his person to disguise the smell of turpentine and linseed, he descended for dinner. The morning-room clock was striking the quarter-hour as he entered. For the second time that day he was late.

# Chapter Twelve

It was only as the dinner was well underway and the servants had loaded the table with the second course – large tureens of boiled pike and cabbage, and venison ragout – that Joshua made his excuses. His tone was grave, his expression suitably sombre.

'Forgive me, Mr Bentnick,' he said, 'but since Mrs Mercier is gone to London, I think it best I too return there for a day or two. The portrait is well advanced, but I prefer not to continue with it until I have both of you to sit. Painting one without the other may affect the delicate rapport between your figures and spoil the whole.'

All this of course was utter hogwash. He wanted to be gone because he was eager to continue his enquiries into the mysterious John Cobb's death. Most pressingly, he wanted to call on Bartholomew Hoare, the attorney who had visited Cobb at the inn. Nonetheless, Joshua's smoothly delivered excuse was convincing enough to take in Herbert completely. Anxious that nothing should impair the perfection of the painting, Herbert agreed to let him go without complaint. He too had much to occupy him. It would help him to have the hours he should be sitting to attend to other matters. They thus cordially agreed that Joshua would remain in London until such time as he received word of Mrs Mercier's return, which Herbert estimated would be no later than the end of the week.

* * *

The truth was that, having spoken to Sabine and viewed Herbert in the light of his conversation with the landlord Dunstable, Joshua had grown deeply suspicious of them both. The more subterfuge he encountered the more certain he had become that Cobb hadn't died from natural causes; someone had murdered him. Joshua was not meddlesome by nature, but he was inherently curious when it came to humankind. Having passed exhausting hours examining myriad physiognomies and laying down his opinions of them on canvas, his expertise when it came to interpreting character was redoubtable. Recent tribulations had caused him to underestimate his own proficiency – he sometimes doubted he read faces with his former incisiveness – but they hadn't altered his passion for portraiture or his eagerness to learn more about his given subject. Here, he thought, was an opportunity to do just that. The extraordinary happenings of the past two days were unlike anything he had previously encountered. But while his enquiring mind had been sparked and craved more, a part of him prevaricated. Beyond all shadow of doubt, some form of injustice had been perpetrated at Astley, but what right had he to delve furtively into it? If he did so would he not be as guilty of duplicity as Herbert and Sabine?

Dwelling on this dilemma, he became conscious too that his perpetual melancholy had receded with his absorption in these matters. Perhaps pursuing poor Cobb's cause would melt his own problems away, allowing him to escape the misery that had dogged him since Rachel and Benjamin's deaths. But was that reason to engender the wrath of his patrons and, bearing in mind there was a murderer on the loose, jeopardize his own safety?

By the time he had eaten a large bowl of ragout, and a modest portion of cabbage and butter sauce, his anxieties were settled. Having died in such a curious manner, Cobb deserved someone to pursue his cause. And perhaps, in helping the unfortunate Cobb, Joshua might also help himself. His professional standing was sufficient to weather any criticisms that Herbert Bentnick might circulate. Moreover, he told himself sternly, the possibility that in so doing he might endanger himself was remote.

Having reached this conclusion, Joshua pondered briefly whether he should broach the subject of his visit to the Star and Garter, and mention the argument that Dunstable, the landlord, had overheard between Herbert and Cobb. He speedily decided against it. If Herbert had wanted to be open about Cobb's death he would have confessed before now to the meeting. Raising the matter would only annoy him and put him further on his guard.

Nevertheless, Joshua couldn't help reflecting on Herbert's reticence. Until today he had thought his patron so harmless and his idiosyncratic dipping into all manner of subjects endearing. And on what had he based this judgement? No more than a smooth round face and placid expression and the opinion of others, who probably saw him only thrice a year. Was this a sound basis for his appraisal? Bearing in mind Dunstable's testimony, he doubted it was. He began to question Herbert, to wonder what lay behind the unruffled countenance and insatiable desire to poke beneath the surface and learn something from everyone he encountered. And the more he wondered, the more dubious he became. Perhaps, in this instance, he had entirely misread Herbert. Was it something more than conviviality that lay behind that courteous smile?

He considered what he knew about the corpse. Sabine and Granger had both described it in some detail. Assuming Cobb had been murdered, what had happened? Cobb showed no signs of an assault upon his person. The only significant indication of what had happened was the fact that he had vomited immediately before he died. Although Joshua was no expert in the field, it seemed probable that poison might account for this evidence, and he resolved to look further into this. Were his patrons capable of such an action? Joshua remembered that Sabine's father was a medical man and that Herbert took a keen interest in matters scientific. Either one might have been capable of ministering a dose of poison. Furthermore, Herbert's perfunctory treatment of Cobb's death and his concealment of his meeting with him would make sense if he were somehow involved in it. But was he a murderer, an accomplice, or merely trying to conceal something for reasons unknown?

Just as Joshua tendered these alarming questions to himself, Herbert put down his knife and fork and dabbed his chin with his napkin. 'By the by,' he said in a soft voice that Joshua now feared signalled sham rather than genuine amiability, 'if you can make yourself ready quickly after the meal is over, I can offer you a ride to the Strand. I intend to go there myself on urgent business. I leave within the hour.'

Joshua muttered a few words of thanks and having bolted his dessert, rushed to his rooms to gather his few belongings together. He collected his brushes, spatulas, pots of ground pigment and bladders of mixed paint and stowed them in their mahogany carrying case, leaving the canvas on the easel to await his return. He went to the work table, wherein he had secreted Sabine Mercier's precious jewel in its case. He half opened the drawer and speedily removed his possessions: his watch and a ring left to him by his father, his pocket book and a silver snuff box – both gifts from grateful patrons. He stowed these treasured objects in his coat pocket, then closed the drawer.

Before making further preparations to leave, remembering his promise to Sabine he rang the bell in his room to summon a servant and sent him for Sabine's maid Marie. While he waited for Marie to come he took out his clothes from the closet, placed them carefully in his portmanteau and buckled it in readiness for the journey. But five minutes later, when all this was done, the servant had yet to return. Joshua rang the bell again, pacing impatiently about his room as five minutes more ticked by and still no one arrived. He threw open his door and scoured the corridor for signs of the servant. Herbert had impressed upon him that he was to prepare himself to leave promptly and Joshua fancied he could hear voices down below. Was Herbert already waiting for him? Anxious not to rile him, Joshua decided to descend with his possessions in each hand. He would find another servant downstairs and give them instructions regarding the necklace.

No sooner had he reached the hall than the carriage drew up at the steps and Herbert bustled down the stairs, bidding farewell to Violet and his children, and a pair of pugs bouncing at his heels, as fulsomely as if he were intending to leave for America rather than an overnight trip to London. What should Joshua do? Perhaps the reason Marie had not come to him was because she was not yet returned from Richmond. In any case, even if she had, it would take him several minutes to ascertain where she was. The wait would only annoy Herbert, and Joshua had no desire to antagonize him; nor did he wish to miss his ride. But then neither did he want to attract the wrath of Sabine – for he knew how precious the necklace was to her. Crimsoning in his dilemma, he turned round, looking for a servant who wasn't occupied with doing something for Herbert, one he could despatch for Marie.

'Is something amiss, Pope?' said Herbert, observing Joshua twirling about, looking unusually agitated as he tried to attract the attentions of the third footman, who was loading his bags onto the back of Herbert's carriage with monumental slowness.

'Indeed, sir, there is something it is imperative for me to do before we leave, but I am loath to cause you the inconvenience of a delay.'

Herbert looked alarmed. 'What on earth do you mean?'

'I sent a servant to perform the commission, sir, but I waited an age and he never returned.'

'Explain yourself properly, sir. What is it? It cannot be as grave as all that. There must surely be a remedy.' He was playing his role as a concerned patron to perfection.

'Mrs Mercier entrusted her necklace to me, since she was in a hurry to leave for London before dinner. I was supposed to hand the jewel to her maid Marie immediately after dinner. I sent a servant for her just now, but she never came. I presume she is still not returned from Richmond. But I don't want to leave without carrying out my undertaking.'

'Where is the necklace now?'

'Where I left it. In its box in the furthest corner of the drawer of the writing table in my room.'

'Ha! Is that all? Such a magnificent lather over such a trifling matter! Don't concern yourself any more about it,' said Herbert. 'The jewel will be perfectly safe.' Then, turning to Violet, he said, 'Dear girl, you heard what Mr Pope has just said. It will be no trouble for you to go immediately to his rooms, retrieve the jewel and keep it safe until you can hand it to Marie for safekeeping.'

Violet regarded Herbert and then Joshua. For the first time since he had made her acquaintance Joshua was honoured with a smile. 'Of course, Mr Bentnick. It will be no trouble at all. I will go directly. Caroline, would you be so kind as to show me the way to Mr Pope's rooms? I don't believe I know where they are.'

# Chapter Thirteen

Joshua's uncertainties regarding his patron Herbert Bentnick made him keener than a frog in springtime to be away from him. Fortunately, with a pair of high-mettled horses to draw them, the journey to London in Herbert's carriage took barely two hours and proved mercifully uneventful. So it was that by six that evening, having sent on his bags to his rooms in St Martin's Lane, Joshua Pope mounted the steps to the door of his mistress's lodgings.

Meg Dunn was an impoverished widow whom Joshua had met six months after the deaths of his wife and son. She was no substitute for Rachel, being at least ten years older than he (she admitted to forty), with a teenage daughter and no education or accomplishments to speak of. But her bed was warm and she was agreeable and clean, and furthermore she flattered him outrageously, something he recognized yet enjoyed. He was in the habit of calling upon her every Wednesday and Saturday, and, since he was generous by nature, more often than not he brought a little present to cheer her when he came. Today, as he was feeling hungry, he had stopped off at a chophouse and bought a meat pudding (Meg was particularly partial to meat pudding) and a bottle of claret with which to wash it down.

He mounted the dingy staircase to Meg's rooms on the first floor and knocked on her door, holding the pudding slightly away so that the fatty juices seeping through the wax-paper wrapping didn't stain his coat. He waited. There was no answer. Where was she? She shouldn't expect his two guineas a month if she was not ready when he called. He always came at about this hour and today was Wednesday, his day. He banged again, louder, more insistently. Hunger gnawed his belly. His fingers felt greasy from the juices of the hot meat pie. He craved the soothing effect of wine and Meg's ministrations. Being forced to wait for them, after such an eventful day, made him feel unusually tetchy.

Some more minutes passed, during which Joshua thumped repeatedly on the door with such force he could feel the hinges groan. He was on the point of retreating and going home, and sending Meg a curt note when he heard the sound of shuffling footsteps and muffled voices in the hallway below. He leaned over the banisters. He could see the top of Meg's head (the bonnet was one he had given her) and the dark triangle of a male hat beside her.

'Meg,' he shouted out, 'where are you? You're late.'

Two faces tilted up: a pale moon surrounded by an aureole of fair hair and yellow straw hat; a florid, fat-cheeked orb framed with a grey periwig. 'Mr Pope? Is it you? I thought you were gone away,' Meg said. Her eyes were round with surprise but she flashed him a smile before jerking her head at her companion, who scowled and bolted out the way he had come.

'Who the devil was that?' Joshua said as Meg hastened up the stairs and embraced him as if she hadn't seen him for a year. 'Careful, careful. Mind my coat, mind the pudding.'

Meg murmured something about how inspired he was to know she was positively starving. Her companion was of no importance – a distant cousin of her dear departed husband's who had come to call unexpectedly. She was delighted to have an excuse to be rid of him; the fellow was the most unutterable bore and had insisted on promenading her around Vauxhall Gardens for the entire afternoon. He had barely let her sit for a second and her feet were quite worn out. From the way she slightly averted her eyes, and the corners of her lips drew tight, Joshua knew that she was not being entirely truthful. But he was hungry and in need of comfort, and in no mood for a squabble just now. He would wait for an opportune moment to probe her more thoroughly on the matter.

After they had eaten the pie and consumed the wine, Meg walked to her bedroom. Through the open door Joshua watched her unpin her hair, so that it ran in a crinkly river of strawberry blonde down her back. She was pretty for her age; her face was round and flower-like, her skin so pale you could see the veins on her breasts. He watched her remove her outer clothing and corsets; she was alluringly rounded with a generous bottom, pendulous breasts and slender ankles, which Joshua greatly admired. She returned dressed only in her chemise and petticoat and stockings to sit on his lap. She opened the ties of her chemise and pulled his head to her bosom. Joshua slid his hand beneath her petticoat and stroked the soft flesh of her thigh. 'Meg,' he said urgently, 'have you missed me?'

'Of course,' said Meg, removing his wig and placing it carefully on the side table before she began stroking his neck. 'I always do, Joshua. You know that.'

He snuggled into the soft folds of her flesh and she sighed contentedly. 'That man you were with? He was not—'

'No, my dearest. I told you, did I not?' She was fingering the buttons of his breeches, prising between his drawers, pressing and kneeding him as if he were dough she were shaping. Joshua became quickly aroused and soon ignored the distinct prickle of apprehension he felt. He knew he should press her further, warn her he expected fidelity (he was petrified of contracting the pox), chastise her even; but faced with imminent pleasure he was helpless. He kissed her, feeling her tongue probe his mouth and savour the taste of meat pudding and claret oozing from it. He stretched out his legs obligingly while she pulled off his boots and stockings and breeches. He stood and kissed her again, this time more urgently, on her neck; then, dropping to his knees, he lifted the chemise to nuzzle the underside of her breasts and curve of her belly while she trailed her fingers across the back of his neck. He tucked one arm around her back and the other under her thighs, raised her aloft and carried her off to her bed.

As he placed her gently down on the mattress, he remarked that the linen was in disarray – usually she was fastidious about such matters; it was one of the things that had drawn him to her – and felt a small shiver of regret. He would have to confront her, or she would presume him to be a fool and continue to take advantage of him. But then, just as he opened his mouth to mention it, Meg caught hold of his shoulders and pulled him down on her belly. For the time being at least, he forgot everything.

An hour later, refreshed and feeling a little peckish again, and still in no mood for a quarrel, Joshua kissed Meg farewell and returned at a brisk walk to his rooms in St Peter's Court, a small alley off St Martin's Lane. As he had stepped away from her door into the dark streets he cursed himself for not having said something. What a fool he had been to let her think she had duped him. The longer he left it the more flagrant she would become, and he would only have himself to blame for the consequences. He shook his head, sternly rebuking himself. Next time, without fail, he would make sure he made plain his requirements regarding her fidelity. Just now there was too much else to occupy him.

The building where Joshua lived was halfway down the court. It was well appointed though no different from countless other brick-fronted, four-storey terraced houses with sash windows, three steps up to the front door, and a semi-basement wherein the kitchen and the servants' quarters were situated.

Joshua counted himself fortunate to live where he did. His rooms were exactly what he needed, being light and airy and spacious. He had moved here only two months earlier, after responding to a notice in the *London Journal*, in the belief that a change might help assuage painful memories of Rachel and Benjamin. The owner of the property, his landlady, was a fractious widow by the name of Mrs Quick, who, on Joshua's application, claimed she had been inundated with responses to her notice. Determined to secure the lodgings, Joshua mentioned his wife had recently died (in the hope of sympathy), that he was a painter by profession (in the hope that she might know his name) and that because of this his patrons – ladies and gentlemen of elevated status – would regularly call on him (in the hope she would be impressed). This last remark had seemed to have the desired effect. No sooner had he let slip the names of a sample of patrons – Herbert Bentnick; the Earl of Lampton; the Countess of Marl – than Mrs Quick softened. She had offered him a cup of tea, and summoned her daughter Bridget to bring it.

Bridget Quick was a large, comely girl with freckled skin, a bouncy bosom that strained at the corsets containing it and glossy auburn hair, which she usually wore braided and coiled beneath a linen cap. She had curtsied demurely at their introduction, rattling the teacups on their tray precariously as she did so. To ease matters Joshua had chivalrously assisted her, carrying a table and taking the tray and placing it just so. He had remarked as he did so to Mrs Quick that should he be fortunate enough to be offered the lodgings, her daughter's charms would surely draw his clients as much as his pictures. He had noticed Mrs Quick's proprietorial eye on her daughter; he had seen too the way Bridget's cupid's-bow lips instantly widened in a smile and the animated sparkle in her jade-green eyes. He had sensed Mrs Quick's marital ambitions for her daughter and that there was more than circumspection beneath Bridget's pretty façade. Several other eligible names had come to Joshua's mind and this had made the tea go very well. Mrs Quick had instructed her daughter to pour them all a second cup and offered Joshua the rooms at the very favourable rent of twenty guineas a year.

* * *

Since Joshua's arrival the household had been arranged as follows: Mrs Quick and Bridget occupied the ground-floor rooms; the maid Kitty and a manservant, Thomas, a lad of sixteen, had rooms in the basement, where the kitchen and coal cellar were also situated; Joshua resided on the first and second floor. His parlour was a sunny south-facing room, furnished with a writing desk and two armchairs, a dining table, a looking glass, a table clock and an Indian rug. The walls were sound enough to display his work and were already hung with a selection of his finished portraits that had yet to be varnished and despatched. Double doors led through to a painting room facing north, wherein he worked, kept his easels, canvasses, pigments, brushes, pencils, bottles of linseed, varnish and spirit. Upstairs was his bedchamber and a closet.

As he had forewarned his landlady, on Sunday afternoons a dozen or more people habitually called at the door, as an alternative excursion to visits to Bedlam and the Foundling Hospital. They visited on the pretext of commissioning him, although most came more from idle curiosity than any real desire to buy.

Joshua couldn't be bothered to waste his time in idle chitchat. When Rachel was alive, they had lived in a small house off Soho Square and she had dealt with the callers, summoning him only when a genuine customer appeared. Having moved in to Mrs Quick's, it was arranged that Kitty or Thomas would open the door. If the callers merited it, Bridget would be summoned to show them to his parlour and make whatever conversation was necessary. He, meanwhile, would remain behind the double doors of his painting room, to continue his work without interruption.

Mrs Quick, as Joshua soon discovered, was a woman of forceful character. Her reputation for ill temper made most people wary of her, although there were a few who, despite her vociferous gripes, claimed she was charitably disposed. Thomas once told Joshua that Mrs Quick had snatched him at the age of ten from the clutches of a sweep who forced him to climb pitch-black chimneys, dressed in rags and with no shoes, and fed him on no more than scraps that you wouldn't give to a dog. Moreover, Kitty had been taken on in the middle of winter when she was found in the gutter outside, starving and half-frozen to death. He claimed that if anyone was in dire need they had only to knock on her kitchen window to be given a bowl of slops. Joshua nodded but privately took these tales with a hefty pinch of salt. He had yet to see a glimmer of charity in his landlady. Rather, he found she was as unyielding as a gatepost. She counted every candle stub and charged him extra for coal or a second helping of mutton broth. If the Sunday visitors disturbed her when she was feeling under the weather, which was often, she was never too ill to come upstairs to castigate him on account of it.

Changes in routine, particularly spontaneous ones, upset her profoundly. Thus, when Joshua reached the door of his lodgings that night, Mrs Quick poked her head out, like a spider alerted to some unfortunate insect just caught in its web. She was dressed with characteristic severity, in a grey high-necked gown with a plain white collar. Her cheeks were hollow, her mouth, owing to an unfortunate lack of teeth, was tight, like a purse pulled in by a drawstring. Her hair was scraped into a large plain bonnet with long lappets, so that not a single wisp was visible. In a voice as harsh as a crow's, she declared herself most displeased by his sudden return. He might have had the manners to send word ahead that he was coming, in which case she would have instructed Kitty to light the fire in his room. The first she knew was when his bags had been delivered less than two hours ago. He had nobody to blame but himself if the bed was damp and he caught his death.

Joshua looked a little sorrowful at this greeting, keenly

aware how different it was from the one he would have received had Rachel and Benjamin been alive. He replied politely nonetheless. He hadn't known till late this afternoon of his return. As for catching a chill: the weather was clement, the month was late May, not February. She should not worry herself on his behalf, but if it was convenient and she could send Bridget up with a little supper on a tray he would count himself most fortunate.

Bridget was the only other bloom that vied with Meg in the wilderness of Joshua's romantic existence. Over the past two months he had remarked her capable manner as she bossed Kitty and Thomas about and bartered loudly with street vendors for the best eggs and butter. Unlike her mother, whose thorns had become more barbed since his residence in her house, Bridget's manner towards him had grown as warm as treacle pudding. Occasionally when she looked at him meaningfully as he came and went, it was on the tip of his tongue to ask her how she was, or where she was going, or if she would care to sit for him. But then he remembered Mrs Quick's irascible temper and how much he relied upon her favourable opinion. His rooms were pleasant, and after so much turmoil in recent months the thought of moving again was insupportable. Mrs Quick saw him as the means of effecting useful introductions for her daughter. He had no wish to disabuse her.

Two hours later, filled with cold mutton and hot ale, he retired to his comfortable bed. He fell asleep still tingling at the pleasant memory of Meg, glad to be among his own possessions and familiar faces, and telling himself that the menace he had sensed at Astley was probably no more than the product of idle imaginings.

Joshua awoke next morning firm as ever in his resolve to pursue the matter of Cobb's death. He rose early and dressed with customary care in a buff wool coat with chocolate-coloured braid, brown breeches and a black silk cravat.

110

Having breakfasted modestly on rolls and marmalade without allowing himself to be distracted by Bridget, who was lingering by the parlour door, he strode out in the direction of Gray's Inn Lane.

He was going to find Mr Hoare, the attorney who had called on John Cobb while he stayed at Richmond. He recalled that Lizzie Manning had suggested this visit, soon after the idea had occurred to him. Lizzie Manning had promised to discover what she could from Violet's maid. He wondered if she had been as good as her word.

He found the place easily. A small tarnished plaque to one side of the door announced that the premises belonged to Messrs Enoch Crackman & Bartholomew Hoare, Solicitors at Law. He entered a narrow corridor leading to a winding stair. Most of the windows had obviously been recently bricked in – a result, no doubt, of the exorbitant glass tax. The few that remained glazed were so blackened by grime and soot as to make any light entering from them worthless. The air smelt musty; even though the day was fine and warm and Joshua was well clad in his woollen coat, a chill penetrated his flesh and he began to fret he might get infected by some distemper.

At the top of the stair he groped his way along another dank passage, towards a door at the far end. The office within was no less dingy than the corridor without. Scarcely any light seemed to enter here, yet he could see the floor and every surface was littered with sheaves and scrolls and pamphlets of paper interspersed with large leather-bound tomes, some open, some closed, scattered about over floor, tables and desks. Several young clerks sat amid this sea of paper writing furiously with their dusty quills, or consulting one or other of the tomes. There was a large partner's desk at the rear of the office. Hunched on one side of it, immersed in writing entries in a vast ledger, was an elderly gentleman.

Since he appeared to be the senior-most person in the office, Joshua went over to him. 'Excuse me, sir,' he said.

'My name is Joshua Pope and I come in search of a Mr Bartholomew Hoare. I believe he has his office here?'

The man raised his head slowly and regarded him. As a portrait painter Joshua made it his business always to remark every oddity of physiognomy, but he was unprepared for this gentleman's features. His face was long and narrow, with a curved, beak-like nose and a strongly cast jaw. What took Joshua aback, however, were his eyes. One was heavy-lidded, deep set into his skull and the palest of blue in colour; the other was a void. Where it should have been was a hollow socket with the skin stretched across and stitched over. Joshua started, blinked, then resisted his urge to stare by looking at the papers on the desk in front of him. The man seemed to take his embarrassed surprise quite in his stride; indeed, Joshua guessed he was quite accustomed to it.

'You believe correctly. There is a Mr Hoare who conducts his business here. I am his senior partner, Enoch Crackman. Have you an appointment?'

'I regret I have not. Is one necessary?'

'It might have helped, for the gentleman you desire to see is not here.'

'Will he return shortly?'

'I would like to think so, though I cannot say for certain. He has been away on business the past few days – longer than expected. On what matter did you wish to consult him? Perhaps I may assist you? Bartholomew Hoare is my nephew.'

'My business concerns Mr John Cobb, a gentleman recently arrived from Barbados. I believe Mr Hoare visited this gentleman at an inn in Richmond a few days ago.'

Crackman paused, swallowing thoughtfully before replying. 'What is it to you if he did?'

'I wish to discover the nature of his business.'

'Does it concern you?'

'In a manner of speaking. I am acting for Mr Cobb.'

Joshua handed him a calling card. The old man looked at it, holding it so close to his good eye it practically brushed his cheek. Then he guffawed and shook his head. 'Forgive my asking. Your reputation is well known to me. I believe you have recently painted an uncle of mine. The portrait hangs in Lincoln's Inn.'

'Judge Lessiter?' guessed Joshua, seeing a vague resemblence now in the august cast of Crackman's jaw and the aquiline curve of his nose.

'The very same. The perceptiveness of your portrait I thought quite remarkable. I don't know how you managed to convey his eloquence, sagacity and wit with canvas and paint, and yet that is exactly what you did.'

Joshua blushed as he always did at such accolades. 'You are most kind. The judge was a delightful man. I recall him well. He had much to occupy him yet he was unfailingly patient.'

'And he was greatly taken with your depiction. Took me to see it.' Crackman halted and looked intently at Joshua again. 'Nevertheless, I regret, Mr Pope, I must ask this. Do you have any letter of authority from Mr Cobb?'

Joshua shook his head.

'Then I am sorry to say you have wasted your time. Whatever the business between Messrs Cobb and Hoare, it is a matter of confidence. Mr Hoare wouldn't tell another soul without good authority or reason and neither will I.'

'Perhaps, sir, I can persuade you. I tell you this, and there are plenty to vouch for the truth of it. Mr Cobb is dead, in mysterious circumstances. I believe he may have been murdered. I am attempting to seek the truth of his death. Are the interests of justice not reason enough to talk to me?'

The old man regarded Joshua with increased interest. 'Cobb is dead? Are you quite certain?'

'As certain as I can be. I was there when his body was discovered in a pineapple house at Astley House, Richmond. You have only to write to Mr Herbert Bentnick at that address to verify it.'

'Astley House, Richmond? That too is a familiar name. And when precisely did Cobb die?'

'Three days ago.'

The old man paused and scratched his wispy pate with the tip of his quill. His single eye gleamed like a nightlight in the dark. 'Unless I am very much mistaken, Mr Hoare was last in this office four days ago. He mentioned he had an appointment out of town. Quite possibly it was with Mr Cobb, for he'd visited him earlier in the week, as you say.' He turned to address a young clerk. 'Posner, look up Mr Hoare's engagements for three days ago, would you?'

Posner briskly did as he was asked. After some minutes he affirmed that, as Mr Crackman suspected, Mr Hoare had made an appointment to call on Mr Cobb at the Star and Garter Inn, Richmond, at three o'clock in the afternoon.

'On what matter?' interposed Joshua. 'I am sure, after all I've revealed, you could give me some indication, Mr Crackman. And in doing so you would be doing poor Cobb a great service.'

There was another long pause while Mr Crackman scrutinized Joshua and regarded his visiting card again. 'I see no reason to withhold the information, bearing in mind that Cobb is dead and you are a highly respectable person. I own I do not know the full story, for the case wasn't mine. I can tell you, however, that their business involves a matter of inheritance – a disputed property.'

'But Cobb had recently arrived from Barbados, had he not?'

He nodded briskly. 'The other party involved in the dispute had also come to England from the same place.'

'Do you know the name of the other party?' Joshua hazarded it must be Sabine Mercier, but he wanted verification.

'I do not recall, but I am perfectly willing for Posner to conduct a search of our records. I will inform you in due course of any discoveries.'

'I would be most grateful, sir.'

Crackman coughed, and twirled his quill thoughtfully. 'I have a very pretty granddaughter, aged about five or six. I have always wanted her painted. I did have a profile done by Hayman, but it does not do her justice . . .'

'Yes, yes, Mr Crackman, of course I will do it, just as soon as I have finished at Astley.'

'And the charge?'

'Shall we say six guineas for a head and shoulders?'

Crackman smiled with delight.

By reiterating his promise to paint the old man's grand-daughter at this extraordinarily reasonable rate, Joshua managed to extract an undertaking from Crackman that he would conduct the research as a matter of urgency and contact him within the next two days. If Hoare returned in time, Crackman would instruct him to write and include an account of what had taken place between Cobb and him; otherwise, Joshua might expect to hear from Crackman himself. And since more than that he would not promise, with this Joshua had to be content.

# Chapter Fourteen

*Barlow Court, Richmond*
*25th May*

*Mr Pope,*

  *I have, as I promised, spoken with Violet Mercier's maid, Marie. This much I can tell you of her: she is Barbadian by birth and has been employed by Mrs Mercier for the past ten years as lady's maid for her daughter and herself. Marie misses her homeland. She is not at all happy with her move to England, displays little loyalty or affection towards the Merciers and longs to return to Bridgetown. I tell you this only so that you understand why she leapt at my offer of some friendly discourse. I easily persuaded her to describe to me the events of their stay in London, in such minute detail that I doubt either one of us would have remarked so much had we been there in her place. I confess myself quite mystified as to the bearing her information has on the death of John Cobb, yet I cannot help my conviction there must be some connection. After all was not Herbert spotted at the Star and Garter arguing with Cobb? I should also say I find it impossible to believe that Herbert, whom I have known since a child, and who has been a kind benefactor to me on several occasions, could be responsible for Cobb's death. His fiancée and her daughter are, to my mind, quite another matter. Perhaps we can discuss this further on your return to Astley.*

The day before Mrs Mercier discovered the body in the pinery, Marie had accompanied Violet Mercier to London. Violet had an appointment with her dressmaker and had been invited to visit the theatre and other entertainments in the company of a relative of Herbert's. They intended to pass the night in town before returning to Astley.

According to Marie, Violet had recently been out of sorts and the day of the visit to the dressmaker was no exception. She stepped into the dress and stood before the looking glass, twirling herself this way and that. The gown fitted miraculously, the trimming was exquisite. There were tiny seed pearls embroidered on the bodice in a pattern of rosebuds, silk roses stitched to her shoulders and neck, satin bows and Brussels lace trimming the neck. To Violet, such details were usually of the utmost importance, but today nothing could vanquish her lacklustre spirits, or spur her to offer poor Mrs Bowles one word of encouragement.

I pressed Marie to tell me what lay at the heart of Violet's misery. Could she hazard a guess? Had it to do with John Cobb? She revealed that there had once been a 'fondness' between Violet and Cobb, but that when Sabine discovered this she had intervened to curtail it. All this took place several weeks ago. Nevertheless, I was right in a sense – it was an affair of the heart that had upset Violet. Since her arrival at Astley, Violet has developed an ungovernable fondness for Francis Bentnick. As soon as Caroline saw this she told her that Francis was as good as promised to me. Nevertheless, according to Marie, Violet thinks I am no match for her and intends to persist in pressing herself upon Francis. As far as Marie is aware, no man has ever refused Violet anything. Francis's elusiveness only seems to make her more determined. You can imagine I wasn't much pleased to learn of Violet's intentions, but though I sensed the maid wanted some response, and I own I longed to say something on the matter, I kept silent.

Once the fitting was over Violet and Marie emerged from Mrs Bowles's premises into the confusion of the Strand mid-morning.

Marie was still unaccustomed to the size and bustle of the city, and it seemed to her that the entire world was returning from somewhere or on their way to somewhere else. The road was jammed with carriages and chairs of every description. The pavements seethed with vendors and shoppers and promenaders and beggars. A cacophony of noise and smells assaulted their senses. They passed down Southampton Street, towards Covent Garden, ignoring a woman in rags who jostled Miss Violet for a penny. They paused to look in the windows of shops selling fans and ribbons and pomades. A straw hat garnished with rose-pink plumes and green ribbons attracted Miss Violet's attentions; then she caught sight of a small powder box enamelled with lovebirds. She pondered whether to purchase one or both or neither of these items before moving on. A pair of sedan chairs pushed roughly past. Marie hastily pulled Violet to the shelter of a doorway to save her from being trampled.

It was while they waited for the commotion to pass that they chanced to look back up the Strand, in the direction from which they had come. Thus it was that they saw Mrs Bowles, the dressmaker whom they had lately left, turn the corner of Southampton Street on the other side of the road and pass by not a dozen paces in front of them. Mrs Bowles had taken off her cap and put on a hat with ribbons and bows and feathers, not much different from the hat Violet had lately admired in the milliner's window. Together with the cloak and gloves she wore, she now appeared almost like one of the gentry. Violet and Marie were going in the same direction and accidentally fell into step some distance behind her on the opposite side of the road. They followed her up Southampton Street, until she came to the piazza and turned into Floral Street. Here they saw her halt in front of a door between a bookseller and a chandler's. She briefly knocked, whereupon the door was opened and she entered as comfortably as if she had been there a dozen times before – or as if she lived there.

They were about to continue on their way – indeed, they had nearly arrived at the corner – when their attention was caught by a second familiar figure approaching from the opposite direction. This person, a gentleman, seemed somewhat preoccupied – so much so, he never saw Violet and Marie though he passed them by on the opposite side of the street. He looked more than once at his pocket watch as if late or pressed for time, though evidently he knew where he was going. He stopped outside the same door, knocked and entered. He was dressed in a dark tricorn hat and a fine brown suit with horn buttons. As they watched from across the road, he entered the upstairs room, removed his cloak and hat and with easy familiarity sat himself in an armchair while a maid brought refreshments. He was a tall man of spreading girth, expansive smile and somewhat spindly legs. Even from this distance neither she nor Violet could fail to recognize him instantly. The man to whom her mother Sabine Mercier was engaged had apparently arranged a secret assignation with her dressmaker. Herbert Bentnick was taking tea in Mrs Bowles's drawing room and looking for all the world as if he was quite at home there.

Is this not a most curious incident? It does of course explain the peculiar conversation between Violet and Herbert that we both remarked the other evening, though it also raises a further question: why did Herbert deny the visit? What was he trying to hide? Perhaps you might call on Mrs Bowles to discover this. I look forward with eagerness to hearing your thoughts and learning how you have fared with Mr Hoare. I will endeavour to call on the Bentnicks in the next few days in order that we may discuss how to advance our strategy.

In eager anticipation,
Elizabeth Manning

# Chapter Fifteen

Lizzie Manning's letter and her account of her conversation with Marie reached Joshua three days after his return to London. He was intrigued by her uncovering of Violet Mercier's fondness for Francis Bentnick, and her frank admission of jealousy. Violet's resolve and dismissive approach to Francis's agreement with Lizzie didn't surprise him. Violet's extravagant beauty was a potent weapon that few men would withstand.

Fascinated though he was, Joshua didn't reply to Lizzie Manning's letter. The reason for his inaction was twofold: first, bearing in mind her animosity towards Violet, he was unsure whether or not it was prudent to involve her in his future enquiries. Second, masculine embarrassment constrained him. The nature of Herbert's assignment with the dressmaker seemed to Joshua to be perfectly obvious. As a recent widower himself, he had found sudden denial of the pleasures of a wife hard to bear, and Meg now slaked those masculine needs. If Herbert felt the same, who could blame him? No doubt Sabine intended to keep her bedroom door closed until the wedding night. If Herbert had an occasional rendezvous with a dressmaker to ease matters, what of it? Denying all knowledge of the woman was, in Joshua's opinion, a manifestation of gentlemanly discretion, and far from being evidence of some malicious subterfuge. Lizzie Manning had merely revealed her naïvety by failing to comprehend this obvious fact, but Joshua had no intention of explaining the matter to her.

The following day Joshua received this note from Herbert Bentnick.

*Astley House*
*26th May 1766*

*Pope,*
*I would be greatly obliged if you would return to Astley without any delay. A matter of the utmost gravity has arisen. I believe you are the only person to help.*
*Yrs,*
*Herbert Bentnick*

The peculiar tone of this letter wasn't lost on Joshua. What could be so urgent as to make Herbert summon him thus? The note was so abrupt, so unlike the effusive Herbert. There was no mention of Sabine's return, which was when he expected to be recalled. Had some other dreadful tragedy taken place? But then, if it had, why would Herbert summon Joshua, when as far as he knew (and hoped) Herbert was ignorant of his enquiries and interest in Cobb's death? Joshua began to worry then that Lizzie Manning might have let slip something of the matter. How foolish he had been to trust her. The intelligence he thought he discerned in her was a delusion. The woman was nothing but a feather-brained chatterbox, incapable of keeping what she knew to herself. She had doubtless pursued her own course, saying nothing to Joshua. Or perhaps she had mentioned something of her conversation with the maid Marie to Caroline or Francis or Violet. Perhaps – Joshua shuddered at this possibility – Sabine had learned of their enquiries and he was being summoned to explain himself.

Thus it was with trepidation and a sense of impending doom that Joshua once more began to pack his artist's paraphernalia in its mahogany travelling box, and then set about choosing clothes for his portmanteau. In carrying out all of this it never once occurred to him to make some excuse and avoid returning to Astley, for having convinced himself that no one but he would be capable of uncovering the truth about John Cobb's death he was determined to get on with it.

In the midst of these preparations there was a knock on his door. Bridget Quick must have heard the clatter and, being an inquisitive soul, had come to see what he was about, on the pretext of offering nourishment. It was barely an hour since Joshua had breakfasted, yet she'd brought a slice of cherry cake and a jug of porter. 'You might care for a little of this.' She smilingly held out the offerings and stepped in through the door before Joshua had the wit to halt her. She was wearing a dress of cream dimity with pale-blue flowers printed on it. Even though her hair was slightly undone and escaped wisps curled about her neck, she made a very fetching picture.

'You are most kind,' he said, groaning silently at the sight of the immense wedge on the plate, but drawn as ever to Bridget's feminine attractions. 'But, as you see, you catch me when I am all a-fluster. I must leave directly for Richmond. An emergency has arisen.'

'Surely it cannot be so pressing you have no time to eat? Indeed, if it is so urgent, my assistance will come in useful. Sit down; let me pack your clothes.'

Joshua would have preferred not to let her among his things. Bridget's helpfulness always made him feel defensive, because part of him yearned to be friendlier with her, but, remembering her mother, he forced himself to hold back. However, on this particular day his mind was preoccupied with Herbert's letter and he was less wary than usual. He mustered no quick excuse. Thus he found himself letting her fold his linens and cravats and stockings. Bending low so that her skirts fanned out like a flower over her broad bottom, she stowed each article with great care in his portmanteau. When she had finished, she stood up and brushed herself down.

'Your costumes are very fine, Mr Pope. I do admire them. I admire any man who takes pride in his garb.' She paused expectantly, waiting for him to say something. Joshua was torn between wanting to reply encouragingly and remembering that circumspection would be wiser. He was also still pondering the reason for Herbert's letter, and thus his usual wit eluded him.

'You too always look very charming – particularly so today, in that gown,' he said rather flatly, stepping away to give himself room to think.

Bridget shot him an unusually penetrating look. 'Sometimes, however, I wonder if our preoccupation with dress is not just a means to deflect attention from deeper worries.'

What on earth did she mean? This was not the sort of remark he expected from his landlady's daughter, no matter how pretty she was. Joshua looked down at the sleeve of his jacket as if he would find the answer inscribed upon it. 'Indeed, Miss Quick. I am vastly grateful for your assistance and compliments. However, when it comes to your last remark, I cannot agree. Surely our outward appearance reflects what lies within.'

She smiled at him, a warm but enigmatic smile. 'On occasion, but not always. Costume permits masquerade – you have only to visit the playhouse to see the truth of it.'

'I would like nothing better. But I fear the playhouse is out of the question for the time being. As I mentioned, I am off to Richmond. I don't know when precisely I'll be back.'

'It's Richmond you go to again, do you? Where shall you stay? Are you still with the Bentnicks at Astley?'

Fearing that this conversation was leading him into uncharted waters, where he did not desire to travel, Joshua was reluctant to confirm his whereabouts. He cursed mentioning the Bentnick commission to her last week. But at the same time, he reflected, she was a kind girl and a pretty one at that. He felt an invitation of some sort was expected and he didn't want to cause offence.

'I tell you what,' he said pleasantly. 'It won't be prudent to meet where I am staying, since I fear something may be amiss and that is the reason I have been summoned so hastily. I will seek out a good place in Richmond; then, if you have the time, we might meet. I will drop you a note of it.' Once he was away he could decide how to proceed. If he thought the better of it he could either plead a lapse of memory or other commitments.

Bridget leaned over and pecked him on the cheek. 'I had best keep our arrangement a secret from my mother. We don't want her knowing our private affairs, do we?'

Joshua wasn't sure whether she said this mockingly or seriously, but it troubled him nonetheless. The threat of Mrs Quick's disapproval loomed larger than ever. 'I heartily concur,' he said, attempting a smile. 'The last thing I desire to do is annoy your mother.'

At this she smiled mischievously. 'My mother's daunting manner belies her real character. She is not as harsh as many people think.'

'Perhaps that is so,' said Joshua, 'but in any case she and I are not on the most cordial terms since my unexpected return last night.'

Bridget would doubtless have defended her mother, but there was no chance of further discussion. Just at that moment Mrs Quick's strident tones were heard bellowing for her daughter.

Joshua shut the door behind Bridget and leaned against it with eyes half closed. His spirits dived; he chastised himself for being a fool. He had not wanted to kindle false hopes in Bridget, and yet, however unwittingly, he feared that was precisely what he had done.

The coach took two hours and left him at the Star and Garter, from where he hired a driver and chaise to take him the short distance to Astley. For most of the journey he spoke to no one, nor, unusually for Joshua, did he examine the faces of his fellow travellers for oddities of physiognomy. Herbert's strange letter and Mr Cobb's death and what he had learned thus far absorbed his thoughts entirely.

Despite his visit to Hoare's premises and Lizzie's letter he felt no closer to comprehending recent events. Assuming Granger was correct in his suspicion that Sabine knew Cobb, why would she deny the fact yet instruct Joshua to look into it? Was it because she was concerned about Cobb's relationship with her daughter but wanted to conceal it from Herbert? But if Dunstable was to be believed, Herbert also knew about Cobb, because he had visited him at the Star and Garter and argued with him there. What was the dispute over inherited property that had brought Cobb to Richmond? The inconvenience of Hoare's disappearance struck him as most unfortunate when Hoare's involvement with Cobb seemed so crucial. If he could trace Hoare, most of his questions would be answered.

He could only hope that, before Crackman wrote to inform him of the name of the other parties involved in this dispute, Hoare would reappear and send his version of events. Joshua felt certain that Mrs Mercier must be one of the people involved. She had been recently widowed and she had come from Barbados. Cobb's story about advising her on her pineapples was surely no more than a concoction to gain entry to Astley. Presumably the wrangle was over property left to Sabine by her second husband. Perhaps she had possession of something Cobb believed was rightfully his. If this were the case it would provide Sabine with a strong motive to want Cobb dead.

A vision of Sabine emerged in Joshua's mind. She was a woman of haunting charms. He pictured her as he had seen her at her dressing table, caressing her necklace. He saw her in the drawing room, wearing the jewel, looking elegant, refined and solicitous. He remembered that something she had said concerning it had the power to terrify Caroline Bentnick. He remembered the last time he had seen her, when

125

she sat for him, and how her grotesquely distorted profile had been cast on the wall. It struck him then that her beauty wasn't radiant; rather, the reverse, it was the beauty of a siren, a distracting allure that hid something deeper, led men astray, made them forget who they were. Thinking of her then he guessed the disputed property must be the necklace. That was why she set such store by it. What if Cobb had threatened to take it from her? Had she decided to resolve the dispute with Cobb by killing him?

Joshua reached the portals of Astley soon after three in the afternoon. He thought it peculiar to see Herbert standing so formally in the doorway waiting for him. Herbert's face registered no acknowledgement that he was relieved or pleased to see him. Joshua had the impression that Herbert looked blankly at his shape instead of recognizing his person. Why was Herbert not sitting down to his dinner? Whatever the emergency, it must surely be a grave one to have caused such a drastic postponement.

It was only when Joshua approached, leaving a footman to carry his bags, that he comprehended Herbert's expression was not one of blankness at all, but of disapproval. He glowered at Joshua as he mounted the steps; he refused Joshua's out-stretched hand. Nor did he respond to Joshua's proffered 'good afternoon'.

'So, Mr Pope, you have come at last.' Herbert's voice was carefully modulated but the displeasure behind it was unmistakable.

'Indeed, Mr Bentnick, your letter asking for my assistance arrived only this morning. I came the minute I could. What is the matter? Has something dreadful happened?'

'In a manner of speaking. And I am doing my utmost to give your actions the benefit of the doubt. Your return here is much in your favour, but at the very least you have some explaining to do.'

Joshua frowned in confusion. 'I regret I do not

126

understand, sir. Have I caused some offence? If so, let me assure you—'

'More than that, sir,' Herbert broke in. 'You have been the cause of the *greatest* distress. I will speak frankly, Mr Pope. You will recall, I take it, the necklace that Mrs Mercier entrusted to you? The necklace you placed in the drawer of your writing table and were supposed to hand to Mrs Mercier's maid?'

Joshua's heart began to sink. 'Indeed I do, sir. For you recall I told you of the undertaking and Miss Mercier said she would retrieve it.'

'That same necklace has disappeared.'

# Chapter Sixteen

Joshua was aghast at the news and his face lost its usual air of calm detachment. Blood surged to his brain; his hands grew clammy; he was aware of a feeling of sickness seeping into the pit of his belly. He felt as if he had been doused with a bucket of freezing water, yet at the same time he was roasting with heat. He could scarcely believe the evidence of his own ears: the necklace was lost and for some reason Herbert thought he was responsible. Although he had not actually come out with it in so many words, accusation was written in his face. It would only be a matter of time before he said so openly.

This, then, was the reason behind Herbert's dreadful stilted letter. Herbert distrusted him profoundly. Herbert believed he, Joshua Pope, whose works were exhibited in elegant salons up and down the land, who was proclaimed the equal of the great masters of history and courted by the gentry and nobility, was no more than a common thief. But as he mused on the ignominy of his situation, his initial sense of dismay and shock yielded to a more considered response. The sense of injustice he had felt regarding Cobb's death was echoed in his own case. He wouldn't concede to disgrace any more than he would let Cobb's death be ignored. He would uncover the truth behind both wrongs.

But along with this determination came a reappraisal of his present predicament. Joshua knew how highly Sabine valued her necklace. He suspected that the necklace had brought Cobb to Astley. He had witnessed the terror Sabine aroused in Caroline Bentnick. If Sabine had killed Cobb to save her necklace, Joshua could not help asking himself what awful justice might she exact if she thought *he* was the perpetrator of its disappearance. Herbert, besotted as he was, might be acting the role of accomplice, summoning him here so that Sabine could make her move.

Herbert escorted Joshua to his study, a room lined from floor to ceiling with mahogany bookcases overflowing with large heavily bound tomes and smelling of leather, musty paper and beeswax. There were cases filled with scientific curiosities – a dodo's egg, the skull of a large ape; the skin of a tiger lay stretched out upon the hearth; teeth from a crocodile and an elephant were ranged according to height along the mantel shelf. Herbert positioned himself in a leather-upholstered armchair behind a vast pedestal desk. Sabine was nowhere to be seen.

'Mr Bentnick,' said Joshua, settling himself wretchedly into a library chair to face him, 'let me assure you I know nothing of the disappearance of Mrs Mercier's necklace. I am completely innocent of any misdemeanour, save the one I admitted – of failing to pass the necklace to the maid in person before I departed. It was only a momentary lapse – you said so yourself.'

Herbert sat facing him, his elbow propped on the armrest, his chin resting in his hand. A look of watchful distrust flickered in his eye. 'I took you at your word when you said you had left the necklace in your rooms. I hardly expected this.'

'The necklace was there when I left. I am quite certain of it.'

'Did you see it when you returned to your rooms to pack?'

'Not exactly, no, but the drawer was still locked, there was no sign of disturbance.'

Herbert regarded him but said nothing. Joshua sensed his responses being weighed, as though Herbert was uncertain how to proceed and was waiting to be convinced of his innocence or guilt. Joshua had no choice but to plead for justice.

'In truth, sir, this is the first I have heard of the loss. I cannot be expected to defend myself until I know all the details. Perhaps there is some logical explanation for the jewel's disappearance. It might be a case of misplacement.'

'I damn well hope so, Pope. Unless we find it, I shall have to call Manning, the justice. When he hears what has happened, he will no doubt have you thrown into jail and branded, or quite possibly transported.'

The varnish of rationality had now all but disappeared. Joshua's knees began to quiver, not with fear so much as with disbelief and outrage at the unfairness of it all. He clenched his hands on his thighs and pressed down hard to hold them still. If Herbert detected his agitation it would only confirm his suspicions.

'Yes, sir, I understand the concerns. I see now why things seem black against me,' Joshua replied, though he very much wanted to say: 'No, sir, this is the grossest injustice. How can you even consider for one second I might be a thief?'

Joshua's apparent acceptance of his probable fate appeared to please Herbert. His mistrustful expression seemed to lift. 'I confess, Mr Pope, that even though you were the last person to have had the necklace in your possession, I have my doubts about your guilt and I have said as much to Mrs Mercier, though she, I must say, regards you more doubtfully. It is fortunate for you that Justice Manning is away – according to his daughter Lizzie he is unlikely to return for a fortnight. At any rate, I am giving you the chance to redeem yourself. I task you with retrieving it.'

Joshua was at a loss to know how he should react. Clearly Herbert considered he had just demonstrated great forbearance and clemency and expected some sign of gratitude, but since Joshua knew he wasn't guilty of taking the wretched jewel why should he be grateful at being ordered to find it?

He was an eminent artist not a contemptible purloiner. It was surely appropriate to put forward a cautious defence.

'Ask yourself, Mr Bentnick, if I had stolen the jewel what reason would I have to return here? You must see that this action alone proves my innocence,' he said quietly, shielding his indignation with politeness.

'Your reason for returning may well be that you do not wish to sully your reputation as an artist. Besides, you have twenty guineas resting on the finished canvas. And if those are your motives, then I declare you are the most brazen criminal I ever encountered.'

Joshua could no longer contain himself. 'May I point out, sir, that I have more commissions than I know what to do with. The sum of twenty guineas is neither here nor there to me. You speak of threatening my reputation. I trust it is so well established that it would not be damaged by a spurious accusation such as this. If you desire it, I can call upon numerous eminent acquaintances to testify to my good character.'

'For the time being that will not be necessary, Mr Pope,' said Herbert, taken aback by the vehemence of this response. 'I am quite well aware of the high esteem in which you are held. I would not have commissioned you otherwise. But be that as it may, I must ask what have you to say regarding the disappearance.'

'What can I say, when I have not the first notion what has happened here? Before I proffer any solutions, you must tell me what took place.'

Herbert seemed willing enough to comply with this request. He told Joshua then that, after they had left for London, Violet, accompanied by Caroline, had gone to his room. They had looked in the writing table and found the box pushed to the farthest corner of the drawer. Violet had taken the box to her mother's room. The maid Marie had just returned from her expedition, and so she handed the box to her without opening it and watched the maid put it away.

Sabine Mercier had returned from London early yesterday afternoon. She had immediately gone to her bedchamber to change out of her travelling garb and taken out from her dressing table the box containing her beloved jewel. On opening the box she had discovered it gone.

'I tell you, Pope,' said Herbert with great feeling, 'you can well imagine her dismay, her disbelief, her distress. She gave a most pitiful cry, then a wail of desolation, then immediately fell into a faint to the floor, knocking her head in the process. So deep was her state of unconsciousness that I feared, when I was called to attend her, she might have died from shock. However, after some time I detected the faintest of pulses and therefore summoned my physician, who came to tend her. Eventually, after several hours of his ministrations, she opened her eyes and sat up. Her first words on regaining consciousness and seeing me at her bedside were, "Dear God! Sweet Herbert, tell me I have been dreaming that my jewel was taken. It *was* a dream, was it not?"

'I suppose my face must have shown what had happened. At any rate, before I could say a word in response she leapt from her bed and hastened to her dressing table, where she found the empty box lying among her pomades and powders. She swooned again, and would have fallen to the ground, only this time I caught her, and wafted salts under her nose to revive her. You can imagine, Mr Pope, how witnessing the distress of one so dear to me has gravely troubled and, indeed, enraged me. I am not by nature a distrustful man, yet you must comprehend why the shadow of suspicion falls upon you. Mrs Mercier entrusted you with the necklace. As far as we know, you were the last person to see it. Neither Violet nor Caroline opened the box, and nor did the maid.'

'But the necklace is a sizeable jewel. Could they not tell from the weight and feel of the box whether there was something inside?'

'Violet says she cannot recall thinking anything about the weight. Caroline never held the box. The maid says she

132

thought she felt the necklace move inside it. But can we trust the maid? She is such a muddle-headed simpleton – how reliable is her testimony?'

Joshua's heart sank but he refused to despair. Certainly Herbert was angry with him. But he had also said that he didn't believe him to be guilty. There must be plenty of other arguments by which he could establish his innocence. He sighed – a heaving exhalation of weariness at the great injustice of it all. 'If the maid remarked nothing wrong when she put the jewel away, that surely indicates all was in order. On your own testimony, the box has been in Mrs Mercier's dressing table since then. Anyone in the household – nay, even an intruder – might have taken the necklace. Of course I comprehend the reason you summoned me and I will comply with your request to look into the matter until Justice Manning's return. But you must confess the case against me is purely circumstantial.'

Herbert thumped his fist on the desk. His withering look signalled displeasure at Joshua's lucid line of reasoning. 'Are you bargaining with me, Mr Pope?'

'No, sir. I am merely putting the matter to you as I see it, in a rational manner.'

'Then as proof of your probity and honest reputation, I trust you will have no objections if I pay a visit to your lodgings and conduct a thorough search of them.'

A slight flicker of Joshua's eyelids was the only outward sign of his surprise at this request. 'You are welcome to look wherever you choose,' he said, eyeing Herbert steadily. His tone was quiet and respectful, but the set of his jaw revealed his refusal to succumb. 'For I have absolutely nothing to hide, either there or anywhere else.'

# Chapter Seventeen

Clearing his name now became a matter of the utmost urgency to Joshua Pope. Despite his protestations to the contrary, he knew that Herbert Bentnick could cause him untold damage. Unless he proved his innocence his reputation could be irredeemably sullied. Quite possibly, even, he might lose his livelihood or his life. Herbert might claim to believe in his innocence, but Joshua sensed he was still viewed with suspicion, and that at any moment Herbert might turn against him. Knowing all this, Joshua had no desire to accompany him to London. Astley was where the necklace had disappeared, where his reputation had been cast into doubt. It was also where Cobb had died. His work was here.

Joshua handed Herbert a letter addressed to Mrs Quick, telling her to allow Herbert into his rooms and to leave him undisturbed there for as long as he wished. He shuddered to think what she would make of such instructions. He would brace himself for a verbal barrage when he returned.

Back in his chamber, he sat down by the window overlooking the garden. It was a fine afternoon, and the sun slipping low had stained the plants and trees and even the pinery with a soft, rosy light. There were no gardeners about, only a few sparrows hopping hither and thither on the gravel path, and an occasional swallow swooping low for a drink from the fishpond. He recognized the tranquillity of this scene, yet it brought him not one iota of peace. With Herbert gone, he felt profound uneasiness to be here, exposed to the unpredictable whim of Mrs Mercier, who had yet to appear and reveal her sentiments towards him.

On first hearing of the necklace's disappearance, Joshua had hoped that it was no more than a matter of simple misplacement. Having considered the matter, it seemed infinitely more complex. Given his suspicion that the necklace was the property at the centre of the dispute between Sabine and Cobb, the disappearance so soon after Cobb's death could hardly be a coincidence. Yet the two events did not fit neatly together. If Cobb had been killed to preserve the necklace, why had the necklace disappeared *after* he died? Was there more than one person interested in possessing it?

This strenuous exercising of his faculties eventually wore Joshua down. He yearned for a familiar face. He wanted Rachel, his poor dead wife, or, if not her, some other friendly companion with whom he might discuss frankly and openly his suspicions and fears. Although it was only Friday, he forgot his earlier doubts and wished he had Meg nearby to console him. And yet he had no one. He tried to shrug off this self-pitying thought. He told himself firmly that despite the shadow into which he had been cast, he should thank God that thus far Herbert seemed willing enough to give him a chance to redeem himself. No sooner had this thought occurred than it was followed by another more sobering one: Herbert's faith would rapidly dwindle without some tangible progress.

What should he do? His instinct was to go directly to the maidservant Marie and press her more closely about what she remembered of the day she had been handed the necklace. Who, strangers or otherwise, had been in Mrs Mercier's rooms since then? Had she remarked any disturbance? But if he went to find her there was every chance he would also run into Sabine, and since Herbert had intimated she viewed him with deep suspicion this was something he wished to avoid for the time being.

Just then Lizzie Manning fluttered into his mind – he had barely thought of her at all until now – and a desire for her company overcame him. This was not from any romantic inclination. Lizzie held no physical allure for him and her tendency to bossiness was irksome, yet her merits were also clear. She was quick-witted (if somewhat naïve in the ways of men) and a doyenne in the art of conversation. More importantly, she knew better than did Joshua the characters involved in this mysterious affair. She had even struck up an acquaintance with the maid Marie. If anyone could extract information from her – assuming there was something to extract – Lizzie would.

But while Joshua craved companionship and assistance, a cautious part of him held back. He had seen for himself how unguardedly Lizzie spoke and behaved on occasion. Discretion in a matter such as this was paramount. Moreover, he wondered whether she was as artless as she first appeared. Did her openness conceal something darker? After only two meetings and a letter it was impossible to be certain. And yet, in his present predicament, he couldn't afford to alienate her. After a brisk deliberation he resolved to move cautiously. He would appeal to her sympathy, tell her no more than she needed to know and thus avail himself of her collaboration. His thoughts he would keep to himself.

Having set upon this course of action he wrote a brief note to her, detailing the disappearance of the necklace as Herbert had related it. In it he declared his innocence of any involvement in the jewel's disappearance. He requested her aid in speaking to the maid and asked her to come immediately to Astley on whatever pretext she could muster for that purpose. He gave the note to Peters, the first footman, to despatch and then, since he was in need of convivial company, he hung his sword about his belt – only a fool ventured out on foot after dark without his weapon of defence – buttoned his coat over it, and set off for the short walk to Richmond, to spend an hour or two at the Star and Garter.

*   *   *

The landlord, Dunstable, remembered Joshua the minute he set foot through his door. Joshua ordered a jar of stout for himself and another for Dunstable.

'The artist returns, I see,' he said with a deep guffaw. 'Have you yet discovered the whereabouts of your friend Cobb? He still has not been for his belongings.'

Joshua winced when Dunstable said this. He had forgotten until this moment that the last time they met he had been wary of letting slip too much and never disclosed that Cobb was dead. 'I still follow the trail. But, yes, I do believe I draw closer.'

'What do you say, sir? Don't beat about the bush. Have you found him, yes or no? I see from your face you hold something back. Let me assure you, Mr Pope, the reason I ask his whereabouts is not to hound him. He has paid his dues right enough. No, all I want is simply to return his belongings. They are naught but a hindrance to me now.'

Joshua reddened. 'In truth, Mr Dunstable, I must tell you – indeed, I should have done before – the reason for my interest in Mr Cobb is not some business I have *with* him, but rather my business is because *of* him. In short, sir, Cobb is dead. He was found lying in the pinery at Astley not five days ago. The death is most suspicious and my enquiries are prompted by my belief that any man, even a scoundrel, deserves better than to be murdered in a strange place and buried with no more regard than a dead dog.'

The landlord's eyes opened round as a pair of billiard balls. '*Murdered? Murdered?* Are you quite sure of it?'

'There is naught but the smallest of doubts in my mind, and it grows more minuscule with each day.'

Dunstable swallowed a gulp of ale uncomfortably then licked his lips, clearly still pondering Joshua's words. 'In that case,' said he, 'tell me, what should I do with his bag? I have no wish to be held responsible for a murder on account of having his belongings under my roof.'

'Do not trouble yourself about that. Give the bag to me. When I return to London I will hand it to his attorney – the same Mr Hoare who you told me was here to see him. Hoare was acting for Cobb in a family matter and will surely know the next of kin, to whom these possessions should rightfully be passed.'

Dunstable seemed happy enough to comply with this suggestion. He excused himself, saying he would go in search of the valise. While Joshua waited he drank another tankard of ale, settling himself by a small window overlooking the back of the inn. The stable yard lay to one side, the gardens to the other. It was growing dark now. The gardens were all but invisible; the stables quiet, horses bolted inside; vacant stalls had been left with doors ajar and there were no grooms to be seen. He gazed at the deserted yard, wondering vaguely what Cobb's bag might contain. Curiosity rather than philanthropy had prompted his offer to take Cobb's bag to Hoare. The bag might yield a clue as to Cobb's fate. A letter from Hoare perhaps.

At this point he remembered the letters Granger said he had handed to Herbert, the letters he had found in Cobb's pocket. Perhaps Hoare had written one of them. If so, it surely would shed some light on this perplexing conundrum. What had become of it? Joshua remembered Herbert tearing up one letter and stowing the other in the writing desk in the drawing room soon after Cobb was found dead. Was the destroyed letter the one that Hoare had written, or was that another communication entirely? He had given no word of explanation for his actions yet Sabine had treated them as if they were nothing out of the ordinary. It had occurred to Joshua then how singular Herbert's behaviour had been. Here was another avenue to pursue. Joshua tried to recall Herbert's expression as he dealt with the letters. Had he seemed furtive? Disconcerted? Angry? He well remembered the dismal set of his face, the slump of his back – he had looked sad, despairing even – yet Joshua's recollection was that there had been no attempt at all to hide what he did, and nor had he seemed enraged. Plainly the letter he had hidden away must be a communication of some significance that he did not want to lose. It was surely worth searching the bureau to discover why. And with Herbert presently in London searching Joshua's rooms, what better opportunity could there be?

Joshua was distracted from these absorbing thoughts by Dunstable's return. He handed over a leather travel bag, initialled with the letters JC, with strict instructions to pass it straight to the attorney Hoare, and to mind nothing went astray. Thankful for the dingy light, which nicely camouflaged his blushes, Joshua assured him that he would meddle with nothing; upon his honour, he would deliver the bag as soon as he was able. Then, as a joking afterthought, he added that the only thing that might stop him was if he met a highwayman or footpad along the way.

Dunstable's expression turned grave. 'The road's no safer than any in these parts, and highwaymen are a common scourge. But since you are armed and a strapping fellow, God willing you should have little to fear.'

And so, brimming with ale and courage, Joshua doffed his hat to Dunstable and set out on the journey to Astley. It was a fine, clear night with a half-moon to light his way. His progress was slowed only by the encumbrance of Cobb's stout bag, which was heavier than he had foreseen. Very soon his arms felt as if they had been wrenched from their sockets and he cursed his wretched curiosity, wishing he had left the bag and come back in a vehicle to collect it. He longed for a carriage or a cart to pass so he could beg a ride, but he met no one save a solitary carter travelling in the opposite direction.

A quarter of a mile on, he reached Marshgate and the bottom of Richmond Hill. The town was now behind him and he strode past the gateposts to Sir Charles Littleton's mansion and very soon was out in open country. Now he was on a flat piece of ground and had only the ominous silver band of the Thames for company. Joshua's detestation of all large expanses of water, and in particular the river, made him uneasy, but the ale helped to numb his fear. He treated the river like an unwanted guest at an assembly and ignored it, although he was relieved when the road turned away from the river's edge. Dense undergrowth now bordered either side of the verge.

He had reached a spot where the road passed through particularly thick vegetation, when a man stepped unexpectedly out of the shadows. Joshua nearly jumped out of his skin at the sudden apparition. The man stood no more than ten feet in front of him. His face was partially obscured by the darkness; nonetheless, Joshua could clearly discern his lanky build, his dishevelled, unwashed appearance and the wild look in his eye.

'Halt, if you please, sir,' said the stranger, taking a pace towards Joshua, then stopping, as if he wanted to see what would happen.

The man's voice was more genteel than Joshua expected, though there was no mistaking the menace it contained. As the man advanced, Joshua saw that his left foot dragged behind him and that he walked with a distinctive uneven gait. He wondered if the man had observed him at the Star and Garter, sitting in the window illuminated by candlelight. He could well have spied Dunstable handing over the valise. Perhaps he had followed him all the way, waiting to reach a suitably deserted spot before making his attack. Presumably he hadn't realized Joshua was armed (his sword being well concealed beneath his coat). He would soon discover his mistake.

'What do you want?' Joshua replied boldly. His heart fluttered in its rib cage, like a bird desperate for freedom. But his mind was icy calm as his hand reached stealthily for his sword.

'My due.'

There wasn't a trace of nervousness in his voice. Joshua was incensed by his audacity. 'And what might the due of a common footpad be other than to hang until you are dead?'

'I am no footpad. I want the bag in your hand. It belongs to me. Drop it if you please, sir, and continue on your way. I give you my honest word I will do you no harm if you do as I ask.'

'I shall do no such thing. I warn you, man, if you approach me, I will defend myself.'

Ignoring Joshua's warning, the man came towards him, until he was so close Joshua could smell gin on his breath and see the gleaming whites of his eyes. The man swayed slightly but perceptibly. Clearly, Joshua thought, the fellow is in drink – that is why he shows not a glimmer of fear; and that is why he is no match for me. Emboldened by this observation, with a single, swift movement Joshua extracted his sword and thrust it towards the man, holding it so that the tip rested on the skin of his scrawny neck.

'I fail to see that this bag is your due. I say again, who are you but a footpad?' Joshua said.

The man gave a barking laugh, which turned abruptly into a coughing fit that had him doubled up. Joshua was forced to withdraw his weapon a little or risk slitting the man's throat. No longer did he feel a glimmer of fear at the miserable specimen before him, merely revulsion. At length, the man brought his spasm under control. He raised himself up, spat a large globule of phlegm to the ground, then looked straight at Joshua.

'My name is John Cobb,' he said.

# Chapter Eighteen

No sooner had this astonishing announcement left his lips than the stranger made a grab for the bag at Joshua's feet. Joshua was so taken by surprise at the man's claim that for a moment he was frozen in shock. Cobb was dead. This man was naught but a fraud, and a pitiful specimen at that. Springing into action then, Joshua grasped his assailant's wrist, while raising his sword to threaten him to submission. The man tried to wrench his hand away, though Joshua held on firm as a manacle. Still writhing and jostling, the man bellowed, 'Now you give me no choice.' With that, he gave a violent contorted tug of his captive hand and pulled out a pistol from his pocket with his free one. He cocked the weapon, pointing its muzzle directly at Joshua's eye. 'Leave me be, sir. Have I not told you the bag is mine? I came to fetch it from the inn, only to see you leave with it before I had a chance to speak to the landlord there.'

With no choice but to concede defeat, Joshua dropped his weapon and handed over the bag. 'You are a bare-faced ruffian and an impostor,' he said, furious to have been outdone when so clearly he had the advantage. 'I do not know how you came to settle upon the name John Cobb. Perhaps you overheard my conversation with the landlord. In any case I will tell you, since you are bold enough to try it, that John Cobb is dead and has been so the past five days.'

The man fixed his gaze on Joshua. In the dark his expression was invisible, though from the gleam on the barrel Joshua was aware he dropped his pistol a fraction. 'Dead, is he? Can you be sure?' he said.

'As certain as if I had seen the corpse with my own eyes,' Joshua retorted. Using the momentary lapse of concentration, he swooped down, retrieved his sword and, brandishing it with a flourish, deliberately wounded the arm in which his assailant held the pistol.

The man gave a yelp of surprise, dropping the weapon and the bag in his haste to staunch the wound. The pistol exploded loudly as it fell to the ground, narrowly avoiding serious injury to Joshua. 'You dare call *me* a scoundrel! It is *you* who are the thief!' he cried out, before loping off into the shadows.

For some minutes after he left, Joshua heard him rustling in the darkness around him, stifling a coughing fit. Joshua knew his assailant was wounded and in poor health, whereas he himself was able-bodied. He might have apprehended him. Yet, as suddenly as it arrived, his earlier courage vanished. He was disturbed by the violence of the encounter, by the thought of how close he had come to injury, and by the vehemence of the man's parting retort. Suppose he had a second weapon about his person and was now lying in wait for him in the thickets? And what was the significance of his remark that Joshua was a thief, not he? Did he know about the disappearance of the necklace or was this a reference to the bag he carried? The shock of the encounter combined with the ale he had earlier drunk made Joshua unusually muddle-headed. It seemed to him there was no purpose in pursuing the man and risking further assault, when all he wanted was to return unscathed to the relative safety of Astley with Cobb's bag and to discover what it might contain.

Having reached this conclusion, Joshua made no attempt to pursue him, or even to shout questions that might have helped him discover what he meant by his strange remark.

(He speedily regretted this faintheartedness.) With no more than a parting glance and prayer that neither he nor any other malefactor would apprehend him again, Joshua let the bleeding, limping assailant disappear into the night and hurried on his way to Astley.

It was nearly midnight by the time Joshua arrived at the door. Finding the house securely locked and all the servants abed, he was forced to wake the housekeeper by knocking on her window, an action that irked her intensely. He murmured an apology when she came, bleary-eyed, to the door to let him in. Taking the lighted stub she begrudgingly proffered, he thanked her and then hurried upstairs to his chamber without waiting for her to chastise him. Once there, he closed his door and turned his attentions to Cobb's valise.

The clasp was unlocked and opened easily. Inside he discovered a small leather case containing brushes, combs, pomades, a razor. Beneath lay a dark-blue woollen coat: clean but plain and of middling quality; a double-breasted wool waistcoat: vertically striped in blue and brown; two pairs of breeches: one black, one buff; two linen shirts: both worn, though of reasonable quality; a pair of stockings; a muslin cravat; three pairs of linen drawers; a nightshirt. At the very bottom, in another leather case, was a travelling walking stick, presently divided into three sections and fashionably capped with a carved pineapple finial. How appropriate, thought Joshua: it seemed there was no avoiding pineapples.

Even by the light of a solitary candle, which was growing smaller every minute, he could see that nothing here was in the least remarkable. Arguably the cane was a little more handsome than Joshua's own walking stick, being made from rosewood rather than mahogany, but then Joshua's had a silver finial in the form of a globe which, on reflection, he deemed superior. All in all it was a perfectly ordinary travelling case of an ordinary middle-ranking gentleman; not quite as fine as his own luggage but not so different either.

Joshua next searched the pockets of the coat thoroughly for

any letter or paper that might offer some clue as to Cobb's untimely death. The only thing of any interest he found was a visiting card from Hoare with the following message inscribed upon it. '*Arrive afternoon of 20th inst. Will call on you directly.*' By some strange coincidence Hoare had evidently arrived in Richmond the same day as he had, and later that same evening Cobb had died. Was this significant? Could Hoare's absence since the meeting with Cobb be a pointer to his guilt? But what reason could there be for an attorney to murder a client? Until he knew more of the business in which both men were involved, and the reason for Hoare's journey, it was impossible to tell.

Joshua put Hoare's card back where he had found it and began to return the clothes to the case. He was halfway through this task, when the candle stub, having burned to nothing, gave a final flicker and expired. There was nothing for it but to fumblingly remove his boots and outer clothes and crawl into bed, whence he fell almost immediately into welcome oblivion.

Next morning, as he stood at his washstand, the thought struck Joshua that since he had never set eyes on Cobb, dead or alive, he had no idea what manner of man he was. Having seen his case he might have expected to learn a little of his tastes and character, yet he was scarcely any the wiser. Was Cobb a proud or a timid man? What sort of figure did he cut dressed in the clothes in his case?

In this spirit of enquiry Joshua turned back to the bag he had opened last night. The coat was lying on the floor where it had dropped when his candle burned out. Joshua was presently clad only in his shirt and breeches. He picked up the coat, put it on and walked to the looking glass. Joshua's middling stature and swelling girth were a source of chagrin, a subject on which he tried not to dwell excessively. Now, however, he was forcibly reminded of them. The sleeves of Cobb's coat dangled three inches below his wrists, the tails swamped him, falling practically to his knees, but the buttons wouldn't meet about his middle. Evidently Cobb was a flagpole of a man.

Joshua was about to remove the jacket to put on his own, when he recalled the card in the pocket. Perhaps there was something he had missed in last night's dwindling candlelight that would stand out in day. But when he groped in the pocket, he discovered to his confusion that the card was no longer there. He fumbled in the pocket on the other side. Still nothing. He looked around the room, then dropped to his knees to scour the floor for the card. It was nowhere to be seen.

Joshua scratched his head and paced about the room, wondering if he had perhaps dreamt he had seen the card, but he was sure he hadn't, for everything else was exactly where it should have been. He had no alternative but to confront a disturbing possibility. Some nocturnal intruder had come into his room while he slept and taken the card away. What other explanation was there for the evidence (or, rather, lack of it) before him? But what possible interest could a card bearing such a mundane message hold for anyone? The encounter with the footpad returned to his consciousness – and seemed a hundred times more frightening in hindsight. The man had demanded Cobb's valise and nearly succeeded in taking it from him. Assuming he had followed Joshua here, gained entry to the house and lain in wait for an opportunity to search Cobb's belongings, he was clearly not the common thief Joshua supposed.

But if Joshua was certain of this much, the rest seemed unfathomably confused. Who was his assailant? What could have made someone so determined to secure Cobb's possessions as to trespass in his room in the dead of night? What had prompted his ludicrous claim to be Cobb? He shuddered inwardly as it dawned on him that the most obvious answer was that the man was Cobb's murderer. Was this Hoare? Perhaps he had taken the card because he feared it incriminated him. Or perhaps he had intended to take the entire bag, but something

146

disturbed him and, fearing apprehension, he fled without it. This led Joshua to a further troubling thought. If the murderer had come to his room while he slept, knew Joshua still had Cobb's bag, and was still determined to recover it, how long would it be before he tried again?

This daunting realization did nothing to shift Joshua's resolve. Rather, he felt a strange sense of satisfaction at having gained some advantage over the murderer. Assuming the bag contained something incriminating, it might serve as bait. It had been in his possession only a few hours, yet already two attempts had been made to interfere with it. The bag should at all costs be safeguarded.

Joshua stowed all the clothes and other objects back inside the bag. He briefly contemplated keeping the walking stick out for his own use, but in the end he decided he had had enough of pineapples and preferred his own. He cast about his bedchamber for a suitable hiding place. He noticed that in a corner of the room, a few feet from the washstand, there was a hinged door set into the wainscoting. On closer examination he discovered that there was a neatly concealed cupboard, probably intended as a linen closet, which contained no more than a few empty boxes and a plentiful supply of cobwebs. Joshua put Cobb's bag inside and pulled his washstand a few feet to the right. He stood back and admired his handiwork. The door was now hidden by the washstand. Unless someone knew the cupboard was there and pulled the washstand away, they would never find it.

But as Joshua sank back in a chair he pondered further on his assailant's identity. He had claimed to be Cobb, but then when Joshua said Cobb was dead the man asked if he was sure. These words, which hitherto he had dismissed, now struck Joshua rather differently. There was a further possible explanation that made sense of the encounter. If the man on the road wasn't Cobb's murderer, intent on taking the bag in case it contained something incriminating against him, then he was no impostor. He was indeed John Cobb.

# Chapter Nineteen

In Joshua's mind, Cobb's death and the disappearance of the necklace now resembled a partially submerged wreck in which only a bowsprit and a mast were visible above the water's surface. From his present vantage point he could see a murky connection between the disappearance of the necklace and the death in the pinery, though how precisely they fitted together remained unclear. The necklace might very well be the disputed property that had drawn Cobb to England from Barbados and that brought about his death. The fact that the necklace had disappeared *after* Cobb's death might point to a co-conspirator, or might be proof of his assailant's story that Cobb wasn't dead. Joshua was still confused after last night's encounter, yet his faculties were clear enough to convince him that he could not consider the disappearance of the necklace without the death in the pinery.

It was still early morning; the clock had yet to chime seven. Joshua went to the window, pulled back the curtain and let his melancholic eye survey the scene. The garden was heavy with dew and a morning mist clung to the ground, but the sky was clear, with only faint wisps of white drifting across the expanse of vivid blue. He looked down over the roof of the vast conservatory gleaming in the early-morning sun. The only sign of life in this tranquil scene was to be glimpsed beneath the glass. Granger was working on the opposite side of the conservatory from the pinery. Accompanied by a couple of men, he was engaged in training a vine into a regular serpentine form, trimming side-shoots where necessary.

Since Granger was the only person apart from Sabine who had seen the corpse, Joshua hoped he might clarify certain details of his appearance. He finished dressing, choosing a workman-like blue woollen jacket, which was well cut and made him feel comfortingly slim around the middle, and a plain blue cravat. Then, having set a dark curled wig on his head, he went off in search of Granger.

By the time Joshua reached him Granger had left the men inside the conservatory sprinkling water like fine rain all over the leaves and was heading towards the kitchen garden.

'Good morning, Granger. I see you are an expert in vines as well as pineapples. What are your men doing?'

Granger stopped walking and turned. 'I have instructed them to water the vine to help the fruit swell and to deter insects. You can only do it before the sun reaches the plant, hence it must be done early.'

'How did you learn such matters?'

'I was taught about vines while I was still an apprentice at Beechwood.'

'Beechwood? The same place you learned to grow pineapples?'

Granger shot him a penetrating glance. 'Your memory does you credit, sir.'

'It's kind of you to say so, but I have come because I wish to put *your* memory to the test. How well did you scrutinize Cobb's body?' he said, leaping straight from vines to corpses with no preamble.

Granger glanced over his shoulder at his men while he pondered and then regarded his callused hands. 'Cobb's corpse?' he repeated.

'Yes. When Mrs Mercier asked you to deal with it, did you take time to look closely?'

149

Granger's leathery complexion darkened to the colour of walnut. He shrugged his shoulders. 'Not especially, sir.'

'Could you describe him for me?'

'Describe him? There was naught remarkable in him, apart from the fact he was dead.'

'How tall would you say he was? My height? Taller than you?'

Granger looked at Joshua. 'About your size maybe. He was lying down, mind, so I can't be exact.'

'I have Cobb's bag. His clothes are those of a tall man – someone, I would hazard, who is considerably taller than I am. An inch or two taller than you even.'

Granger walked a little further down the path and squatted to crumble some earth, as if testing the soil for moistness or some other quality of which Joshua knew nothing. Joshua fancied he began to look a little uncomfortable. Why wouldn't Granger look him in the eye? 'I told you, sir, I can't be precise. He was lying down.'

'But you saw Cobb on the previous occasion, when he came to the garden. You said so yourself. How tall was he then?'

'Yes. He was a tall man; I remember now.'

Joshua sensed that if Granger wasn't lying, then he wasn't being entirely open either. The obstruction exasperated him, but it didn't deter him from pressing home his point. 'Are you quite certain, Mr Granger, that the man you accosted in the gardens and the man lying dead in the pinery were one and the same?'

Granger shrugged his shoulders and fell silent. Though Joshua could not be certain – Granger's back was turned to him – he thought he seemed a little stiffer than usual. Joshua waited for Granger to speak. He would wait all day if necessary.

'I assumed it was him on account of the letter,' Granger mumbled at last, conceding defeat by standing up and turning to look at Joshua directly. 'But maybe, now you come to mention it, it wasn't.'

'What precisely do you mean, Granger? A man is dead, possibly murdered. Was he the same man you met in the garden? I want the truth, not maybes and assumptions.'

Granger lowered his voice and furrowed his brow. There was a new urgency in his tone. 'In truth, sir, I can't be certain of anything. I haven't seen a dead man before. It disturbed me to see the corpse like that, and the smell – on account of him vomiting – and the heat made it worse. In short, sir, I confess I didn't look straight at him. Mrs Mercier had put her handkerchief over his face. I saw no need to remove it. I looked in his pockets, like she asked. Then I called two under gardeners to put him on the cart and take him to the undertaker.'

'So you never really inspected the corpse?'

He regarded his boots once more. 'No, sir. I suppose, now I think on it, I didn't.'

Frustrated by this disappointing confession, Joshua returned to the house. He felt hungry and wondered if it was too early for breakfast. As he opened the door to the hall he remembered the letter Herbert had secreted in the writing desk in the drawing room on the morning the corpse was discovered. It now seemed more imperative than ever to find this communication. He had already formed a shady theory as to whose the corpse was if it wasn't Cobb's, but before he let speculation run away with him he had to unearth certain facts.

To search Herbert's bureau seemed to Joshua a most perilous undertaking. The drawing room was at the hub of the house, at the foot of the stairs. During the morning the family sporadically used the room. Even when they didn't stop in it, they tended to pass through it on their way to the morning room. Late afternoons and evenings were always passed there. At other times servants came and went to perform their duties.

Joshua needed to enter and to remain there for some time without being observed. And yet, since he was unfamiliar with servants' routines, it was impossible for him to be sure at what hour he might be certain of avoiding them. Herbert was presumably still in London, sifting through Joshua's possessions for incriminating evidence. The rest of the household remained at Astley. He had missed his opportunity to search the drawing room last night, when everyone was abed. If he waited until later the family would be about; this evening Herbert might have returned and the task would grow even trickier. Thus, he concluded, steeling his wavering resolve as he did so, the present hour – it was barely eight o'clock and no one was yet risen – was his best chance.

He paused in the hallway. To his left lay the open door to the breakfast room, where he could see the table set for six. Silver-domed dishes had been set out on burners to keep the food warm on the serving table. The bell to summon the servants was in the centre of the table. The room was deserted.

The drawing-room door on the right was closed. Dare he open it? His heart palpitated, but he urged himself to proceed. He walked forward, turned the handle and went in, closing the door behind him. The curtains were drawn back and the room had already been tidied, with the chairs and tables pushed back to the wall. He hoped that meant there would be little threat of interruption by a zealous housemaid with a duster. His pulse still raced but he tried to calm himself. He would be in no danger until after the family had breakfasted. He would be able to hear them descend the stairs and enter the breakfast room.

Having mastered his trepidation, Joshua walked to the far end of the room, where the writing desk was situated. The desk had a front flap that opened out by means of a key, and, as fortune would have it, the key was presently in the lock. Joshua drew up a chair and opened the desk. Inside were two rows of small drawers and pigeonholes crammed with all manner of letters and papers. He sighed. No wonder Herbert felt little need to keep his desk locked. Amid such a quantity of papers how would any prying outsider, himself included, discover what he wanted? He could spend a day sifting through all this writing matter and there would still be more to read.

In this despondent frame of mind he took a bundle of papers from the first pigeonhole and glanced through them. They were, it was clear, letters from Sabine to Herbert, prior to her arrival in England. The missives were full of affection and excitement, coupled with detailed instructions regarding the preparations to be made for her pineapple house. Joshua felt a disconcerting twang of envy and put them back. In the next compartment were various household bills and accounts and a booklet charting the servants' wages and other household expenses. He flicked these morosely to one side, thinking he would never find anything of note. It was some minutes later that he came across something more interesting: a letter sent from London, addressed to Herbert and dated six days ago – the day the body was found. The hand in which it was written was large and rather fanciful, with many twirls and curlicues; by contrast, its message was short and simple.

Mr Bentnick,
*I have done my utmost to exercise my self-control, but you have
tested me to the limit. I see now that after all this time you
have merely feigned sympathy with my cause, yet never truly
listened to a word I said to you. My patience is now at an end,
and none but you have driven me to make this ultimatum. Since
you have not extracted what is mine, I will come immediately and
retrieve it in person.*

The letter was signed with an unintelligible monogram, which could have been almost any letters in the alphabet. Joshua was utterly perplexed not just by the signature but also by the meaning of this letter. Was *'what I asked'* the necklace, or could this refer to some other dispute of which he was ignorant? Was the scrawl Cobb's? This seemed unlikely: the elaborate script looked as if it was a woman's hand. Joshua put the letter between the pages of his pocket book and secreted it in his pocket. He was about to move to the next pigeonhole, when his eye chanced upon a slender folder lying in a large horizontal compartment under a pile of fresh writing paper. On the cover was a label, with the word *daybook* inscribed upon it. Joshua untied the folder. Here was the most recent correspondence Herbert had received and copies of letters he had sent. The last was a folded letter. The paper was mud-stained, but not so badly that Joshua couldn't read the address on the outside; it was inscribed in heavy black ink: *To Mr John Cobb, Star and Garter Inn, Richmond.*

His heart was racing now. He had spent far longer in the room than he intended. Yet this was what he had come to find and, by some minor miracle, he had succeeded. The mud stains were surely proof enough this was the letter Granger had taken from the dead man's coat. Without unfolding the letter, Joshua placed it with the other, between the pages of his pocket book. As he did so he fancied he heard a light rustle somewhere close. The family must be beginning to arrive for their breakfast. He should leave as quickly as possible.

Briskly he closed the daybook, returned it to its compartment under the papers and closed the flap. It was as he was locking the desk that he heard the rustle again. He spun round. Standing in the doorway to the drawing room, a look of unmistakable accusation glinting in her eye, was Lizzie Manning.

# Chapter Twenty

Once he had overcome his initial shock at her sudden appearance, Joshua felt at a loss to comprehend Lizzie Manning's ferocious expression. He was disappointed too in his own misjudgement, and the sentiment was manifest in a tightening of his lips and a gathering of his brows as he examined her minutely. Last night his reasons for summoning her hither seemed so unequivocal. Yet here she was, the woman he had hoped would assist him, giving him a look that was blacker than his boots. What had possessed him to believe her presence could be beneficial? She was naught but a hindrance and an unpredictable one at that.

'Miss Manning,' Joshua said quietly, masking his sinking heart with the flicker of a smile. 'I did not hear you enter. Nor did I know you had arrived and were staying in this house.'

'Evidently,' said she with *froideur*. 'I received your letter, in which you told me of the disappearance of Mrs Mercier's necklace and requested my assistance to prove your innocence. I came as speedily as I was able, only to find you rifling through the Bentnick family's private possessions. Tell me, Mr Pope, what do *you* think I should make of it all?'

'Why, madam,' he said, drawing himself up, 'surely you don't think *I* was doing anything wrong? I searched the desk for evidence. I saw Mr Bentnick place a letter there on the day the body was discovered in the pinery. There is a chance it was one of the letters that Granger the gardener handed him, and it might therefore have some bearing on these perplexing matters in which we have become embroiled.'

'*We*? Do you infer *I* am also fallen under a shadow of suspicion? I think not, sir.'

Joshua's eyes flashed; exasperation simmered inside him but he smothered it. Did she, too, doubt his integrity? Could she not see the urgency of his predicament? The answer to both questions was plainly yes. Yet he should not blame her for these shortcomings when it was he who had ignored his own instincts and deluded himself about her usefulness.

'No, madam, I did not mean what you think. What I meant was—'

'Never mind that, Mr Pope. Just tell me straight what is important. Did you find anything?'

'I cannot be certain.' His retort was unusually sharp, bordering on curtness. He hoped it would remind her who he was.

'How very muddling. Please explain yourself a little more lucidly, Mr Pope. I confess I cannot follow your drift thus far.'

He took on a tone even more lofty than hers, one that implied it was she not he who was acting out of turn. 'Forgive me, Miss Manning, for not making myself clear when it is plain you are in a state of confusion. I *have* found a letter that may be relevant. It is addressed to Mr Cobb at the Star and Garter, but I have not yet had a chance to read it. And I found another letter that is certainly most perplexing. But just now, I fancy, is not the moment to linger among Mr Bentnick's correspondence.'

'May I see the communications?' Her tone was a shade more conciliatory. Clearly, Joshua thought, the way to manage her was not to attempt to pacify her but to vie with her instead.

'I will gladly show you the letters. But may I suggest we first take some breakfast? Not to join the family at the usual meal-times might arouse suspicions, which, I am sure you would agree, could be most detrimental to our enquiries. Afterwards,

156

we will find somewhere quiet and secluded, where we will not be interrupted, to peruse the letters and discuss them at our leisure.'

Lizzie nodded her acquiescence without a trace of ill temper, and thus they adjourned to the breakfast room. Joshua hungrily consumed two poached eggs, a bloater and a cup of chocolate. Lizzie toyed with a small roll as she regarded Joshua in wary silence, which he noted but ignored.

Soon after they had sat down at the table, Francis and Caroline made their appearances. They were surprised and glad to see Lizzie at their table, for they hadn't expected her before the ball. To what did they owe this unexpected pleasure?

Joshua observed with interest that Lizzie explained herself without a flicker of self-consciousness. She had come on impulse to ask a great favour of Herbert and Sabine and Mr Pope. She wanted to make a gift to the happy couple to mark their engagement and she thought it would be a fine thing indeed if she could draw a pineapple for them. She wished, therefore, to beg a lesson or two in drawing. This was a hobby of which she had always been excessively fond, but hopelessly inept, unlike her dear friend Caroline. Did they think Herbert or Sabine would have any objection? Would Joshua agree?

Caroline's face registered her astonishment. 'My dear friend, of course I am delighted at this ambition. Though I confess you surprise me – you have always said you thought drawing the most tedious of pursuits.'

Francis intervened. 'Caroline, don't be harsh with poor Lizzie. We are all entitled to a change of heart on occasion. Our father is presently away from Astley. Thus, as far as I know, Mr Pope is free to instruct you if he has no objection.'

Joshua hastily assured them he would be honoured to tutor so keen a pupil. Botanical art had never been his forte, but he would do his utmost to teach her the rudiments.

In the middle of this discussion Violet arrived. Having smiled pleasantly at Francis, and bade a surprised good morning to Lizzie, she sat herself down at the table. Joshua's heart sank at the sight of her. He was sure now that at any moment Sabine would enter. What would her reaction to his presence be without Herbert to temper her wrath? Was he about to be subjected to a barrage of inquisition or some far more fearsome assault? Mercifully his agitation was short-lived. Violet directed a servant to take a breakfast tray to her mother in her room, where she was occupied with her correspondence.

During the half-hour that followed, Violet made polite conversation with Francis and passed one or two desultory remarks to Caroline and Lizzie, but by and large seemed much preoccupied by her own thoughts and spoke not a word to Joshua.

Since Joshua was greatly relieved to know that he was safe from Sabine for the time being, this did not duly concern him. Besides, he had on his plate the last morsels of a particularly succulent bloater to consume. When not a fragment remained save for a pile of wispy bones, he rose from the table and addressed Violet. 'I do not know if your mother desires to resume her sittings for the portrait. Perhaps, Miss Mercier, you would be kind enough to tell her I am at her disposal whenever she wishes, although it might be best to wait for Mr Bentnick's return. In the meantime, as you no doubt have gathered, I shall occupy myself with instructing Miss Manning in the art of drawing.'

Violet nodded and complied willingly with this request, though she took a minute or two to register what Joshua asked of her. Once again he had the feeling she was distracted by something else, so that her mind was scarcely aware of what was going on around her. He wondered what this might be. Remembering her maid's testimony that Violet had been fond of John Cobb, he thought it probable Cobb's fate had something to do with it. He made a mental note to persuade Lizzie to talk to Violet, to probe her further on this matter, and turned then to his would-be pupil. 'Miss Manning, I believe the weather is fine this morning. Let us go out into the garden and practise botanical studies. I have yet to see the pineapple house. Shall we meet there in an hour?'

Some ten minutes before the agreed hour, Joshua, laden with sketchbooks and pencils, emerged from his rooms onto the landing, but just as he was about to descend the staircase he heard Herbert's sonorous voice on the half-landing below. He peered over the balustrade at the very moment, as misfortune would have it, Herbert heard his step and looked up. Their eyes locked. Herbert's upturned face crimsoned.

'Mr Pope,' he said, 'the very man I desired most urgently to see. Will you be so kind as to accompany me directly to the library.'

It wasn't a question, more a summons. Joshua knew it and so did Herbert, for he turned on his heels to lead the way without waiting for a reply. Joshua wondered what in God's name it might be that had caused him to speak in such a tone. He did not at all relish following him, and he hoped he wouldn't now be late for Lizzie Manning, but, caught as he was, he could do little but comply with the order.

Herbert stood with his back to the unlit fire, his head framed by two large silver candelabra, which in Joshua's mind resembled the antlers of a gigantic stag. 'As you see, Mr Pope, I have returned from my search of your lodgings.'

'Indeed, sir. And I trust you found nothing to incriminate me in the disappearance of Mrs Mercier's necklace.'

'In that respect I found nothing untoward. What I did find, however, has raised new uncertainties in my mind. It concerns a letter I discovered at your rooms – a letter that I haven't read, although its contents have been outlined to me. That letter has occasioned my acute astonishment, not to mention anger; it reveals that you have been meddling in matters that are no concern of yours.'

Herbert regarded Joshua as if he were waiting for a

confession. Joshua's mind was racing. What letter could he have discovered? Who could have written it? What might it say? He thought immediately of the letter Lizzie Manning had written concerning her interview with Marie, the Merciers' maid. But then he dismissed the notion. He knew for certain he had brought the letter with him.

'Forgive me, Mr Bentnick. I have absolutely no idea of the communication to which you refer.'

'Nor could you,' said Herbert. 'You haven't read it yet. Your landlady's daughter, Miss Quick, asked me to pass it on to you. She thought it might concern a matter of urgency, since it was delivered by hand by a messenger from an attorney in Gray's Inn. I took it upon myself to call upon the said firm, their name being familiar to me and their address being clearly written on the letter. You will well imagine my consternation, sir, when I found that the letter relates to Mr Cobb's death at Astley. Mr Crackman, the senior partner at the firm, was the author of the letter and he told me that the general topic of the letter concerns 'the sudden and suspicious death of his partner's associate, Mr John Cobb'. He refused, however, to tell me more, trusting in my honour as a gentlemen not to pry. So what I desire, sir, is an explanation of your precise involvement in all of this.'

Here Herbert opened his jacket and rummaged around in his pocket. He removed a letter, which he then proceeded to waft accusingly beneath Joshua's nose.

'Mr Bentnick, sir,' said Joshua helplessly, 'I pray that you give me leave to read this letter, in order that I may discover its contents and report them to you.'

'Very well,' said Herbert, 'take it. And by the by, Crackman told me to inform you that his partner, a Mr Bartholomew Hoare, has still not reappeared.'

Joshua broke the seal and unfolded the letter swiftly.

It contained both surprising and expected news, in some ways confirming his suspicions; in others only serving to muddy matters more. 'The letter says that Cobb was also an attorney-at-law; that he and Mr Hoare were both engaged upon the same case: a matter of a disputed necklace – presently in the possession of a Mrs Sabine Mercier – a rare jewel made in medieval times in the form of a serpent.' He nodded knowingly. In this last respect his guess had been correct that the necklace lay at the heart of the dispute. But he was surprised to learn that Cobb was an attorney acting for another. He had assumed Cobb must have been pursuing his claim on his own behalf.

'And who is the other claimant?' said Herbert quickly.

'He says only that, since she is a woman much concerned for her privacy, he cannot reveal her identity without her permission. Under these exceptional circumstances he has written to obtain it.'

Herbert sighed with evident annoyance. 'Well,' he said, stepping closer to the paper in Joshua's hand as if he would have liked to snatch it away. 'That is not the point. What I want is an explanation for your meddling. What the devil d'you mean by prying into my family's private matters? I employed you to paint my portrait. I have since asked you to recover a necklace that has gone missing thanks to your carelessness. Those are your duties; I see no reason for you to be calling on attorneys to discuss matters that are irrelevant.'

Joshua watched Herbert thoughtfully. He noted the unusual tautness of his mouth, and that his neck was so tense a muscle was twitching visibly. Why was Herbert so reticent when it came to the subject of Cobb? He would have liked to probe him on the reason for his meeting at the Star and Garter but prudence held him back. 'I believe, sir, that the disappearance of the necklace is intertwined with the death in the pinery.'

'You did not know of the necklace's disappearance when you called on Crackman. Come, Pope, take me for a fool and you will be sorry for it.'

Joshua responded smoothly. 'I see I have no alternative but to speak candidly, even though I am breaking a confidence in doing so. It was Mrs Mercier who asked me to look into Cobb's death, sir. She requested that I question Granger, as she was anxious to know more about Cobb. Since I found myself in London, I thought I would please her if I pursued the matter a little further.'

Herbert snorted sceptically. 'Indeed? You should have said so from the beginning, then.'

'She asked me to act in confidence.'

Herbert glared at Joshua, but he did not question Sabine's order. Nor did he criticize her instruction.

Joshua took advantage of his silence to press home his argument. 'Of course, Mr Bentnick, you have every reason to chastise me for meddling, as you see it. But that was not my intention. Furthermore, the missing necklace places a new complexion on this matter. As I said before, the two are almost certainly linked. Mr Crackman clearly states both Hoare and Cobb were acting in a dispute over the necklace with Mrs Mercier. It cannot be coincidence for two such events to take place so close in time and there be *no* connection. If you want the jewel found you must let me pursue the matter of the body in the pinery.'

'Why? What is one to do with the other? And why do you persist in calling it "the body"? It was John Cobb, as we very well know.'

'We believed it was John Cobb. Now I'm less sure.'

'But the letters in his pocket had the name of Cobb on them.'

Joshua looked inscrutable. 'Perhaps they were letters intended for Cobb that had yet to be despatched. Or perhaps they were planted on him. You still do not recall what they said or who wrote them?'

'They were nothing significant.'

'Was one written by Hoare?'

Herbert shook his head as if plagued by a wasp but didn't answer. He still refused to be diverted from his principal concern. 'What makes you doubt the body was Cobb's?'

'Last night on the road I was accosted by a man. I believe

he was no ordinary vagabond. He said his name was John Cobb,' said Joshua gravely.

Herbert's reaction to this information was most unexpected. His eyes opened wide; he began to sway, a slow revolving movement, like a packet boat rolling hither and thither in a hefty sea. He reached out an unsteady hand to the back of a chair to support himself.

'Sir, are you ill?' said Joshua, growing alarmed – was he witnessing a fit of some kind? – 'I see you are taken sick. Allow me to help you to a chair. I shall go directly to call assistance.'

Herbert grunted an unintelligible response as Joshua lowered him into a chair, lifted his feet onto a stool and loosened his cravat. He was muttering, 'I can't credit it. The letters, the letters.'

Realizing there was nothing much to be garnered from Herbert in his present condition, Joshua summoned the first footman, Peters. He asked him loudly to attend to Herbert, then he took him to one side. 'There is one further errand I would ask of you,' he said *sotto voce*.

'Yes, sir,' replied Peters.

'Be so good as to despatch one of your hall-boys to the undertakers in Richmond. I would know the size of the coffin made for the dead man that Mrs Mercier found in the pinery.'

'The size of the coffin?' said Peters, as unruffled as if he had been asked for a hat or a cloak or a glass of brandy.

'Yes, Peters, the size. That is all.'

Then, feeling greatly relieved to be away from Herbert, and quietly satisfied that he had discovered the means to circumnavigate Granger's failure to examine the dead body, he stepped outdoors in search of Lizzie Manning.

# Chapter Twenty-one

The conservatory, an imposing mound of wood and glass, rose before Joshua. He lifted his eyes to the sparkling cupola, then lowered them to the figure of Lizzie Manning, who paced sentinel-like outside the door. She twirled her parasol in her gloved hand, biting her upper lip with evident impatience at having to wait in the heat for a drawing lesson that should have begun half an hour ago. In her high-necked gown of pale grey she looked, he reflected, like a moth fluttering before an ice sculpture. Joshua's awkward interview with Herbert was still fresh in his mind. For the time being it dispelled his ambivalence towards Lizzie Manning and, rather, he felt a strange sensation of apprehension mingled with amusement as he approached.

His levity was rapidly dispelled by Lizzie's greeting. 'Mr Pope,' she exclaimed crossly, 'are you in the habit of keeping your pupils waiting?'

'My dear Miss Manning,' replied Joshua, the faintest glimmer of a smile playing about his lips, 'Being unused to instructing pupils, I have never formed any habits, either good or bad.' His thoughts raced swiftly on to the pinery, which he was all eagerness to examine. 'But tell me,' he said, 'why did you chose to wait here and not inside this remarkable edifice?'

'I found the atmosphere within unbearably oppressive. Moreover, Granger is engaged in tending to his pots in the pinery. I thought it better we seek a more private spot.'

Joshua concurred. Not wishing to conduct their discussions within Granger's earshot, they walked a short distance, to a place where a stone garden seat was set into a niche of yew. Then with no further delay (they were each as hungry as the other to discover what was contained in the letter Joshua had retrieved from the desk) they set to reading.

*20th May 1766*
*Mr Cobb*
*After the encounter in the gardens today I must reiterate what I have already told you. Our association is at an end. It is fruitless to believe that by pursuit of me you might change my mind. Quite the contrary – you succeed only in strengthening my resolve and souring any sympathy I once may have had. How dare you come to Richmond and threaten me in one breath and declare your affection in another? The necklace will remain in my mother's possession. Your threats to tell her of our association will not alter my determination. I would rather she knew all – indeed, I have half a mind to tell her myself. My only wish is that you would return to Bridgetown to do the same.*
*Violet Mercier*

Joshua regarded Lizzie and then returned to the page. To begin with he was puzzled. Ever since he had begun to doubt that the dead man was Cobb, he had privately assumed that the corpse must be that of Hoare, the attorney who had called upon him and subsequently disappeared. At first sight, the letter seemed to conflict with this hypothesis. Why would Hoare have a letter addressed to Cobb from Violet about his person? And for that matter, if it wasn't one of the letters Granger had taken from the corpse's pocket, how had it come into Herbert's possession? But on further reflection he realized the letter did nothing to prove or disprove the identity of the corpse. Assuming it had come from the corpse, the man could have been Cobb, or Hoare.

For the time being, however, Joshua remembered his earlier resolve with regard to Lizzie Manning. Keeping most of his conclusions to himself, he told her only what he had to of his recent discoveries and adventures. That a man calling himself Cobb had accosted him last night and demanded Cobb's bag, which Dunstable had earlier given him; and that a letter written by Crackman revealed Cobb was an attorney working on the same disputed claim for the necklace as Mr Hoare.

'Do you believe Cobb is alive?' said Lizzie, thunderstruck.

'I don't know. I was hoping this might help us decide,' he said, gesturing to the letter. 'But it only confirms what we already know: that the necklace and the death are linked and that there was a relationship between Violet and Cobb that soured.' He stated the obvious to see what response it might elicit from Lizzie. 'Cobb, in his capacity as attorney acting for an unknown claimant, came searching for the necklace. But he had more than one reason for coming: he was still fond of Violet.'

'Perhaps in the beginning Violet agreed to assist Cobb in his attempts to recover the jewel and then changed her mind,' suggested Lizzie.

Joshua recalled that, according to the maid Marie, Sabine had put a halt to the relationship between Cobb and Violet. Clearly the fondness, from Cobb's side at least, lasted longer than Sabine (and Marie) thought.

'At any rate, whatever was between them appears over now,' he said. Inwardly he cursed Herbert for destroying the second letter Granger had given him; the very fact he had destroyed it surely revealed its significance. Did it follow, then, that the keeping of this communication was intended to mislead?

'Suppose Cobb didn't take the necklace,' he said. 'Someone else did.'

She looked a little crossly at him, as if he were taunting her by his cryptic postulations. 'Who?'

'I don't know yet. But there is another letter that may have a bearing on it. I discovered it in Herbert's desk. Tell me what you make of it.' Here he took out his pocket book and showed her the other letter.

*Mr Bentnick,*
*I have done my utmost to exercise my self-control, but you have*
*tested me to the limit. I see now that after all this time you*
*have merely feigned sympathy with my cause, yet never truly*
*listened to a word I said to you. My patience is now at an end,*
*and none but you have driven me to make this ultimatum. Since*
*you have not extracted what is mine, I will come immediately and*
*retrieve it in person.*

Reading this again in the light of the letter from Violet to Cobb, Joshua couldn't help thinking how convenient his discovery of both letters was. Would Herbert have left such letters in his unlocked desk if he didn't intend them to be found? Both were most convenient pieces of evidence to incriminate someone else. He mused regretfully again on the other letter Herbert had destroyed. There must have been some reason why he kept these and threw away the other. Suppose the lost letter revealed his or Sabine's involvement in the intrigue. That surely would be a reason to destroy it and keep these.

'Can you fathom anything from it?' Joshua asked when she had read it.

Lizzie thought for a short while before she spoke. 'The letter is undated, which is irksome, for if we knew when it was written it might have helped us. The writer addresses Herbert as if he or she is quite well acquainted with him and has known him for a considerable time. The tone is definite, threatening, yet at the same time it attempts to draw sympathy.'

'Very good,' he said, impressed by her line of reasoning. 'But can you hazard what it is about or, more importantly, who might have written it?'

She looked up from the pocket book. 'It must relate to the necklace. But as to the author, the signature is indecipherable. Can you read it?' she asked.

He shook his head, to indicate that he was no wiser than she, then decided to give her a little assistance to see where it might lead. 'If Cobb was acting on behalf of another in trying to retrieve the necklace, then this letter might have been written by the person he represented. Perhaps that person grew tired of waiting for the legal process and has carried out their threat. If that is the case, then Herbert knows perfectly well who has taken it. The writer of this letter. But that poses a further question: why accuse me, and order me to look into the matter?'

'To keep the truth of the matter from Sabine,' postulated Lizzie cautiously.

Joshua was disappointed. 'But Sabine must know who the claimant is, since the necklace is hers. Or are you perhaps suggesting Herbert is involved in some form of conspiracy against Sabine whom he is shortly to marry? If so, it seems improbable.'

Lizzie's face revealed her annoyance that Joshua could pick holes in her argument almost before she had strung it together. Seeing her patience was wearing thin, he addressed her more gently.

'My next action will be to try to seek out the man who accosted me last night. I regret letting him slip away. Meanwhile, there is something you can do that would help me greatly to untangle all this. Speak to the maid about what happened with the necklace the day I left. Perhaps she will say something to you she didn't tell Sabine or Herbert. Then question Violet over the same events, to see if her account tallies with the maid's. Try to persuade her to confide in you over the matter of Cobb, and ask her how reliable she believes the maid's testimony to be. Do not under any circumstance divulge to her that Cobb might be alive.'

'Why not?'

'Because to judge from the tone of the letter she wrote she was tired of his pestering – perhaps she was tired enough to wish him dead. We believe she visited Cobb at the inn, perhaps soon after this letter was written. I am no medical man, yet I believe the symptoms of death are consistent with poisoning. If so, Violet might well be the person responsible.'

'Her mother might have more reason. Remember, Sabine's father was a physician and taught her a great deal about the medical properties of plants. If Cobb represented the claimant to her necklace, she may have killed him to save it. But in any case you have just said Cobb might not be dead.'

'Someone is, though. Suppose Violet, or Sabine, or Herbert, or the man on the road, whoever he was, tried to kill Cobb and failed – the poison killed the wrong person. There is every possibility that on discovering the error the guilty party might try again, is there not?'

'But whose was the corpse?'

Joshua hesitated, looking sadly into her grey eyes. He noticed their lustrous gleam and that her pupils were dilated with the excitement of the discussion. There was something attractive in her fervour, although at the same time he was aware that for her this was no more than an intriguing diversion, while for him and the poor dead man in the pinery it was a matter of life, reputation and death. Nevertheless, without her he would have no ally at all. He had to make her think he trusted her.

'I have yet to prove it categorically, but I suspect it was Hoare's,' he said quietly.

After this conversation they went to the pinery with their sketchbooks and pens to carry out the agreed drawing lesson. Botanical drawing was an art to which Joshua laid no claim to greatness but Lizzie was adamant that pineapples were what she wanted to draw. And, since Joshua was curious to view the building that had played such a central role in this affair, he was happy to comply.

The effect of walking into the pinery for the first time over-whelmed him. He was staggered by the scale of the roof soaring above and the kaleidoscopic shafts of light radiating through the myriad panes. In front of him was the atrium, a circular arena with tables and chairs set out by the fountain, and orange and pomegranate trees positioned like sentinels around the edge. Vast double doors led off to the right and left. On one side was the vine he had seen Granger tending, beyond lemon trees heavy with fruit, and melons twisting up trellises. Opposite was the door leading to the pinery. It was in this direction that Lizzie turned and he followed.

Deep raised beds, some six feet wide and filled with decaying tan bark, stretched the length of the building. In the centre was a tiled path bordered by a pit containing steaming manure – which added to the heat supplied by the tan bark and the stoves and sun. The beds were filled with ranks of silvery leaves and knobbly green fruits rearing up from the centres of the largest specimens like Venus appearing from a shell.

There being no seats in this part of the pinery, they perched themselves sideways on the low wall of one of the beds with their sketchbooks on their laps. Lizzie appeared unperturbed by the discomfort of such a seat or the risk of mud to her hem and set to with alacrity.

She was an awkward student, far too quick to put down on paper what she believed lay in front of her, unwilling to look at the way each leaf curled slightly differently or the way the light altered the hue of each plant before she proceeded to draw it. They chose the largest plants with fruits that, though green, appeared almost fully formed. Joshua drew the same plant as Lizzie and tried to teach her by example. An hour later, Joshua's first study of the pineapple was not quite complete and Lizzie had made several execrable attempts; there were blots and smudges all over her page and her patience at his criticisms was wearing thin.

'Miss Manning,' he said, anticipating an imminent outburst

of ill temper, 'I think we have done enough for one day. You have made great progress, but I feel your style would be better suited to the broader sweeps of landscape painting than to the meticulousness of botany. Tomorrow, if you wish, we will try our hand at depicting some scenes in the park. I have no doubt Sabine would welcome such a subject as a gift. Until then I believe we should cease our lesson.'

She agreed willingly and went off in search of Violet and her maid Marie, leaving him to put the finishing touches to his drawing. He made notes as to the hues of foliage and fruit, which would serve him as an *aide memoire* when he transferred this image to his canvas. All the while he was dimly aware of Granger coming and going. When finally he gathered up his crayons and papers and turned to leave, he nearly fell over Granger halfway along the path. Apparently the gardener had come into the pinery to sink the new pots into the bark beds.

'Yet again at your labours, Mr Granger,' Joshua said cordially.

'Forgive me,' said Granger, moving aside.

'Are these new plants you have reared?'

'Why, no, sir,' he replied. 'They are the latest arrivals from the nursery, to fill up the places in the beds of those that died.'

'Are these any different from the other plants you have growing here?'

If Granger was surprised by his sudden interest in horticulture his face betrayed none of it. He answered solemnly. 'Several varieties grow in this country. In the beds there are already Black Antigua, Cayenne, Enville and Jamaica Queen. These are Providence; they make fruits that weigh fourteen pounds or more. Mrs Mercier has requested they be the centrepiece at her wedding breakfast.'

'Then it will indeed be an occasion of Providence. This is my first visit and the whole house strikes me as a remarkable achievement. I congratulate you on it.'

Granger regarded his surroundings and then looked

uncomfortably at the plants in his hand. 'In truth, sir, I've done what I was asked to do. Nor more or less. The building was all here before my arrival. When all's said and done, the pineapple is not so difficult a fruit to grow. Once you balance the water with the correct light and heat, it flourishes. Modulating the heat is the only aspect that can be difficult.' He paused, looking at his mud-logged boots, before smiling briefly. 'But you have no need to be asking me about pineapples. You could ask your drawing pupil, Miss Manning. She is another enthusiast.'

'Surely you mean Mrs Mercier?'

'Mrs Mercier too, but you already know that.'

'Does Miss Manning know about the cultivation of pineapple plants?'

Granger gave another narrow-lipped smile. 'She's as knowledgeable as Mr Bentnick on most aspects of horticulture – that's why he's so fond of her. They used to spend hours discussing their prized plants. The gardens at Barlow Court are said to rival Astley's, or they used to, at any rate. Sir Lancelot Brown, who had much to do here, was also, I believe, employed at Barlow Court and at my previous estate after I left it. He lives in Kew, just a mile from here – I hazard that's why he is so popular in this vicinity.'

'His pre-eminent reputation may also have something to do with it,' said Joshua not unkindly.

'Of course his reputation is unrivalled. But in any event, under his direction Miss Manning took charge of much of the planting. I know she tried to grow pineapples there. She asked me for advice, though whether Mr Brown had anything to do with it, and whether she succeeded, I couldn't say.'

This information baffled Joshua. How peculiar, he thought, that when he had marvelled aloud his impressions of the pinery Lizzie had not passed a single remark – had said nothing to imply she had any interest in horticulture whatsoever.

'You say the garden at Barlow Court used to outshine

Astley's. Has something changed that it's no longer so fine?'

Granger surveyed him closely. 'Ask her about her brother Arthur. What I know's only gossip.'

Joshua dimly recalled Herbert mentioning Lizzie's brother, though she had never spoken of him. 'Tell me what they say, then.'

'That he always loses when he plays; has played unceasingly for the past four years, and lost a veritable fortune at quadrille. His father, William Manning, is the local justice in these parts and has all but ruined himself to pay off his son's debts. He only keeps Barlow Court by the skin of his teeth and the goodwill of money lenders. The place is falling down; there is not the wherewithal to maintain the house let alone the gardens that were once one of the wonders of these parts.'

'I had no idea.'

'Aye, well, you might have noted Arthur Manning doesn't show his face around here – there is talk of him being in Italy and suchlike. That's all hokum.'

'How do you know?'

'I have seen him skulking about the grounds and in the vicinity.'

'Then why do they say he's abroad?'

'To save face. He recently borrowed a large sum from Miss Caroline; money left to her by her mother, I believe.'

'Was she not foolish to hand it to him if she knew his reputation?'

'She was fond of him and his family, and was taken in. You can't blame the girl. He told her he wanted the money to pay back his father for part of the debt; he took the money and never repaid a penny to his father.'

'Is Mr Bentnick aware of this?'

'How should I know? If he is, he wouldn't bring it up with William Manning or his daughter. To do so would bankrupt the one and shame the other to no purpose.'

'And what of the contemptible Arthur?'

'Still at Barlow, I presume. He has no money to go elsewhere.'

173

While Joshua pondered the significance of Arthur Manning, Granger knelt down and began to embed the two pots in his hand in the steaming soil.

Joshua watched him going about his business with purposeful efficiency. But as he took his leave and began to walk slowly back to the door, suddenly something struck him. 'I thought you had saved the other damaged plants by your repotting,' he said.

'Some of the others overheated,' replied Granger.

'How did that come about?'

Granger paused and frowned. Joshua sensed his reluctance to answer and thus paid careful attention to his reply. 'As I told you before, it's controlling the heat that's the most difficult part of rearing pineapples. This house is so large it needs vigilance both day and night. There's a boy by the name of Joe Carlton whose duty is to guard it at night and make sure the heat's neither too great nor too cold. I doubt you know but new bark can get so hot it bursts into flames.'

'What of this boy?' said Joshua.

'He fell asleep at his post. The pinery overheated. Some of the plants near the door survived; those furthest away perished from too much heat.'

'When did this happen?'

'Five nights ago, or thereabouts.'

'The night before the man was found dead?'

Granger paused, scratching his chin thoughtfully. 'Yes, now you mention it, it was that night. Funny thing, if he hadn't fallen asleep he might have seen what happened, mightn't he?'

'Mr Granger,' said Joshua, speaking quickly as a new notion raced through his brain, 'what might happen if a man lay comatose in this glasshouse while it overheated?'

Again Granger stopped what he was doing; this time he looked over his shoulder at Joshua from the corner of his eye. 'I'm no medical man, but I hazard the heat might be sufficient to kill a man. Ask anyone who knows and they'll tell you the

174

same. As I said before, I have heard glasshouses with similar methods of heating can burst into flames for want of care. Nothing fanciful about that, sir.'

'In other words, Granger, you are saying the corpse might have cooked to death?'

'Yes, sir, that's about it.'

# Chapter Twenty-two

In his rooms, Joshua turned his attentions to the portrait. Painting was his greatest passion. If Herbert took against him, and he couldn't recover the necklace, he might never be paid for the Bentnick portrait, yet he could not restrain himself from tinkering with it, adding highlights and details to items of dress and defining the background in greater detail.

As he painted he mulled over his discoveries. He considered Granger's suspicions that Cobb might have died accidentally, as a result of overheating. All the descriptions he had heard of the corpse's condition mentioned the stench, and until now he had assumed this was due to his vomiting prior to death, which pointed to death from poisoning. But had the sweet smell also been caused by the effect of the heat on the flesh? He had reached no conclusion, nor had he fathomed a way to prove or disprove the theory, when a knocking on his door interrupted his musing.

'Come,' Joshua said at last, wrenching himself from his thoughts and putting down his brush.

A maidservant brought him a letter on a silver tray.

*28th May 1766*
*Mr Pope,*
*Perceiving you to be a man of reticence, I will take matters in hand in order to make headway. Before you left for Richmond*

*you invited me to where you are staying, though in your embarrassment you never told me when or where to come. Today Mr Bentnick came to look through your rooms and tells he sees no reason we cannot meet for an excursion on the river, or what about a stroll on the hill? Indeed, he could hardly believe it when I said I had heard of Richmond but never visited. He described the place most pleasantly and said I would enjoy a promenade in the gardens at Astley. So, Mr Pope, I'll be arriving on the midday stage at the Star and Garter, next Sunday. Will you meet me there or will I walk to the house? Mr Bentnick says it is only a short distance. If you're not there I will ask directions and come for you.*

*Yours in expectation,*
*Bridget Quick*

Reading this message, Joshua's spirits surged and then plummeted almost as quickly. Bridget was the flower he had determined not to pick. How could she tempt him thus? Today was Friday; she would arrive the day after tomorrow. It was too late now to stop her. There was no way to avoid their meeting. If he wasn't at the Star and Garter, she would arrive at Astley. With so much to occupy him, he had no time for diversion, and in any case the thought of taking her boating on the river was something he would never contemplate. Nor did he feel inclined to take her for an excursion on the hill. Furthermore, he had no desire to explain the multitude of reasons why to her. The only thing he could think of was to go and meet her, then fashion some excuse – a make-believe malady, perhaps – for which reason he would curtail their outing.

'Sir,' said the maid, intruding into his thoughts once again, 'I've two other messages for you. The first is from Peters, the first footman, who bade me tell you that the hall-boy has run the errand you asked. The measurement you wanted was "five foot nine". That was all. He said you'd know what it meant.'

Joshua thought for a moment, then nodded. 'Five foot nine'

referred to the dimensions of the coffin. The clothes in Cobb's bag were those of a man well over six foot. The dead man certainly wasn't Cobb, though the lanky assailant on the road could well have been. Bearing in mind the other circumstantial evidence: Hoare's appointment with Cobb on the afternoon of the death, his disappearance – his theory of the body being Hoare's now seemed highly likely. Assuming he was correct, an obvious suspect for Hoare's murder was Cobb himself. Why else would he be living as a vagabond, attacking passers-by, entering bedrooms in the dead of night? But what might his motive have been?

'And the other message?'

'The mistress, that is, Mrs Mercier, she bade me ask you if you would meet her at the pavilion on the northern borders of the lake – I can point it out to you if you wish. She'll be waiting for you.'

Hearing this compounded Joshua's downcast frame of mind. His usual composure deserted him. He forgot Cobb, he forgot Hoare, he even forgot Bridget's letter. Foremost in his mind was the fear that Sabine had called him to this secluded spot to perpetrate some evil act of vengeance for the loss of her necklace. If only he had some information pertaining to the jewel to divulge to her he might deflect her wrath. And yet, apart from Violet's letter, which he couldn't show her – for how would he explain his discovery of it? – what did he have to appease her with? Could he express a vague inkling that the body she had found was in some way linked to the necklace's disappearance? No – for that might lead to a discussion of Cobb and Hoare's activities, which might in turn lead her to conclude Joshua thought her own claim upon the jewel uncertain. Sabine had a clear motive for wishing both Cobb and Hoare dead. In their professional capacity they had threatened to take the jewel away from her. If Sabine had killed once to protect her jewel, to what lengths might she now go to avenge its loss?

Yet within a minute or two his sense of purpose returned.

He had to face Sabine sooner or later. There were questions he had to put to her. If they were alone together she might speak more freely than in company. And so he donned his buff coat braided with corn-coloured silk, arranged his lace cuffs and cravat nicely, and made his way to the appointed pavilion with a heavy heart but his sights clearly set. He would do his utmost to placate Sabine while eliciting as much as possible. If his scheme failed, he would give himself up to whatever dreadful fate lay in store.

The lake lay on the southern side of the house. Joshua had seen it from the drawing-room windows but had yet to view it from close proximity. His morbid dislike of large expanses of water had kept him at a distance, even though he had heard it said that this portion of the garden was where Mr Lancelot 'Capability' Brown had exerted himself most brilliantly. It was only now that he fully appreciated the reason for Astley's sublime reputation. Brown had formed a gentle slope leading to a serpentine stretch of water fed by a stream at one end and with a small island disguising the limits at the other. Neat mown lawns studded with single trees and shrubs ran down to the shore. On the far side of the lake, clumps of beech and thicker woodland met the water's edge, their reflections gleaming in splashes of dark and light on the still expanse. A path meandered along the borders of the lake and led to Joshua's appointed meeting place.

The pavilion was set on a rocky escarpment overlooking the water and its fringe of trees. Shaped in the form of a rotunda, with a colonnade supporting a domed roof, and a circular seat in the middle, it was open to the landscape all around. Joshua mounted the slope to the building, trying to ignore the uncomfortable sensation that gripped his insides. To his surprise, however, when he reached the steps supporting the colonnade he found that the place was deserted. Sabine, far from lying in malevolent wait, was nowhere to be seen.

Joshua paced about; he sat down then stood, then sat once more; all the while, he scoured the landscape to see if she might be anywhere about. As his eye skirted a small copse some twenty yards away, he thought he caught sight of the shadow of a figure skulking in the trees. Instantly the thought occurred that perhaps this was Cobb, whom he had determined he must find at the earliest opportunity. He screwed up his eyes and focused intently, uncertain if in the glancing shadows and light he had merely seen a branch moving in the wind. He thought he caught another flash of movement and was on the point of careering down the slope towards it, but at that very second there was a rustle close behind. He wheeled round. 'Mrs Mercier!' he exclaimed. 'I didn't hear you come.'

'Good morning, Mr Pope,' she answered softly. 'My apologies for keeping you. I had something to discuss with Granger.'

'It is no matter, madam. I have been enjoying the view,' Joshua replied courteously. He scrutinized her features as he spoke. Her countenance seemed unruffled. Her eyes were expressionless, unblinking, her mouth relaxed, her brow smooth. Was this the face of a dangerous murderess? Or someone about to accuse him of the theft of something she held most dear? He detected no trace of menace, but he viewed her nonetheless with the respect he would accord a sleeping viper.

'I dare say you have guessed why I summoned you here: the necklace is uppermost in my mind, Mr Pope. I gather you have protested your innocence and that Mr Bentnick has given you leave to try to recover it. You must think yourself very fortunate.'

Fortunate was the last thing he considered himself at this instant, but he desisted from saying so. 'I assure you, madam, I am doing my utmost to find the jewel. God willing, it is just a matter of time.'

'Granger tells me you gave Miss Manning some instruction in drawing in the pinery this morning. Tell me, do you believe that tutoring her might aid the recovery of my jewel?'

Joshua felt the blood rush to his cheeks but he refused to capitulate. 'Miss Manning requested it. I thought an hour in her company might be useful in other ways. She is intimately acquainted with the workings of the Astley household. Moreover, the drawings I made while instructing her will serve for the portrait.'

'To my mind, spending the morning in the company of a young woman implies you are shirking your duty to find my necklace. And to me that only points to your guilt. Tell me, what progress did the morning's endeavours yield?'

'It enabled me to learn something from Granger, which may be most significant.'

'What?'

'A detail, of which you are doubtless aware – something concerning the temperature needed for pineapples to grow.'

She looked slightly surprised, which pleased him no end, but not for long.

'I presume you refer to the night the boy fell asleep and several plants perished? I don't see what importance that has with regard to my jewel. What intrigues me more is learning of Miss Manning's interest in gardening. She has never said a word to me on the subject. And Granger says he instructed her about how to grow pineapples at Barlow Court some years ago, and she even gave fruit to Mr Bentnick for his table. Her reticence is most peculiar, is it not? Do you think it points to a darker purpose? You know her family is lately impoverished. Perhaps *she* stole my jewel.'

Joshua was momentarily silent. His instinct was to deflect Sabine's attention from Lizzie – heaven forbid he should lead her into danger. He shrugged his shoulders as if Lizzie and pineapples were matters of equal unimportance. 'God may know the workings of Miss Manning's mind, but I am not privy to them. You are right. I consider her as a possible suspect, but then I view everyone in the same manner.'

'Answer me this, then, Mr Pope. Do you truly believe that the dead man was not Cobb?'

'What makes you ask?'

'Mr Bentnick told me you believed as much. He said you were accosted last night by a man claiming to be Cobb. Is that true?'

'Yes.'

'What did the man want?'

'Money, I presume.' He held her gaze, revealing not a flicker of guilt.

'Did he take it?'

'No. I kept hold of my purse.'

'Then if it wasn't Cobb's, whose *was* the body I found?'

'I believe it may have belonged to an attorney called Hoare, who was pursuing the dispute over the ownership of your necklace and chanced to be visiting Cobb the day before you found the corpse. And on that subject, may I ask you, madam, have *you* ever met John Cobb?'

'No, or I would have known it wasn't him when I found him, would I not?'

He nodded, acknowledging to himself that even if she were lying she would not easily ensnare herself. Nevertheless, she did seem to be answering his questions more candidly than he dared hope. Now was the moment for his most crucial question. 'Madam, I must ask, who is the other claimant for your necklace?'

Sabine regarded Joshua severely. For a while she said nothing and he had the impression that she was weighing up in her mind whether to answer him or tell him to go to the devil. At length she raised her chin and caught his eye. 'I could ask you how you know anything about this private matter, but Mr Bentnick has already told me. I understand that you travelled to London to make enquiries on my behalf and that you visited the premises of the attorney who is pressing the claim against me. I presume that is why you ask me this?'

He nodded wordlessly. He was still observing every shift and nuance in her face and voice. Until this moment

182

her expression had been controlled, now he felt the icy blast of her disapproval. He braved it, knowing that she offered him an opportunity to learn something he needed desperately to discover. 'It is for this reason I would like to ask who—'

'But it wasn't true that I asked you to enquire into any of this.'

'Not in so many words. But you had revealed your noble sentiments when you asked me to look into the death and question Granger on your behalf. I forbore to mention it then, but I too felt outrage at the way his death was glossed over without further inquiry – and so I felt assured of your concurrence, and took it upon myself to explore the matter further when the opportunity presented itself.'

She looked mollified by his manipulation of the truth, but not entirely content. 'Perhaps you are right and it is this business that lies behind the jewel's loss. But I would not have you waste more time than necessary on Hoare now my necklace is gone. Moreover, I must emphasize, the claim was an utterly spurious one.'

'That may well be. But unless I learn the details, how can I be expected to judge? And how can I find the necklace? Cobb was a member of the legal profession pursuing the claim. Moreover, he was interested in your daughter. Hoare was also involved. It is lunacy to pretend that this may not have some bearing—'

'Very well,' broke in Sabine, her eyes flashing in a manner that might have made the knees of a gladiator buckle, 'since you insist, I will tell you briefly all I know. The jewel was left to me by my second husband, Charles Mercier. He had a child out of wedlock before we were married. It is she who is pursuing this ridiculous claim.'

'And her name?'

Sabine laughed as if the question were one only an imbecile would ask. 'If I knew that, the difficulty would be solved. She is intent upon retaining her respectability and wishes no one to know of her sordid birth; thus she wishes to remain incognito.'

Joshua recalled Crackman's letter made reference to the claimant's desire for privacy. He judged she was telling the truth and was as frustrated as he by her lack of knowledge. He considered raising the matter of the letter in Herbert's desk, which he was sure had been sent by the claimant, but suspected to do so would only incur her wrath and prove pointless. Plainly the scrawling monogram was as illegible to her as to him. Perhaps this was what the sender had intended – the letter was sent as a taunt. Having reached this impasse, he veered onto another train of thought. 'Then, may I ask, ma'am, the purpose of your recent trip to London?'

She blushed and her lips twitched with annoyance. 'It was private – nothing to do with this matter.'

Though he sensed she was holding back, he let the matter drop. 'One last favour I would ask of you, madam. May I question your maid about what happened during that interval?'

Her face registered surprise. 'I cannot for the life of me think what you would learn from a servant, but if you wish it you might call on Marie early this evening. We will resume our usual routine of sittings from tomorrow, Mr Pope – that will give you the opportunity to apprise me of your advances. Remember, finding my necklace must take precedence over your enquiries into Hoare.'

Then, without waiting for his response, she left.

Joshua watched her sweep down the path and head back to the house, her pale-blue skirts billowing out behind her like a wind-blown sail. For some time after her figure had receded into the distance he remained, pondering over the meeting. She had clearly been most disturbed by his reference to the dispute over the necklace, and furious that he had been to see Crackman regarding the body in the pinery, but he believed he had convinced her that this was necessary. It was most unfortunate that even she did not know who was the other claimant for her necklace. And yet, all things considered, she had behaved far better than he had dared hope. He had, after all, survived the encounter.

# Chapter Twenty-three

After Sabine had gone, Joshua remained in the pavilion. All about him was now motionless, tinged with golden evening light, as tranquil and mellow as a landscape by Claude Lorraine. Although he was too absorbed in meditation to register much, when a beam of light flashed out from the shadows he was instantly distracted.

One minute it was there, the next it had gone – a blinding flare, as if for an instant someone had held a mirror and magnified the sun. Joshua peered at the spot where he thought the light had originated. It was now past five o'clock in the evening. The shadows were long and purplish, the light falling over the leaves and across the water dazzling by contrast. Had he been distracted by a ray reflected off the water? He thought not but it was impossible to be sure. He remembered the shadow of movement he thought he had glimpsed prior to Sabine's arrival. Was this Cobb?

Without further thought Joshua began to make for the copse. The park was now deserted. Nevertheless, after his satisfactory encounter with Sabine, his earlier apprehensions had gone. He felt fired up, determined to track Cobb down, to settle the matter of the corpse's identity, to put to him the questions he should have posed the night before.

When Joshua arrived at the edge of the wood he found it far darker than he expected. He was forced to slow his pace, turning around from side to side as he advanced towards the centre of the wood, scouring the undergrowth for any sign of the person he knew was concealed there. Nothing he saw or heard alarmed him until, just as he approached an open grassy glade surrounded by a clump of ancient beech trees, something stirred.

Was it a cracking twig, or the rustle of leaves, or a squirrel jumping from one tree to another? Joshua didn't know, but he sensed an unknown presence close by. The realization brought shivers of disquiet. What was he doing, prowling around in this godforsaken place, chasing after an imaginary beam of light? What a folly it was ever to enter this wood in such a fine costume where brambles might ruin it. He half made up his mind to retreat to the house and call for a glass of Hollands gin, but some unconscious sense drove him to move a little to the right, towards the direction of the sound.

Behind the beech trees were dense thickets of hazel. The only way forward now was to cross the open expanse, but to do so might expose him to the view of whoever watched him. His steps now were short and hesitant, as a reluctant child's might be. His breath was heavy and he was conscious of blood pounding his veins and an uncomfortable tingling at the roots of his hair.

He had almost reached the heart of the glade before he saw him. A tall man, wearing a dark costume and a black hat upon his head, lay slumped in a pool of sun against one of the beech trees. To judge from his position he was presently asleep. An empty bottle lay alongside him – the source of the beam of light that had caught Joshua's eye. The man's head was tilted forward, so that his face was invisible beneath the brim of his hat. Joshua stood there for several minutes looking down at him. Was it Cobb? It was hard to tell because the previous night when they had met it had been dark. The stature seemed about right, though it was difficult to judge when the fellow was sitting down.

Before Joshua tried to wake the man something disturbed

him; his right hand began to claw as if trying to grasp some invisible object. When he clutched at air, his head jerked up. Joshua could now make out a little of his countenance: a narrow, pallid face, eyes as dark as mahogany, cavernous cheeks, an unshaven complexion – the face of a gypsy yet the garb of a gentleman. Not Cobb, Joshua was fairly certain. He was aware now that he too was being watched. For some time they eyed each other, neither moving a muscle, like two foxes stopped in their tracks.

Suddenly, as if a wasp had stung his posterior, the man sprang to his feet. He reached out and grasped Joshua by the scruff of the neck. His face was purple with fury. 'Damn you!' he shouted out. 'How dare you come creeping up on me? Where's the bottle you snatched from my hand?'

'I took nothing,' Joshua replied flatly, though he felt his eyes narrow at the shock of the assault. He could smell the brandy on the man's breath and guessed that he was scarcely conscious of what he was saying for drink. 'The bottle is lying there, and by the look of it and you it's empty.'

'You impertinent devil. I'll teach you to steal from me. I saw you with my own eyes, sir. Felt you too. D'you take me for a fool?' With that, Joshua felt himself shoved away, as the man unsheathed his sword and began brandishing it about under Joshua's nose.

'Sir,' Joshua said, raising his hands to show he was unarmed and intended no harm. 'I beg you, listen to me a minute. When I came upon you you were fast asleep. Your notion that I robbed you was simply a dream. Search me if you will. You will find nothing on me.'

The man appeared briefly to be confused but still no less dangerous. Joshua pressed confidently on. 'In any case, if it's merely brandy you are after, you have only to come with me to the house over there and I will procure you some.' At least, reasoned Joshua, if the man could be persuaded into the house, he would have him apprehended and be safe.

The man squinted through the trees at the distant silhouette of Astley House. 'You invite me to go with you to the house? Who are you, then, for I know everyone in that place and you are a stranger to me?'

'Why, sir,' Joshua said, more intrigued now than ever, 'I had no idea you were a family friend. Allow me to present myself. I am Joshua Pope. Perhaps you have heard of me? I am an artist by profession, commissioned by Mr Bentnick to paint his marriage portrait. Whom do I have the honour of addressing?'

The man stepped forward again. His eyes were bleary and bloodshot, his complexion as white as his shirt; when his mouth lolled open, the smell of alcohol emanating from it was overpowering.

'Since you promise me brandy, I suppose you must be a decent fellow. I will tell you, then – my name is Arthur Manning.'

The name took Joshua by surprise. He remembered what Granger had told him of Arthur Manning: that he had ruined his family and disappeared after relieving Caroline Bentnick of her inheritance. Joshua looked at him more closely. It was all he could do to control his urge to chastise him roundly or hit him on the nose. And yet, he reminded himself, Granger had confessed what he knew was only hearsay; perhaps there was more to discover.

'I was with your sister this morning,' Joshua said coldly. 'She asked me to teach her drawing. She never told me her brother was coming to call.'

He shrugged his shoulders. 'She and I rarely speak.'

'Come, sir,' Joshua pressed. 'Let us go to the house and on the way you shall tell me why you and your sister have quarrelled. Whatever it is, it will easily be forgotten. Such a delightful girl as she would not harbour a grudge for long.'

Arthur Manning now abandoned his earlier hostility. Perhaps the effort of maintaining it was too much in his present inebriated state. He sheathed his sword and lost his scowl and draped his arm about Joshua's back as if they were old friends reunited. 'I cannot go with you, Pope,' said Arthur Manning, shaking his head with exaggerated solemnity. 'Best thing to do is this. You go back to the house. Bring some brandy and some food – I have eaten nothing all day and, by God I am famished. It's a fine evening for a little supper outdoors, is it not?'

Joshua recoiled at this familiarity. It struck him nonetheless that Manning's face might have looked quite pleasant had he shaved and paid a little more attention to his toilet and were it not for a wolfish gleam in his eye. Feigning ignorance, he said, 'Why cannot you accompany me into the house? As Miss Manning's brother you would surely be most welcome.'

'It's a long story – won't go into it now. Be a good fellow, get the brandy, come back, then we'll discuss it.'

Seeing it would be futile to urge Arthur further, Joshua conceded. He returned via the garden door to the dining room, helped himself to a cut-glass decanter of brandy and a pair of glasses and draped his coat over this contraband in case he ran into Herbert or someone else on his way. In fact his fears were unwarranted. The gardens near the house were deserted; there was no one about in the dining room and nor did he spy any servants. The family had presumably repaired to their rooms to prepare for the evening. He was back at the glade within the thicket in less than half an hour.

Arthur Manning was sitting back against a beech tree, smoking a long clay pipe. 'Ah,' he said, snatching the brandy decanter and pouring a considerable quantity directly into his mouth without troubling about the glass, 'I knew I could rely on you. Good man. What did you say your name was?'

The fog of brandy had grown thicker and, to judge from the speed he was gulping from the decanter, would swiftly grow thicker still. Within a very short space of time Arthur Manning would be incoherent. However, his present condition, uninhibited, garrulous – though admittedly not entirely lucid – provided Joshua with a valuable opportunity.

With a little pressing regarding his circumstances and history, Arthur readily confided his misfortunes, describing them quite differently from Granger. He had been tricked by a charlatan (who he was sure now had used weighted dice and marked cards), in a room at the Swan in Water Lane in Richmond, into gambling more than he should. Had he known he didn't stand a cat in hell's chance of winning he would never have stayed in the game. Guilt over his losses had spurred him to accept Caroline Bentnick's offer of a loan. She had pressed the money on him; he never petitioned her for it. He had taken the money reluctantly, intending to repay his father with it directly, but then further misfortune had befallen him. Passing through Sheen, on his way to meet his father, he had been held up by a highwayman who had relieved him of the lot. He had been so incensed by the robbery that he put up a struggle and only narrowly escaped with his life. Furthermore – iniquity of iniquities – no one believed him! His father had treated him as a veritable outcast; his sister sulked. So furious had he been at them he had left Barlow Court for a fortnight to stay with friends in Bath. Since his return he could not bear to speak to his father or Lizzie, for he still felt aggrieved by their doubts. Joshua had only to speak to the watch in Richmond and they would back up his account. He had every intention of repaying the money somehow, though as yet he was unsure how.

Joshua listened, nodding and making sympathetic noises when he thought it necessary, but he was far from taken in. Arthur Manning, to judge from all he had seen of him, was a drunken reprobate, a liar and a thief. He had stolen from his family and from their close friends the Bentnicks; he had taken advantage of Caroline Bentnick's fondness; he wouldn't put anything past him.

Nonetheless, when the story of his woes came to an end Joshua put on a friendly expression. 'I am sorry to hear all this. No one should have to endure such misfortune. By the by, what have you heard of Mrs Mercier and her daughter?'

Arthur laughed, a trifle grimly. 'Caused quite a stir, them coming to Astley, so soon after Jane Bentnick's death. Handsome woman, though – can't say I blame old Herbert. And as for the daughter, Violet – a dainty dish, very dainty. Can't think what old Francis is waiting for. Surely not my sister!'

Joshua was perplexed. 'Are you acquainted with the Merciers, then? I thought your disgrace took place before their arrival?'

Arthur pushed out his chin sheepishly. 'My most recent troubles happened only a fortnight ago. Told you, Pope, it's impossible for me to enter the house openly. But that doesn't mean to say I cannot go there at all.'

'What are you saying, Mr Manning? That you have been in the house clandestinely?'

He laughed, spluttering half-swallowed brandy down his front in the process. 'In a manner of speaking.'

'How, then? Tell me what you saw.'

He looked bleary-eyed into the middle distance. He was dribbling a little and slurring his words quite heavily now, so that Joshua had to struggle to decipher his meaning. 'I go in, sometimes, at night. I swear, Pope, if you let this be known I will kill you.'

'For what purpose?

He shrugged his shoulders. 'Idle curiosity, I suppose.'

Joshua didn't believe this for a minute. 'Did you enter my rooms two nights ago?

'Possibly.'

'You removed a card from my pocket. Why?'

There was a long pause during which Arthur blinked slowly, licking his lips as if he was parched. 'I was looking for something. I thought it might be there. You stirred in your sleep and I feared you would waken. I left with the card by mistake.'

'You were looking for something? What, precisely?'

Arthur looked mulish. 'I caught sight of your return. You were clutching something. I thought I would see what it was.'

He was lying, Joshua was certain of it. Had he witnessed the encounter on the road? 'Did you know a man named Cobb?'

Joshua could scarcely have anticipated Arthur Manning's response. At first he seemed quite taken aback, for his eyes opened wide, so wide Joshua could see the tracery of veins crisscrossing the jaundiced whites; then for some unknown reason the question struck him as extraordinarily amusing and he began to guffaw with laughter. His gales of mirth were of such resonating rowdiness that Joshua feared they might be heard. He begged him to compose himself, warning him of the dangers. But by now Arthur was incapable of comprehending a word Joshua said.

Only when he was quite exhausted by his paroxysms of laughter did he eventually become calmer. Even then, a residue of amusement remained. He looked down at his brandy-stained front, as if deep in contemplation, mulling over the tremendous joke, giving the occasional chortle as he reflected on it. Between these outbursts there were pauses which gradually became longer and longer, until at last he fell entirely silent.

'Mr Manning,' Joshua said, 'answer this last question, I beg you. Did you see me meet Cobb? Did you ever know a man named Cobb?'

But in place of the answer he so urgently wanted came a loud and protracted snore.

# Chapter Twenty-four

Next morning Joshua spent over an hour at the breakfast table waiting for Lizzie Manning to appear. By nine, when she still hadn't descended and all the other members of the household apart from Herbert had begun their breakfast, he ventured to ask where she was. When he posed the question Caroline was on her way out of the room, her progress hastened by the arrival of Sabine, Joshua presumed. She turned back from the doorway to answer.

'Miss Manning left yesterday afternoon. She is not expected back before the ball in a week's time. Good morning to you, Mr Pope.'

Joshua maintained a look of disinterest; he didn't wish to arouse suspicions, but the news frustrated and perplexed him. There was a catalogue of questions he now wanted to ask of her. Had she found the opportunity to speak to Violet or her maid? What had she discovered? Why had she concealed her knowledge of horticulture? Above all, why had she left when she could easily have stayed on the pretext of continuing their drawing lessons?

After a minute's reflection Joshua put down his coffee cup. He would tackle Violet Mercier himself. Perhaps, if she was amenable, he could arrange an opportunity to talk to her in private and find out directly what he needed to know. He began cautiously. 'I wonder, Miss Mercier, whether Miss

Manning showed you any of her drawings yesterday? She made sterling progress.'

Violet raised a perfectly arched brow. Her lips gathered in a pout. 'Drawings, Mr Pope? I don't recall seeing any. Was there some reason I should take an interest in them?'

Joshua persisted. 'But, Miss Mercier, you did see Miss Manning yesterday before she left?'

'Why do you ask?'

'Because I am puzzled by her sudden departure. I thought we had agreed to continue our tuition today.'

'Evidently you were mistaken, Mr Pope. And, since you ask, we did have a brief conversation, but she said nothing whatsoever of you or your drawing lesson.' With this, she put down her porcelain tea bowl carefully in its saucer, bowed her head, then left the table.

Joshua was ready to follow her but Sabine thwarted his departure. 'More drawing lessons, Mr Pope? What did you hope to garner from them today may I ask?'

'As I told you before, madam, there are insights Miss Manning can provide that are most beneficial. In any case it seems I shall have to manage without them, for she isn't here.'

'Then before you disappear in search of other insights, Mr Pope, may I remind you of our appointment for a sitting this afternoon?'

'I had not forgotten, madam.'

'I am glad to hear it, Mr Pope, for I must take you to task over your bad manners in neglecting another appointment. You asked my permission to question my maid yesterday afternoon. On my instruction Marie waited for you, yet you never went to speak to her. Tell me, Mr Pope, are you in the habit of making arrangements and then ignoring them whenever it suits you? Or is this merely occasional treatment you have accorded me and my staff, along with frequent tardiness and losing my necklace?'

Joshua thought rapidly. He had forgotten the appointment because he had become caught up with Arthur Manning. He had thus succeeded in doing the very thing he wanted to avoid: further annoying Sabine and heaping yet more disapproval upon his own shoulders. And yet for all this his steely purpose kept him calm. He had to fathom a means to appease her unless he was to become the target for her wrath and who knows what else besides. But there was no reason to reveal his meeting with Arthur Manning just at this moment. Manning might serve a further purpose if he could gain his trust. What did his outlandish reaction to Cobb's name signify? If he told Sabine about him she would doubtless tell Herbert and then there was no knowing what action they might take.

He shook his head as if ashamed of his error. 'My profound apologies, madam, to you and your maid. I was waylaid yesterday evening by my painting. By the time I put down my brush I thought it too late to trouble her.'

'Then I shall expect to see great progress in the work when I come for my sitting today,' said Sabine in an unmistakably menacing tone.

'As I am sure you shall, my dear,' said Herbert, entering the room and the conversation at that moment.

'You may rest assured on it,' answered Joshua smoothly.

Herbert sat down with a heavy sigh to two coddled eggs and a slice of toast. 'Well, Pope, any progress to report? Have you discovered the thief yet, or had any more nocturnal encounters, or caught the hapless killer of Mr Hoare?'

Joshua didn't know whether to resent his whimsical tone or be glad of it. This was the first occasion he had been in the same room with Sabine and Herbert since the necklace's loss. At least, for the moment, neither of them was accusing him of thieving.

'No, sir,' he replied solemnly, 'though as I told Mrs Mercier, I believe both matters are wrapped up with the dispute over the jewel. May I ask, sir, did you ever meet either Mr Hoare or Mr Cobb?'

Herbert raised his eyes from his egg-laden toast for an instant. 'No, I never did,' he said.

Recalling the evidence of the landlord Dunstable that he had seen Herbert embroiled in a quarrel with Cobb, Joshua recognized this for a bare-faced lie, but nonetheless he kept quiet. If Herbert had something to hide, he would pursue another tack to discover it.

'I told Mr Pope yesterday that I am not convinced the dispute has anything to do with the necklace's disappearance and that he should not waste more time than necessary on Hoare's death,' interrupted Sabine.

'Quite so,' said Herbert soothingly, 'but if Mr Pope believes the matters are connected we must allow him a certain freedom to investigate. After all, I am sure he has not forgotten, his reputation depends upon it.'

Joshua was not so troubled by this implicit threat that he failed to notice the silent communication that passed between the couple. Sabine met Herbert's gaze. He sensed from the set of her chin and the quizzical raising of her brow that there was some response she would have liked to make. But clearly his presence impeded her. She said nothing.

Sabine's maid, Marie, was a small, dark-skinned, dark-eyed woman, aged about thirty, with purple circles about her eyes and a disgruntled, down-turned mouth. When Joshua left the breakfast table he went to find her directly.

Having listened to him explain his business, Marie gave a hefty sigh. 'How many times more must I go over it all?' she exclaimed petulantly.

'Who else has been to ask you?'

'Mrs Mercier, Mr Bentnick, then yesterday Miss Manning came. Is that not enough?'

'Come, come,' said Joshua, drawing himself up and puffing himself out and looking down his nose at her. 'A valuable jewel has been lost. You can't expect it to be treated like losing a button.'

'So long as I don't get the blame,' she said, 'when *you* were the last to have it.'

Joshua surveyed the flowers woven into the Aubusson carpet. Why was it everyone in this house seemed so wary, so reluctant to speak openly to him? Was there no one without some secret grievance, something they wished to conceal? A man of less composure might have felt the desire to take Marie by the shoulders and shake her for her impudence. But Joshua mastered such weak sentiments. 'No one is accusing you of anything,' he said gently. 'Just show me first where the necklace box was kept when Mrs Mercier was away.'

Marie moved towards the dressing table, where on his previous visit to this room Sabine had fingered the necklace so lovingly. She opened the top drawer on the right-hand side. The shagreen box lay inside. Marie took it out, opened the lid and held the empty box out to him.

'This is where the necklace was kept. And this is what madam found when she opened the box. No necklace.'

Joshua closed the box and held it in his hand, pausing to reflect. It seemed perfectly obvious to him the box was empty, but was that just because he knew there was nothing inside? 'Tell me what happened when Miss Violet brought the box to you on the day I left for London.'

She answered readily, as well she might, for the story was one she had related several times before. 'I took the box from Miss Violet, put it inside the drawer, where it is always kept, and locked the drawer.'

'What happened to the key?'

'I put it where madam always keeps it.' She pointed to a small silver box on the dressing table.

'Was anyone else present when you did all this?'

'Why, yes, sir. Miss Violet was here and so was Miss Caroline.'

'Tell me,' Joshua said, 'and please think carefully before you reply, do you believe that the box you put away on that day was empty?'

She answered with scarcely a moment's pause. There was an expressionless note in her voice that suggested she was repeating her response, rather than thinking carefully about it. 'I can't be certain. But I have held the necklace in the box so often I am sure I would have noticed if it was as light as this.' Here she waved her hand at the object in Joshua's hand.

'Between the time of Mrs Mercier's departure and her return two days later, did anyone enter this room, apart from yourself?'

She shrugged her shoulders. 'The room wasn't locked. Anyone might have come in. I can't be expected to stay here every minute of the day.'

'What was the purpose of Mrs Mercier's trip?'

Marie looked puzzled. At last, thought Joshua, a question she hasn't answered before. 'I don't know.'

'Whom did she visit?'

Marie shrugged.

'Come,' said Joshua smiling winningly, 'you must have some idea. I can see how bright and observant you are. Did she let nothing slip?'

Marie blushed coquettishly. 'There was a note . . .' Her voice trailed away.

'A note,' said Joshua, trying to conceal his excitement. 'Do you have it?'

'I'm not certain if the mistress . . .'

'She needn't know,' said Joshua, smiling persuasively again, 'and if it helps retrieve her jewel I will ensure you benefit handsomely.'

Marie looked at him and then turned to a small *bonheur du jour* at the side of the room. She opened the fall front and went unhesitatingly to one of the compartments, from which she extracted a folded paper. Clearly, thought Joshua, there was not much that escaped Marie's eye.

Joshua took the paper and unfolded it. The hand was curlicued and curvaceous, unmistakably the same as that on the note with the illegible signature he had found in Herbert's desk. There were but two lines written on it.

*Come at 6 o'clock.*
*Your offer is much overdue.*


No name, no signature.

'Who sent this? Do you know?'

Marie shook her head.

'And when Mrs Mercier returned from London, she gave no indication of where she had been?'

'None. She seemed at first greatly relieved when she came back. But of course that didn't last. She went to put on the necklace; but when she opened the box she saw that it was gone.'

'And what was her reaction?'

'She was incredulous at first. Shook her head as if she didn't believe it. Then she became very distressed. She sent for Mr Bentnick, but before he came she had fainted. We laid her on the bed and summoned a physician; but even after he arrived it was some hours before she regained consciousness.'

# Chapter Twenty-five

Joshua adjusted the easel just so, before turning his attentions to his mahogany carrying-box of pigments. The powders had been ready ground and he began to mix them with linseed and spirit to the consistency he required in order to set them out on his palette in his usual orderly fashion. He was preparing for Sabine's arrival, which he expected in an hour or two. He knew he would have to work hard to show the progress she expected, but there was plenty of time and he worked with the unhurried confidence of someone who knew precisely what he was about.

All the while his hands performed these routine tasks his mind wandered elsewhere, running over the contradictions he had learned thus far. The note the maid had showed him was most intriguing. It suggested that the purpose of Sabine's recent journey was to meet the claimant and resolve the dispute. And yet both she and Herbert pretended not to know who the claimant was. Was this why the disappearance of the necklace had come as such a shock? She had believed the matter settled, only to return and find the necklace gone. Perhaps, then, she spoke the truth when she said the dispute had nothing to do with the necklace's loss.

But since there was no evidence of disturbance, it appeared the theft of the necklace was not the work of a casual intruder. The thief had known where to look. This suggested someone inside the household, or at very least someone familiar with the house.

Sabine had raised Lizzie Manning's name, citing her family's poverty as a possible motive. Joshua had disregarded this, but having discovered Arthur Manning, who was well acquainted with the house, he could not avoid the conclusion that he might easily stoop to theft. But was he a murderer? Before he could ponder further on this, the timepiece in the corridor chimed the hour, and Sabine, dressed in her finery, swept in for her sitting.

She walked immediately to the easel and examined the canvas. Evidently the work he had completed convinced her that progress was being made, for as she sat down, plumped her skirts around her and waited for Joshua to arrange the finer details of her pose she complimented him on the fine manner in which the light reflected off her skirt and gave it such richness and volume. 'It is still incomplete,' said Joshua modestly. 'When it is finished there will be more highlight, still greater lustre.'

Joshua was burning to ask her more about the visit to London. And yet he had questioned her once on the matter and feared if he did so again she might suspect he had read the note. In any case, once he picked up his palette and brushes and began to scrutinize his subject, a curious transformation came over him. He forgot his other preoccupations, his wariness of Sabine, the danger she represented. He was struck by her luminous complexion; her eyes had a depth he hadn't remarked before. He comprehended what it was that had so smitten Herbert. She was mesmerizing, siren-like; a man might drown in her embrace, forget everything that he was or would be – or go to any lengths to keep her.

During the following hour Sabine spoke not a word. Joshua, meanwhile, painted unceasingly. He began with her face – he would not allow himself to be distracted to any other part. He worked on the structure of the lips, painting them slightly parted, using glazes of vermilion and red lake to emphasize their voluptuous fullness, the way they came forward from the rest of the face and the corners tipped upwards a trifle, as if she were half smiling. He concentrated then on the eyes, on their relation to her nose, on the way the eyelids hung heavy and sensual, on the deep iridescent hue of the iris and the light reflected in it.

Sometimes when he painted, Joshua thought he would never end. He worked day after day adding highlights, deepening shadows, touching up details such as locks of hair here, the smallest nuance of brows and lashes there. At worst, even when he forced himself to believe a picture complete, it was no more than a sum of its parts – a nose, two eyes, a mouth – soundly delineated, a good likeness, but lacking in some intangible soul. At best, without warning – sometimes within ten minutes or twenty – a mysterious alchemy took place. Canvas and paint transmuted; parts came together to transform to a composition with its own life, its own spark. In the Bentnick painting the transformation took place in that hour on that day.

When the clock chimed five and the sitting was over, Sabine rose and swept from the room as grandiosely as she had entered. Only then did Joshua put down his brush. He stood back and looked at his handiwork and knew it was his best work thus far – perhaps the best he would ever paint. The realization made him feel two things. On the one hand it seemed quite miraculous to be the creator of such a work. On the other he felt a curious detachment, as if its brilliance removed it from belonging to him, it was too good to be his. Some other hand had created it; Joshua Pope was a spectator at the exhibition of a stranger.

# Chapter Twenty-six

Barlow Court lay off the Sheen Road, some three miles distant by road from Astley House, on a wide stretch of land fronting the river Thames. The house was all but invisible from the road, being set low down a long drive behind a dense screen of willow trees and reeds that flourished in the swampy ground.

Joshua arrived at the house early, feeling flustered after having to follow a course that passed uncomfortably close to the water's edge. He had rallied his courage by telling himself that Lizzie Manning would be waiting for him and the thought was curiously pleasant. He had sent her a note the previous evening saying he would call on her first thing and, having donned a smart but simple blue coat, clean breeches, a black silk cravat and a dove-grey waistcoat, had left Astley bristling with expectation. His eagerness was thwarted, however, by the inappropriateness of his mode of transport. At the Astley stables he had been told by the lugubrious head groom that one spare horse was lame, a pair of bays were needed to pull the chaise, Mr Bentnick's mare was never ridden by anyone without his personal permission, and the same went for Francis's chestnut. The only mount available was a barrel-bellied old piebald, used to pull wagons round the park, that refused to travel at anything faster than an amble.

Nevertheless, it was only nine o'clock when this lowly

beast, with its handsome cargo, had plodded the short distance to Barlow Court, so that when Joshua asked a manservant for Miss Manning, the response was not what he expected. 'I regret, sir, Miss Manning is not at home.'

'Not at home? Where has she gone?' he cried, infuriated that once again she had eluded him. He had warned her of his visit and her absence coupled with the ignominy of his ride left him feeling more than a mite insulted.

'I'm not certain, sir,' said the manservant. 'I'll search out the housekeeper. Perhaps she will know.'

Left alone in the drawing room to wait, he morosely surveyed his surroundings. On his previous visit to Barlow Court, the day Lizzie had stopped Herbert's carriage and saved him from the downpour, he hadn't gone inside. Now, there was time to take in the place more thoroughly. The room he was standing in was of moderate proportions, with sage-green painted wainscoting and a large wooden chimney piece positioned opposite two long sash windows. There were no ornaments on the mantel shelf; the walls were without a single adornment, though from the faded marks on the paint-work Joshua judged that numerous pictures had lately been removed. The furniture was sparse and simple: a single settee, two arm chairs upholstered in brocade that must once have been sumptuous but was now threadbare and torn, a plain walnut cabinet, a small round tea table. Nothing more. The furniture needed polishing, cobwebs hung from the wall sconces, motes of dust clung to the bare oak boards. The whole place had a run-down air suggestive of owners in straightened circumstance with too few housemaids at their disposal.

Somewhat depressed by the gloomy interior, and still feel-ing ill-tempered on account of Lizzie's absence, Joshua turned to consider the gardens, of which Granger had spoken so highly. The windows looked south across a small raised terrace, with steps leading to lawns bordered by parterres. Columbines, marguerites, lavender, periwinkles, pinks of various kinds, as well as a multitude of roses of every possible hue, bloomed in lush profusion, though most were overgrown, poorly staked and infested with weeds. Between the parterres was a winding pathway, which, like the flowerbeds, seemed poorly tended, for grass had encroached upon its borders and docks sprouted along it like candlesticks set out on a dining table. Beyond lay sweeping parkland, punctuated with copses of trees, that led down towards the river, where a small summerhouse nestled among a bed of reeds.

After some minutes had passed, the housekeeper, a girl of no more than twenty, appeared. 'Have I the pleasure of addressing Mr Pope, sir?' she said.

'I thought Miss Manning expected me,' said Joshua, crossly brushing a speck of dust from his perfectly pressed lapel.

'I believe you sent her a message. She told me to make apologies and to say she had an urgent call that wouldn't wait. She went out first thing this morning. She said to let you know she would be back later this afternoon if you care to call back.'

'Assuming I have nothing better to do,' said Joshua. But no sooner had he made this petulant retort than a shrewder thought occurred to him. Lizzie's actions suggested whatever had taken her out this morning had some relevance to him. Why else would she ignore their rendezvous, depart so early, yet leave word for him to call back? 'Did she mention where she was going?' he asked casually.

'I believe it was to visit a nurseryman at Chertsey.'

Joshua's eyebrows knotted. 'A nurseryman?'

'Aye, sir, I believe that was it.'

'But today is Sunday. Did she say *why* she was calling on him on this of all days?'

'No, sir, she did not.'

Joshua was now consumed by a spirit of inquiry. He considered following her, but then dismissed the idea. On his ancient mount he had no time to get to Chertsey and back in time to meet the midday stage with Bridget on it. In any case, if she discovered anything, he would learn of it in due course. Sooner or later, if he didn't come back, she would come looking for him. In the meantime he might as well pass the hours before Bridget's arrival by pursuing another equally pressing avenue.

'Tell me, then, is her brother, Mr Arthur Manning, at home?'

The girl shook her head, blushing and looking uncomfortable. 'No, sir, he's not been seen here for some time.'

'Since when precisely?'

'Two or three weeks. I thought he had gone abroad. That was what Miss Manning said, at any rate.'

'So you have no idea where I might find him?'

'No, sir, I haven't.'

Doubly thwarted, Joshua headed back towards Richmond and the Star and Garter, where he intended to drink an ale or two with the landlord while waiting for Bridget's arrival. A drink or two might spur Dunstable to remember something more of relevance pertaining to Cobb and Hoare. Above all, Joshua longed to trace Cobb's whereabouts. Perhaps here too Dunstable might help.

As he passed by the spot where Cobb had apprehended him, Joshua drew in his reins and, having halted, surveyed the scene about him. He knew it was too much to expect Cobb to be waiting for him and the spot was, not surprisingly, deserted. How different it looked by day. The bracken that had seemed to loom so menacingly was now harmless lacy fronds in a delicate shade of yellowish green; the thickets of elder, hawthorn and bramble that had impeded his way were not impenetrable as he recalled. To his left the terrain rose quite steeply towards the hill. To his right it shelved away equally precipitously, giving a view of the river snaking ominously through the town of Richmond below.

He had begun to move slowly on, when his eye was caught by a mound of stones and a lichen-covered wooden beam lying among a patch of brambles. He stopped and forced his mount to back up; he looked more closely and glimpsed, further down the slope, crouched between a cluster of boulders and some straggling hawthorn trees, the corner of a stone wall.

Was this wall a boundary or did it form part of an old building? From his present vantage point the undergrowth obscured his view and it wasn't possible to tell. There was no pathway leading to it, which seemed to suggest it was not a building. And yet it occurred to Joshua that if Cobb was living rough in the vicinity this might be the type of shelter he would chose. Like a hound who catches a faint scent of its quarry, Joshua's enquiring spirit was thus fired into action. Ablaze with energy and heedless of danger, he dismounted and led his horse to the verge, where he tethered it to the sturdy branch of a hazel. He began to make his way impatiently down the slope towards the wall. To begin with he thought he could scramble down easily. He had travelled barely five yards before realizing the folly of this plan. The hill was steeper, the ground softer and moister, than he had anticipated. His boots were hopelessly inadequate to the task of giving him a foothold in the muddy soil. He began to slip and skid down the slope. On several occasions he saved himself from losing his footing altogether only by clutching helplessly for branches or rocks or whatever else he happened to pass. His breeches caught on brambles, his coat was spattered with mud, but his craving for truth made him unusually careless of such matters and propelled him on. There was never an instant where he thought of retiring.

By the time he approached the wall near enough to see it was not just a boundary, but formed part of a tumbledown building, his boots were laden with clay, his hands scratched by and bleeding from brambles, and his clothes all but ruined by the mud. But still he scarcely noticed his dishevelment. He was panting heavily, both from his exertions thus far and apprehension at what lay ahead. Sweat clung to his brow, his eyes had darkened with concentration and a hawkish, predatory expression had entered them. There was only one thing on his mind: his mission to find Cobb.

The building had no windows to the rear or on the side he could see. The thatched roof was rotten and had fallen in. The stone walls were in a similar state of disrepair, with crumbling mortar and missing sections. Now that he had drawn close Joshua became aware of the scent of wood smoke. He looked again at the broken roof and thought he saw a wisp of smoke rising through. But then the wind blew and he was uncertain whether he had imagined it.

Presuming that the door and any windows faced the river, Joshua rounded the corner, forcing his way through chest-high brambles to do so. As he approached this side of the building he felt the first prickle of apprehension. To recover his breath he stood for a moment with his back pressed against the solid wall of the building. The smell of smoke suggested this was some form of human habitation. If it was Cobb's hide-out and he was inside, he could hardly fail to have heard Joshua's approach. Would he be lying in wait as he rounded the corner, making for the door? But then Joshua remembered Cobb's feeble health: his cough, his limp, the wound to his arm he had given him. Cobb wouldn't escape a second time.

He came to the point where the side of the building met the front wall. Crouching down, he edged forwards on all fours, arming himself with a large stone as he went. Turning the corner, Joshua saw that the building was a dilapidated barn. There were no windows and the only way in was through a wide doorway – wide enough to allow a cart entrance. The door stood ajar, blocking his view of the interior.

Inching his way forward he came to the door jamb, where there was a wide crack between the wall and the gaping door. Joshua pressed his eye to this aperture. The interior was gloomy but the hole in the roof afforded enough light for Joshua to make out sheaves of hay and straw heaped up against the back wall and a broken ladder leading to an open loft above, where more sheaves were stacked up. In the centre of the floor was a mound of ashes and charred remains of logs – the source of the smoke he had seen. As far as he could tell, the barn was deserted. Joshua stood up and went in.

He kicked about in the ashes; those underneath still glowed red, proof that the place had been inhabited recently and it wasn't long since the fire had died. There were numerous footprints visible in the soft mud of the floor and a couple of bones, as if someone had consumed a repast here. For some reason the sight of them made him nervous and a faint rustle overhead made him jerk his head upwards. As he did so he had the curious impression of a large black silhouette, resembling a gargantuan bat or monster eagle, looming over him from above. The black shadow seemed to flit downwards and something struck his forehead. He felt a heavy thud and his skull seemed to crumble like a blackbird's egg; then came a dull throb of pain as his legs gave way beneath him. He lay helpless on the ground, aware that a hot trickle of blood oozed from the wound to his head. Now too dazed and shocked to feel any real sense of fear, he was aware only of feeling furious at having been caught out, of rough hands taking a grip of him, of being trussed with rope and gagged and hauled upwards, feet first, into the sky. Then the trickle of blood became a torrent. He saw it form a luminous pool in the dark earth beneath him. And then there was nothing. Blackness smothered him.

# Chapter Twenty-seven

When Joshua came to, he found his arms and legs still tightly bound together and a gag in his mouth. He lay on his side in a bed of damp straw that pricked through his breeches and scratched his posterior. His face was caked with dried blood. His skin felt as if it were made from parchment and any facial movement would crack it. His tongue was swollen and tender, as if he had bitten it, and the gag was salty with the taste of blood. The pounding in his skull was so great that even the smallest movement made his head spin. From the corner of his eye he could see the floor of the barn beneath and some form of pulley attached to a long rope net dangling overhead. Presumably the usual purpose of the contraption was to lift hay and straw to the loft, but Joshua strongly suspected that it was by this means he had himself been hauled up here.

Now that he had wakened he wasn't in any sense muddle-headed. His recollections of what had happened until the moment he was struck were clear as candlelight. He remembered entering the barn, looking about him, and being aware of a sense of something looming over him. He remembered too how indignant he had felt to be captured so ignominiously. But he had no recall at all of the appearance of his attacker who had jumped down from above so unexpectedly; he had never seen his face.

Who was he? The obvious answer was John Cobb, the man

he had come to find. Cobb had been Joshua's quarry and, despite Joshua's physical supremacy, had managed once again to take him by surprise and escape. But this solution posed more questions than it answered. If all Cobb wanted was to avoid Joshua, why had he bound and tied him? Was Cobb intent on killing him? If it wasn't Cobb, who else could it be?

He lay there for some time, still boiling with anger, waiting for Cobb, or whoever it was, to return. When nothing happened, his frustration and fury shifted. What was the purpose in waiting for his captor's return? He became imbued with energy, a determination to act rather that wait passively. He forced himself into a sitting position. Immediately his brain seemed to lurch about, like a weathercock in a tempest. He felt sick with dizziness, but by biting hard on the gag, imagining it was his captor's arm, he managed to revive himself.

He searched for some means to release himself. He needed only a scythe or a plough, or even a nail, to work his bindings free. But he could discover no such convenient object. There was nothing save straw and hay and the embers of the fire below and the broken ladder leading to the floor.

To escape he had to get down from this loft, which would be no easy matter with hands and feet that were bound. But in his present steely frame of mind nothing could deter him. After a minute's reflection he shuffled forward to where the top of the ladder jutted out over the floor. The instant he looked down his head began to swim again and he had to grip the edge between his legs to stop himself from falling prey to vertigo. The ladder wasn't secured at the top. The gradient at which it descended seemed almost vertical; the floor lay some fifteen feet below; too high to jump without risk of serious injury. To add to his woes, the first two rungs of the ladder were broken.

Joshua fired himself with cantankerous thoughts about what he would like to say and do to the villain Cobb who had put him here. He would string him up by his ankles. He would

212

knock him out cold and leave him for dead in some god-forsaken spot without food and water. Meanwhile, without dwelling on the risk, he propelled himself forward, took hold of the broken rung with his bound hands and launched himself off the loft floor. He felt the wood yield and sag under his weight, but his hand hold stayed in place just long enough to allow him to get his boots on the lower rung before the wood came away in his hands. Letting it fall to the ground, Joshua pressed his body forwards and grabbed at the side supports. The ladder juddered alarmingly from side to side under the sudden shift of weight. But it remained upright.

With his chin jutting forward to prevent himself from over-balancing backwards on the ladder, Joshua moved his legs caterpillar-like down a rung, then slid his hands down and began the whole looping process again. He had managed three or four of these arduous moves before he turned to look over his shoulder to see how far he was from the floor. As soon as he did so his weight was thrown back and the ladder pulled away from its resting place above his head. He threw himself forwards again – but too late. For a long moment the ladder seemed suspended in midair and Joshua felt like some circus clown performing a balancing act for the amusement of spectators. The ladder teetered and all at once began to lurch backwards. Joshua lost his hold and pitched to the floor.

His landing left him bruised, shaken, but triumphantly alive. The ladder was beside him, stretched across the embers of the fire. He picked himself up. His hip and thigh had taken the impact of the fall, but somehow his head must also have received a knock, for the wound had begun to bleed again, a copious flow that coursed down his cheek and neck. At the same time as he took stock of his injuries he realized that, if his attacker should return and find him still bound, he would be unable to defend himself. He saw that the fire was smoking around the ladder, a part of which was now beginning to smoulder vigorously, as if it were about to burst into flames.

Joshua rolled away from the fire, not wishing to add burns

213

to the catalogue of his wounds, and sat up. It was then that inspiration struck him. Far from threatening him, the fire offered salvation.

He quickly retrieved the broken rung that had earlier fallen to the ground and shuffled back to the fire, where small tongues of flame were already wrapping themselves around the ladder. Joshua thrust his broken piece of wood into the largest flame. In no time the fire took hold. He retracted the flaming wood and then shuffled some distance from the fire. With legs outstretched in front, he jammed the torch between his feet and held it there, so that the flame burned aloft like a large candle. Then, holding his hands in front, he dipped their rope manacles towards the flame. The fire sizzled as it caught hold. There was an acrid stench of burning jute and tar. At the same time he felt the heat searing into his wrists. For as long as he could – a matter of a few seconds, though it seemed infinitely longer – he held his hands in place, watching the flames consume the rope. When the heat became unbearable he lifted his hands away, flailing wildly as he did so. The rope had burned through; his shackles yielded and fell to the ground. His hands were free.

Briskly he untied his feet, wincing with pain at the raw flesh on his wrists. He rose unsteadily to his feet and hobbled to the open door. Every step was agony, but since he was aware Cobb might return at any minute he tried to dismiss the pain. With all the speed he could muster he dragged himself out the same way he had arrived and began to heave himself up towards the road. The distance was only fifty yards, yet it might have been fifty miles for the effort it cost him. He was feeble as an old woman and negotiating the nettles and brambles had him panting and sweating and forced to stop to regain his breath every few yards.

He didn't notice he wasn't alone until he was nearly at the roadside. He heard him first, a rasping cough, followed by a gasping sound, as if someone was fighting for breath. As Joshua approached, he saw a man standing beneath a tree at the verge on the far side of the road. In the intervals between his spasms of coughing he was attempting to untie Joshua's horse. His figure was lanky, his hair ill kempt, his dark cloak spattered with mud. Joshua recognized him instantly, even though the last time they had met was in the dark. It was the cough that gave it away. He was the man who had assaulted him on the road; the man whom Joshua suspected more strongly than ever had knocked his head and left him trussed like a turkey in the loft. The man who called himself John Cobb.

Joshua didn't pause, he didn't consider. In that instant he forgot his injuries. Rage, pure, unadulterated and sweet, brought him strength.

'You miserable, villainous devil!' he bellowed. 'I'll thank you to leave the beast alone, for he belongs to me.'

Astonished by this voice from the wilderness, the man looked up with a start. As Joshua lurched onto the verge and hobbled across the road, the man's eyes widened in horror at the apparition caked in mud and blood, careering wildly towards him.

'Yes, villain,' Joshua said. 'Your handiwork makes a fearsome spectacle, does it not? And I intend to see you brought to justice for it.'

'What do you mean?' said Cobb, taking a step back. 'I have not encountered you since the other night, when I tried to retrieve my bag and you would not let me have it. And as my scars testify, it was *you* who injured *me*.'

'Then you confess you are John Cobb.'

'I told you so the other night, did I not? It was you who chose not to believe me.'

'Well, now I do believe you. And I will have some explanation.'

'Explanation for what? For being who I told you I was, or not being who you believed me to be?'

'Don't try your tomfoolery with me, you miserable rogue. Tell me first, what is your purpose in skulking about the

215

countryside assaulting innocent men such as I? And what were you about to do with my horse?'

Cobb looked guarded, but Joshua discerned none of the guilt he expected. His breast heaved, as if it pained him to speak. 'I do not understand you, sir. My only interest was in my possessions. The bag you took – I must have it, for it contains something of great value. As you see, I am in dire need of a change of clothes and the little money I had is all gone. Everything I have left is in that bag.'

He paused, looked at Joshua's incredulous face, then sighed again and continued. 'I don't believe you are the type of man to withhold something from its rightful owner, but that is what you are doing. I cannot say I blame you for not believing me the other night. How were you to know I was not a footpad? I may as well confess to you that the reason I was standing by your horse was because I have come in search of you. I wanted to beg you again to return my bag to me.'

'How did you know the horse was mine?'

'I waited by the entrance gate to Astley and saw you go out. I didn't want to apprehend you within sight of the house, where those who threaten me might see me, so I decided I would wait here for your return. I suppose I must have fallen asleep while I waited, for I never saw you pass by. But as good fortune would have it, when I came to I saw your horse. I guessed you would return before long.'

Cobb's candour didn't convince Joshua one jot. Indeed, with all the fuss the rogue made over his bag, Joshua now began to wonder if the necklace might be contained inside. Yet he had searched it and found nothing.

'If you are willing to admit all that, why won't you tell me honestly for what purpose you just now leapt on me, struck me on the head and tied me up?'

'I swear to you I did no such thing.'

'Is not that shelter down the slope where you have been sleeping?'

216

'Yes. But I go there only at night. I am fearful that if I stay there during the day the owner might apprehend me.'

'Then if it wasn't you, who was it that attacked me just now?'

Cobb looked towards the building, where smoke from the still burning ladder rose in a plume from the roof. 'I regret I cannot say. It may be that your assailant mistook you for me. My own life has recently been threatened. It wouldn't be the first time another man had suffered in my stead.'

Joshua was torn between disbelief and a desire to hear what Cobb had to say. He still suspected Cobb had attacked him – his mere presence seemed evidence of that – yet Cobb's face and manner betrayed no sign of guile. Rather the reverse, he appeared genuinely confused by Joshua's condition. Moreover, seeing Cobb again reminded Joshua how feeble he was. He looked barely capable of supporting his own weight, let alone leaping from a hayloft, beating him about the head and hauling him twenty feet in the air. Perhaps he should listen to what Cobb had to say before he condemned him.

'What do you mean when you say your life has been threatened?'

'Hoare was killed. I should have gone to that rendezvous.'

This was what he wanted: confirmation of his suspicions. 'How can you be certain the dead man was Hoare?'

'I will explain properly on one condition.'

'Name it.'

'As I said before, I am in the direst need. Without my bag, I have no money for the basic necessities of life. Give me your word you will return my belongings to me immediately and I will tell you everything you ask.'

There was a note of desperation in this plea that Joshua sensed was genuine. The suspicion he had harboured about Cobb began to fade. The man might look like a reprobate – he was gaunt, dirty, ailing from some dreadful malady that might well be contagious – but then, how much better did Joshua

217

look in his present condition? Moreover, Cobb was the key to this entire business, and without his co-operation it might be impossible to unravel. Joshua thought of his endangered reputation; he thought of the dead Hoare; he thought of the missing necklace. All in all, he needed Cobb as much as Cobb needed his bag. More, probably. He would be a fool if he didn't play along with him for the time being at least.

'Very well,' said Joshua. 'I will return your bag as soon as I am able. But you must answer me now about Hoare.'

'How do I know I can trust you?'

'I might ask the same of you. How do I know it wasn't you who attacked me just now?'

'You have only to look at me,' replied Cobb. 'I am not accustomed to this climate and contracted a cough from the day I arrived here. The last days have had an even more drastic effect on my health. I have been subjected to physical attack by you and others. In short, I am no match for you. Do you honestly believe such a thing would be possible?'

Joshua glanced at him and tried to think clearly, but after his recent ordeal his mind lacked its usual clarity and he felt as if he was running through fog. Cobb held the key to events. Having lost him once, he didn't want to lose track of him for a second time. If he refused Cobb's request, there was no knowing where he would go or what he would do. Clearly Cobb believed himself to be in serious danger. It would be foolish, then, to let him stay in the vicinity of Richmond. In addition, his health was weak and likely to grow worse if he continued to live rough.

Joshua had little option but to give Cobb the benefit of the doubt and agree to his terms. What had he to lose? More if he didn't risk it than if he did.

'Very well,' said Joshua, 'These are my terms. I will give you sufficient money to make your way to London and have a good meal . . .'

'London?'

'Yes, London. Until I return the bag you must stay at my

218

lodgings off St Martin's Lane. St Peter's Court. Here's the key. I will send word to the landlady. No one will trace you there and I want to keep you safe where I can contact you when I need to. I will bring the bag to you as soon as I am able. But before you leave you must tell me what you know. Do you agree?'

It seemed ironic to Joshua that Cobb pondered this proposal every bit as warily as he offered it. Neither of them trusted each other, yet both were forced to co-operate. It was an uneasy alliance and Joshua wondered who would breach it first. Nevertheless, having shaken hands on it, Cobb needed little further prompting to relate his story. He spoke in a rush, as though he was eager to reveal what he knew and feared being apprehended before he had finished.

'I arrived in this country three months ago. A London solicitor, by the name of Bartholomew Hoare, engaged me. He had been commissioned to pursue a claim relating to a dispute over the will of a man by the name of Charles Mercier, who had lived all his life in Bridgetown, Barbados. Charles Mercier had left most of his possessions to his wife, who also resided on the island. But he had a daughter by an earlier relationship who lived in London. On his death this daughter was bequeathed an important piece of jewellery – an emerald necklace. But Mrs Mercier, being particularly fond of this jewel, resolved to ignore the bequest and keep it for herself.'

'But who *is* the daughter?' Joshua asked impatiently, intruding on Cobb's flow.

Cobb signed and shook his head. 'I regret that is something I have never discovered. Hoare knew, but in the interests of his client's reputation he never divulged it. In any case, that has nothing to do with it. Hoare was killed in error. *I* was the intended victim.'

'What makes you so sure?'

'Hoare attended a rendezvous at Astley in my place and died as a result. A message was sent to me. *I* should have gone that night.'

'And the motive for wishing you dead?'

Cobb's gaze shifted uneasily. 'I don't know. I presume it is my involvement in the dispute over the necklace. What other reason is there? I am only lately arrived in this country. I have no friends here, no family, and none but the most casual of acquaintances outside my profession.'

'Come, come, Mr Cobb!' Joshua said, annoyed by his guile. 'Your professional dealings are all very fine, but let us not beat about the bush more than necessary. I have read a certain letter written by Violet Mercier to you. The letter speaks of an association and implies you have been pursuing her. Are you sure your actions and acquaintances are all as innocent as you profess them to be?'

Cobb winced as if Joshua's words caused him physical ache. 'How did you find the letter? Hoare took it from me.'

'That is no concern of yours. Just answer the question.'

He looked down at his feet and sighed. 'Since you know, there's no reason for me to pretend otherwise. My involvement with Violet began some time ago, soon after the death of her stepfather, when I was first commissioned to reclaim the necklace. At that stage Mrs Mercier cited her reason for keeping the necklace was her desire to hand it on to her daughter. My intention was, therefore, to inform Violet of the facts of the dispute, trusting her integrity would prevail and that she would persuade her mother of the folly of her ways. I explained that not only had her mother refused to hand on the necklace but that she had also curtailed all payments to Charles Mercier's daughter. The girl was suffering great privation as a result. I think Violet saw reason and felt pity for the girl. But when she approached her mother, Mrs Mercier refused to discuss the matter with her. By then, having met Violet several times, I had fallen for her charms. Why, sir, tell me, as an artist, is she not quite the most beautiful creature you ever saw?'

'My opinion of Miss Mercier's beauty is neither here nor there, Mr Cobb,' Joshua said firmly. 'What interests me more is whether or not you took the necklace. For I will tell you frankly I have been accused of the crime and unless I recover it soon I may expect to be hanged and very probably dissected by some devilish surgeon.'

Cobb's face became a picture of confusion. He drew his brow up, his chin jutted forward, his jaw gaped. 'What are you saying? The necklace is gone? I cannot credit it! Why did you not tell me so at once?'

'I fancied you knew. I assumed you had taken it. The thought even crossed my mind it might be in your bag and that you killed Hoare on account of it.'

'For what reason would I take it clandestinely? Have I not told you I am a solicitor, an officer of justice? It would be contrary to professional ethics to do so. And why would I kill Hoare? He didn't own the necklace any more than I did.'

'And do not professional ethics preclude attempted robbery and clandestine meetings with the daughters of interested parties?'

Cobb waved an airy hand, as if the argument was too pathetic to warrant serious response. 'That is different. I told you the reason for it. I love Violet. And I accosted you to retrieve my own property. It is quite another thing to purloin a priceless necklace and kill a man. In all honesty, I have not the faintest idea who took it, nor who killed Hoare.'

# Chapter Twenty-eight

Joshua hadn't finished with Cobb. He was poised to broach the subject of Arthur Manning, when the slow clopping of hooves and creaking of wheels apprised him there was traffic coming their way.

A gig driven by a scruffy urchin wearing no shoes and clothed in only the grimiest of rags approached from the direction of the town. The vehicle was drawn by an aged moth-eaten bay, its shaggy coat clogged with dust, a myriad flies buzzing about causing it to twitch and toss with annoyance. What struck Joshua most about the vehicle, however, was not its sorry horse nor its disreputable-looking driver, but the passenger who was seated in front beside him.

It was Bridget Quick, his landlady's daughter. She was clad in a muslin-sprigged gown; her hair was nicely curled beneath a straw bonnet trimmed with roses and forget-me-nots; her cheeks were pink as carnations and her eyes shone. In short, this was a Bridget more enticing than ever – as sweet and wholesome as a ripe plum.

'Why, Bridget, how well you look!' Joshua stammered.

'Joshua Pope! Is it you? What a fright you gave me!' she exclaimed, peering down from her seat. Joshua sensed her take in his torn clothes and bruised and bloody face. He knew he looked more hideous than the most revolting ruffian she had ever seen in the gutter of a London street and wondered how she would respond.

'Yes, Bridget, it is I.'

'Then you must be expecting me. I sent a letter to you soon after Mr Bentnick's visit. Since you weren't there to meet me, I did what I said and decided to make my way to the house. Perhaps I should not have come without waiting to hear from you. What a state you are in. What on earth have you done to yourself?'

He was relieved that Bridget's tone conveyed concern rather than revulsion, but he could not forget his grotesque appearance. 'Forgive me, Bridget. I have met with a misadventure just now. I have been knocked unconscious and tied up, and I only narrowly escaped with my life.' Why not embellish a little? he thought. 'And with all this drama I quite forgot that I had intended to be at the Star and Garter to meet you.'

'I see,' she said in a tone that still sounded concerned. 'Then I have come at an inopportune moment. Perhaps I can assist in some way? Otherwise I should turn back to London immediately.'

A flood of disappointment enveloped Joshua. He had intended the catalogue of woes to elicit sympathy, not make her run away. After all he had endured, how pleasant it would be to have an hour or two in Bridget's company without fear of apprehension from her gorgon of a mother. Although there were the pressing matters of Sabine's necklace, Hoare's death and his own reputation to occupy him, none of it now seemed so urgent.

'No, Bridget, forgive me for greeting you like this. But the wounds are superficial, and you cannot leave when you have only just arrived. Let us proceed to Astley. I will attend to myself and then we will take a stroll on the hill. The prospect from there is said to be very fine. Afterwards, perhaps I can offer you some refreshment before you return.'

The temptation of seeing Astley seemed to tip the balance.

Bridget hesitated. 'I have heard Astley's gardens are most remarkable. Certainly it would interest me to see them.' Thus she agreed.

All the while this conversation continued, Cobb had entirely fled Joshua's mind. Only now did he recall his presence and the wisdom of his invitation to Cobb to stay in his lodgings immediately seemed dubious. What had possessed him to act so rashly? He couldn't be sure Cobb wasn't guilty of attacking him. More worryingly, he didn't know whether he was guilty of killing Hoare. Joshua speedily determined to alter the plan. He would make an excuse and send Cobb to a lodging house to wait for him. But when he turned to do so he found Cobb had melted away and was presently limping at a surprising rate two hundred yards down the road, in the direction of the Star and Garter and the London stage.

'Who was that man you were with?' demanded Bridget, spotting Joshua staring after Cobb's retreating figure.

'That,' said Joshua with a sinking heart, 'was John Cobb.' For the moment he remained silent on the subject of the strange events in which Cobb and he were embroiled. There would be time enough later to work out how to break the news gently that he had just invited a man who might or might not be a dangerous malefactor to stay in her mother's house.

Since Joshua was incapable of riding in his present condition, they tethered his nag to the back of the cart and he took a seat behind. In this way they made the mile-long journey to Astley. Herbert was reading a book in the garden when their bedraggled procession arrived. He looked astonished to see Joshua, dishevelled and bloody, and Bridget, winsome and pink, driven in an ox cart by a ragged urchin.

Throwing down his volume, he bustled towards them. He recognized Bridget from his recent visit to search Joshua's rooms, and seemed pleased to see her, but words failed him when he regarded Joshua. He turned chalk white, his eyes bulged while he drank in every cut and bruise and blemish, and yet although he asked what had happened – which Joshua briefly told him – he offered no word of sympathy.

After this Joshua had no energy left for social niceties. He was racked with pain and craved a bath and clean clothes. It was all he could do to stagger indoors after asking Herbert to show Bridget the gardens. Herbert took this request quite in his stride. The last thing Joshua heard as he unsteadily scaled the steps to the door was: 'Now, you will recall I told you of my damask and musk roses. If you would care to come this way, Miss Quick, I will show you some that are particularly splendid . . .'

Once in his room, Joshua called for Peters, the first footman, to send for a servant to fill the bathtub and bring bandages and ointment. An old manservant by the name of Henderson, with chalk hair, a wizened face and a humped back, arrived carrying pails of steaming water. Having filled the copper tub and tested the temperature, the manservant helped Joshua to discard his filthy clothes and step in. Joshua steeped himself in hot water – all bar his wrists, which were so painful he couldn't submerge them and had to lay them on the rim of the tub. He demanded a cloth and gingerly washed the blood from his face. Only then did he dare ask Henderson for a looking glass.

Joshua hardly recognized himself. His left eye was livid and swollen, and there was a deep cut beneath it. The wound to his forehead, white skin gaping open to reveal a cavern of red, was some four inches long. No wonder Herbert and Bridget and Cobb had viewed him with such incredulity.

He dried and dressed laboriously with the assistance of the hunched servant, flinching whenever the towel touched a bruise or a graze, which was often. But when he asked Henderson to tend to his wounds, the old man frowned and shook his head. 'You must excuse me, sir. I will send immediately for someone better fitted to such a task.' Then he bowed and left.

Joshua had not asked who would come. He expected that the person would be one of the female members of staff – the first housemaid, the housekeeper even. While he waited he examined his burns, which were by far the most painful of his wounds. The skin was heavily blistered; there were pouches of skin, with watery liquid beneath; in places the skin had burst, to reveal raw red flesh beneath so excruciatingly tender that the thought of anything touching his wrists, let alone wearing his shirtsleeves buttoned, was unbearable.

Strangely, for one who had always been much preoccupied by imaginary maladies, Joshua felt surprisingly calm when faced with real injury. The burns were severe. If they didn't heal, the repercussions on his career might be grave, yet he didn't fret. What would be would be; there was nothing much he could do about it.

Not long after the old servant left he heard a gentle knock and his door opened.

'I gather you have been hurt and require assistance, Mr Pope?'

His eyebrows shot up and his cheeks reddened spontaneously. To his astonishment, there stood Caroline Bentnick carrying a tray of ointments and bottles.

'Miss Bentnick. Forgive me for troubling you. I would not have done so, only Henderson said he couldn't dress my wounds but would send someone better suited.'

'And will I not do, Mr Pope?' she said, pursing her lips as she came closer to peer at the gash on his head. She gently picked up first one wrist, then the other, to inspect them. 'He was right to do so. I have a little medical knowledge, taught to me by my mother. I will do what I can, but if there is no improvement soon, you should see a physician.'

With that, Caroline Bentnick unstoppered a small brown bottle and poured a draught into a glass. 'Take this, Mr Pope.'

'What is it?'

'Something to alleviate your discomfort.'

226

'Laudanum?'

'No. If you must know, a mixture of ingredients closer to hand. Honey and water and wine and powdered rush. Drink it and you will feel better.'

Joshua drank the bitter-sweet liquid. Almost immediately, his pain diminished. When Caroline applied with a feather a preparation made, so she told him, from trefoil and sweet oil and treacle and then placed wadding and bindings to his wrists, he was scarcely conscious of it.

'I won't be able to paint if you wrap the bandages so tight,' he protested.

'Then you must find some alternative occupation for a day or two. Perhaps you could continue your instruction with Lizzie Manning?'

'Miss Manning's application was wanting,' said Joshua. 'Besides, she is too busy to see me. When I called on her today she had gone out.'

Caroline Bentnick smiled and met his eyes. 'Lizzie Manning is the most charming girl. From hearing her speak to you, I sense in what high opinion she holds you. She would not mean to slight you. If she missed your visit, there must have been a pressing reason.'

'That is all very well, Miss Bentnick. But what was the reason?'

# Chapter Twenty-nine

Ater Caroline Bentnick left him, Joshua meant to go in search of Bridget, but the potion he had taken was stronger than he knew. Loath though he was to yield to sleep, his head began to swim, his eyes grew heavier than a handful of sovereigns and minutes later he lost consciousness.

He awoke, bathed in perspiration and filled with such longing for Rachel as he hadn't experienced for many months. For a time he tried to console himself with thoughts of Meg and their last encounter, but for some reason that only increased his sense of loneliness. It was morning. His father's timepiece read just after seven o'clock. An entire night had come and gone and he remembered nothing. Outside, a chorus of birdsong echoed; inside, the house was silent. At some stage during the hours of his unconsciousness someone had undressed him. He was presently clad in his nightshirt and nightcap; his clothes were neatly folded on the chair. Who had performed this service for him? He had no recollection at all of being undressed but prayed it was the footman Peters or one of the other manservants and not Caroline Bentnick.

The cup with the dregs of the draught she had given him still stood on the night table. Propped against the cup was a bulky letter. Joshua didn't recall seeing this before and could only presume it had been delivered after he had fallen asleep. His first thought was that it must be a message from Bridget, whom he had abandoned to Herbert Bentnick. Fearing the letter would contain a reprimand for having left her after urging her to stay, he now began to fret. He was already in an awkward predicament, having sent Cobb to his lodgings, the wisdom of which now seemed undeniably flawed. He relied upon Bridget's goodwill towards him to pacify her mother. He grabbed for the letter, full of dread at what it might contain.

Then, even before he opened it, a second thought flashed upon him. He should have realized as soon as he saw the hand that the letter wasn't from Bridget – it was from Lizzie Manning.

*30th May 1766*
*Barlow Court, Richmond*

*Mr Pope,*
*I gather from my housekeeper that you came to Barlow this morning and were somewhat put out to find me absent and unable to greet you. Forgive me for missing you. I went to question a nurseryman on the subject of pineapples. Forgive me also for quitting Astley without first apprising you of my conversation with Violet. The minute I finished with her I received a message from my father that made it imperative for me to leave more speedily than I would have liked.*

*That apart, let me recount my most interesting conversation. I took Violet for a stroll on her return from another trip to London for fitting her dress – has any garment in Christendom required such an excess of attention? – and still it isn't finished. Can you believe it, Mrs Bowles, the unfortunate dressmaker, will deliver the dress in the next few days, and Violet says she will have to stay at the house to make any alterations necessary, or she will not be paid.*

*In any event, to the matter in hand. I told Violet we believed Mr Cobb might still be alive and that he might be responsible for the disappearance of the necklace. You may rest assured I made* no mention of the letters we discovered – how would I do so without incriminating you?

On hearing it wasn't Cobb who had died, but, we surmised, Hoare, her face seemed to brighten. Seeing this, I asked whether she was still fond of him, to which she replied rather sharply that there was nothing between them and, on the contrary, I should know there was someone else who now held sway over her feelings. I presume this 'someone else' was Francis and that she did not say so for fear of incurring my wrath.

When I questioned her about the necklace's disappearance, she declared I must have been recruited by Cobb to pursue her, for he had pestered her interminably for assistance in persuading her mother to hand over the jewel, but that despite all her efforts her mother was determined to keep it. I assured her I was entirely open-minded on the subject of Cobb and the necklace, and that it was in her mother's interest that we recover the jewel. With these reassurances she became calmer and told me a little of the history behind the necklace. The story was an intriguing one, and even if it is not entirely pertinent to our business I think it worthwhile recording here.

Charles Mercier, Violet's stepfather, was a shipping clerk, a kindly, prudent soul, with a great antipathy to risk-taking and gambling of any sort. His strange aversion resulted from an incident that took place when he was a young man, and he often spoke of the episode as a way of keeping Violet from the perils of gaming.

When he was aged no more than three and twenty he attended an assembly at the governor's residence, where he was introduced to a newly widowed countess, a woman of substantial means who was lately arrived in Bridgetown to inspect her estates on the island. During the evening Charles Mercier engaged the countess in conversation, upon which she cajoled him to join her in a round of ombre. By some extraordinary quirk of fate, Charles, who as far as anyone knew could scarcely tell a jack from an ace, won every hand. His winnings included a promissory note from the countess for a valuable emerald necklace that had belonged to her

230

family for centuries. Next morning she sent her maid round with the necklace — hoping perhaps that in due course she would have the opportunity to win it back.

The maid, whose name was Emma Baynes, was by all accounts a titian-haired beauty, and Charles Mercier, still heady with his successes of the previous night, was much struck by her. He asked her to try on the necklace so he could see it well displayed. When Emma opened the case and took out a necklace fashioned as a serpent, he was more than a little shocked. But then he laughed and proclaimed it most fitting, since the serpent of temptation had surely led the countess astray the previous night.

The meeting led to a romantic liaison in which Charles Mercier fell deeply in love with Emma Baynes. Meanwhile, much to the chagrin of the countess, he refused all invitations to play her at ombre — or any other game, for that matter. Three months later, by which time the disgruntled countess had virtually ruined herself with losses, she decided to return to London.

At about the time she announced this intention, Emma Baynes discovered she was expecting a child. Charles Mercier immediately offered to marry her, but Emma Baynes — a foolish, headstrong girl, to judge by her actions — had other ideas. She detested the climate in Barbados and missed her homeland. Moreover, she had a sweetheart in London whom she believed to be so besotted with her beauty he would marry her despite her present condition. Thus, with scarcely a thought for propriety or the wellbeing of her child, she turned down Mercier's proposal.

Charles had grown deeply attached to Emma Baynes, and while he was greatly saddened by her refusal he stood by his responsibilities. He promised to make arrangements to support the child and her mother, who would no longer be able to continue in service once the child was born. Emma never divulged anything of her hopes of marriage in London and agreed eagerly to accept his financial assistance.

All this took place fifteen years before Sabine met and married Charles Mercier. He was always scrupulously honest about the daughter he had never met. He told Sabine frankly of her existence and warned her that he intended to do as much for this child as for any legitimate offspring he might father with Sabine. In the event Sabine and Charles's union was childless; and while Charles grew fond of Violet, and often called her his daughter, his pledge to remember his natural child was never forgotten.

Soon after their marriage, Charles showed Sabine the emerald serpent and told her the history behind it. Sabine, much taken with the unique beauty of the jewel, asked if she might wear it from time to time – a request to which Charles Mercier agreed. For the next ten years Sabine proudly wore the emerald necklace whenever the opportunity arose. As far as anyone knew, Charles never actually told Sabine the jewel was hers, but neither did he give her any inkling of his intentions to bequeath it elsewhere.

It was only a year ago, after Charles's death, when the will was read, that Sabine discovered his decision to leave to his illegitimate daughter this most precious object among all his possessions. The reason he gave was simple. The necklace had been brought to him in the hands of Emma Baynes. Were it not for that jewel, his daughter would never have been born. In his eyes it was only fitting, therefore, that she should have it after he was gone.

It is not hard to imagine Sabine's feelings of outrage and resentment. She had no qualms about flouting the will, arguing that it had been written many years ago, in the early days of her marriage. Charles had in the meantime changed his mind – why else would he have allowed her to wear the necklace so frequently? Moreover, Violet had been more of a daughter to him than a child he had never seen. And she, Sabine, had been more of a wife than Emma Baynes. What claimant could possibly oppose her?

Soon after Sabine's determination to hold on to the necklace became clear, a Bridgetown attorney by the name of John Cobb contacted Violet and asked her to meet him, 'over a matter in which you might be able to give someone less fortunate than yourself some assistance'. Violet, who knew only the bare rudiments of the dispute, agreed, perhaps a little naïvely, to Cobb's request, never suspecting that he was acting on behalf of her mother's adversary.

Cobb told Violet that Charles Mercier's daughter in London was of similar age to herself; that Emma Baynes had recently died, and unless her daughter received her rightful inheritance she would be forced to scratch a living in the streets of London as best she could – an outcome that Charles Mercier had expressly intended to prevent. Did she not feel a sense of duty to do right by this poor girl who, in the eyes of God, if not the law, was a half-sister?

Violet listened carefully to all Cobb told her. He was a tall, handsome fellow – being the focus of his persuasive charms was agreeable. Remembering how good her stepfather had been towards her, she felt a twinge of conscience. She went so far as to mention the matter to her mother, but Sabine was unbending. She wouldn't consider relinquishing the necklace. Her only compromise, by way of appeasement, was to promise to make alternative financial arrangements if Emma Baynes's daughter agreed to give up her claim to the necklace.

So Violet seesawed between the two camps, continually pursued by Cobb, whose every argument was refuted by her mother. How was poor Violet to know which of them was telling the truth? Before long, Cobb began to profess his romantic interest in her, promising that if she reciprocated his affection he would do his utmost to work in her best interests with regard to the necklace. Perhaps the claimant would accept a financial settlement rather than the jewel itself.

At this juncture in her account, Violet became visibly distressed. Tears coursed her cheeks as she declared that although she found him pleasant and handsome, she had no romantic inclinations in that quarter. She did everything possible to discourage Cobb's attentions, writing to him and telling him to his face that she wanted nothing to do with him and nothing to do with the necklace if he was part of the bargain.

She had thought herself rid of the wretched man when they left Bridgetown and moved to Astley. Thus you will understand that, the day she went for a stroll with Francis Bentnick and met Cobb wandering the gardens, she could hardly believe her eyes. In a turmoil of disbelief she told her mother of her encounter and begged her to give him the necklace so that she could live her life in peace – after all, why did she need the wretched necklace when she had Herbert who would buy her a dozen more?

Sabine had seemed unsurprised at the news of Cobb's appearance. She told Violet not to concern herself about the necklace. Her resolve was unchanged. She had no more intention now than before of handing it over. Herbert knew the details of the matter; he intended to call on Cobb and would advise her how to proceed.

I think it was at this juncture that Violet seemed to realize the ambiguity of her words. 'Miss Manning,' she said, 'the reason I said nothing of all this to you before was because I feared if I admitted to knowing Cobb I might in some way incriminate my mother of some involvement in his death. The necklace has inordinate significance in her eyes; who knows to what lengths she would go to keep it? However, now you have told me Cobb is alive, and someone else is dead, there is no reason whatsoever not to tell you the truth, is there?'

I didn't point out the obvious – that Hoare may have been killed because he was mistaken for Cobb; and that if this was the case, her mother might well be guilty. I did ask, however, if her mother had ever met Cobb. 'No,' said Violet without hesitation. 'Cobb knew my mother's animosity towards him and kept out of her sight. To my knowledge she never did meet him.'

Surely, my friend, this is further corroboration of our most promising theory. If Sabine didn't know what Cobb looked like, she could easily have killed Hoare by mistake. What do you think?

Yours,
Lizzie Manning

What Joshua thought took him some minutes to acknowledge. He was as intrigued as much by the motives of Lizzie Manning as the content of her letter. She had written cordially, apparently following his instructions. But there were questions left unanswered, instructions ignored, which spoke volumes about her true character. What had her father said to cause her to leave Astley so precipitously? What was so pressing about pineapples to make her go to a nursery the morning he arrived, and yet neglect to mention it? Why had she deliberately ignored his warning not to tell Violet that Cobb might be alive? The lengthy history of the jewel was all very intriguing, but much of it he had already learned from Cobb. She had entirely ignored his request to question Violet closely about the day Joshua had left Astley. He wanted to know the details of how she had given the necklace to the maid, to see whether this agreed with the maid's account. He wanted to know how reliable Violet thought the maid, how long she had been in their service, and would she be capable of theft? Yet such crucial matters were either not mentioned at all or glossed over. What had made her ignore these crucial instructions, forget there was a noose hanging over his head?

He shook his head, nostrils flaring in disappointed comprehension. It was simple, now he thought on it. And in a sense he had only himself to blame for not realizing much sooner. She acted carelessly not from malice – doubtless it didn't occur to her she was hastening his ruination.

Lizzie's central concern was Francis. Her family predicament could only add to her anxiety that no one should threaten her marriage to Francis. Compared with this, her own future, what would his downfall matter to her? In short, why should Lizzie Manning give a jot about him when she had Francis Bentnick to worry over?

But having reflected further, Joshua began to see her actions in a more intriguing light. It was surely most significant that Lizzie had never mentioned her brother to him; neither had she mentioned the family's straightened circumstances, nor her interest in horticulture. Why had she pressed so insistently to involve herself in his enquiries? Was there more than innocent fondness for Francis?

Fired with new insight Joshua sprang up from his bed, only

to be reminded by the aches and throbs that yanked at every sinew of his being that he was far from recovered from the previous day's ordeal. There was a bulky dressing wrapped around his forehead. Bandages were bound around his wrists and palms, leaving only the tips of his fingers free. Dressing was thus a tricky ordeal and it was a good half-hour before he accomplished the feat of pulling on buff breeches, buttoning a brown coat with ochre frogging and tying a yellow cravat. Then, having tied his dark hair back – a wig was out of the question with the bandage – and manoeuvred himself into his boots, he glanced at himself in the mirror. All things considered, he looked not too bad. With this consoling thought he hobbled downstairs.

He found Bridget seated in the breakfast room with Herbert and Caroline Bentnick. The trio looked perfectly at ease and seemed neither eager nor relieved to see him. Rather the reverse. 'Mr Pope,' said Caroline, 'are you quite well and recovered? I had expected you to sleep until late and said as much to Miss Quick. You look better, though still a little peaky, if truth be told.'

'I am very well,' Joshua replied, rubbing the dressing on his head, which was pounding uncomfortably and making him unsteady on his feet. 'And as you see, I am perfectly recovered.'

Joshua turned to Bridget. 'Miss Quick, you are still here. My apologies for abandoning you like that. I feared you would have lost patience and returned to London.'

'Not at all, Mr Pope,' replied Bridget, replacing her cup lightly in its saucer. 'Miss Bentnick was kind enough to apprise me of your condition and to offer me a bed for the night. And I have enjoyed a promenade in the gardens with Mr Bentnick as a guide. All in all, I have been most hospitably treated.'

Joshua was struck by the ease of her manner as she spoke. She held her head high; her neck was longer and more slender than he remembered; her bosom swelled enticingly within her bodice; her hair was attractively arranged – was that a rose in it? Most importantly, she seemed not at all put out by his absence the evening before. After the antics of Lizzie Manning, this was welcome relief.

In a more optimistic frame of mind, he turned then to Caroline Bentnick. When she had come to attend to his wounds the previous day he had perceived a certain softening in her manner; he saw now he had not been mistaken. Her demeanour was amiable; she met his gaze with a friendly directness. What had effected this transformation?

'Miss Quick is a most welcome guest,' said Caroline, as if she had read his thoughts. 'She has been most practical in her advice regarding preparations for dinner and is welcome to stay longer, if she chooses. Why, Mr Pope, after all the help she has given, you should bring her to the ball on Friday.'

Bridget glowed with delight at Caroline's offer. Joshua thought she would accept. But remembering her mother, and what she might do if crossed, he swiftly intervened.

'Your offer is most generous, but Bridget – Miss Quick, I mean – has to return to London or her mother will be anxious. And she is kept very busy in town. I doubt she has time to socialize . . .'

Bridget frowned. 'Not at all,' she interposed. 'I told my mother I might stay the night with my aunt at Twickenham. If I don't return, she will presume I am there.'

'You can hardly remain here another three days. Think of your duties to your poor mother . . . her rheumatism.'

'Then if she must go, she shall return tomorrow. London is no more than a couple of hours from Richmond after all,' cut in Herbert, in a voice of authority that countenanced no refusal. 'Meanwhile, Mr Pope, since you are unable to paint, you might turn your thoughts urgently to recovering Mrs Mercier's necklace. I hear Sir William Manning, the justice, is due to return any day now. As soon as he does, if you have made no progress I intend to put the matter in his hands. I

237

don't say *I* think you are guilty, Pope. If I did I would hardly invite you to my table. Nonetheless you must see things might look different from other perspectives. As I told you before, Mrs Mercier believes I have shown you excessive leniency.'

With this chilling announcement, before Joshua had a chance to remonstrate, Herbert discarded a crust of toast on his plate, dropped his napkin on the table and stalked from the room. Joshua's head was now pounding intolerably; frustration overwhelmed him. He felt horribly aware of the fragility of his position. His paintings were hung in mansions and palaces, he was held in esteem by their eminent owners, and yet his entire future seemed to depend upon Herbert's whim.

'It's settled, then,' said Caroline, disregarding his torment as if her father's outburst and Joshua's imminent doom were no more than a trifle. 'You will spend the morning taking Miss Quick on a drive to see a little of the local region, Mr Pope. That will give you something to do – and I wager you have yet to take a stroll on the hill, or in the gardens at Kew. Your bandages should stay on your hands for at least two days. I have told my father you will be unable to paint until Wednesday at the soonest. And since today is only Monday you have plenty of time to fill. Miss Quick is extremely sensible and will make sure you don't over exert yourself after your recent ordeal.'

'But the necklace . . . You heard what your father said. I really should do something more,' Joshua objected.

'Do not worry yourself about that odious object,' said Caroline, wafting an airy hand as if whisking away a blue-bottle. 'I warrant my father's threats have no substance whatsoever. In my opinion we are all better off without the wretched thing.'

# Chapter Thirty

Thus it was agreed that Bridget Quick, whom Joshua had spent the past weeks keeping at arm's length for fear of falling out with her mother, was to be his constant companion for that day and, unless he could muster some plausible excuse, his partner at the forthcoming ball as well. Joshua accepted the situation with outward good grace – Bridget was undeniably appealing – but, inwardly, emotion raged. A clutch of evils was gathering against him like waves on the horizon. If he didn't act, the storm would break and wash him away. He was a man at the peak of his profession, threatened with the loss of all he had accomplished. In this turbulent sea Bridget Quick, however attractive, represented a further peril, one which, had he only made some glib excuse, he could have easily escaped. But he had been so flabbergasted by Herbert's menacing manner he had said nothing. The tracing of a murderer, the discovery of a lost heirloom and the avoidance of his imminent disgrace were his priorities. Amusing a lady, however pretty, did not feature in his plans. How could he be expected to make any form of progress when he was thus hampered? Herbert might as well manacle his feet, tether him to a tree and demand he run a hundred yards.

When Bridget left the breakfast room to prepare for their outing, Joshua turned to Caroline Bentnick, with whom he was now alone. Avoiding the subject of Bridget, he sought to salvage something from her amenable mood. 'I am most grateful for your kindness in dressing my wounds yesterday. Indeed, I hardly know how to thank you. I was in the most intolerable discomfort and you soothed it miraculously.'

Caroline looked slightly taken aback and dabbed her lips with her napkin several times. 'It was no more than I would have done for anyone. But your burns are severe and you must take care of them.'

'Where did you acquire your medical knowledge?'

She smiled, a mite oddly, he thought. 'I have no great knowledge, Mr Pope. The little I know is from my mother, who was well versed in the medicinal properties of herbs, as are most housewives. I have her book of receipts, which I believe she inherited from her mother. I have some success in preventing the first occasion of sickness. I do not pretend to be capable of any more.'

'Then tell me,' Joshua said, to test her, 'I am often bedevilled by agonizing aches of the head. I have one now that feels as if a monster fist has wrapped itself about my skull and would wring the brains from it. What do you recommend?'

'Have you a cold when the headaches come?'

'Not necessarily. They are brought on by extremes of humour. If I am anxious, or when I become agitated, I am in danger of starting one.'

She nodded and thought for a minute. 'According to my mother's Culpeper, lettuce cools and moistens and the juice mixed or boiled with oil of roses and applied to the forehead and temples procures sleep and eases the head. I will make some for you to try if you wish.'

'You are most kind,' he said. 'Perhaps, in return, I can offer you something.'

'What have you in mind?'

'Some instruction in drawing. I know from your father you are an enthusiast – I fancy you will have more application and diligence than your friend Miss Manning.'

Caroline smiled. 'I would be honoured to have such an eminent tutor. You implied last night that Lizzie had annoyed you. Let me remind you of what I firmly believe. Lizzie can be headstrong and she is frequently outspoken. Yet she has an extraordinary capacity for life. You cannot deny it.'

Joshua gritted his teeth and managed a smile and a nod, even though the elusiveness of Lizzie Manning and her attempts at deceiving him were still a source of annoyance. 'Without doubt she is a remarkable person. I understand there is some romantic attachment between Miss Manning and your brother?'

'More than an attachment: an unofficial engagement. It has been known to both the families for some time. The wedding date is not yet set, nor is it likely to be under the present circumstances.'

'What do you mean by "the present circumstances"?' he probed.

'My father's impending marriage,' she said flatly. 'Lizzie would not dream of stealing his glory. That's why her engagement to Francis has not been discussed, even though it was as good as settled before Sabine arrived.'

Joshua winced as he reached forward for the butter and felt his muscles complain. 'I gather the Mannings' fortunes have lately been unhappy. Perhaps that also has something to do with it?'

'Arthur Manning has been the cause of a great deal of unhappiness. He has disappointed me and his family. I would prefer not to discuss him.'

'Miss Bentnick, may I speak frankly to you?'

'What about?'

'You have made no secret of your dislike of Mrs Mercier. A moment ago when you spoke of your father's marriage your disapproval was plain. What is it about her you find so objectionable?'

She pursed her lips and twirled her spoon on her saucer.

Her eyes had a mournful look; her long face looked more elongated and gaunt than usual. 'Why should I discuss this with you? What business of yours are my feelings towards my future stepmother?'

Joshua held up his hand. 'I do not pry willingly. You heard your father's demand that I find the missing necklace. I am unjustly accused. Through no fault of my own, my reputation – indeed, my life itself – has been cast under a shadow. I may add I have no allegiances, to your father or anyone else. I am utterly objective. My only aim is to clear my name and discover the truth.'

Caroline leaned back in her chair and tilted her head to one side. Her eyes were still sorrowful but now they glittered with unusual intensity. 'Very well, Mr Pope. I trust that if I speak you will listen with a sympathetic ear. You won't think me fanciful and what I say will go no further than this room?'

'You have my word on it.'

'I cannot rid myself of the feeling there is something unwholesome about Sabine Mercier. I know she is beguiling in her looks and manners; I know my father is entirely taken in by her. Perhaps you think I am swamped by jealousy, a grown daughter who should have a lover of her own and feels excluded from their happiness. But I give you my word that has nothing to do with it. Sabine deserves my doubts. There is something that makes me distrust her. I hate to say these words, but why should I not since I have thought them often enough? It would not surprise me in the least to learn that she had a hand in Hoare's death, or in her previous husband's, or my mother's.'

A heavy silence now hung between them. Joshua was taken aback. The matter of the earlier deaths was something he had considered briefly but dismissed, since there was little chance of learning more about them. 'Do you have any grounds for your suspicions?'

'I know that a few moments ago you were testing me on my knowledge of plants. I presume you believe that Hoare was poisoned?'

Joshua nodded.

'Sabine has a wide knowledge of the medicinal properties of plants. Her father was a physician and taught her much; she has studied the subject and learned a great deal more. She makes no secret of the matter – indeed, I would say she revels in her expertise. The little I know of my mother's death is also compatible with poisoning. To slip something in my mother's food that made her fall ill was well within her capabilities. My father would have been easily duped. He would have thought Sabine was doing all she could to help.'

This statement was uttered in such a calm, unapologetic tone that Joshua was quite disturbed. There was no vestige of doubt in her voice. She might have been reading an account from a newspaper.

'That is a grave accusation. Do you really believe her capable of such a thing?'

'Without a shadow of doubt. Even the pineapples in which she takes such pride may be poisonous.'

Joshua smiled. 'Come, come. A pineapple is an edible fruit, much lauded for its perfume and sweetness.'

'The ripe fruit is just as you say. But perhaps you are not aware of the harmful effects of the unripe fruit. Violet mentioned the subject once when we went on a tour of the pinery. And how would she know such a fact if not from her mother? Unripe fruits are a powerful purgative. I know this not only from Violet but from family acquaintances who lived on an estate called Beechwood where pineapples were grown. I recall hearing that a sailor who returned to the village from a voyage to the Indies and found his wife expecting another man's child stole an unripe fruit and forced her to eat it to cause a miscarriage.'

'But are unripe fruits fatal?'

'Not usually, but by all accounts Hoare vomited prior to death. That is a symptom of eating unripe pineapple.'

Joshua held his neutral expression, though he thought to himself that there were countless other concoctions that

243

might have had the same effect. 'Let us put the earlier deaths of your mother and Charles Mercier to one side, for how could we properly prove such a thing? Do you honestly believe Mrs Mercier had a hand in killing Hoare?'

Caroline flushed uneasily, lowering her gaze. 'Of course. If it was not Sabine, who else could it have been? As for why she did it, I didn't comprehend the motive before, but now, having heard a little of the dispute surrounding it, I see it must be the necklace that she was so eager to preserve for herself. I will wager, moreover, he was poisoned by pineapple – have you thought of that, Mr Pope?'

Joshua remembered that an unripe fruit had gone missing. He remembered too that Lizzie Manning had visited a nurseryman who, by her own admission, was an expert in pineapples.

'Did you mention this theory to your friend Miss Manning?'

'Yes.'

'One final question, Miss Bentnick. On the night Miss Manning came for dinner and met the Merciers for the first time – the day after the body had been found, if you recall . . . We were seated in the drawing room. I was playing cards with your brother and father. I saw Mrs Mercier engage you in conversation. And all at once you seemed most powerfully affected: a complete change came over you. If I had to describe it I would say you looked frightened, nay, terrified. What did she say to cause such a reaction?'

It was as if he had pressed an invisible trigger and caused a wall to descend between them. Joshua's perceptive eye took in the shift in Caroline's entire demeanour. Her voice became wary; she blinked rapidly and twined her fingers together.

'Were my feelings so transparent?'

'I doubt anyone else noticed anything at all, Miss Bentnick. It is my business to look at faces.'

She raised her eyes to meet his. Her expression was half trusting, half wary, as if she was judging whether he was a saviour or a snake. 'Very well, I will tell you. In any case, you must have heard part of what she said. She asked me if I would care to wear her necklace at the ball.'

'Why did that distress you?'

'It did not to begin with. It merely struck me as strange that she should offer me something that I knew to be so precious to her.' She halted and looked down again. Her clenched hands twitched and trembled as they had on the night they were presently discussing.

'I cannot help you, Miss Bentnick, if you do not tell me what it is that frightens you.'

'Well, then I remembered what Violet had said earlier concerning the superstitions associated with the necklace. And that made me wonder why she was offering me her necklace, when she knew I disliked her and regarded my mother's death as being . . .'

'Suspicious,' Joshua hazarded.

'Quite so.' Caroline appeared to swallow hard before continuing. 'I realized that there was evidently more to the offer of the necklace than first appeared. You must remember, I was sitting on that settee, under her gaze. I could feel her looking at me and it seemed to me that the emerald serpent around her neck was also fixing me with its ruby eye. For some reason the wretched necklace seemed to draw me, as though it were magnetically charged. I could not tear my eyes from it. Nor could I stop thinking of the malevolent power it was supposed to have. I promise you it was a most frightening sensation.

'And all this while I was aware that she kept on at me. "What have you to say, Caroline? I take it you accept?" Of course I did not want to accept. It seemed to me that the serpent embodied her murderous tendencies. I opened my mouth to say no, but just at that moment she interrupted. Her voice was entirely different, no more than a whisper – no one else could have heard it, yet at the same time it was peculiarly penetrating.'

'What did she say?'

'She said that my silence was a great affront to her in view of the efforts she had made. I was naught but an ungrateful girl. And – this was what struck me most vividly – that the necklace had a potency of its own. I should remember that serpents have long been forceful symbols and if I had any sense I would treat her offer with greater respect.' She paused, searching his face for some sign he comprehended her meaning. The anguish in her eyes was plain. 'So now you see why I said we are all better off without it.'

# Chapter Thirty-one

Caroline Bentnick's revelations and the presence of Bridget Quick brought Joshua an unlooked-for advantage. Caroline was so relieved to have voiced her suspicions to someone outside the family, and so taken with Bridget Quick, she insisted they borrow a chaise and two lively chestnuts from the stables for their tour. The moth-eaten piebald that Joshua had been obliged to ride the previous day was thus put out to grass. Newly polished harnesses were buckled and fixed, and a vehicle that Joshua was proud to drive was delivered to his charge and Bridget's travelling bag stowed in it. He sat in the driving seat with sentiments more mixed than usual. Though he knew he should find some excuse to rid himself of Bridget at the earliest opportunity, nevertheless the prospect of an hour in her company was not entirely unwelcome. The air might help clarify his thoughts; a quick tour of Richmond Park would do him good.

So many different trains of intriguing thought intertwined in his mind that, like ribbons on a maypole, he hardly knew which to pursue. To add to his difficulties the road to the park skirted the river, which only compounded the feelings of apprehension sparked by Herbert's cruel remarks about the necklace. Moreover, they were but a short distance into the journey when it dawned on him that the advantage of the carriage did not entirely outweigh the disadvantage of Bridget

Quick's presence. Although she was fair and her manner was circumspect, her curiosity was inescapable.

She began most unexpectedly some few minutes after they had set out on their drive. They were on high ground and the road looked down over the expanse of the river. 'Tell me, Mr Pope,' Bridget said abruptly, 'why is it that whenever the road closely skirts the river you look in the opposite direction? Yet the river makes such a charming picture. Being an artist, I would have thought you might appreciate it . . .'

Joshua was dumbfounded. This oddity of his had never been remarked by any other acquaintance. 'If I do,' he stuttered, trying to muster a plausible answer, 'it is involuntary.'

'Are you afraid of water?'

'I cannot swim.'

She raised an eyebrow and made a purse of her lips. 'Few people swim, yet they do not cringe at the sight of a river.'

Joshua pondered in silence as he sought something to say that would make her quit this painful subject. After a long pause, adopting an air of lofty composure he declared, 'This is a matter of the greatest delicacy, Miss Quick. Something I never discuss with anyone.'

He underestimated her persistence. The pause allowed her to glimpse the weakness in his carapace and the point of her sword was in.

'What exactly do you never discuss? Your fear of water, or the cause of it?'

He shook his head and gave her a rueful smile. 'The water makes me desolate and lowers my spirits whenever I look at it. There, does that satisfy you?'

'No,' said Bridget, 'for you still have not told me why.'

Suddenly he felt too tired to parry with her. He could deflect her with a half truth but she would no doubt return to the subject before long. Once he said what he had to say, the matter would be over. There would be no more discussion. And – this thought above all propelled him – she might leave him in peace.

'You know my wife died recently. She drowned on the river.

She was with our child at the time. He perished too. They were swept away in a boat. It happened one year ago, almost to the day. That is why I took the commission and came away. I detest the sight of the river, or any stretch of water, for that matter, because of the memories it awakens.'

The vehemence in his voice must have been obvious, and he expected her to look awkward or ashamed at having forced such a painful admission and thus to fall silent. Yet, to his amazement, he was only partly right. She was forthright in her solicitude, revealing no hint of shame. Nor did she bother with platitudes.

'I am sorry for your dreadful loss, but it is a mistake to spend so much time worrying about death that you never live. Water was the source of your tragedy, but it is also the source of life,' she said, and patted his arm.

Until this moment Joshua had always pointedly avoided the subject of Rachel and Benjamin's deaths, expecting it to resurrect his feelings of loss and thus multiply his feelings of melancholy. Moreover, he detested the idea that anyone might feel sorry for him. A man such as he, successful, well established, highly esteemed, had no need of anyone's pity. Thus it surprised him to discover that after this conversation he felt curiously lightened, as if a breeze had blown a gap in a heavy cloud that had shadowed him for the past year. He was surprised too that Bridget showed no sign of pity. Nor did she wish to dwell on the matter. Instead her attention moved rapidly to other more immediate subjects.

She had heard from Caroline how Mrs Mercier had found the corpse of a man recently arrived from Bridgetown, Barbados, believed to be called John Cobb. Caroline had explained that the corpse was not Cobb's but that of a man called Hoare, an attorney whose practice was in London, and that both men were acting for an anonymous claimant in a dispute over a necklace. She had witnessed Herbert's threats about the necklace. But how did all this fit with what had happened to Joshua yesterday?

Under different circumstances Joshua might have been reticent to discuss matters that were none of her concern. But after the admission he had just made, he felt more mellow and more open than usual. He explained that he had gone in search of Cobb, when he had been brutally assaulted, tied up and left for dead. After managing to escape, he had discovered Cobb standing by his horse, just before Bridget came upon him.

'And what did this Mr Cobb say when you apprehended him?' asked Bridget, much perplexed.

'He denied he was responsible for attacking me and declared he did not know who my attacker was. He said that he dared not return to the Star and Garter, for fear of being attacked. And that since I had taken his bag and possessions, he had been forced to use the barn as a shelter. He suggested that my attacker had mistaken me for him. No doubt seeing the state I was in made him even more fearful for his safety and that was why he ran off at the earliest opportunity when you arrived.'

Joshua remembered with a twinge of anxiety that he had sent Cobb to his lodgings – her mother's home. He knew he would have to choose an opportune moment to break this news, but he wasn't ready just yet. He swooped instead to a subject that he knew would be bound to interest her: Lizzie Manning. Explaining that she was the daughter of the local justice and a close friend of Caroline and Francis Bentnick, he said, 'There is more to her than I first realized. She is unofficially engaged to Francis Bentnick, for whom Violet has also formed an attachment. Lizzie concealed her interest in gardens and the existence of her brother. She went to visit a nursery yesterday when I had told her I would call on her, and I am determined to discover why. She is undeniably flighty and capricious; and I cannot decide whether the inconsistencies in her behaviour are part of the usual female psyche or something to do with her distrust of Violet, or whether they have deeper significance.'

'You have a great deal to say on the subject of Miss Manning. She sounds a most fascinating character,' observed Bridget dryly.

'I assure you she is nothing of the kind. Far from fascination, I feel annoyance when I think of her. She disappears whenever I want to see her.'

'Have you heard anything from her since your escapade with Cobb?'

'She sent me a letter with details of what she had learned from Violet.'

'And that did not satisfy you?'

Joshua reflected for a moment. 'Most of what she told me I had learned from Cobb already. There was much she could have said that she did not. She was decidedly vague on the reason for her departure and said nothing at all of why she wanted to visit a nursery.'

'What do you think her reasons were?'

'Lizzie Manning has a scoundrel for a brother. I met him the other night. If it wasn't Cobb who attacked me yesterday, it was most likely Arthur Manning. He has ruined his family as a result of gambling losses and has apparently taken it upon himself to leave the family house for shame. As I said before, Lizzie has never mentioned him to me, which shows, I suppose, she is ashamed of him. It would not surprise me to learn a misadventure of some sort had befallen him and that was why she left.'

'And the visit to the nursery?'

'The reason for that is easier to divine. Her friend Caroline Bentnick has a theory that Hoare was murdered by being poisoned by unripe pineapple. I think Lizzie went to consult an expert in the subject to see if such a thing might be possible.'

At this point they arrived at Richmond Gate and entered the park. The road passed through plantations of ancient oak and beech and ranked saplings of various size and form. Here and there herds of deer grazed on long tussocks of sun-bleached grass. Bridget was mesmerized by the scenery. She had never imagined there were so many tints of green and, enthralled by all she saw, she fell temporarily silent.

Joshua could not pretend any great knowledge or interest in the subject of horticulture. To his way of thinking, nature was all very fine when viewed through the frame of a window, or on a promenade through a park, but he had never comprehended the urge to meddle with it. People, with their multitude of history, thought, hope, character, weakness and strength were what intrigued, bemused and baffled him. That was why people were always what he wanted to paint.

Nevertheless, the view was prettier than he thought it would be, and the ancient oaks particularly impressed him. Perhaps this was why, having echoed Bridget's sentiments on the sublime character of the surroundings, it wasn't people on which he began to muse, but on the more urgent matter of pineapples.

Granger had said he believed Cobb had cut an unripe pineapple, although he did not *see* him cut the fruit. Having just sent Cobb to his lodgings, and feeling far from happy about the decision, Joshua was anxious to convince himself of Cobb's innocence. Assuming the fruit had been used to poison Hoare, who else might have done such a thing? Both Sabine and Violet knew pineapples were poisonous, though Sabine, who was constantly coming and going in the pinery, seemed more probable.

But how likely was it that pineapples had anything to do with Hoare's death? From Caroline's account, pineapples brought about miscarriage and were used as a purgative, but they weren't fatal. And yet scores of plants that grew readily in the garden certainly were fatal; Joshua was no expert, yet even he knew certain narcissus, nightshade, yew, reeds and aconites were all capable of killing Hoare very effectively. Why, then, would anyone bent on murder bother to use a plant that might or might not kill his or her victim? Why not

252

use something that was definitely lethal? Or was the answer perfectly obvious? Pineapple had been used precisely because it was *not* lethal.

Just as he came to this conclusion the carriage turned a sharp bend. Joshua found himself jolted close to Bridget, so that he pressed against her soft arm and could smell the scent of rosewater behind her ears. A minute later the carriage straightened and so did he. In that moment he was struck by how pleasant his proximity had been. Bridget was no longer an encumbrance; even her questions did not irk him as Lizzie Manning's did. On the contrary, she aroused feelings of warmth. Perhaps he would put her on the second stage to London, not the first.

It was then that he remembered something less pleasant: the piece of news he had still to tell her concerning Cobb. But, before he had time to broach the subject, Bridget's contemplation, interrupted by the same jolt, abruptly ceased and a further bout of questions tumbled forth.

'What attempts have you made to discover the claimant to the necklace?'

His guilty feelings regarding Cobb being at the forefront of his mind, Joshua answered with as much candour as he could muster. 'Hoare must have known, but since he is dead I cannot ask him. Cobb could not tell me. Mr Hoare's senior partner, Enoch Crackman, knows but so far refuses to say until he has permission of the person concerned. When I return to London I will call on him again.'

'Doesn't Herbert know?'

'He claims not. But I believe that, despite her claim to the contrary, Sabine knows, and that she recently visited her in London to reach some sort of compromise.'

Bridget leaned towards him in the carriage and put her hand on his arm. The gesture felt curiously natural. 'Are you sure Cobb was telling the truth?'

'He had every appearance of doing so.'

'But Cobb has been engaged in this case for some time –

months, if not years. The client must have paid him during that time. He *must* know who she is.'

'Not necessarily. I wager it was Crackman who engaged Cobb, and who paid him too. Such arrangements are far from uncommon,' said Joshua, in a voice of authority. 'Cobb probably never knew who was behind the claim. He told me Charles Mercier's mistress, Emma Baynes, married on her return to this country. Her child probably took the stepfather's name. Their identity has doubtless been closely guarded to avoid embarrassment to the daughter, who after all must now be of marriageable age.'

Bridget looked pensive. 'Cobb said he came to pursue the case, but Hoare had been employed here to take care of the London side of things. Cobb did not have much of a reason to come to England, did he?'

Joshua swallowed uneasily. He had to admit that on the surface things looked black against Cobb, and bearing in mind Cobb's present whereabouts he could hardly avoid feeling sheepish. 'He implied it was his affection for Violet that brought him. That aside, Cobb's true motive may have been pecuniary gain. As well as being beautiful, Violet is an eligible young woman. Once her mother marries Herbert Bentnick she will be well provided for, with or without the necklace.'

He fell silent as he mentally drew the threads of his argument to its inevitable, unwelcome, conclusion. Cobb had several motives to want Hoare dead. Hoare knew but refused to name the claimant of the necklace and, furthermore, he stood between Violet and Cobb. With another lawyer watching him, Cobb hadn't the earlier freedom he had enjoyed in Barbados to persuade Violet to respond to his attentions. Or perhaps he did not need to persuade Violet. Perhaps she was a willing conspirator. She might have told Cobb that unripe pineapple was harmful but that it wouldn't kill; they could use it as a means of making Hoare ill so that he would be forced to retire back to London. Hoare arrived at the inn and Cobb persuaded him to eat the fruit, disguising it somehow or other.

When Hoare was taken ill, Cobb transported him to the pinery, to disguise his involvement. Hoare was sick enough to lose consciousness. He might not have died but for a further misfortune. Joshua recalled Granger's confession. The boy in charge of regulating the temperature in the pinery had fallen asleep that night. The ground grew hotter than it should. The heat had been sufficient to kill Hoare.

No sooner had he reached this unpalatable conclusion than Joshua dismissed it. His hypothesis was obviously flawed. Why would Cobb need to take Hoare to the pinery if he didn't expect him to die? Some other person must have been involved whom Hoare expected to meet at the pinery. Joshua recalled Cobb's assertion that Hoare had gone to a rendezvous in his place. Assuming that much was true, who was the rendezvous with? Violet might have arranged a nocturnal rendezvous with Cobb, perhaps intending to kill him to prevent him pestering her. But she would not have confused Cobb with Hoare.

Joshua struck his head with his bandaged hand at his own confusion.

Bridget observed the gesture. 'What is it?' she asked.

He released the reins a little. He had to tell her sooner or later. Now was as good a time as any. 'I have a confession to make that you may not take kindly. When I met Cobb by the side of the road yesterday, I was not myself. I believed at first that he had attacked me, but he persuaded me otherwise, saying he lived in fear for his life and that everything he possessed was in his bag which I had taken. I was muddle-headed and gave him the benefit of the doubt. On reflection I am less certain than I was of his innocence. Although it still seems unlikely that he killed Hoare, he nevertheless had plenty of reasons to wish him out of the way and I cannot be sure he didn't have a hand in it somehow or other. But in short, my confession is this: I gave Cobb a key to my rooms and insisted he make himself at home there until I returned with his bag. I have several more matters to ask of him. I wanted to have him where I could interrogate him whenever I needed to. Furthermore, his health is fast deteriorating. I confess I felt sorry for him.'

Joshua naturally expected to see Bridget grow hysterical at this information. In letting Cobb, a possible murderer, have entry to his rooms he had permitted him entry to her home too.

Bridget rose immeasurably in his estimation by her response. She did not cry or reprimand him. Any terrors she felt were carefully controlled. Her voice was quietly determined. 'In that case,' she said, 'should you not return to London to question him?'

'I cannot, Bridget. If I run away back to London now, Sabine and Herbert will read it as a sure signal of my guilt.'

'But assuming you are correct in thinking Cobb is innocent, you may be in grave danger here. You have been attacked once. Next time you may not escape so lightly. Tell Herbert you believe the answers lie in London and he will let you go.'

'I will come directly. But first I have matters to attend here.'

She furrowed her brow with concentration. 'Then, for my mother's sake, I must return straightaway.'

As he turned the chaise to head for the Star and Garter, Joshua observed Bridget sitting erect, looking away into the far distance. Her green eyes had misted over in deep contemplation; she looked unusually pale and serious, and although he hazarded the nature of her preoccupation was her concern for her mother, she said not a word, and thus he was not entirely convinced he hazarded correctly.

# Chapter Thirty-two

Since there was still half an hour before the London stage was due to depart, they decided to leave the chaise and stroll across the grassy slopes of Richmond Hill to the stage post at the Star and Garter. The sky was a clear ultramarine blue, with only a few strands of white cloud suspended low over the horizon. The town, with its red roofs and chimneypots and thoroughfares and dense clumps of trees, spread out like a map beneath them. The river, a great serpent of silver, cut its way between the habitations.

As they turned in the direction of the inn, about fifty yards from the gate Joshua caught sight of two figures – a man and a woman – walking ahead in the same direction. Unthinkingly, he found himself gathering pace and, drawing closer to the two figures, his suspicions were confirmed. The woman was small and slender, dressed in a drab grey cloak and plain straw bonnet; russet curls whipped about its brim. The gentleman with whose arm her own was entwined was unusually tall and handsomely clad, in a blue coat and breeches and a black tricorn hat.

'What has got into you, Mr Pope? Are you determined to lose me?' said Bridget indignantly when she caught up with him. 'Why do you stare so at that couple? Are you acquainted with them?'

'Forgive me,' Joshua said, suddenly recalling where he was and slowing. 'The suddenness of seeing those two scattered my senses. In answer to your question, unless I am very much mistaken that is Elizabeth Manning out walking with Francis Bentnick.'

'Am I to infer that you are offended because you entertained hopes in that direction yourself?' said Bridget curtly.

'Certainly not,' Joshua said emphatically. 'If I seem annoyed it is only because she must know I have things to say to her, and she certainly has matters to discuss with me, yet for the past three days she has avoided me – deliberately, I believe. Would you excuse me for one moment?'

Before she could remonstrate, Joshua had left Bridget trailing on the path as he spurted swiftly ahead until he caught up with Lizzie and Francis. 'Good day to you, Miss Manning and Mr Bentnick,' he said, in mock gentility. 'A thousand pardons for disturbing you. I trust you are enjoying your quiet promenade? What a delightful surprise to run into you.'

'Mr Pope!' said Lizzie Manning, withdrawing her arm from Francis's without a flicker of awkwardness. 'The very man we wanted to find! I came to speak to you this morning on the subject of our drawing lessons. I was disappointed to find you absent. Caroline said you had gone out with Miss Bridget Quick, your landlady's daughter. We were heading in the direction of the Star and Garter to look for you. Where is your companion? Is that her coming now?'

Just then Bridget came up, red-faced and puffing with exertion. Mud had splattered the hem of her dress. The breeze had dishevelled her hair. But what did a few specks of mud and a tangled ringlet or two matter? Bridget had passed an entire morning in his company without once disappearing.

Having effected brisk introductions, Joshua turned to Lizzie. 'I haven't time to talk now. Miss Quick has the stage to catch and I want to see her safely on it. However, I would be most grateful for a little of your precious time at the earliest convenience. Shall we say later this afternoon? I have something to tell you that concerns your brother.'

Lizzie's sudden flush of astonishment, anger even, wasn't

missed by the observant eye of Joshua Pope, and it brought him unmistakable satisfaction. 'My brother! What do you know of Arthur? Have you seen him?' she stammered.

He raised a quizzical brow and gave her an enigmatic half-smile. 'That, Miss Manning, is what I wish to discuss. But for now the subject must wait. Enjoy your promenade. Good day to you both.'

He could sense her infuriation but he ignored it. He raised his hat, took Bridget by the arm, and they walked briskly away in the direction of the London stage.

# Chapter Thirty-three

Wilderness House, the home of Lancelot Brown, was an inappropriately named yet pleasant-looking red-brick building, situated a few hundred yards west of the Lion Gate to Hampton Court. The house was of modest dimensions and unremarkable style, with little in its outward appearance to suggest it was the home of a legend of landscape design. Were the wistaria and ivy clambering about its façade more cleverly pruned than others in the street? Were the topiaries of yew and box better shaped? Joshua's untrained eye discerned nothing notable about them. And what, indeed, did he care for such things? He had modified certain of his preconceptions, but he had not altered his belief that landscapes and trees were all very well to pass an hour or make a journey less tedious, and gardens were pleasant to stroll in, but people were what he desired to paint.

He had come here after a sudden burst of inspiration had struck him as soon as Bridget had stepped onto the London stage. His meeting with Francis Bentnick and Lizzie Manning had placed them uppermost in his mind. Lizzie's reaction to his comment regarding her brother was most revealing. Joshua knew Arthur Manning was somehow embroiled in this business. The sound of his laughter at the mention of Cobb's name still reverberated in his memory. He had a niggling feeling that one person alone could not have been responsible for these events. Even if Cobb *had* killed Hoare, his feeble condition made it unlikely he was responsible for the attack on Joshua at the barn. Nor did it seem probable he had stolen into Astley unobserved and removed the necklace. He was not familiar with the layout of the house. How would he have known where Sabine's room was, let alone where she secreted her jewels? Arthur Manning, on the other hand, though he had no reason to wish Hoare dead, was strong, violent of temper, knew the house well and had admitted he had entered Joshua's room while he was asleep. And having ruined his family, Arthur was desperate for money. Since Joshua's reputation rested on the necklace, finding Arthur must be his first priority. The question was: how?

According to the housekeeper at Barlow Court, Arthur was not living at home. Was he, then, hiding somewhere in the grounds of Barlow Court? Or was he lurking in the grounds at Astley? Joshua was in no mood to contemplate a search, which might take hours and expose him to another vicious attack. He had no wish to involve Granger, for that might cause gossip which would reach Sabine and Herbert before he was ready. And in any case Granger had no knowledge of Barlow Court. But after pondering the matter for a few minutes more, a way to avoid all these obstacles came to him.

He recalled Granger telling him the gardens at Barlow Court and Astley had both been designed by Lancelot Brown and that the great man lived nearby at Kew. Who better than Brown to suggest plausible hiding places? Joshua felt greatly pleased by his inspiration. Quite apart from helping him discover the whereabouts of Arthur Manning, there was a chance Brown might remember something of further interest pertaining to the relevant gardens. And, since Brown no longer had anything to do with either household, there was no danger that word of his visit would reach Herbert or Sabine or any of the other involved parties.

Joshua knocked upon the door to Wilderness House and was

shown into a small hallway with four doors leading off and a wide flight of stairs rising to the floor above. A servant ushered him to a small library at the rear. The room was simple but comfortably furnished with a large desk, a folio chest filled with papers, and a pair of leather-upholstered armchairs. One wall was lined from floor to ceiling with books; the others were panelled in oak. Prints of sublime landscapes – parsley trees, craggy rocks and mountains, with the occasional lake or coastal view for relief – were scattered about the wall. A portrait of the great man himself hung over the chimney piece, and showed a bright-eyed, florid face with a nose of disproportionate grandeur and a smallish receding chin.

Having surveyed his interior surroundings, Joshua moved to the window, which gave onto a small walled garden consisting of a lawn, an apple tree and a couple of rose bushes. In a niche at the end stood a life-size marble statue of a nymph holding a sheaf of flowers with flowers emerging from her lips.

Joshua knew Brown's reputation was every bit as elevated as his own. Like him, Brown sat down at the table of every lord in the land. He had the ear of kings and queens and princesses. And how had he accomplished this feat? Not by painting with sublime inspiration, not by sculpting or architecture, or any form of artistic genius Joshua recognized. He had arranged the gardens of palaces at Kew and Kensington and Windsor. He had strayed further – to Stowe, Petworth, Burghley, Warwick, Blenheim and Alnwick. In each of these estates – and countless others, great and small, besides – his brilliant contribution came down to this: softening straight lines and formality with arbours and Elysian Fields and lakes and gentle green vistas, which resembled nothing so much as what was there before the formality was introduced. Thus as Joshua peered from the window the question that he asked himself was: can this be art?

'Behold the nymph Chloris transformed to goddess Flora!' said a booming voice that interrupted Joshua's unresolved contemplation.

Joshua spun round to see a man, aged about fifty, jowly-faced, with bright boot-button eyes set at a soulful slant, offering him his hand.

Brown gripped Joshua with a firmness that made him wince. 'Good morning, Mr Pope. I have heard of you by reputation. I am honoured to make your acquaintance.'

'The honour is all mine,' said Joshua decorously. 'And to return to your charming statue, I take it that Zephyr, who transformed the nymph into the goddess of flowers, is you!'

Brown laughed at Joshua's wit and clapped him on the back. 'What a delightful notion! The figure was given to me by one of my patrons. No one else has interpreted it thus. If only I could transform all my patrons to Flora I would indeed be the happiest man alive. As it is, I content myself with their gardens. Now, tell me, Mr Pope, what brings you here?'

Joshua recited the story he had prepared. He was staying at Astley, to paint Herbert Bentnick's marriage portrait, and had grown friendly with Lizzie Manning, who had recently done him a great favour. Since he had learned of her interest in horticulture, and pineapples in particular, he had thought to buy her two dozen pineapple plants. Would Mr Brown object to advising Joshua where he thought it best to position the frames for this purpose?

'Pineapples, that most redoubtable of fruits!' Brown exclaimed. 'The holy grail of every gardener in the civilized world. What would you say, Pope, if I indiscreetly let slip that, in addition to my handsome salary as His Majesty's master gardener, I am paid a fee of a hundred pounds for raising those luscious plants?'

'I should say it reflects the fact that you are held in the highest regard by His Majesty. And I should repeat what I have learned from Mrs Mercier and Mr Granger, the head gardener at Astley. Pineapples are the most fragrant and delicious of fruits. In form they are pleasing to artists and craftsmen of every medium. To grow the fruit in this climate challenges any gardener's skill. Can we wonder that they are so coveted, or that anyone able to produce one for the table is held in the highest regard.'

Brown snorted. 'That is hokum and we both know it. Fashion, Pope – frivolous fashion – that is what has put a hundred pounds into my purse this year and last year, and the one before that, and will do so in the future, I dare say. Please don't imagine I believe it worth this elevated price. And what is the impetus behind this fashion, when there are cherries and apricots and peaches and grapes and apples and plums and pears galore that will grow with the minimum of fuss and taste equally delicious?'

'Man's desire for novelty? Human curiosity?' answered Joshua. He felt astonished by Brown's thoughts but drawn to his jovial candour.

'No, sir. It is the desire for the unattainable. The yearning for what is impossible. Consider this, Mr Pope. I give them lakes and copses as beautiful as any that existed in the king-dom of Flora. They applaud me for my achievements. Yet give them the choice and before we know it they'll be demanding palm trees and bananas in place of oaks and elms and ash.' Brown burst into a gale of laughter, partly occasioned, Joshua suspected, by the astonishment on his own face.

'I never thought you would disapprove of the fashion for pineapples. Forgive me, I had no intention of giving offence. If that is how you feel I can't expect you to assist me.'

'Stay awhile,' said Brown. 'My private views don't mean I won't help you. I have yet to fall out with a single one of my employers, Pope, but that doesn't mean I agree with them. I will confess to you, while I grow pineapples for His Majesty, I see them as an embodiment of much that is foolish in society today. Simplicity in nature, as in most aspects of life, is in-finitely preferable to conspicuous display. I am most successful where I am invisible.'

'Is not civilization built upon advance, whether artistic, scientific or in the landscape? Can you say that foreign plants and trees have not enlivened our gardens?'

'They are all very well in their place, Mr Pope. But I prefer to improve the *natural* beauties, rather than import *foreign* ones. To continue your allusion, I believe, since my work is set in England, it is best read in English too. Phrases in other languages, whether from the Indies, or Africa, are unnecessary and incomprehensible. But, as I said before, I always keep my patrons happy. Why shouldn't Miss Manning have a pine-apple pit at Barlow Court if she so desires one? I believe I have copies of the drawings for her gardens somewhere here. Let us consult them.'

Brown stood up and went to a mahogany folio chest and began to open its drawers one by one and rummage about in them. A short while later he extracted a large cloth-bound folio and brought it to a library table that stood in the centre of the room. Inside was a large drawing folded into three, and several smaller sheets on which were details such as a planting of trees around the shore of a lake. He unfolded the large drawing and pointed to various features dotted over it. 'Now you see, Mr Pope, to continue our literary metaphor further – here is a comma, there a capital letter, there an exclamation mark and here is a new chapter.' With this he took a new sheet. 'And all of it is, you will see, written in our native tongue, so you and I, and anyone else for that matter, can easily read it.'

The smaller page showed the kitchen garden placed at the rear boundary of the house, on the eastern corner. 'I confess, Pope, this situation for a pine pit is not ideal. It would be best set to the south, so it gains maximum benefit from the sun. But here the only wall facing south is taken with a vine, upon which Miss Manning insisted, having heard of the plan to plant one at Hampton Court.'

'I gather Miss Manning is something of an enthusiast in horticulture?'

'Miss Manning? I agree, she was remarkable – someone of enthusiasm, imagination, intellect and ambition.' He replied with the same goodwill in his voice as earlier in their conversation.

Emboldened, Joshua pressed further. '*Was?*'

'Her circumstances changed and, inevitably, that altered her.'

'Do I gather, then, you know about her brother Arthur?'

A wistful expression came to Brown's eyes as he looked at the ceiling and considered before replying. 'Not all my employers are the owners of great estates. I have worked most satisfactorily for some who possessed less than half an acre. Anyone may have the misfortune to find themselves in financial difficulties. I tell you in confidence that at present the Earl of Northampton finds himself in an awkward predicament. Work underway at his estate Castle Ashby has recently been suspended. To return to Miss Manning – I designed this scheme for Barlow Court several years ago and told the dear girl she could execute as much of it as she chose each year. We were proceeding quite happily, until some months ago I received a most poignant note from her.'

He stopped for a moment and looked at Joshua quite sharply for a moment. 'I still have the note in my possession. Perhaps it would not be indiscreet of me to tell you what it said.'

'As God is my witness, it will go no further,' Joshua said, raising his palm as if taking the oath at the King's Bench.

Brown rose and rummaged among a file of papers in his desk, and at length removed a small folded letter from a bundle tied with a green ribbon. He took up an eyeglass, perused the paper, then looked up at Joshua.

'Very well then, I won't read it to you, it's too personal for that, but I'll tell you broadly what it says. The letter is dated in April this year. It declares she is much obliged for the favour I did her in coming and making such inspired suggestions for improvements to the gardens at Barlow Court. But, owing to an unfortunate encounter between her dear brother and a stranger of dubious integrity, regrettably she can no longer continue, our schemes must wait. She does not blame her dear brother – she remains fond of him as ever – she

266

only rues the dreadful fate that led him to take the actions he did. Touching, is it not?' said Brown, looking up, having reached the end of the page.

'Very affecting. I had no idea she was so devoted to her brother. She has barely mentioned him to me. Indeed, he seems to have entirely disappeared from the scene.'

Brown shook his head. 'Her loyalty and devotion to Arthur cannot be called into question.'

'Did you ever meet him?'

'Once or twice, but only to pass the time of day. We never engaged in conversation. His interests lay some distance from the parterre and potting shed, I hazard.'

Joshua's eyes gleamed brightly. His brain was now cantering ahead like a horse that has unseated its rider. Lizzie's letter surprised him. Her relationship with her brother surprised him. He wanted to speak candidly to Brown. But could he trust him enough to speak openly to him? What had he to lose, apart from possibly riling this amiable man and leaving his house with a flea in his ear?

'Mr Brown, I am going to speak to you with the same openness you have shown to me. If what I have to say offends you, forgive me. I speak from the highest of motives, I assure you.'

Brown sat back in his chair, steepling his fingers beneath his chin. He indicated that Joshua should proceed.

'In the past week, while I have been staying at Astley there has been a suspicious death in the pinery. I met Arthur Manning in the grounds of Astley a few nights ago. He struck me as something of a scoundrel. I don't believe he was involved in the death, but he may have taken a valuable necklace. I have been implicated in its disappearance and the only way to prove my innocence is by recovering it. In truth, the purpose of my visit is not to discuss pineapples, but to see if I might persuade you to help me clear my name and discover the truth. What I want to know is this: is there anywhere in the grounds of Barlow Court or Astley you think Arthur

267

Manning could conceal himself and quite possibly the necklace as well?'

Brown gazed at Joshua, scratching his head. A bemused smile slowly stretched over his face, though behind it Joshua detected his astonishment at what he had just heard. 'I can scarce credit a member of the Manning family would comport himself in such a way. But who am I to judge a man after two cursory meetings with him? If all you want is to reach the truth, and save your skin, I see no reason why I should not help you. A hiding place you're after, is it? Well then, let me see.'

He turned back to the large plan and unfolded it. 'Here is the river; there's a summerhouse, but that's of no consequence since it floods every high tide. Over here is a small folly – but, again, it would make a poor hiding place: there are no windows or doors. No, in short, there is nowhere I can think of in the grounds of Barlow Court where a man might conceal himself. If it was Astley, on the other hand, I might suggest a few.'

'That is also a possibility,' said Joshua. 'But why do you think it more likely?'

'For one thing, the park is ten times the size. Let me show you, my friend.' With that, he went back to his folio chest and withdrew a folder with *Astley Park* emblazoned upon it. He unfolded the plan; the sheet was far larger than that for Barlow Court, measuring perhaps eight feet across. When he opened it the sheet flopped over the sides of the desk and fell to the floor. The lake formed a long, gently meandering strand across a half of the surface; in places where it widened there was a sliver of green to denote an island. Carefully marked around its borders were clumps of trees and shrubs. Elsewhere were marked paths, fishponds, enclosures for fowl, bridges, gateways, temples, fountains, the cascade, and further splashes of green of varied form and size denoting plantings. In one of these, Joshua reflected, he had met Arthur Manning.

Brown took up a ruler and pointed it to the eastern corner of the lake, where a series of blue steps was marked. 'Now, over

268

here is the Temple of Neptune, but it is a local beauty spot where ramblers often walk. I doubt he would hide there, for fear of being noticed.'

'And this?' Joshua said, indicating a craggy outline halfway along the cascade and separated from it by a faint line.

'The grotto. It is a series of tunnels and underground chambers, some natural, some enlarged under my direction. Herbert lost interest in it halfway through and it was never finished. I dare say since then it has scarcely been used. The entrance resembles the mouth of a cave, concealed behind rocks. There are iron gates, which I assume are kept locked to prevent anyone inadvertently wandering in there and becoming lost. The light inside is poor: it would be a gloomy place to hide, and dangerous, too, if he got lost. But if he had been able to gain access to it, a man might live there unnoticed.'

'What are the dangers?'

'Apart from losing himself in the maze of tunnels, there is a risk of drowning. The grotto is indirectly linked to the cascade through this building here, which is also a possible hiding place.' He pointed to an outline at the lake end of the cascade labelled 'Octagon'.

'It was built to disguise the overflow for the lake. It is conceivable, I suppose, for a man to hide in the basement, though that too would be precarious.'

'Why so?'

'Because of the constant changes in the water level of the lake. Assuming the water level remains low, as at present – you will recall there has been no significant downpour for several weeks – the basement would be dry. When the level in the lake rises, that changes very swiftly. The overflow system is designed to reroute the water to the river to prevent the ground around the lake becoming flooded. In winter or in prolonged spells of wet weather the basement is flooded more often than not. Even now, if the weather breaks, only the most foolhardy of men would pass the night there. And if the water rose, it could seep into the grotto. So in either event he would put himself in peril.'

'Do you think Arthur Manning recognizes the dangers of these places?'

Brown looked dubious. 'I don't know, Mr Pope. As I said before, to my knowledge he took little interest in such matters. In any case all this is no more than speculation. Who knows, Arthur Manning may be hiding somewhere else entirely. But if he is in one or other spot and he isn't warned, I fear that before long there may be another death at Astley.'

# Chapter Thirty-four

Joshua returned to Astley as fast as the chaise permitted. But as he rattled over the cobblestones and ruts of Richmond roads, he found that instead of dwelling on the urgent matter of where Arthur Manning was hiding, and whether the necklace was with him, a stream of other thoughts distracted him.

Brown's words echoed and confounded him. The great man seemed untainted by the elevated status he had reached, mentioning no more than a couple of his illustrious patrons, though admittedly one was the king. He aspired to simplicity – the plainness of his dress bore testimony to this desire. Foreign fruits he deemed frivolity; and yet he was willing to accommodate others' opinions and desires. Was there a lesson here for Joshua? Turning gloomily into the gates of Astley, Joshua saw the great porticoed and pedimented entrance ahead of him. Within were paintings by Correggio and Guido Reni, chairs made in Paris, tapestries from Flanders, Italian damask. Was the house richer or poorer on account of it? He couldn't persuade himself that the interiors would be improved without these embellishments. Nevertheless he acknowledged that within the husk of Brown's hyperbole there was a kernel of truth. No one could deny the misfortunes at Astley all stemmed from pineapples.

* * *

271

Francis Bentnick and Lizzie Manning were on the rose terrace outside the drawing room. Joshua saw them as he rounded the corner to leave his carriage at the stables. He felt a flicker of interest seeing the pair seated in companionable silence, reading. This was the second time in recent days he had found them alone engrossed together. Surely this was a sign that so far Lizzie's fears regarding Violet were unfounded, Francis remained true.

Having learned of the most likely hiding places where Arthur might have concealed himself, Joshua had reasoned that the way to avoid further attack (assuming Arthur was his attacker) was to persuade Lizzie Manning to accompany him. Arthur could hardly attempt an assault with his devoted sister present. But Joshua knew it was crucial he put the proposal to Lizzie alone. If Francis discovered the scheme he might grow protective, insist he came too, which, bearing in mind Arthur's unhappy history with the Bentnicks, would only make it harder to lure Arthur out of hiding. The question was how to lure Lizzie away from Francis.

'Good afternoon, Miss Manning, Mr Bentnick.'

Francis looked up and greeted him in a polite but distant manner. Lizzie said not a word. She remained frozen with her book in her hand, her chin set firm, her knuckles white. Joshua presumed the reason for her coolness was that she felt he had offended her when they had met on Richmond Hill. At the time he had felt a sense of satisfaction at having ruffled her. After all, she had irked him by disappearing when he needed her. Now, having learned of her affection for her brother, and formulated his plan, he felt differently. Without her co-operation, Arthur would be harder to find.

He hadn't foreseen this frostiness, but since that was what he encountered he set about thawing it. Bearing in mind Francis's presence, however, he took a circuitous route.

'I am just returned from a visit to Mr Lancelot Brown.'

'Is that so?' said Francis. 'He once was employed here, you know.'

'So I gather,' responded Joshua. 'And at Barlow Court too, I believe?'

Lizzie's head remained bent stubbornly downwards. 'I believe so, yes,' said Francis levelly.

Joshua ignored him and leaned over slightly so that his face approached Lizzie's. He spoke softly, in a voice intended to convey a certain sympathy. 'Miss Manning, the reason I raise this subject is because Mr Brown gave me a message for you. I wonder if I may ask you for a moment in private to deliver it?'

Silence again. Not a word. She pointedly turned her page, making a show of reading, as though oblivious to Joshua's presence. Francis coughed and stood up. Holding out his right arm, he beckoned like a convivial host who wishes to welcome a late-coming guest. 'I think, Pope, it might be best if you and I take a turn together.'

And so, since he could see Lizzie was not about to respond, Joshua followed Francis back down the steps to the path leading from the terrace to the flower gardens. They walked along a wide strip of lawn flanked on either side by trellised roses planted under with clumps of columbine and lavender.

As soon as they were a safe distance from Lizzie, Francis spoke without preamble. 'Mr Pope, you can see that Miss Manning has no desire to speak to you. If you want to know why, I will tell you. It is because you wounded her deeply this morning by your tactless reference to her brother. She is devoted to him but as you know he has brought much shame on her family and she hardly ever speaks of him. Take my advice, Pope: leave the poor girl alone for the time being; and keep off the subject of Arthur. She has enough to endure without you adding to her burdens.'

'It is for that very reason I came,' Joshua said, regarding Francis's handsome and now troubled face with measured caution. 'I sensed I spoke out of turn and wanted to apologize. Moreover, as I said, I have a most urgent message to give her.'

'What is the message? Give it to me if it is so important – and I will pass it on to her.'

Joshua hesitated. He didn't think there was any side to Francis, but he had encountered treachery where he least expected it several times in recent days. Besides, he was determined Francis should not spoil his scheme. 'I know, sir, you are as good as affianced to Miss Manning, but I gave Mr Brown my word I would deliver the message to her and no one else. I will tell you in confidence my message concerns her brother; thus, despite your advice to avoid the subject, I think I am right that she would be eager to hear it.'

The heat was suddenly bothersome to Francis. 'Concerns her wretched brother, does it?' he said, mopping his shiny forehead with a lace-trimmed handkerchief and looking suddenly plum red with the heat.

It was no surprise to see evidence of ill feeling between Arthur and Francis. Arthur had, after all, relieved Caroline of part of her inheritance. While the opportunity presented itself he decided to press the subject further. 'Has Miss Manning said anything about her brother to you?'

Francis shook his head. 'No, but that does not surprise me. You know, I suppose, what he did to my sister – borrowed a sizeable sum with the aim of paying back some of his debts and then lost the lot.'

'He said he was accosted on the road by a highwayman.'

'A very convenient encounter, I would say.'

'D'you have proof the story was a fabrication?'

'He reported nothing to the beadle or the constable, though both were on duty in the town when the assault was supposed to have taken place. Manning is notorious for his love of play. He's the mainstay of half a dozen gambling houses in Richmond. You have only to walk down Brewers Lane and ask anyone in the Magpie or Lilliput, or go to George Street and visit the Black Boy or the Flying Horse, to learn the truth of it.'

'Do you believe him capable of theft?'

'Was not that what he did to my sister?'

'In a sense, I suppose – but might he have taken the necklace?'

Francis shook his head impatiently, as if the subject was a beggar he wanted to be rid of but who followed him none-theless wherever he went. 'I tell you this, Pope – but not a word to Miss Manning. Arthur was fair enough when sober, but for as long as I have known him he has always been a man of dubious character when in drink. It was a bottle of Hollands gin that did for Barlow Court – that and a couple of aces in his opponent's hand, I dare say.'

'Nevertheless, sir, you would do me a great favour if you would tell Miss Manning I wish to tender my apologies, and that I have a message concerning her brother.'

Francis seemed irked that Joshua wasn't more forthcoming. He nodded curtly and returned to the terrace. Joshua strolled the gardens a while longer, wondering what, if anything, Francis would tell Lizzie of their encounter, and what his next move should be. Half an hour later he had resolved that his best course was to assume Francis had said nothing. He would return to find her and apologize profusely, while hinting that he knew where her brother was. This, with any luck, would win her round and they could arrange a rendezvous in private to discuss Arthur.

Joshua returned to the house, intent on pursuing his scheme. He came to the terrace to find that Francis, Violet and Sabine Mercier and Caroline Bentnick were all seated beneath their parasols, drinking tea in the evening sun. Granger had brought a basket of strawberries and was presently engaged in conversation with Sabine. There was no sign of Lizzie.

Joshua could hardly pass by the assembled party without at least bidding them good afternoon. No sooner had he approached than he found his natural inquisitiveness inflamed. It was most strange to find Francis and Caroline willingly sitting outdoors conversing together with the Merciers as if they were old friends, when Caroline believed Sabine was responsible for the death of her mother, and possibly the death of Hoare as well. Thus, when Caroline

Bentnick began to question him on the whereabouts of Bridget Quick, and how his wounds progressed, he was unable to resist the opportunity to probe.

'Miss Quick returned to London this morning, after we spent a most enjoyable time touring the region. My wrists are not troubling me, though I am impatient to remove the bandages. I dare say you are all busy with final preparations for the ball?'

A shadow darkened Caroline's face. Her eyes flitted in the direction of Sabine and Violet. Then she lowered her gaze to her teacup and stirred it so roughly the whirling liquid spilled into the saucer. 'There's something I have remembered that I wanted to tell you,' said Caroline. 'It concerns Mr Hoare. I will come to you at ten tomorrow morning and examine your bandages. Wait until then before removing them,' she said.

Joshua turned then to Violet, who, from a purely aesthetic point of view, looked as enchanting as a bird of paradise, in a robe of azure blue that matched her eyes. 'Miss Mercier, how well you look in that particular shade. You are a treat for any artist to behold.'

Violet immediately looked towards her mother, blushed and said thank you, in a small voice that suggested she would prefer it if he didn't compliment her in future.

Sabine dropped her teacup into its saucer and shot a pointed look in Joshua's direction. 'I wonder you have time for frivolous compliments, Mr Pope, when there are so many pressing matters to concern you. Need I remind you that you still have a portrait to paint and, more importantly, my necklace to recover? As far as I am concerned, until you accomplish the latter you remain under a cloud of suspicion. I had hoped to have the jewel for Caroline to wear.' She cast a brisk sideways glance in the direction of Caroline Bentnick, who flushed and regarded her hands. 'Apropos of that, I would like a word with you, in private, if you please.'

Sabine rose and led the way to the drawing room. After the warmth of the sunny terrace the interior seemed dark and foreboding. She walked to the chimney piece, above which hung the Gainsborough portrait of Jane Bentnick, and turned to face him. Joshua looked bleakly from the canvas face of the past Mrs Bentnick to the flesh-and-blood visage of the future one. He couldn't help thinking there was some deficiency in Sabine's beauty – was it a lack of warmth, an absence of animation or indeed any expression? He wasn't sure, but neither was he able to contemplate how Herbert could share his bed with this woman. He would prefer to sleep with a statue.

'You are no closer to finding my necklace?' said Sabine.

'I have not forgotten it. But you know, I believe, the matter is wrapped up with the claimant, and until I trace her I can do little more.' Mindful of the letter Marie had shown him from the claimant to Sabine agreeing a meeting, he hoped this might elicit some useful response. A name perhaps.

He was disappointed.

'I told you before that is naught to do with it,' said Sabine crossly. 'The answer to the disappearance lies here, in this house. Yet you have been gadding about all morning and drawn no conclusions. If you cannot tell me something, or at least where you have been, I will assume you are wasting time and not doing all you might. In which case, I will summon Justice Manning, with or without Herbert's say-so. He is due to return late tomorrow. I want my necklace returned in time for the ball.'

Thus cornered, Joshua knew he had to respond. Anger at his own predicament began to smoulder within him. Should he confront her over the letter? It was on the tip of his tongue to do so, but at the last minute something restrained him. How could he mention the letter without revealing how he had found it? He had no desire to lose Marie her position. Yet he must say something. 'I have been to call on Lancelot Brown.'

'Lancelot Brown the landscape gardener? Whatever for?'

'I have only one suspect: Arthur Manning, Miss Manning's brother . . . I believe he may be concealed somewhere in the vicinity. Brown knows every nook and cranny of the grounds.'

'What makes you think it was Manning and not Cobb?'

'I was attacked yesterday. That is how I sustained these injuries.'

'Cobb attacked you before.'

'Yes,' said Joshua, 'but this man was powerful. Cobb is in poor health. I don't believe it was him.'

She didn't appear in the least surprised, although he noticed her gaze didn't meet his but seemed to flash over his shoulder when he said the name. 'And what do you propose to do next?'

'I intend to go in search of Manning.'

Again there followed the rapid flicker of a glance over his shoulder. 'What delays you?'

'Nothing. I intend leaving at the first opportunity. Tomorrow morning at first light I think would be best.'

Sabine thought for a while before she nodded curtly, signalling that their interview was at an end. Her onslaught had begun so swiftly after they entered the drawing room that Joshua had assumed they were alone. It was only now, as she turned to leave, that he heard a faint rustle of papers behind him and spun round.

At the far end of the room, Lizzie Manning was seated at Herbert's writing desk. She appeared to be busy scribbling a note. Sabine must have seen her, but had done nothing to warn him; but then, Sabine cared little for the feelings of others. Lizzie must have sensed their gaze fall on her, for she finished her note, put down her pen, sanded her paper, then stood up and came towards them. She was dressed in her customary grey, though Joshua noticed that the shade was paler and more becoming than usual and it seemed to bring out the warmth in her hair and the lustrous depths of her eyes.

'Mr Pope, how fortuitous you should find me here,' she said, with the slightest of tremors in her bell-like voice. 'I have this note to give you.'

Joshua felt uncharacteristically flustered. The blunder was

no fault of his. He had wanted to keep his suspicions concerning Arthur Manning silent for the time being. It was cruel coincidence that Sabine had forced him to speak out just when she was in the room.

He looked down at his name inscribed upon the thick paper in Lizzie's elegant hand. Lizzie Manning was probably the only one who could help him find Arthur, yet knowing how deeply she cared for him he recognized his gaffe. Every endeavour seemed doomed, foiled by Sabine. She knew who the claimant was and concealed it, and now she had hampered his pursuit of Arthur Manning and his best chance of saving his skin.

# Chapter Thirty-five

*Astley House*
*Sir,*
*I understand from Francis that you wish to tender your apologies*
*and that your message from Mr Brown concerns my brother. I*
*too am anxious that we discuss these matters in private. In order*
*that we may be sure we will not be overheard or interrupted, I*
*will come to your rooms this evening at ten o'clock.*
*Until then I am, sir, yr obedient servant,*
    *Elizabeth Manning*

Joshua had opened the note with trepidation. Reading these
words, his spirits soared. He had feared that after she heard
him betray her brother he would never persuade her to
help him. Yet here she was agreeing to a meeting. This was
good fortune indeed.

Throughout the evening, Joshua noticed that Lizzie seemed
to avoid his eye, although he did not read this as an ominous
sign. She had planned the rendezvous, thus she could not feel
entirely hostile towards him, and once he was alone in her
presence he would explain the reason for his actions.

Anxious to avoid giving further offence, he concentrated
on what he would say, and, thus immersed, joined in little of
the conversation. As soon as was decent after supper Joshua
left the assembled party and went to his rooms to compose

himself. To pass the time until the appointed hour he took up paper and pen and began to write a letter explaining his actions as honestly as he thought wise. This was no easy matter because of the encumbrance of the bandages, and after a short time, frustrated by his clumsy efforts, he gave up and poured himself a glass of claret.

He sipped the wine and watched the hands of his father's timepiece move close to ten. His heart began to race a little faster than usual. When ten chimes rang, he listened for every creak of the floorboard. But the corridor was silent. There was no sound of approaching footsteps, no rustle of skirts or petticoats to indicate that the person he expected was coming to keep her appointment. Another half-hour came and went; the clock sounded eleven; a further half-hour passed. Still there was nothing: no knock, no muffled footsteps, no sound at all apart from the thunderous roar of blood in his ears.

By now, feelings of despair overwhelmed those of hope. A cloud descended. Without Lizzie, without discovering Arthur Manning, there was no reason for Sabine not to summon Justice Manning. He was on the very brink of ruin. Joshua struggled to comprehend why Lizzie had said she would come and then failed to arrive. Was this retaliation for his offence? Or simply her characteristic unreliability? Then in a blinding flash he comprehended: she had written the note *before* she had overheard him betraying Arthur to Sabine. Having heard, she had been infuriated and changed her mind about coming. Knowing how eagerly he wished to speak to her, this was a particular torture devised to punish him for his latest misdemeanour.

Sitting in his chair staring moodily at the door, the heat in the room seemed stifling. He walked to the window, threw it open and gulped the air, but this didn't satisfy him – the air outside was too warm. Instead it brought a great thirst upon him. He turned back to the room, poured himself a second glass of claret and gulped it down, then another and another.

By the time his timepiece sounded twelve the decanter was drained and Joshua was numb with claret and disappointment. He staggered to his feet and discarded his shoes, his velvet breeches, his silk coat, his stockings, cursing the bandages that made this task so slow and dropping each article carelessly on the floor before he unbuttoned or untied the next. Then, dressed only in his shirt, he kicked the heap of clothes out of his way as if it were a pile of rags, extinguished the candle and fell in a stupor on his bed.

Joshua thought that he would never sleep, and yet he must have quickly lost consciousness. Nonetheless the claret proved a poor sedative. At some stage during the hours that followed he became dimly aware of the sound of footsteps, the door catch opening, the floorboards creaking, the soft sounds of someone walking about his room disturbing things in it. He rose slowly to the realms of consciousness, opened his eyes and thought he was still dreaming. Surely his eyes deceived him. By the paltry flame of a nightlight he saw that Lizzie Manning had at last arrived. She was walking about his room, holding the candlestick, dressed only in her nightgown.

'Miss Manning,' he murmured, 'is it you? You kept me waiting half the night.'

She seemed to start at the sound of his voice. Turning towards him, she said after a moment's pause, 'I didn't mean to anger you. Violet kept me talking for hours and then, when I went upstairs and saw the hour, I did not dare call for fear you were already abed. I went to bed myself but then the thought of the message you had concerning my brother kept me from sleeping. So here I am. You may save yourself the trouble of expressing your apology, for I have already read what you wrote and left on the table. I took the liberty of looking at it in case it was sent for me from Mr Brown.'

The nightlight illuminated the underside of her chin and face, leaving much in shadow. Feeling profoundly uncomfortable at her proximity and state of undress, he lowered his eyes. It crossed his mind that the contours of her body would have been visible were it not for the dimness of the nightlight. He could scarcely believe she was there, but he did his best to muster his reasoning faculties and conceal his surprise with a yawn.

She came towards him, placed her hand on top of his and shook him. 'Mr Pope, did you hear what I said? Rouse yourself. I want you to tell me what you know about my brother.'

'I heard you,' said Joshua. He was still so hindered by sleep and wine he could hardly articulate a word and yet already the piercing insight that had earlier deserted him returned with more than its usual force. The oddity of her visit struck him with the force of a fist in the belly. He knew enough of Lizzie Manning to comprehend this nocturnal visit had been carefully orchestrated. Even her flimsy gown was calculated to distract him. The question was: what precisely was her motive?

'I will tell you what I know if you tell me why you have come here at such an uncommonly late hour.'

'Why does that matter?' she said softly. Now that she saw he was fully awake she straightened and began walking about the room. 'Is it not enough that I am here and read what you wrote?'

'But you could have waited till tomorrow morning. That would have been a more proper hour to come calling, surely?'

'I have not seen my brother for two weeks. He said he was going abroad and would send word of where he was, but no letter has come. He is younger than I, and all I have, Mr Pope, apart from my father, who is often called away on business. I know he has his faults, but I feel responsible for him. Moreover I cannot believe him guilty of theft or murder, which is what you have suggested.'

As Joshua regained proper command of his faculties he observed that as she continued her perambulations she appeared to be scanning the walls and furniture, albeit surreptitiously. Was she looking for something? He recalled then his semiconscious impression of there being someone in the room. Why did she not say what she wanted? It wasn't hard to guess what it was.

'It seems to me,' said Joshua sternly, 'that quite apart from your anxieties for Arthur you are here for another reason. Why else would you come to my bedchamber in the dead of night? I hazard you are searching for something.'

'What?' said Lizzie curtailing her searching to look at him as if he were suggesting something quite preposterous. 'I have not the faintest notion what you mean.'

'I presume the object of your interest is the bag belonging to Cobb?'

Lizzie halted. She shrugged, then, half-smiling, approached him. 'Very well. If you want to know why, I will tell you. It occurs to me there may be more contained in Cobb's bag than we realized. If the necklace is inside, it would prove my brother's innocence.'

'Do you think I haven't looked? What a fool you must consider me, Miss Manning.'

There was a pause as she stood over him and met his gaze. Joshua caught a gleam of something in her eye before she turned her head away. What was it he saw reflected there? Shame? Concealment? Whatever it was, it seemed she had her doubts about Arthur too.

She positioned herself on a chair not far from the bed. 'Please tell me all you know concerning my brother, and what you have done with Cobb's bag.'

Joshua sensed he was on dangerous ground and that unless he told her what she wanted to know she might leave, and then he would lose his best chance of finding Arthur and surviving the encounter. 'I gave the bag back to Cobb,' he lied, 'but not before I searched it thoroughly. And so, I believe, did your brother. I met him three days ago in the grounds by the lake. He told me he had come to my room one night. Neither of us found anything in it.'

'You saw Arthur here?'

'Yes, as I said, in the grounds.'

'And was he well? Where is he staying?' The relief in her voice was unmistakable.

'He seemed quite well, though perhaps a little inebriated. He didn't say where he was staying. That was why I called on Brown.'

'I do not understand. What was the message you had from Brown?'

'It's not a message in a straightforward sense, it is something I learned from him. I went to visit Mr Brown because I believed your brother might have stolen the necklace and be hiding with it at Barlow Court.'

'Impossible. He may be misguided, but he is not a thief. And if he had the necklace, why did he search your room?'

'Perhaps he was looking for something else of value to him.' Joshua paused, waiting for some furious reaction or denial, but when there was none he assumed he was correct and wondered what it might be. 'Brown's conclusion was that it would be impossible for him to conceal himself for any length of time at Barlow Court. However, he also pointed out there were two suitable places a man might conceal himself at Astley. Considering my recent conversation with your brother took place in these grounds, I think it is a possibility worth investigating.'

'What places did he suggest?'

'The grotto and the basement beneath the octagon tower that houses the overflow chamber for the lake. According to Brown, both places are perilous if the weather breaks and a storm arrives. That is why I believe we should go together to find him and warn him.'

The whites of her eyes gleamed. Joshua heard her sharp intake of breath. 'Of course I will come; you need have no fear of that. Shall we go now? Will you get dressed?'

'No,' Joshua said firmly. 'It is out of the question. We will see nothing in the dark and only endanger ourselves. And in any case the weather tonight is fine. Even if he is there he will

285

come to no harm. We will wait till first light. I will knock at your bedchamber door.'

After some moments Lizzie concurred with this arrangement. And so with no further discussion she left his room. Joshua tossed and turned, pondering the motive for her nocturnal visit. Did she really believe the necklace was in Cobb's bag? Or was there something else it contained? He had thoroughly examined every object in it twice and there seemed nothing untoward. Nevertheless, the thought that he might have overlooked something bothered him. It was some time before he slept.

As soon as the first fingers of dawn began to illuminate the room, Joshua opened his eyes and saw that several things were not as they had been the night before. The clothes that he guiltily recalled kicking under the bed had been picked up and now lay piled on a chair. The papers on his writing table were disarranged. Several of his possessions – his father's timepiece, his pocket book, and a brush and comb left on the dressing chest – had been moved. The bottom drawer was slightly open. The door to the linen press in which his clothes were stored stood ajar.

He realized instantly what this signified: Lizzie had not been taken in by his lie that the bag wasn't here. She must have returned again and searched the room more thoroughly while he slept. Neither of them trusted the other. He shifted his gaze in the direction of the washstand that hid the closet wherein he had secreted Cobb's bag. It was with relief, and a surge of triumph too, that he saw the washstand remained exactly where he had left it.

He leapt from his bed, resolving to ignore the headache pounding in his temples. What had possessed him to drink so much wine? Having poured cold water in the bowl in the washstand, he performed his toilette and felt somewhat revived. He dressed as speedily as his injuries allowed, choosing plain black breeches, a white linen shirt (leaving the cuffs unbuttoned), and his blue everyday topcoat. Then, having tied back his hair with a ribband, he went to rouse Lizzie Manning and begin the search for her brother.

# Chapter Thirty-six

It was after six by the time Joshua and Lizzie stepped outside. Dawn had lifted, although the air remained still and heavy. A large orange sun hung low in the sky and the western horizon was fringed with mounds of purple clouds. A few swallows darted about, dipping low over the fishpond to drink, or catch the fragile insects that hovered there. Hedgerows and shrubs were alive with the shrill sound of bird song, which seemed only to emphasize the strained silence between Lizzie and Joshua.

Lizzie's eyes, appearing darker and more brooding than usual, had purplish circles beneath them. She looked innocent and fragile, which only went to show, he thought ruefully, how deceptive appearances could be. Even when they were side by side on the path he was aware that she walked as far from him as possible. He sensed hostility emanate from her.

Joshua felt his headache worsen. 'The air feels uncommonly oppressive,' he said. 'It is well we have come early: the weather might break soon.'

She glanced at the heavens, screwing up her eyes slightly, as if to verify the truth of what he said. 'In that case, we shouldn't waste any time in finding my brother,' said she curtly. Then: 'Not that way. It will be quicker by this path.'

She turned at right angles from the track Joshua was following, taking another, which appeared to lead towards a dense copse of trees. Joshua's earlier feelings of confidence, brought on by the fact she had tried and failed to find Cobb's bag, were now interspersed with rumblings of irritation. His headache made him unusually short-tempered. He was tempted to ask what she meant by her uncivil tone. Yet, remembering how important her presence might be, and to what lengths she had gone to pursue her aim, he ordered himself to act benevolently and say nothing.

'Have you been to the grotto before?' he questioned her instead. 'Are you certain this is the best path?'

'I have heard of it often enough and since I know this garden almost as well as my own I am sure I will be able to find it.'

The serpentine path Lizzie had chosen now veered away from the lake, traversed a small woodland plantation, and then, to his chagrin, turned back towards the left side of the water, where the cascades and grotto were situated. Proximity to the water speedily distracted Joshua from all other considerations. A wretched hollow feeling gripped the pit of his stomach. He clenched his jaw and looked as his feet as a way of containing his fears, but he remained unsettled – so much so that when the path turned a sharp bend, and he came face to face with the head gardener, he nearly walked straight into him.

Granger was carrying what appeared to be a small scythe in one hand and a bundle of rooted box cuttings in the other. The sight of him going about his everyday business temporarily distracted Joshua and brought him to his senses. 'Good morning, Mr Granger. I wonder to see you in this part of the garden so early.'

Granger bowed slightly and gave a wry smile, which seemed to stretch the scar on his cheek as taut as a violin string. He looked Joshua straight in the eye, but if he was surprised at seeing the two guests out so early he betrayed not a jot of it. 'My cottage is two hundred yards in that direction. I am on my way to my office in the kitchen garden.'

There was an awkward silence while Granger toyed with the ends of his cuttings and Joshua, surveying the shrubbery over his shoulder, wondered how little he could say to allay Granger's suspicions. Plainly he would have to offer some explanation for their early-morning excursion.

'We were on our way to visit the cascade and grotto,' said Lizzie, intervening, as if waiting any longer was unbearable. 'Mr Pope was curious to see them – he wonders about putting some such natural yet picturesque feature in the background of his painting. He tells me the light at early morning is advantageous for an artist's needs. And, besides, I thought it might make a pleasant surprise for Mr Bentnick and Mrs Mercier. So if you will excuse us, Mr Granger, we'll be on our way before the early light is gone.'

Joshua was all too aware that this was a lame excuse. Granger might well have asked why, if art was his purpose, Joshua had apparently brought no drawing materials with him. And yet, perhaps he understood he had intruded in a matter of some delicacy, for he nodded as if a promenade at six in the morning were the most normal thing in the world.

'In that case, it's most fortuitous we have met. You will require a key to enter both places; the grotto has been kept locked for many months now. As you know, Miss Manning, it was devised by Mrs Bentnick with the assistance of Mr Brown. It was unfinished when she and Mr Bentnick went on their voyage to Barbados; since her death all work has been curtailed. Mr Bentnick told me he can't bear to visit the place, for it reminds him too much of her. As for the octagon house, that is kept similarly secure to discourage vagabonds from entering there in search of shelter and falling into the water.'

'How often do you inspect the buildings, Mr Granger?' said Joshua. He was surprised to hear the buildings were kept locked. This was something he hadn't considered.

'It varies according to circumstances. At present, I go to the octagon house once a fortnight; more, if there's a severe storm and the overflow is in use.' With this, Granger took out from his pocket a large ring on which several keys were suspended. He began to inspect the bundle.

'When did you last visit?'

'I don't remember precisely, but it would have been the last time we had rain. Last week, I believe that was. Why? Is it important to your study?'

Joshua shrugged his shoulders noncommittally, adopting an air of mysterious authority. 'And you noticed nothing untoward?'

'Not that I recall. Should I have done?'

Joshua ignored the question. 'And the grotto? Do you recall your last inspection there?'

'I don't rightly remember. I have little call to go there now the work's been stopped. A month or two ago perhaps.'

Joshua met Lizzie's gaze. 'We should proceed at once, Miss Manning.'

She nodded. 'I said the very same five minutes ago, Mr Pope,' she said tartly.

Granger was still holding two keys in his hand. He seemed reluctant to pass them over. 'Would you like me to accompany you, Mr Pope? It would be a wise precaution, bearing in mind that neither one of you is familiar with the grotto. There was an accident there, some months ago, in which several lives were lost. The tragedy happened when an excess of water entered one of the natural passages and drowned three men. The place is a veritable maze; it is poorly lit and no doubt extremely treacherous in places.'

Lizzie intervened. 'As I recall, after that tragedy a metal gate was installed to prevent the water entering the passages, was it not?'

Joshua noted that her tone towards Granger was cordial, whereas whenever she addressed him she was downright insolent. The realization made his headache and temper worsen.

Granger nodded. 'Even so, miss, if you wandered into one of the tunnels it would be all too easy to lose yourselves for days in the darkness – perhaps, though I shudder to say so, with the direst of consequences.'

Lizzie's face grew pale. Her dark-circled eyes looked larger and more bruised than ever. Joshua wondered if she were faced with real peril her testiness might ebb. He waited, but she showed no sign of accepting Granger's offer. Nevertheless, he wasn't so foolish as deliberately to court danger, even if she wanted to. Speaking in a composed tone that concealed his own trepidation he said, 'In that case, Granger, we most gratefully accept your offer to escort us.'

And so the three of them trouped off together, Granger leading the way, Lizzie and Joshua walking in brisk, but slightly less hostile, silence behind. They skirted the lake then branched off on a trail that led up a steep incline parallel to the cascade. On their right a torrent of water gushed down a series of stone steps and splashed noisily into the lake. The water created a fine mist of droplets that seemed to hang low over the ground like a layer of gossamer. Through this delicate veil Joshua discerned mossy boulders, between which sprouted clumps of reeds, tall grasses and purple flags. Elsewhere the garden was planted as an artful wilderness. Vast granite boulders reared up here and there, interspersed with ferns and willow trees and flowering shrubs, all of which appeared to flourish in the damp atmosphere.

A hundred yards further on, a large rock set upright in the ground like a gigantic black tooth guarded the entrance to the cavern.

'This way,' directed Granger, stepping behind the massive pillar.

A yawning black maw, barricaded by metal railings, confronted them. Through the railings they could see a passage and main chamber beyond. The cavern was roughly oval in form, extending to some thirty feet at the widest point, with a ceiling that soared up perhaps twenty feet. What struck Joshua most, however, was not the cavern's scale but its decoration. Every inch of the walls and ceiling was studded with shells of various form and hue, arranged in mosaic-like concentric circles, spirals and flowers, creating a richness akin to a gentleman's embroidered waistcoat. On one wall a small fountain gushed from the wall into a basin hewn from rock. The surface of the floor and walls around it was encrusted with moss and lichens, and here and there filigree ferns had found crevices in which to grow, giving this corner the appearance of a subterranean garden.

A gate was set in the centre of the railing. At present it was fastened by a large padlock, which didn't appear to have been tampered with, but Joshua reckoned Arthur Manning might easily have entered here. The railings were only about eight feet high and there was a gap of several feet between the top and the roof of the tunnel. It would be simple enough for an agile young man to scale this barrier and clamber over if he had wanted to.

Judging by Granger's lengthy efforts to open it, the lock had not been used for some time. Eventually, after much jiggling and manoeuvring, the mechanism yielded and the hasp came free. The door creaked loudly as Granger pulled it open. Before stepping aside to allow them to pass, he turned and gave Joshua a quizzical look. 'I don't pretend to know your purpose in coming here, Mr Pope, though I surmise it has naught to do with painting. In any event, that's none of my business. But I would remind you, most emphatically, that since we have brought no torches with us, and we have a young lady present, it would be the gravest folly indeed to venture into the tunnels.'

Ignoring his remark, Joshua looked past Granger into the grotto. The interior was shadowy and mysterious; towards the back of the chamber he could see the shadow of a passage meandering into darkness. Joshua shuddered inadvertently, then looked back at Granger. 'Fear not, Mr Granger, we have taken your warnings to heart. We neither of us have any desire to lose ourselves in the labyrinth.' He paused, then added rather condescendingly, 'By the by, Granger, I thank you for your discretion. We have come here on a delicate matter, one that we are not at liberty to discuss.'

'In that case,' said Granger, brightening a little and retreating so that they could pass through, 'I will wait here until you have finished and then escort you to the octagon house.'

'There's no need for that, Mr Granger,' interposed Lizzie sharply. 'You have had Mr Pope's assurance. I know the way to the other building very well. Give us the key, and we will return it to you the instant we have finished with it.'

Granger's furrowed brow registered renewed disquiet. 'There are dangers there too, miss. Suppose one of you should fall in the water?'

'I thank you for your concerns, Granger, but Mr Pope is perfectly capable of seeing where the water is and avoiding it. I am equally familiar with its dangers. You have our assurance we will leave the place secure as we found it.'

Granger smoothed his ruffled brown hair with a hand. His countenance still seemed troubled. Did he honestly believe they wanted to kill themselves? 'Very well. If that is your wish, then I can do no more for you. I will leave you alone.'

With that, he disappeared up the trail that had brought them here. They heard the crunch of his boots as he descended the slope. Some minutes after, when there was no sign of Granger, Joshua wondered whether it was prudent to have sent him away, and half wished he could call him back. If the unpredictable Arthur Manning should suddenly chose this moment to make an appearance, and if he should take against Joshua, the presence of Granger could have proved mightily useful.

Without a further word to each other, Lizzie and Joshua entered the cavern. They stood in the centre and looked up at the roof and its elaborate encrustations, then they circled the perimeter, allowing their hands to brush over the thousands of shells that had been so meticulously collected and arranged. Joshua made no attempt to speak to her – what was the point of courting further put downs? – and instead occupied himself by searching for signs that another person had recently entered here.

The floor was covered in stone flags; there was no trace of any footprint. Joshua didn't know what else he might have expected to find – a piece of clothing, perhaps? – but in any event the chamber was entirely devoid of evidence of any human life. As he searched, Joshua wondered if his protracted silence might provoke Lizzie to say something, to give some hint of her thoughts and feelings, but she remained mute, touring the chamber, staring at the elaborate patterns in brooding silence.

Joshua was disappointed but not entirely surprised they had found no evidence of an interloper. After all, they had made no attempt to arrive quietly, so even if Arthur had been here he would have had time to disappear. He was about to say as much to Lizzie, but then, since she had refused to speak courteously to him all morning, he decided to hold back. He understood the reason for her rudeness. It was always annoying to be refused something you wanted, especially if you were as accomplished at charming people as she was; doubtless her intentions towards her brother were noble. In these respects he felt sympathy. Nevertheless his patience was not limitless. No one, no matter how captivating and clever, triumphed all the time. Her sulks were becoming decidedly tiresome.

On reaching the fountain at the opposite side of the cave from where she stood, he bent forward and lowered his head to drink from the stream of water that fell into the basin below. As he did so, he caught sight of something in the bottom of the bowl. He angled his head to look more closely. No mistake: a small transparent object lay in the bottom of the basin, though he couldn't fathom precisely what it was.

Joshua looked surreptitiously round at Lizzie; she was still frozen in silent contemplation with her back towards him. Without a word, he put his hand into the basin and fished towards the bottom. The water was not much more than a

295

foot deep and he reached it easily, though he soaked the bandages that still bound his wrists in the process. Grasping the object between forefinger and thumb, he brought it to the surface.

Now that he held it in his hand he recognized it instantly. It was one of the crystal brandy glasses he had taken with him on the night when he had met Arthur Manning. He was so astonished to see the glass that, without thinking, he released it and it sank back to the bottom of the basin.

Plainly Arthur Manning had been here. Should he go in pursuit of him immediately? What should he say to Lizzie? What effect would knowing he was somewhere in the vicinity have upon her? Furthermore, Joshua couldn't help asking himself, would his discovery make her treat him a little more civilly? Minutes ticked by. Joshua paced about, scratching his head, rubbing his chin pensively, while all the time Lizzie stood ignoring him as before.

In the end he decided to opt for caution. Assuming Manning had fled into the cavern at the sound of their approach, what chance would he have of apprehending him in the dark tunnels? At the very least, he needed another able-bodied man to support him, and some torches.

Joshua wondered whether or not to explain his reasoning to Lizzie and in the end decided against it. In her present contrary mood she might insist they immediately set out together on a search for him in the maze. If he refused she might go alone, and he would still be obliged to go with her to protect her.

Just as he reached this decision, Lizzie spoke.

'We have seen all there is to see here, Mr Pope. Nothing has presented itself. Let us leave now and hope the other place will be more fruitful.'

'As you wish, Miss Manning,' said Joshua, smiling as he ushered her out of the gate ahead of him with a flutter of relief in his heart.

She barely waited for him to secure the padlock. When he

turned she was already some yards off on a path that meandered through stands of birch trees and led up the incline and along towards the cascade. Joshua sprinted a short way to catch up with her and was vexed when this exertion, coupled with the steepness of the slope, had him puffing and panting like an old man, while she showed no evidence at all of strain.

Some two hundred yards further they clambered down a steep slope and came to the octagon house, a two-storey building nestling between two large willow trees on the corner where the cascade tumbled into the lake. They circled the building. There were no windows at ground level, all of them having been set high up under the eaves, but there was a wide arched aperture on the side nearest the lake. The door, a heavy Gothic structure studded with iron nails, stood on the opposite side. It crossed Joshua's mind that if someone had forced entry here, he would have had to do so by this entrance. Since there were no signs of an intrusion, this indicated that an interloper would have required a key to enter. Bearing in mind the glass he had found, it seemed more probable than ever to Joshua that Arthur Manning was not here but hiding in the grotto. However, since he didn't want to reveal his discovery to Lizzie, he resigned himself to going through the motions of a search.

'The key, if you please, Mr Pope,' said Lizzie imperiously. Joshua stepped forward, frowning as he did so, for by now, despite his earlier resolve, he found it impossible not to be exasperated by her rudeness.

The door opened easily to reveal an eight-sided galleried chamber, with a hole in the middle through which the basement was visible. A metal ladder fixed to the side wall appeared to be the only method of descent to this lower space. Lizzie briefly explained the workings of the system as they had been related to her by Herbert.

'The water of the lake is held back behind the arch by a brick parapet. When the level rises, during sudden storms, the water gushes over the parapet into the lower chamber, where it is carried off to the river by a system of underground pipes. At present the water level is below the parapet, but when the volume of water grows larger the entire chamber fills with water.'

Joshua shivered, imagining vividly what it would be like to be in this building with a torrent of water gushing over the parapet. Thank God for dry weather, he thought. He noticed a small metal door several feet above the basement floor. 'What is that opening?'

'The door that was installed after the men were killed last year. During a storm the water penetrated through the basement wall in that spot, and found its way into the tunnels leading to the grotto. Until then no one knew the lake and grotto were linked. It was thought that Brown's excavations might have weakened the rock and caused the tragedy.'

'I should descend to search for signs of your brother,' said Joshua reluctantly. Even though there was no water in the lower chamber, it was the last thing he wanted to do. He straddled the metal parapet and clambered down the narrow ladder. The bandages on his hands hampered his progress; nevertheless in a few minutes he had reached the bottom and was able to walk about. The tiles were slimy with algae and every now and again his boot slipped and he skidded forward. He looked up and saw the arch, and the face of Lizzie Manning looking down. He trembled inwardly, again picturing what it would be like to be caught here in a flood – the place would become a hellish vortex of water. Tension made his head pound dreadfully, as if someone were striking his brain with an anvil. Nothing on earth would persuade him to pass an hour here, let alone a night.

To disguise these awful fancies he walked around, pretending to scrutinize the ground, as if he might find some sign of Arthur Manning. As he expected, he found nothing and, having searched fruitlessly for several minutes, climbed back up the ladder.

Outside, with the door closed, he felt his pulse subside.

They stood for a moment on the grassy slope. 'Lancelot Brown was certainly correct when he said that this would be a perilous place to hide. It doesn't in the least surprise me we found no sign of your brother there.'

'Why not?'

'Because that door would be impenetrable without a key. If he had forced entry there we would certainly have seen signs of it. I strongly suspect he is hiding in the grotto.'

'What makes you say so? We found no signs of him there either.'

Joshua nodded sagely, without a glimmer of guilt. 'Having seen both places, instinct tells me it would be a far more likely place for him to hide. He might easily have climbed over the bars. The tunnels would be a convenient hiding place where he would run little risk of detection.'

For the first time she looked at him with something approaching interest. 'In that case, why did we leave there without searching them?'

'We needed to come here in order to be certain. Moreover, I take seriously Granger's point that it is dangerous to venture there, and so should you.'

She tossed her head and held her chin high, but some of the earlier hostility was gone. His warning had struck home. 'What do you suggest we do?' she said.

'Prepare ourselves properly and formulate a careful plan to find him. The early evening, I hazard, would be the best time, when he is least likely to be prowling about the grounds or attempting to enter the house. If we return to look for him tonight, we could ask Granger to accompany us.'

Lizzie's eyes looked distracted. 'Then you believe we should confide the details of this matter to Granger?'

'Not necessarily. The less we divulge to anyone the better. We will inform him merely that we need to search the cavern and request that in the interests of safety he accompany us. Let him draw his own conclusion as to the whys and where-fores of our action.'

*  *  *

After a hearty breakfast of fried sweetbreads, bacon, eggs and parsley crisps, Joshua felt greatly restored. As soon as he left the table he went outdoors again. He intended to go in search of Granger, to return his keys and to ask him to join them that evening on their return to the grotto. He felt thankful to be alone, free from Lizzie Manning's unsettling sulks and silences.

They had spent several hours together and he had not troubled himself to ask her about her visit to the nursery, or to take her to task about the way she had questioned Violet and told her Cobb was alive. He now recognized that to do so was pointless. Her concerns for her brother and Francis influenced everything she said and did. That was why she blew hot and cold with him; that was why she had offered to help in the first place. Whatever the answers to his questions they would be prompted by her own interests.

Joshua thought longingly of the morning spent with Bridget. Her straightforwardness and lack of guile seemed suddenly greatly desirable. Even her questions about Rachel had been unexpectedly consoling. He wondered, with a sudden pounding concern, how Bridget was faring with Cobb and Crackman and when he would escape Astley to see her. Not before he found Granger and persuaded him to accompany him for this evening's adventure at any rate.

Granger stood by a stone bench next to the fishpond. Seated on the bench, conversing with him, was a woman Joshua didn't recognize. She was plainly dressed in a dark-blue gown and white linen bonnet; her hair, a gleaming crown of the richness of burnished copper, was arranged in coils beneath it. Was this his wife or betrothed? She seemed too finely dressed. Perhaps she was a member of the local gentry come to beg a favour. Curiosity began to smoulder. 'Mr Granger,' said Joshua, 'forgive me for intruding in your tête-à-tête, but I have come to return your keys and to make a request.'

'And what might that be?' Granger replied. The tightening

of his jaw and a faintly perceptible tic in his cheek suggested he was a little put out to be so disturbed.

Joshua shot a meaningful glance at his companion. 'Perhaps I should return later when you are not so busy. I do not wish to inconvenience you or this lady by interrupting your conversation.'

'It's no matter, I assure you,' said the woman, turning towards him. 'I was just quizzing Mr Granger on his duties. In any case I have to resume my work.'

'Are you a member of the household staff? Forgive me, but I do not think I have had the pleasure of making your acquaintance,' said Joshua niftily.

'This is Mrs Bowles. She's a seamstress from London, come to deliver some work and assist with other preparations for the ball,' said Granger. Then, gesturing to Joshua, he turned to his companion. 'And this, madam, is another visitor come to Astley, on a special commission. Mr Joshua Pope, the portrait painter.'

Joshua bowed, thinking to himself that Mrs Bowles was a striking woman. He remembered instantly who she was. Violet had said she saw Herbert calling on this woman and he had assumed she was Herbert's mistress. Lizzie had made some mention of her coming to deliver Violet's dress. Presumably that explained her presence. Perhaps, since she was here, he should verify the precise nature of her arrangement with Herbert.

'Mrs Bowles – why, yes. I have heard a little about you. Indeed, there's a matter in which you might be able to help me. I met with a mishap two days ago and a good jacket of mine was torn. Might I call on you later this morning to see if you are able to repair it?'

Mrs Bowles seemed a little taken aback, though whether this was from natural shyness or some other cause Joshua couldn't discern. At any rate, her now crimson complexion only added to her allure. 'I will be at my work all day, and it's my habit to take my meals in my room, rather than in the

301

servants' hall. You may come whenever it pleases you, though I don't promise I will be able to help you.'

'You may expect me within the hour,' responded Joshua with a small bow.

She stood, curtsied by way of return, then took her leave.

Joshua had decided to secure Granger's co-operation for an evening excursion by hinting that he believed Arthur Manning might be somewhere in the vicinity of the grotto. He explained briefly that Lizzie was anxious to trace her brother and he was anxious to assist. He refrained from mentioning that he thought Arthur might have taken the necklace and nor was he entirely honest as to why he felt the need for Granger to accompany them. There was no reason to terrify him with stories of wild assaults. Let Granger assume it was because the grotto was a treacherous place that he was needed. It was partly true, after all. They agreed to rendezvous at nine o'clock. Then, having successfully achieved his aim, Joshua returned the way he had come.

Mrs Bowles worried Joshua. He knew why she had come; he knew she was expected (Violet had told Lizzie, who had reported it in her letter); it was the fact of seeing her for the first time that rattled him. Her looks – her russet hair, her creamy complexion, the arch of her brow, those deep-blue eyes – these were features not easily overlooked by any man, and an artist of Joshua's imagination and sensitivity was naturally struck by them even more forcefully than most. His musings on the subject of Mrs Bowles then shifted, not surprisingly, to Herbert Bentnick. He, after all, was the person with whom she was most intimately associated in Joshua's mind.

He remembered that Herbert had been seen paying a visit to her house. What was the reason for his visit? Was it, as Joshua first supposed, that she – a more radiant version of his own sweet and probably duplicitous Meg – warmed his bed or was there something else?

Suppose Herbert had become involved with the claim for Sabine's necklace. Suppose he had decided, as any besotted bridegroom might, to protect the interests of his future bride. He had called on Cobb and tried to persuade him to drop the claim. Dunstable had confirmed Herbert had been seen arguing with Cobb, which seemed to bear the theory out.

Having failed to deter Cobb, what might Herbert have then done? The obvious next step was to search out Charles Mercier's illegitimate daughter directly and try to persuade her to drop the claim. Herbert said he didn't know who she was, but he might be lying. After all, there was the letter in his desk with its indecipherable signature. Herbert had never mentioned its existence, and it was quite possible that he knew who the author was. Moreover, there was the letter to Sabine that her maid had shown him – the letter arranging a meeting. Soon after his visit to Cobb, Herbert had been seen by Violet calling on the dressmaker. Was this strange visit in some way connected?

Joshua's fertile mind made a precipitous leap. Like a huntsman flying over a hedge that conceals a ditch, he landed where he did not expect to land, in mud and murky water. Was it fanciful to think another reason for Herbert's visit might be that Mrs Bowles was Charles Mercier's daughter?

# Chapter Thirty-seven

Joshua put his head round the door and his eyes swept the morning room, where the family and guests often gathered at this time of day, but he found the place deserted. He walked through to the breakfast room, but apart from Peters, who was sampling a slice of sweetbread, and a couple of housemaids clearing the table of toast crusts, bacon rinds and crockery there was no one there either. Impatient to discover if his imaginative surmise was correct, he shook his head in disappointment. Was Mrs Bowles the claimant for the necklace? Was she the one Sabine had visited on her recent trip to London? She who had written the letters? Was that why Herbert had called on her?

There were three people he could press on the matter. Mrs Bowles he intended to call upon within the hour. The others were Herbert and Sabine.

But neither of these two were anywhere to be found, and perhaps, Joshua reflected stoically, it was as well. If he did ask them outright about Mrs Bowles, the question was likely to incense them and provoke them to drastic action. It would be better to speak first to the dressmaker herself: she at least had no hold over him.

It was now a little after half-past nine – not enough time to call on Mrs Bowles, he fancied. He didn't want to have to rush with her and Caroline had agreed to come to his rooms at ten this morning to examine his wounds.

Joshua returned to his rooms to wait. He sat down on a large Windsor chair by the window. His eyes narrowed until they were no more than flinty slivers in his face. His brain was still wrestling with thoughts sparked by his recent encounter: Mrs Bowles and Granger. What were the two discussing? Why were they discussing anything? Then there was Mrs Bowles and Herbert. What was there between these two? Here were multiple trails to follow.

He sat up in the chair, eyes open, and unconsciously began to fiddle with his tattered bandages. They were still uncomfortably damp from the soaking he had given them in the grotto and stained with rust and slime from descending the ladder in the octagon house. He looked across at his easel, his palette, pencils, hog's-bristle brushes, the bladders of pigments ranked in their box, and felt a sudden craving to use them. Unless he could paint he was worthless.

The wait for Caroline Bentnick had become insupportable. The bandages felt like manacles impeding his freedom. Taking matters into his own hands, he whipped off the dressing from his head and examined his face in the looking glass. The wound was healing; air would dry it faster, and at least now he would be able to wear a wig if he desired. Then he turned his attention to his hands. Using a dextrous combination of teeth and the fingers of his left hand, he untied the knot on the right and began to unravel the linen band. He twirled his arm in a corkscrew gesture, watching the sodden bandage spiral to the floor like a dirty white worm. As the last layers peeled away they tugged the skin, but discomfort was outweighed by great relief when he saw that new skin had begun to grow. Thus encouraged, he removed the bandages on his left wrist and found that similarly improved. Released from his bonds, he rolled back his shirtsleeves to prevent the cuffs rubbing. Then, since Caroline had yet to arrive, he decided to make an attempt at painting.

He picked up a bladder of lead white, unstoppered it with a tack, and squeezed a little on the palette. He did the same with red lake, vermilion and yellow ochre. Then he turned the easel towards him. It was some days since he had looked at the composition and as always after such an interlude he saw it with a useful objectivity. His first reaction was entirely unexpected.

Sabine reclined indolently upon her seat, her head thrown back to gaze up at Herbert. The arm with which she held out the pineapple to Herbert was bare from the elbow down. One foot was thrown forward as if she were on the point of reclining, the underside of her chin and neck were portrayed in deep shadow. The serpent necklace coiled about her neck glittered with green lights. Her eyes, heavy-lidded, large and dark, were redolent of mystery, passion, promise. Herbert, standing behind, hand on hip, looked down. His eyes did not meet hers. They rested instead upon her pale bosom, and on the jewel at her throat. There was warmth in them and something more besides: an expression of possession and adoration.

He had represented with great fineness and detail the costumes, the skin tones, the rich embroidery and the folds and creases, the bravura landscape. The likenesses of Sabine and Herbert were so well caught and so animated that they almost breathed with life of their own. And yet, though he recognized the accomplishment of his painting, he didn't feel the sense of achievement he might have expected. Instead he felt distracted; his eyes were inexorably drawn to the necklace – as if that rather than the couple were the focus of the painting.

Joshua wondered whether he should alter Herbert's pose, so that the couple's eyes did meet, or adjust his expression so that it was riveted less on the necklace, or darken the necklace so that its highlights were less prominent. In the end, however, he decided against tampering. What was the purpose? In all probability it was his own preoccupation with recovering the necklace that distorted his view of his work. No one else would interpret it in the same way.

Joshua took up his palette and delicately added further details to the background, which was all that remained to be finished. But despite his earlier urge to paint, his work failed to hold his attention as it usually did. Too many other thoughts distracted him. This morning's adventures – finding the wine glass and meeting Mrs Bowles with Granger – made him sense that he was on the brink of a great breakthrough, elevating his spirits. But then the fact he had heard nothing from Bridget Quick since her departure to London depressed them. He couldn't help wondering what was taking place in St Peter's Court. Cobb was probably innocent of involvement in Hoare's death. Joshua still clung to this belief, but until he knew who was to blame there remained a doubt he could not entirely banish.

Bridget had promised to call on Crackman, to try to discover the identity of the claimant. The fact he had heard nothing was a further source of disappointment. Of course, if his hunch was correct and Mrs Bowles was the claimant, he could resolve the matter here and now. And all being well, this evening he would find Arthur Manning and recover the necklace. There would then be nothing to prevent him returning to London tomorrow to rejoin Bridget.

No sooner had he set upon this course of action than he grew desperate to set events in motion. He glanced at his timepiece. Ten o'clock had come and gone and still Caroline Bentnick had failed to appear. He dimly recalled that there was something she wished to tell him concerning the day of Hoare's death. Presumably it wasn't of great significance or she would have told him already. Whatever it was it would have to wait. Glad that he had taken it upon himself to remove his bandages, he delayed himself no longer.

He took up the torn and soiled brown coat that he had worn on the day he was attacked and asked the third footman where he might find Mrs Bowles. The footman escorted him to an attic staircase leading to the garret, where most of the servants' quarters were situated. He found her in a pleasant, though stiflingly hot, room. The sloping ceiling was punctuated with a shuttered window that gave a bird's-eye view of the kitchen garden, the pinery, and Richmond Hill beyond. Glancing through it, he saw it was practically the same view he had from his rooms below. The sky was becoming increasingly overburdened with lowering clouds, but at the moment he entered the sun broke out briefly and spears of sunlight radiated across the room in a dazzling fan, which disappeared almost instantly.

A gown of pale-blue satin embroidered with seed pearls in a trailing vine pattern stood in one corner of the room on a tailor's dummy, which reminded him of the lay figure he used for his portrait. Mrs Bowles sat on a stool nearby, busy at her craft, apparently stitching a pair of crimson velvet gentleman's breeches. She had removed the bonnet she wore earlier and put on a small linen cap, with lappets hanging on each side of her face. He caught a glimpse of strands of russet hair beneath the cap.

As before, Joshua was struck by the richness of her hair and by Mrs Bowles's radiance. He recalled the story of the maid, Emma Baynes, who had delivered the jewel to Charles Mercier and so bewitched him that she subsequently bore his child. Was this the child Charles Mercier had fathered? Or was she no more than Herbert's mistress? She was certainly lovely enough to distract the most upright of men.

He cast about, looking for any scrap of paper containing a sample of her handwriting. If it were the same hand as he had seen on the letters to Herbert and Sabine her identity would be confirmed. There was nothing visible, though he noticed a closed book on the table next to her. Was this an order book perhaps?

Joshua coughed. 'Mrs Bowles, forgive my intrusion. I have brought my coat. It was badly torn in a misadventure that befell me two days ago. I wondered if you could repair it.'

She took the coat and began to finger the rips to the sleeve and lapel. 'I hesitate to say I can mend it so well it will be as good as before. And certainly I am too occupied just at the moment . . .'

'I would not expect it,' said Joshua. 'I see you are kept busy by the demands of the Bentnicks.'

'It's the reason I have come here, sir.'

'Is it often that you are called here from London by the family?'

'No, sir. Indeed, it's the first time.'

'Did Mr Granger tell you anything of the recent events that have taken place here?'

'A little.'

'Perhaps, then, he also mentioned that I have been ordered to look into them?'

'He did say something of the kind, but since it all took place before my arrival I do not see what possible help I can be to you.'

'Madam,' said Joshua, in a more authoritative tone, 'what you know of the family may have a bearing on these events, even if you are unaware of it. Thus I would ask, how did your connection with the family come about?'

'I come originally from a village near Luton in Bedfordshire. The Bentnicks are acquainted with the Seebrights, owners of Beechwood, a large estate in the county. When I ventured to London, after the death of my husband, Frances Seebright recommended me to all her friends in the vicinity, among them Jane Bentnick. I presume that after Mrs Bentnick's death, Miss Caroline must have passed my name on to Mrs Mercier and her daughter.'

'That was most fortunate for you.'

Mrs Bowles smiled wryly. 'Miss Violet, I may say, is a most demanding customer; she insisted I personally deliver the gown I have made for her, in case any alterations are necessary. Now that I am here, Mr Bentnick requests that I adjust his breeches, for he complains they have always been too tight.'

The name Beechwood was familiar to him, though he

decided to take things in a logical sequence and wait before he pursued it.

'Tell me, Mrs Bowles, a little of your background. Are your parents still alive?'

'Both my parents are dead, sir.'

'Lately so?'

'My father died when I was an infant; I never knew him. My mother perished two years ago.'

'Was your mother ever in service?'

'She worked as cook to Mrs Seebright.'

'She never went abroad with her?'

'No, sir.'

It occurred to Joshua that, though her replies did not tally, there was plenty in her family history that fitted conveniently with what he knew of Charles Mercier's daughter. But if she was the claimant for the necklace she was an accomplished actress, for she gave no flicker to indicate that she had other reasons for being here. If only there were a sample of her handwriting to be seen, he could resolve the matter instantly. Joshua decided to press more roughly. 'Are you personally acquainted with Mr Bentnick?'

She looked up from her work and, catching his scrutiny, her complexion seemed to turn a shade paler. 'I am not sure what you mean, Mr Pope. I have told you the nature of my acquaintance with the family. Mrs Mercier and her daughter are my customers. Mr Bentnick has naught to do with it. I am adjusting his breeches as a favour; under usual circumstances his tailor would do it.'

Joshua stood up. He was puzzled by her vehement tone. He knew there was more to her relationship with Herbert than she admitted, and yet she hadn't the demeanour of a liar. He walked a little closer towards her and stood next to the table on which the book was resting. 'You told me about your dealings with the ladies in the Bentnick family, but that doesn't mean you haven't worked for the gentlemen. I should like to know, does Mr Herbert Bentnick often avail himself of your . . . services . . . in town?'

The pause and the look he gave her made his meaning as clear as spring water. She stopped her work and raised her eyes to his. As she did so, he saw her expression transform from puzzlement to shame. Her hand began to tremble; she bit her lip as if trying to subdue the rising tide of emotion. 'I am not entirely sure of your meaning, Mr Pope, but you may rest assured there has never been anything improper in my relations with Mr Bentnick, nor indeed with any one of my patrons.'

'Then may I be so bold as to ask why, less than two weeks ago, you were observed entering a house off Floral Street and, minutes later, Mr Bentnick was also seen to enter the same premises? You were then observed in intimate conversation with Mr Bentnick in a room on the first floor. Do not think me over-zealous or prying, Mrs Bowles, but, as I have already made clear, in view of the fact that a man is dead and a valuable jewel has gone missing I must press you for an honest response to these questions.'

Her pale-blue eyes now grew round as marbles. Her lips worked as though she would speak and yet for several moments no utterance came. When at last she managed to compose herself sufficiently to speak, her voice trembled with emotion.

'I do not know who has provided you with this malignant slander,' said she, with what vestige of dignity she could muster, 'but I can assure you my character has been most unjustly traduced. There is a confidence I would have preferred not to break, but since you appear intent upon besmirching my reputation I will tell you. Nothing untoward has taken place between Mr Bentnick and me. Nothing whatsoever. He has paid several visits to me at my residence, in order to commission two ball gowns – one is a surprise for Mrs Mercier, the other is for his daughter. '

Joshua was taken aback and not entirely convinced. He looked down at the book again. 'If that was all, what reason did he have to visit your private dwelling?'

'He didn't wish Violet to catch him. He is a man of great generosity and kindness. He didn't want the surprise to be spoiled.'

Her outrage and mortification seemed genuine. She appeared to be telling the truth. Joshua reached down towards the book and opened the cover. The handwriting was small and regular, a copperplate hand. It was nothing like the writing on the letters. She couldn't be the claimant.

He wanted to apologize for upsetting her, but before he had a chance to make amends he heard the pounding of heavy footsteps mounting the staircase to the garret and a voice bellowing his name. An instant later the door burst open. Francis Bentnick stood there, wigless and coatless, his face red and moist with his recent exertions, his straw-coloured hair plastered to his forehead with perspiration. 'Mr Pope,' he blustered, 'you must come at once. A terrible tragedy has taken place.'

# Chapter Thirty-eight

Caroline Bentnick was dead. Granger had found her lying at the entrance to the pinery beneath the glazed cupola, some half-hour or so after Joshua had left him. By the time Joshua arrived at the scene, the rest of the family had already learned of the tragedy and were gathered outside the pinery door, shock and distress plainly written on their faces. Herbert, Francis and Joshua went inside, where they found Granger keeping vigil over the body. Granger looked unusually agitated. He caught Joshua's eye as if there were something pressing he wished to say, but he didn't want to speak out in front of the others. The corpse remained as he had discovered it: sprawled face upward on the path, one arm outstretched, the other lying across her breast.

'Yes, sir,' he said very quietly, as if Joshua had asked the obvious question. 'She is dead. I have examined her; there's no pulse at all.'

Joshua was entirely unprepared for the ferocity of Caroline's expression. Her wide lips were drawn back in a strange grimace; her tongue, purple and swollen, protruded. Her eyes were glassy and open and seemed more bulbous than he remembered; the whites were visible, the pupils half disappeared in their sockets, as if she had looked up to heaven at the moment of death.

Even more shocking than the wild strangeness of Caroline

313

Bentnick's face was the presence around her neck of a collar of glittering green. The serpent necklace had returned as a terrible talisman of death to the person who detested it most. It was wrapped about her throat, its smooth green body gleaming, its single ruby eye winking malevolently.

'Sir,' whispered Granger urgently, 'there's something—'

'Yes, yes, Granger. All in good time. Just let me look first, if you please.' Joshua sensed Granger's perturbation, but his own thoughts were also thrown into turmoil and he had no words of comfort to spare; it was all he could do to contain his emotions. Death, violent death, once more. Memories of poor Rachel's corpse returned to his mind. He looked at Caroline and he saw his wife: Rachel's soaked body, Rachel's wrinkled flesh. Kneeling by her side, he felt his head swim with horror and unreality. He leaned forward, clawing at the ground for support, in an effort to master a rising tide that threatened to submerge him.

It was that gesture which somehow brought him back from the brink of unreality. His eyes had deceived him; he was incapable of hearing what anyone said. But for some reason the grittiness of the earth, the sensation of soil beneath his nails and on his palms, revived his senses. It was that which forced him to see.

With a feeling of revulsion, he picked up the necklace between forefinger and thumb. He noticed that the links were slightly speckled with soil. Holding the necklace to one side, as if it were a venomous writhing thing that might strike at any moment, he looked at Caroline's neck where the necklace had been laid. Etched upon her throat was a livid circle of bruising, the sort of mark that a noose pulled tight to prevent her from breathing might make. The sight of this mark further helped him. An uneasy instinct that something was wrong made him bend forward to examine the wound again more closely. There was a light powdering of soil on Caroline's neck. The mark, however, was the width of a narrow cord; it didn't correspond to the form of the necklace.

The necklace had been placed there after she was strangled.

He looked again at the rest of her body and noticed that her right hand, the one lying across her, was clenched and that there appeared to be soil on it. Taking the hand in his own, he gently prised it open. There were faint soil marks, like an imprint, across her palm. They were in the shape of the necklace.

He turned to Granger. 'I presume what you want to tell me concerns the necklace?'

Granger started back, his eyes widened, his leathery face bleached with shock. 'Yes, in a manner of speaking,' he said. 'In God's name, how did you know that?'

It was obvious to Joshua that the necklace had been held firmly in Caroline Bentnick's hand immediately prior to her death, and earlier it had somehow come in contact with soil. But he didn't answer Granger. He had no patience now for explanation; he was unable to tear himself from the corpse.

'Just tell me what it was.'

'When I found her, her hand was closed and across her neck. I lifted it, and the necklace dropped out, as you see it now. I never touched it.'

Joshua nodded wordlessly. His eyes were half closed as his mind ran on to a torrent of further questions and suppositions. What possible reason could there be for such a killing? What was the significance of the necklace? Was it merely disguising the wound, or did it serve as some macabre adornment? Had the necklace been buried and then dug up? Was the murderer of Caroline the murderer of Bartholomew Hoare? If this was so, it must mean Cobb was innocent – assuming he was in London.

He compared the two methods of killing: poisoning and strangulation. Poisoning seemed the easier of the two. Anyone, man or woman, weak or strong, might administer poison. You didn't require physical strength; you needed only stealth and detailed knowledge of the chosen substance.

Caroline Bentnick's murder by strangulation was very

315

different. Though a slightly built woman, she was nevertheless young and in her prime. To kill her in such a manner would require considerable force but no particular knowledge. Joshua stood up and looked down at the body again. The clothes were not unduly disarranged; there was no evidence to suggest she had struggled before death. She must have been taken by surprise. And yet there was that ghastly look on her face – a look of recognition, surely.

'Tell me, Granger, how you happened to find her.'

'There's not much to tell, sir,' said Granger. 'I entered the pinery in order to tend to the plants and check the heat, and there she lay. I could hardly miss her.'

'How long ago was this?'

'About ten, fifteen minutes at the most, sir.'

'And you saw and heard nothing untoward prior to that?'

'Nothing in particular that I recall, sir.'

'So you didn't see Miss Bentnick when she entered the pinery?'

'No, sir.'

'And where were you immediately before you came here just now?'

'Over there, sir, by the melon frames.' He pointed to a spot some twenty feet from where they stood. The frames were partly concealed by a trellis, up which a cucumber scrambled; apart from this obstruction there was a clear view of the pinery.

'So if anyone had passed, you should have seen them?'

'I suppose so, sir, but in truth I was kneeling down, tending the plants. It is possible someone could have passed without my noticing. Also, I was only there for ten minutes or so. Before that, I was attending to matters on the other side of the house. If someone had entered then I wouldn't have seen them.'

'In that case, perhaps you would be good enough to go now and question your men and discover if they remarked anything unusual.'

Granger nodded and left. Joshua turned back to look again at the face with its dreadful contorted expression. He remembered the fear her face expressed that evening in the drawing room. He remembered too the kindness she had displayed towards him and Bridget. He felt ashamed now to have been so ungrateful that when she failed to arrive for their appointment he had felt no glimmer of foreboding. Perhaps if he had, and if he had gone in search of her, he could have prevented her death.

What conceivable reason could there be for someone to kill her? A terrible answer sprang to his mind. He remembered so clearly the words she had spoken the previous day that he fancied them ringing in his ears. She had something to tell him concerning Hoare. She had announced it to him in front of all those assembled on the terrace. Had this innocent remark thrown her into peril? Was this the reason she had been killed?

This notion so distressed him that he could hardly bear to consider it objectively. His mouth was dry; he swallowed uncomfortably, aware that his turmoil was subject to the astonished scrutiny of both Granger and Francis. Then another thought came to him. If Caroline had been killed because the murderer feared being identified by her, would his own involvement place his life in danger? Was he next? If so, what grim fate had the murderer in store for him?

He pushed past Francis and Granger, desperate now to get outside.

Violet and Lizzie were standing together close to the door. Lizzie's head was bowed and she was crying quietly, holding a handkerchief to her eyes, dabbing each in turn. Violet looked tremulous but had thus far managed to control her tears. She held a pink silk fan in one hand and was fluttering it rapidly in front of her face. A short distance off stood a cluster of three or four under gardeners gathered to wait for Granger – who now advanced towards them – presumably to follow his instructions and help him discover where each of them was at

317

the crucial moments earlier that morning, and what if anything they had seen.

Herbert and Sabine stood apart from the rest. Joshua noted Herbert's agonized expression, his pinched and pale face. His shoulders trembled and his eyes gleamed with suppressed anguish – plainly he was having difficulty in preventing himself from sobbing openly. Sabine appeared unusually agitated. She held his hand in both of hers and rubbed it gently, as if by this soothing gesture she could erase the pain of bereavement, but all the time she looked about with jerky, wary movements that reminded Joshua of a bird about to take flight.

Joshua steeled himself and went over to Herbert. 'I believe, sir, that this is the missing necklace,' he said. 'I am only sorry that I have to restore it to you in such unhappy circumstances.'

Herbert took the jewel and handed it to Sabine. 'What does this signify, Pope? I beg that you will explain it to me.' He spoke in a dull, expressionless monotone. Joshua had never seen him look so subdued or uncertain of himself. He seemed dazed, as if he had entirely lost all sense of who he was.

'I don't know who did this, but I do know my poor sister has been killed by that accursed jewel,' whispered Francis Bentnick, before Joshua had a chance to reply. He had followed Joshua out of the pinery. His glassy eyes were haunted by the sight of his dead sister and he fixed his gaze on Sabine, as if by a look he could wordlessly accuse her.

'What do you mean?' said Joshua to Francis.

'Isn't it plain?' said Francis.

Joshua noticed that while he responded to his question, he refused to meet his eye. His gaze was locked on Sabine.

Eventually Francis scratched his head and looked at the ground. His shoulders were still trembling and the spasms seemed more violent now. Hearing the discussion, Violet approached the group and threaded her arm through Francis's. 'I confess I am utterly confused,' she said quietly. 'Caroline always claimed to despise it, but if she was not responsible for the necklace's disappearance why is the jewel now recovered?'

Francis turned towards her, horrified at this theory, and shook off her arm in an undisguised gesture of distaste. He stepped closer to Lizzie and took her hand in his. 'Impossible! I won't even honour such a dreadful notion by refuting it,' he cried.

Seeing that the conversation could only become more heated, Joshua tried to prevail upon them all to be reasonable in their grief. He too was still in emotional turmoil and for this reason recklessly yielded to uncertain destiny and voiced his thoughts. 'It seems most probable to me that the thief and the murderer of Mr Hoare and Miss Bentnick are one and the same. The assassin feared Caroline knew his or her identity and probably killed her just now because the opportunity presented itself,' he said. 'Perhaps the necklace was returned to avoid detection. In any event, I believe the reason for her death was something she said yesterday which may have made the killer believe she knew more than she did.'

'What's this?' said Herbert, looking up and suddenly taking note of Joshua's drift. 'What did she say?'

'First, sir, I would like to pose a question. I believe you have had some correspondence with the other claimant for the necklace, a letter threatening to remove the jewel if you didn't co-operate with her wishes. Who wrote it?'

'How do you know the letter threatened me? Have you been among my private papers? said Herbert in icily controlled tones.

'He has,' said Lizzie between sobs. 'I was there and saw the letter. Forgive me, Mr Bentnick. It was only my concern for my brother made me desperate to involve myself with him.'

'That letter may lead us to the murderer of your daughter, sir. Surely that is more important than whether I read a letter that you should have showed me,' said Joshua quietly.

'What a fool you are, Pope. I don't know who wrote the

letter. If I did, would I have asked you to find the jewel? I could have gone straight to the claimant myself. Now, tell me, before I also commit murder, what it was my daughter said that made her fall victim to this crime.'

Joshua thought swiftly. He dared not let slip that the maid Marie had shown him the letter sent to Sabine arranging a meeting with the claimant, for he didn't want to cost Marie her job. Perhaps Herbert was telling the truth when he said he didn't know who she was, but Sabine, who was listening to every word and saying nothing, certainly did. Nevertheless, now, in the midst of tragedy, was no time to expose her deceit. He would wait for a more opportune moment.

'Yesterday she declared she had remembered something of importance regarding the day of Hoare's death. She said she would come to my room and tell me what it was at ten this morning. Most of the household, apart from you, sir, were present when she made this arrangement. She never came.'

Herbert blinked and pulled himself up so that he seemed to tower over Joshua like a man-of-war looming over a longboat. 'Then it was you who caused her death. Yet again it was *you*, Pope. You have brought about this great tragedy.'

'No, sir,' protested Joshua, 'she passed the remark without provocation from me.'

'Nevertheless,' said Herbert, who desperately needed someone to blame for his misery, 'if you had not insisted that the matter of Hoare's death was linked to the necklace, none of this would have happened. I told you to find the necklace. I did not want to provoke a further murder. Let alone that of my only daughter.'

'It was hardly my intention to do so,' said Joshua, so consumed with remorse – for he had to admit there was a certain dreadful logic in Herbert's onslaught – he hadn't the heart to mount a robust argument against it.

'And, as it transpires, the disappearance of the necklace has nothing to do with Hoare's death.'

'I still cannot be certain of that,' replied Joshua, looking penetratingly in the direction of Sabine, who ignored him entirely, 'although I believe I may be close . . .'

'However close you are, do not expect to progress further with my blessing. I say again, your meddling with Hoare and Cobb has resulted in the death of my daughter. You have enjoyed my forbearance long enough. The portrait must by now be practically finished – I have never known an artist procrastinate like you, and that's the truth. You can complete it in your own premises. Remove yourself from Astley forthwith.'

'But, sir,' said Joshua, aghast at the unreasonable turn Herbert was taking against him, 'I believe I am close to discovering the reason for these strange events. I beg you, let me remain here one more night.'

'One more night be damned!' shouted Herbert. 'You have brought about a calamity. I planned a ball, but now I must hold a funeral. Your services are no longer required.'

'In that case, pardon my freedom, but I earnestly entreat you to summon an officer of justice to look into this.' Joshua remonstrated with as much force as he dared. 'If Miss Manning's father is still absent, then call the constable. There is a murderer in your midst and you ignore that fact at your peril.'

'Pope,' said Francis, now intervening on his father's behalf, 'do not make matters worse by arguing. We have suffered a family tragedy. What we do is our business, not yours. It is only right that you comply with my father's desire.' His voice was less forceful than his father's, yet Joshua could sense he too was implacable.

Rocked though he was by his perfunctory dismissal, Joshua had no option but to acknowledge defeat. There was such glaring danger here, how could they ignore it? Why did Sabine not confess she knew the claimant's identity? Should he speak out? He glanced towards her again, but she refused steadfastly to meet his eye. He sighed and bowed curtly to them all. 'Let me in parting offer my condolences for these terrible events. If at any juncture you change your mind and desire that I should pursue them for you, I would willingly do so.'

Only now, having refused to meet his scrutiny and observed the exchange in uncharacteristic silence, did Sabine at last deign to speak. She raised her head and shot a baleful look in his direction. 'Thank you, Mr Pope, but I believe you have done quite enough. More will not be necessary,' she declared with soft yet unmistakable finality.

As Joshua returned dolefully towards the house, it seemed to him that destiny had played him a cruel hand. His driving desire to seek justice had gone horribly awry. The charge of theft had been replaced by that of causing the death of Caroline Bentnick. Even though part of him recognized this as a misjudgement, the accusation wounded him because in his heart of hearts he felt in some sense culpable. There was no doubt in his mind that it was Caroline's conversation with him that had drawn the murderer's eye. If he hadn't looked into Hoare's death, if she hadn't mentioned his wretched name, she might be alive still. He wished he had never agreed to set foot in that house, never picked up a brush to paint the wretched Bentnick portrait.

All the while he packed his possessions and equipment, his thoughts were in turmoil. He ricocheted between relief at the prospect of leaving this strange unhappy house, a sense of failure in quitting under such a cloud, and a heavy burden of guilt. Also, he no longer knew if his reputation was salvaged or irrefutably condemned. What would Herbert do? Despite having discovered the necklace, he feared Herbert's wrath – or, worse, that he might publicly condemn his conduct.

Prior to leaving Astley, in between assembling his own possessions, retrieving Cobb's bag from its hiding place and giving orders for the packing of canvas and stretcher and easel and paints, he searched high and low for Lizzie Manning. When he finally met her on the stairs he reminded her of his arrangement with Granger and told her not be so foolish as to venture into the grotto in search of her brother without Granger as escort. It was on the tip of his tongue to say that he feared Arthur Manning might be responsible for the death of Caroline and the mysterious return of the necklace, but no sooner had he finished the first part of his speech than she thanked him coolly and walked off with her nose in the air, as if she were examining the mouldings on the ceiling. A few minutes later she was back, wanting to know what had become of Cobb's bag.

'I have undertaken to return it to him. Its whereabouts are no concern of yours,' he replied coldly to her.

'So you lied to me the other night when you said you had already given it to him. I thought as much.'

'You too have been less than honest with me, madam. It is not customary in any circles I know for a young lady to enter a gentleman's rooms in the dead of night and search them without his say-so.'

She looked as if she would fly at him for this retort, but by then his goods were safely loaded and tied onto the roof of the carriage and, unless she fancied climbing up there, he knew she would never find Cobb's bag.

Lizzie Manning and the Bentnicks of Astley were a black chapter in his life. But the chapter was now closed. London was where his future lay.

# Chapter Thirty-nine

It was mid-afternoon by the time the carriage drew up outside Joshua's lodgings. He knocked tentatively at his front door. Having given the key to Cobb, he had no means of opening it. He still felt uneasy whenever he dwelled on the subject of Cobb. If Hoare's murderer was also Caroline Bentnick's, Cobb was unlikely to be guilty. Nevertheless, with so much shift and alteration in all the characters he had encountered, Joshua's assurance in his own capacity to read human nature was shaken. Filled with doubt about his own ability, he felt less certain of everyone. It would no longer greatly surprise him, he thought as he stood on his threshold, if everyone within this house had been slaughtered.

It was with some relief, therefore, that after several minutes the door jerked open to reveal the ancient face of Mrs Quick, in the same formidable humour as ever. She glowered balefully when she discerned it was he. Some things never change, thought Joshua ruefully.

'Mr Pope. You return, having sent your unwholesome deputy in the meantime. Can we expect the pleasure of your company for long?'

Joshua raised his hat to her, trying to muster some semblance of dignity. 'I am pleased to say I have no intention of leaving for some considerable time, Mrs Quick. My business at Richmond is over. It remains only for me to resolve things with Mr Cobb. I trust you have taken good care of him.'

'Trust all you like, sir,' she replied sourly. 'Next time, though, I would thank you to send such disreputable personages elsewhere. It may surprise you to learn you do not reside in Newgate prison or a sewer. Though some of your acquaintances would certainly be well-suited there.'

Joshua gushed contrition. 'Forgive me, Mrs Quick. I suffered a misadventure and had no chance to write. I had thought that Bridget would have explained matters to you.'

'How could she? She wasn't here at the time!'

'Is your daughter about?'

'As you see, she is not.'

'You expect her soon?'

'In half an hour, perhaps a little more.'

Just then Kitty came out with the empty coal scuttle, which she was on her way to fill. Taking advantage of the interruption, Joshua cannily altered tack.

'May I ask you, madam, what became of Cobb? I take it from your earlier remark he isn't here?'

'Why, what would you expect me to do with him? What was I supposed to think of a wild-eyed stranger who looked as if he hadn't washed for several weeks, and entered my abode without warning in the dead of night and ransacked my larder?'

'He ransacked your larder?' Joshua echoed, incredulous at Cobb's stupidity.

'He woke poor Kitty and scared her half out of her wits; she very sensibly screamed, whereupon Thomas came to assist her. When they woke me I told them to summon the watch and call the constable and apprehend your Mr Cobb for breaking and entering.'

Joshua swallowed and concealed his dismay. He knew enough of Mrs Quick's unpredictable character to be sure that if she caught the slightest whiff of anxiety she would clam up like an oyster or launch into a virulent tirade. He thought it wiser, therefore, to adopt a more neutral approach. 'You had him arrested?'

She nodded. 'I did, sir, and I don't need you to criticize,' she said stoutly.

'Of course I shouldn't dream of criticizing, Mrs Quick. The fault was entirely mine for not forewarning you of the circumstances of Mr Cobb's distress. I know had you been apprised of the situation your charitable sentiments, for which you are well known, would have been stirred.'

'There's charity, Mr Pope, and there's preservation. And, let me tell you, when a vagabond comes into your home and ransacks your larder, charity flies off with the speed of a bat. You do as Kitty did – open your mouth and shriek for assistance.'

'Quite so, ma'am. May I ask, do you know where Cobb is now?'

'Still in the Roundhouse, for aught I know or care.'

'I see,' said Joshua, looking away from her. He was uncertain how to proceed now she had delivered this astonishing blow. Bearing in mind Cobb's unsavoury demeanour and his idiotic behaviour, he had to admit she had reason to be alarmed. Indeed, remembering his own doubts about Cobb, perhaps the Roundhouse was the safest place for him.

'Of course I comprehend your awkward dilemma. Indeed, I cannot think how I overlooked it before. My profound apologies for the inconvenience, madam.'

'Won't you wait for my daughter?'

'No,' Joshua said. The last thing he wanted was to see Bridget again under the scrutiny of her mother, who would monitor every move and every word and give them no peace. 'There is no time just now to wait. There are matters I must attend to immediately. Be so kind, madam, to tell her I will call on her tomorrow morning at nine.'

Mrs Quick gave him a knowing grin. 'It's no use you going to visit your other lady friend, Mr Pope.'

'What,' said Joshua, blanching at this astonishing remark, 'what lady friend?'

'That widow you've been calling on. Mrs Dunn, isn't it?

No good going there. She's going to be married to some cousin of her husband's. Came round two or three days ago to break the news to you. Bridget spoke to her and told me.'

'I see,' he said curtly, as he took his leave.

Joshua mounted the stairs to his rooms with a heavy heart. Was there anything more in his miserable existence that could possibly go wrong? Although he had suspected that Meg was stringing him along and half expected something of the kind, he was surprised how dejected he felt to have his suspicions confirmed.

He wished it had been Bridget rather than Mrs Quick who had opened the door. Her practical sense and good heart might have helped him decide what he should do about Cobb, who languished in a cell not a hundred yards from his door.

Joshua's resolve to detach himself from events at Astley hadn't altered, yet he felt obliged to act. Whatever Cobb's role in this intrigue, he could not have killed Caroline Bentnick, and thus it seemed doubtful he was the murderer of Hoare. Assuming Cobb was innocent, his misfortunes were even worse than Joshua's. In sending him to his lodgings – believing he would be safe there – Joshua had directed him straight into the jaws of peril in the unlikely form of Mrs Quick. How could he feel otherwise than honour-bound to save him? But that was all he would do.

The Roundhouse was the headquarters of the local watch, where malefactors in this part of London were held prior to being brought before the magistrate. The building stood in the main thoroughfare of St Martin's Lane, opposite St Martin's Church, a mere three hundred yards from Mrs Quick's house. Joshua picked his way past a cluster of spectators at the stocks that stood outside it – presently occupied by two men who had been found guilty of cursing and swearing in the street – and a whipping post – presently vacant. The building was about the size of a summer pavilion with the guards' office and an entrance hall on the ground floor and a holding cell in the

327

basement beneath. On questioning the guard, Joshua learned to his surprise that Cobb was still held a prisoner in its cell and had yet to be charged with any offence. Mrs Quick, being uncertain whether or not he was a vagabond, had paid the constable a florin to hold him till Joshua's return, whereupon, if Joshua was willing to vouchsafe his good character, she would drop all charges. This action, thought Joshua, might well have saved Cobb from heinous punishment. It was also the only sign he had ever seen of Mrs Quick's supposed compassion.

Thus encouraged, Joshua pleaded Cobb's case. He was told it would be impossible to release him that night, since it was late and the constable was no longer on the premises. Joshua handed a shilling to the guard and reiterated his wish to see Cobb freed as soon as possible. The sweetened guard swiftly changed his tune. Joshua might view the cell. Provided he could identify Cobb, the guard saw no reason why Joshua shouldn't take him away.

Two guardsmen escorted Joshua down a spiral staircase to a circular cell in the bowels of the building. In this crowded, unventilated space, the air was foul, filled with the unwholesome smells of human sweat, rank breath and excrement. There was naught but damp straw on the floor and open buckets were the only method of sanitation. Through the gloom he glimpsed the dismal prisoners. Males and females of every age, size and demeanour imaginable were sequestered together and lay or sat in uneasy poses, some hunched and stooped or prostrate, while others stood immobile, as if frozen by their dreadful predicament.

As Joshua and the guards approached the door, several of the more energetic prisoners, alerted by the light of their lantern, began crying out and rattling the bars, in the vain hope that Joshua might take pity on one of them and pay to have him released. Cobb wasn't among these more strident prisoners. Joshua searched about and for some time he couldn't see him. Eventually he discerned him by his rasping cough, which Joshua well remembered from their previous encounters. He was crouched against the wall, at the furthest point from the door. He appeared half asleep, for his head was slumped forward, resting on his knees, as if he were tired of the effort of living in such a noisome, hellish place. Despite the commotion he didn't once raise his head.

'Cobb,' Joshua called out to him, 'it is I, Joshua Pope. I am here to have you freed.'

Cobb lifted his head slowly, as if the weight was almost more than his neck could bear. Joshua heard another racking cough. 'Pope! Not only have you taken all I have, look where you have put me!' he spluttered, before sinking back to his former position.

Joshua was so shocked that words failed him. He nodded to the guards to indicate that this man was indeed Cobb, whereupon one unlocked the door and ordered the other in to retrieve him. Before entering, the guardsman picked up a club and, as he walked through the miserable mêlée, Joshua saw him swing it and kick viciously at anyone who attempted to approach him. He reached Cobb, pulled the poor fellow to his feet by his collar, as though he had no more feeling than a corpse, and half dragged him out of the cell. With similar roughness the other guard helped manhandle Cobb up the stairs, then they thrust him towards Joshua.

Cobb was thin as a toasting fork; his flesh was grimy and unwashed; a foul odour, the origins of which Joshua couldn't bear to contemplate, emanated from him. He was incapable of walking, incapable almost of standing, and the wound to his arm looked foul and infected. He had been ill when Joshua last saw him, yet how much worse now was his condition. Joshua recoiled from this miserable, stinking wreckage. The last thing he wanted was to take him to his home. But then he sharply reminded himself that he was partly to blame for Cobb's state. Cringing inwardly, he draped Cobb's arm about his shoulder and, battling to prevent himself retching from his close proximity, they staggered back to Joshua's lodgings.

As they entered the door, Joshua prayed fervently that Mrs Quick would not apprehend them, for there was little doubt that if she caught a glimpse or a whiff of Cobb she would banish him. In this instance, however, Joshua's prayer was answered. Mrs Quick did not emerge. Joshua was able to haul Cobb through the hallway and up the stairs. He fancied that through the door leading to Mrs Quick's parlour he could hear the sound of female voices in animated conversation. He wondered if this was merely Mrs Quick ordering Kitty about or if Bridget had returned.

In the sanctuary of his parlour, Joshua lowered Cobb down onto a daybed and rang for Kitty, whom he ordered to fetch hot water and a bathtub and towels. Cobb meanwhile lay semi-comatose, his head lolling this way and that, his eyes rolling as he muttered insensibly to himself. Beneath the grime and filth his skin was pallid and damp with perspiration. Joshua put a palm on his brow; his flesh burned with fever. He poured a tankard of ale from a flagon he kept on a side table and held it to Cobb's lips. Most of the liquid dribbled down the side of his mouth, but he managed to swallow a little and it must have comforted him, for he lay a little more peacefully after that.

Presently, when the bath was brought and filled, Joshua asked Kitty to assist him, telling her that there would be sixpence for her trouble if she mentioned none of this to Mrs Quick. They stripped him of his stinking clothes and bundled them up for Thomas to burn. Then they lowered him into the bath. He gripped the rim with knobbly fingers, as if fearful he might slip and fall under the water. Kitty seemed to take entirely in her stride the shocking sight of him naked, scrubbing his arms and back and belly as if there were no more to it than scouring a copper pan.

Cobb offered no resistance to these ministrations and, indeed, after a short while the water seemed to soothe him, for he released his grip on the rim of the tub, and lay back with eyes half closed, smiling to himself. Every now and then, however, he was racked with a spasm of coughing and, while Kitty held a cloth to his mouth, more than once Joshua saw blood stain his spittle.

Between them they lifted him from the tub, dried him and, having dressed him in a nightshirt taken from his bag, laid him back on the daybed. Kitty then departed in search of some nourishment.

Cobb seemed a little revived after all this, for he opened his eyes and looked at his clothes. 'Did you bring my bag?' he suddenly said.

'Yes,' said Joshua. 'I have it safe. You are wearing your nightshirt from it. Do not concern yourself about it any more.'

Cobb's spirits seemed to lift. 'I thank you, Pope, for what you have done for me just now. You are not entirely the bad fellow I took you for.'

This sudden display of gratitude reminded Joshua of his earlier doubts. 'Perhaps, on the contrary, it is *you* who is the bad fellow, Mr Cobb.'

He looked alarmed. 'What d'you mean, Pope? I came here at your invitation. You said I would be safe, yet I found myself arrested like a common prisoner. You have extracted me from that hell-hole of your own volition.'

'I am sorry for your ordeal, but I fear it was partly your own fault for going scavenging downstairs at the dead of night.'

'I was half dead with hunger. What would you expect me to do?'

Joshua refrained from telling Cobb that if he had had an ounce of intelligence he would have washed himself, waited till morning and sent for the maid to announce his arrival in the proper manner. Although he had determined to dwell no more on the events at Astley, having Cobb before him Joshua's curiosity was once more kindled. Interred in the Roundhouse, Cobb could have had nothing to do with Caroline Bentnick's death, yet he was irrefutably involved with much that had earlier passed. Where was the harm in putting a question or two to him? It could only help allay certain matters in Joshua's mind, and that might bring him peace. 'Tell me frankly, Cobb, what it was that brought you to this country?'

'I came because I was charged to do so. I am an attorney at law. I was engaged in a matter of disputed property.'

'Yes, yes, I know all that. But as I understand it, Hoare took care of things at this end. You were employed to work for him in Barbados. *You* had no real reason to come to this country.'

Cobb looked thoughtful a moment. Joshua thought he caught something hidden in his expression. 'Very well, I will tell you in all honesty what I told you before. Violet was my reason. You have seen her, Pope. Surely, then, you can understand how I was driven to follow her.'

'And did she offer you any encouragement?'

He paused and rolled his eyes skywards as if casting his mind back over past times. 'She *was* fond of me in Bridgetown. Otherwise I would not have come here. It was only after she came to Astley her mother found out and tried to intervene.'

'What did Violet do?'

'She said it wasn't wise to cross her mother. That was why she pretended to fall for Francis Bentnick and said she wanted no more to do with me.'

'Pretended?'

'Aye. We still communicated from time to time, by letter and rendezvous in the garden.'

'But in Herbert's desk I found a letter addressed to you in which she declared the relationship at an end.'

'She wrote that as a ploy, to convince her mother that our relationship was over,' said Cobb.

Joshua was unsure whether or not Cobb was deluding himself; certainly he seemed convinced of the veracity of what he said. But would Violet really be capable of such duplicity? 'How did Sabine know about the letter?'

'Sabine sent Herbert to the inn to plague me over my

relations with Violet. I showed him the letter, as proof there was no longer anything between us.'

'In that case how did it find its way into Herbert's desk?'

'When Hoare came he also pursued the matter with me and I gave him the same letter to read. But he took it from me and refused to return it.'

'So Hoare also took exception to your relations with Violet?'

Cobb swallowed thoughtfully and nodded. Joshua had struck a cord, he was sure of it. 'He said my behaviour was extremely unprofessional. To grow romantically involved with a person opposed to one's client defied common sense as well as every legal rule of conduct he could think of. I was dangerously jeopardizing the outcome of our client's case. He tried to get me to leave. But I wouldn't. I wanted Violet, you see, Pope. Wouldn't leave without her.'

'Tell me about the day Hoare died. You said you believed your life was in danger and that you were the intended victim. What makes you say so?'

'The evening before Hoare was found dead, I received a message. I believed it to be from Violet. The note asked me to meet her in the pinery at ten. It said she had something to tell me that would lift my spirits. I hoped that meant she would agree to come away with me.'

'So why did Hoare go in your stead?'

'Hoare happened to be present when the message was delivered and grew suspicious that there was still something between us. We sat together for some hours arguing about it. I denied that the message was from Violet and refused to say who it was from. I said it was no concern of his. During this time he made me take too much brandy. I fell asleep. He had drugged me, Pope, I'm certain of it.'

'What happened when you woke?'

'It was after midnight, so I had missed my rendezvous. I looked in my pocket and found the message gone. I went to Hoare's room and found it empty. Guessing he had gone in my place to turn Violet against me, I went to the pinery to try to rectify matters.

'When I got there I found the place was like a furnace. I could hardly stand the heat, but I saw Hoare lying there. I don't know if he was dead, but before I could ascertain what had happened to him I heard footsteps approaching. I wasn't about to let myself be apprehended for trespass or whatever misadventure had befallen him, so I followed my instincts and ran. Even then, I fancied the footsteps were following me. I grew terrified. I dared not go back to my lodgings, for fear of being apprehended there. So I went into hiding, intending to bide my time till I could recover my belongings. But then you appeared and took them before I had found a chance. And when you told me about the corpse, I realized that Hoare had been killed in my stead – and that I must have been the intended victim.'

Joshua remembered clearly the whiff of brandy on Cobb's breath the night he had accosted him on the road. It didn't surprise him in the least to know he had drunk himself into a stupor, but he let this pass and pressed home with his chief concern.

'What made Hoare so anxious to keep you from meeting Violet? She wasn't directly involved in the disputed property. Did he believe you wanted to persuade her to steal the necklace? Was that why Hoare wanted you away, because he thought you were after the necklace for your own gain? Did *you* kill him on account of his objections?'

At this Cobb paused, gazed incredulously at Joshua, then broke into a mocking laugh. 'What an imbecile you are, Pope, even to entertain such an idea! I had no need of the necklace. I told Hoare as much. That was partly why he grew so incensed with me.'

'So he did accuse you?'

'Yes, until I showed him my fortune. That maddened him still more, for despite my protestations he knew I was lying. He could see there was no way to hold me from pursuing

Violet and, as I said, the prospect of us eloping jeopardized the case and contradicted his notions of professional etiquette.'

'A fortune?' Joshua repeated. 'What do you mean?'

'I had a stroke of good luck not long after arriving here.'

Joshua's face must have shown his bewilderment, for Cobb elucidated. 'The tables, Pope.'

'I had no idea you were a gambling man.'

'I have found that for a stranger in any town it's an efficacious way to forge acquaintances and pass a convivial evening.'

A worrisome seed now sprouted in Joshua's brain. 'Is that what you did when you got to Richmond? Went gaming?'

'Haven't I just told you as much?'

The memory of raucous laughter now began to reverberate like an echoing gong in Joshua's head. He vividly remembered his encounter with Arthur Manning and Manning's reaction to the mention of Cobb's name. 'And do you recall with whom you played?'

For a moment Cobb tilted his head and swallowed silently. When he spoke he looked Joshua directly in the eye. 'Of course,' he said evenly. 'I won two thousand pounds in a run of only three nights from a man called Arthur Manning. Never dreamed of making such riches so easily. That was what I told Violet when I met her in the gardens. I had money enough to allow us to go back to Barbados, buy a house and some land, and our future would be assured. We had no need of the necklace or her mother's approbation. It was only later I understood that making a fortune overnight is only a good thing if you live to enjoy it.'

'What do you mean?'

'Isn't it obvious? A fortnight after I had beaten Manning so roundly Hoare was killed after he went to a rendezvous in my place. The message I was given agreeing the rendezvous can't have been in Violet's hand, though it was close enough to fool me. Two days after Hoare's death I was assaulted on the road up to the Star and Garter by a masked highwayman, whose physique bore a remarkable resemblance to Manning's. The man shot me in the foot, giving me the limp that now afflicts me. That is why I determined to hide out until such time as I could regain my bag and then save my skin by returning to Barbados. Give it to me now, I beg you.'

Joshua went to the corner where Cobb's bag had been left, picked it up and carried it over to him. 'I will gladly give it to you, but I regret to tell you I doubt what you left there is still inside. I searched twice and found nothing of value.'

Cobb smiled grimly. He grasped the bag, delved inside and retracted the leather case containing his travelling walking cane. He opened the case and took out the top section with its carved pineapple top. 'I bought this before leaving Bridgetown to store my correspondence from Violet. It is cunningly made with a hollow compartment inside,' he said, unscrewing the pineapple finial.

Joshua watched in astonishment as Cobb shook the tube and a clutch of large white banknotes fell into his lap.

It seemed to Joshua that recent events had taken on an entirely new and undeniably intriguing complexion. Ignoring his determination to forget what had taken place at Astley, he was again so caught up in what he had learned he couldn't prevent himself from further contemplation.

Cobb with his fortune won from Arthur Manning had no reason to kill Hoare or steal the necklace. In view of Cobb's story of the message and the subsequent attempts on his life, it seemed probable that Hoare had been killed by mistake. Cobb was the intended victim. What did that signify? Obviously the murderer couldn't distinguish between Cobb and Hoare. That eliminated Violet and Arthur Manning, who both knew what Cobb looked like. He could also discount Herbert, who had called on Cobb at the Star and Garter, and Francis, who had met Cobb in the gardens at Astley. Sabine remained suspect, not having met Cobb.

But there was also another name which sprang to his mind,

one that he had never considered until now. Arthur Manning had been deprived of his fortune. His sister Lizzie had demonstrated her apparent devotion to him in innumerable ways. She had meddled in matters that were none of her concern. She had come to Joshua's rooms in her nightgown in the dead of night and searched his room while he slept. She was frantic to trace her brother. Until now he had assumed this was simple sisterly devotion. Now it seemed there was more than this: her determination to find Cobb's bag showed she was bent on retrieving the fortune her brother had lost. And if she was prepared to risk her reputation for her family fortune what other risks might she be prepared to take for it? Murder perhaps?

Joshua poured himself a brandy from a Bristol glass decanter and thought back to the night she had entered his room so unexpectedly. He had known before that she was fickle; he had guessed her purpose, but he hadn't properly understood. He should have questioned her more rigorously at the time, demanded to know why she wanted the bag. It had nothing to do with the necklace. Having learned that Cobb was living as a vagabond and was eager to recover his bag, she must have guessed her family fortune lay inside it.

Joshua pondered the question of the necklace and the murder of Caroline Bentnick. Was Lizzie responsible for these two evil deeds as well as Hoare's murder? In the case of poor Caroline, there was an obvious motive: Lizzie might have overheard Caroline declare she had seen something that would lead him to the murderer. In other words, Lizzie may have killed her dear friend Caroline Bentnick in order to save her own skin.

But what about the necklace? Could Lizzie have taken that too? Here Joshua grappled to find a clear reason for her doing so. If she had stolen the necklace because she was intent on saving her family fortune, why return the jewel after Caroline's death? It seemed implausible that Lizzie was responsible for the theft. The disappearance of the necklace was separate from the murders. Either Arthur had taken it – unlikely, for if he had he wouldn't have needed to come looking for Cobb's bag either – or, most likely, as he first supposed, it was stolen as a consequence of Charles Mercier's disputed will. Mrs Bowles was not Mercier's daughter. More than ever he needed to find who was.

Having recovered his fortune, Cobb seemed suddenly overwhelmed by his exertions. He lay back on the daybed and closed his eyes. Joshua covered him with a blanket. The fever was rising again; perspiration had gathered on his brow and he looked unhealthily flushed. Joshua thought about calling for Kitty again or going downstairs to ask Bridget for her advice, but in the end he managed alone. He gave Cobb a hefty dose of an elixir he took regularly to soothe his nervous maladies and an opium pill. For good measure, he took a spoonful himself to help calm his own feverish thoughts. He passed the next two hours sitting by Cobb, sponging dry his head whenever the sweats appeared.

In between these ministrations, Joshua leaned his head back in his hands, stretched his toes within the embroidered slippers he favoured, and considered what his next actions should be. He wanted to know what Bridget had learned from Crackman. Had he given her the name he so urgently desired? If he was still prevaricating, Joshua was determined to pay him a call first thing and extract the information himself. He considered confronting Lizzie Manning, but the thought of returning to Astley and subjecting himself once more to the oppressive atmosphere of that house and its inmates was far from tempting. He told himself, not for the first time, that whatever she said would skirt the truth. And what had gone on at Astley was now no longer a concern of his. Why endanger his own life to avenge the death of Hoare, a man he had never known? And yet, though he could not entirely convince himself he should go, neither could he resolve that he shouldn't, and in this state of indecision he decided it was time to retire.

# Chapter Forty

Crossing the hallway from the parlour to his bedchamber, Joshua chanced to look down and saw to his surprise that a packet had been pushed beneath his door. He bent to retrieve it and, after a cursory glance, saw that it was a message from Bridget, enclosing another letter. He carried both communications to his bedchamber and, having shed his clothes, donned his nightshirt and nightcap and swaddled himself comfortably in bedclothes, he settled down to read.

*Joshua,*
*I didn't like to trouble you this evening, for Kitty told me you recovered Cobb and that he was unwell and you were occupied with looking after him. Nevertheless, I was much relieved to learn of your safe return. I have been fearful for your safety ever since I left Richmond. I thank God you weren't attacked again and have left that ill-fated place once and for all.*
*    I must tell you that I called on Crackman, but found his office closed, but for a solitary clerk who was bundling up letters and papers. Crackman has fallen victim to some virulent distemper and is dead, and since Hoare is also deceased, there is no one to continue the business of the firm. I couldn't ascertain from the clerk who will take over the affairs of the clients belonging to the company. He said that he had no knowledge of Crackman's business concerning a dispute over a necklace, but that if I left my*

*particulars he would write as soon as there was any news to*
*impart.*

*I enclose herewith a letter that arrived for you yesterday.*
*I am, sir, your obedient servant,*
*Bridget Quick*

At the news of Crackman's demise, Joshua shook his head
in frustration so vigorously that the tassel on his nightcap
swayed back and forth like a pendulum. Crackman knew who
the claimant was and now he was dead. Once again malicious
fate seemed to conspire against him. But then, before he had
time to work himself into an overly morose frenzy, he
reminded himself that there must be records of the wretched
woman's identity. Thus calmed, he glanced at the second
letter. He saw by the sender's address it was from Lancelot
Brown. Immediately he was overcome with interest at what
had prompted that great man to put pen to paper. He opened
the seal and unfolded the page.

*Sir,*
*You had no sooner left me than something occurred to me*
*concerning a member of the household at Astley. In view of recent*
*strange events I think I should apprise you of it. I would impart*
*the information in this letter, only since it is long and rather*
*complicated I think it easier to tell you in person. I propose we*
*meet at the Roebuck Inn on the terrace of Richmond Hill on*
*Wednesday afternoon at three o'clock.*

*I am, sir, yours in expectation,*
*Lancelot Brown*

Joshua refolded the letter, placed it on the side table and
snuffed out his light. His mind was soothed by the draught he
had taken, but for some minutes he resisted the desire to sleep.
His dismay at learning of Crackman's death was eclipsed by
Brown's letter. What had caused Brown to write so urgently?
Which member of the Astley household did his information

concern? Would he corroborate Joshua's suspicion that Lizzie was the culprit? In his present state of exhaustion it was far beyond Joshua's imagination to guess what his information could be, but his determination to have nothing further to do with Astley and its inhabitants was forgotten. Wednesday was tomorrow. He would take the midday stage to Richmond to meet Brown.

Next morning, Cobb's face still looked pallid and two crown-sized red stains had appeared on his cheeks. Joshua called Kitty for some barley gruel and rice milk, which Cobb ate with reasonable appetite. Joshua dosed him again with his elixir and an opium pill and judged him a little better. Before Cobb fell asleep Joshua took his leave, saying he would be out for much of the day and possibly the next night too. In the meantime Cobb should stay where he was. The servants would bring him whatever he desired in the way of nourishment and Bridget Quick, his landlady's daughter, would look in on him.

Joshua buttoned his best blue coat and descended swiftly to the ground floor, where he knocked on Bridget's door. She opened it immediately and when she saw it was Joshua she gave him a blushing smile. He noticed she was dressed in a sprigged muslin gown which was cut low over her ample shoulders. Her mass of toffee-coloured hair was bound up beneath a linen cap, but wisps of curls had escaped and wound about her ears. Compared with the pallid Cobb, she looked as plump and full of life as a rosebud on the point of unfurling. Joshua felt warmer than ever towards her. If he hadn't such urgent business to attend to, he would have asked her there and then to accompany him on a promenade.

He stood awkwardly on the threshold. 'Forgive me for calling so early, Miss Quick, but I have a great deal to do and intend to return immediately to Richmond. I come with some damnably sad news that I thought you would want to know.'

341

'Oh,' said Bridget, suddenly crestfallen. 'In that case you had better come in. I thought you were finished with that dreadful place.'

She invited him into the parlour and indicated to a settle at the side of the hearth. Bending distractingly low in front of him, she sat down on a low stool opposite. Joshua was temporarily mesmerized by the sight of her. He noted the edge of lace about her neck, from which her breasts seemed to swell like smooth rocks from a frothy sea; he imagined the comforting swell of her hips beneath her hooped skirts, and thought that her eyes seemed immeasurably larger and more lustrous than he remembered them. He had been drawn to her from the minute he had seen her in the cart at Richmond, but had fought his feelings ever since. How cowardly he had been to allow himself to be deterred by her mother! And Meg was nothing but a distraction. He would do whatever it took to pacify the daunting Mrs Quick. Perhaps if he offered to paint Bridget she might warm to him.

Having acknowledged these feelings to himself, he longed to announce them to the object of his affections. But he deemed it inappropriate to speak of such matters when there was sad news to impart. He contented himself with leaning forward, taking her plump white hand in his, and giving it a gentle squeeze.

'There has been another tragedy. Caroline Bentnick was found dead in the pinery yesterday morning.'

Instantly Bridget retracted her hand from his tender grasp and held it to her mouth. 'What? Caroline? Miss Bentnick? I should have known that house would bear witness to more tragedy.'

Joshua nodded mutely.

'What happened?'

'She was found strangled and with the necklace upon her. Immediately afterwards, Mr Bentnick took against me, for meddling in Hoare's death, which he believed was the reason Caroline was killed. He ordered me out of the house. I shall finish the portrait in my rooms here.'

Bridget's cheeks were marble pale. She swallowed uncomfortably and looked at her hands. 'The necklace is returned. That means your reputation is safe, which is something to be thankful for, I suppose. But in that case why did you tell me just now you intend to return to Astley? Would it not be foolhardy to annoy your patron further and again risk unnecessary peril?'

'I go not to Astley but Richmond, because Mr Brown has asked me to meet him there this afternoon. He has something important to tell me. Moreover, I have found out something from Cobb of crucial importance. But until I hear what Mr Brown has to tell me I would prefer to keep an open mind who the murderer is. Once I know, it seems only right I should inform Herbert of my discoveries. What he does about them will be his own affair.'

Bridget raised her eyes briefly to meet his. 'So you do intend to go back there?'

'Not necessarily. I can send word to him from the town.'

'What was it you learned from Cobb?'

'That Lizzie Manning's brother Arthur lost the family fortune to him at cards. Cobb became acquainted with Arthur Manning in some gambling hole in Richmond and, after a few epic evenings at the tables, took everything he had.'

'How is that significant?'

'Miss Manning is devoted to her brother – that is without question. She has been prepared to go to extraordinary lengths to discover the whereabouts of Cobb's bag, which contained the money he won from her brother. Suppose she had been so bent on retrieving the lost wealth that she was prepared to kill Cobb for it? Cobb says he received a letter, apparently sent by Violet, calling him to a rendezvous in the pinery but that Hoare went in his stead. It is possible that Lizzie sent that letter, that she killed Hoare, believing he was Cobb, and then killed Caroline Bentnick, believing she knew something that might lead to her murder being discovered.'

343

All this while Bridget had met his regard without blinking. Now her eyes flashed away; she was lost in thought for some time. 'Could Lizzie Manning be capable of such an act? Miss Bentnick considered her a dear companion. To commit such treachery against an innocent, affectionate friend – why, it's beyond me even to contemplate it . . .'

'I would prefer to believe it wasn't so, but I tell you this frankly: Miss Manning has amply demonstrated to me her capacity for duplicity. She is a woman who uses the truth when it suits her purpose, and when it doesn't she will invent whatever she fancies. Whether she is also a murderer remains to be seen.'

Bridget bit her lip uncomfortably, as if suddenly overcome with emotion. She took from her pocket a lace-trimmed handkerchief with which she carefully dabbed her eyes. 'Now you have explained, I suppose I comprehend your predicament, Mr Pope. I see why you have determined to go, although I urge you to exercise the greatest caution.'

Touched though he was by Bridget's evident concern, something in her demeanour surprised him. She seemed less open, no longer her usual straightforward self – the trait he most admired in her. He suspected she was more frustrated at his sudden departure than she revealed. And since he too felt unable to speak as freely as he would have liked, an awkwardness descended between them.

Joshua recognized the strain and its presence infuriated him. Just when he had awakened from a solitary nightmare to find himself at the portals of romantic paradise, circumstances again seemed to conspire against him. He wanted to declare himself, yet any declaration would be doomed under the present strained state of affairs. Nevertheless, no harm could come from giving her some inkling of his feelings. 'I thought,' he said, squeezing her hand again and looking earnestly into her eyes, 'that after I return we might take an excursion. I hear the Ombres Chinois is an entertainment worth seeing, or we could take a promenade in Vauxhall Gardens.'

Bridget coloured deeply as she rose and led him to the door. 'Let us look forward to that safe return, Mr Pope. Then we will have no more to do than discuss the merits of Ombres Chinois or Vauxhall. Until that time, God speed . . .'

# Chapter Forty-one

Outside, the fine weather of previous weeks had vanished. The storm that had threatened yesterday and never arrived felt imminent now. Lumpy pewter clouds were piled precariously behind the rooftops. A piercing wind had begun to blow. Rain would come soon and he prayed it would not fall directly upon his best blue coat. After everything else that had gone wrong he had no desire to see it ruined.

He took a chair to the Eight Bells in the Strand, from whence he would take the midday stage to Richmond. A cacophony of sound and smell assailed his senses. Iron wheels creaked on cobble stones, the stench of rotting pies and pickled herrings mingled with the ordure of the open gutter – the carcass of a dog, offal discarded by a butcher, the contents of chamber pots. Within the arcades, the cries of orange sellers and vendors of vegetables and damask roses vied stridently with the bellowing calls of passing chair carriers and hackney coachmen.

On the way, since he had a few minutes to spare, he impulsively directed the bearers up Gray's Inn Lane, to the door leading to the premises of Crackman and Hoare. Joshua had been much frustrated by the news Bridget had given him of Crackman's sudden demise. But thinking about it further he had reasoned that even though she had been unable to extract much information from the solitary clerk on the premises, his own confident manner and powers of persuasion might unearth something more. The records relating to the case would certainly reveal the name of the claimant for the necklace.

As he stepped down from the chair, he chanced to glance up at the grimy windows of that establishment. A figure was visible at the window. Joshua could have sworn that the man he saw was Enoch Crackman, but then he told himself that he must have been mistaken. He entered the door, charged along the dingy corridor and up the stairs and threw open the door to Crackman's office. The place was exactly as he remembered it. There was no sign that the office was being closed down. Rather the reverse, it seemed busier than ever. Several clerks were employed at their desks; an old man clad in a dusty black coat was crouched with his back towards him. 'Mr Crackman,' he said to the humped figure, 'is it you?'

The old man turned. His one beady eye lighted on Joshua, he gave a curiously stern smile. 'Why, it's Mr Pope returned, is it? Yes, sir,' he said, 'who else would you expect to find here?'

'Forgive me for bursting in on you so rudely. A friend of mine came to call on you a day or two ago. A Miss Bridget Quick. She was told by a member of staff that you were . . . no longer in practice.'

Crackman shook his head, his mouth down-turned with annoyance. 'You are confused, Mr Pope. I recall Miss Quick's visit quite clearly. I told her that I was disappointed not to have heard from you sooner. My partner Hoare has never returned and I must presume some terrible misadventure has befallen him. He had no family to speak of apart from me – I am his uncle. Did you receive my letter? I asked for any news you could give me. You never acknowledged it.'

Joshua was filled with shame that temporarily eclipsed any astonishment he felt over Bridget's deception. How could he have omitted to let Crackman know of his partner's death? Thank God there was no wife or children starving on account of his thoughtlessness. 'The letter arrived. My apologies for not replying, but that is why I was anxious to call on you. You are correct in your surmise that something dreadful happened to Hoare. It was he who was found dead in the pinery, not Mr Cobb at all. Forgive me for my negligence in not informing you sooner.'

'Hoare is dead?' Crackman shook his head forlornly. 'Poor fellow. I suppose I knew something of the kind must have happened.' He put down his pen and looked out of the window. His mouth remained taut. He blinked slowly, repeating, 'Poor fellow, poor fellow.'

Joshua looked at his boots. He deserved a scolding for his insensitivity. This was the first time anyone had expressed any vestige of emotion for poor dead Hoare and Joshua was glad to see it. Nevertheless his head was in a state of confusion. Bridget had told him Crackman was dead. But why? What had possessed her to she say such a thing? Before he could ponder this properly he had to extract the name of the claimant from Crackman. He was loath to do so in Crackman's present distressed state, but his dismay at Bridget's deception made him more ruthless than usual.

'I know this is a difficult moment, sir. But I remain convinced your nephew's death is bound up with the dispute over the necklace. Therefore I have to ask: who is the claimant for the necklace?'

Crackman turned back and subjected Joshua to a baleful glare. 'I will tell you what I told Miss Quick. The claimant was anxious to preserve her anonymity. That was why I did not write it in the letter I sent you. But in view of recent events there is no longer any reason to conceal her name.' He paused as if weighing his decision. 'Her name is Nell Lambton.'

'Nell Lambton,' said Joshua, repeating the unfamiliar name for which he had searched so long, as if he were fearful of forgetting it. 'And where may I find Nell Lambton?'

Crackman paused, scrutinizing Joshua, weighing his words. 'For several months she was a resident of a hovel near Smithfield. The street's name is Cap Alley.'

'And now?'

'Now she is no longer there.'

'Then I ask again, where may I find her?'

Crackman gazed unblinkingly at Joshua, which gave him the feeling he should have known the answer. 'She lies in the paupers' graveyard at the church of St Swithin's nearby. Shall I spell it out, Mr Pope? She died ten days ago. And since she had no family to take up her cause, the case is closed. And, incidentally, I will never be paid.'

'Died?' reiterated Joshua. 'How?'

'How?' Crackman gave a mirthless laugh. 'Let me tell you what I learned from the constable. Ten days or so ago, her landlord made his way to the vile hole she rented from him and found what he thought was a bundle of rags. When he looked again, he found beneath the rags a body so emaciated from want it was naught but skin and bone. She had died, sir, though whether from hunger, thirst or disease, only God knows.'

'Dead!' said Joshua, scarcely comprehending.

'Aye, dead, sir.'

He thought immediately of Sabine's rendezvous. Was this why she had been so surprised to find her necklace gone?

'Was there anything suspicious in it?'

'You know as well as I that no one gives a jot for those without means. How many like Nell die in abject misery with none to remark their deaths, I shudder to think. But what I will say, as God is my witness, is that Mrs Mercier has much to answer for. Indirectly it was she who killed Nell. If she hadn't refused to adhere to her husband's clearly stated will, Miss Lambton would have lived in respectable lodgings, with enough to eat, as he intended, and I believe she would still be alive today.'

Joshua shook his head. He could hardly take in the fact that after all his endeavours to trace Nell Lambton she had died before he found her. She could have had nothing to do with the murders or the theft of the necklace or its return.

The answer lay elsewhere.

# Chapter Forty-two

Outside the window the city clocks began to chime. It was half-past eleven; unless he hurried he would miss the midday stage. With a brisk word of thanks to the still stony-faced Crackman, Joshua fled downstairs to his waiting chair, which he directed to take him to the Eight Bells in the Strand as speedily as possible.

He made the coach with just minutes to spare. It was only when he was ensconced in his seat, gazing from the window at the juddering scene, that he allowed himself to contemplate Bridget's part in all of this. He was rocked by her trickery. He felt he had been subjected to the gravest of assaults. How crass he had been, how blinded by his own stupid assumptions. He had taken for granted that there was nothing underhand in Bridget's eagerness to please him. Even this morning when he sensed that there was something she was holding back, he had put it down to her feelings for him. And yet now it transpired her fondness was feigned, her motives not at all what he had assumed. But what had possessed her to lie about Crackman and pretend he was dead?

He had yet to come to any coherent conclusion when they entered the village of Hammersmith and the impending storm that had threatened for two days began to break. Large heavy gouts started to fall with gentle regularity but soon gathered pace until they pelted down with torrential force. Within half an hour the road was reduced to a quagmire of mud and rubble, and every unfortunate pedestrian they passed was drenched. Then there was a violent clap of thunder: the startled horses reared then slipped and the carriage lurched and wavered alarmingly. The stress of the sideways wrench proved too much for the front axle, which gave an audible crack that sounded like a gun being fired, and snapped; the next thing Joshua saw was a wheel careering off like a spinning coin into the overflowing ditch.

The carriage veered sideways and ground to a halt at an alarming angle to the general groans of those within, who were thrown all over one another. The postillion clambered down from his mount and went off to recover the wheel and summon a carter to make temporary repairs. As soon as he returned, all the passengers, Joshua included, were forced to leave the carriage and wait forlornly on the verge, while the rain saturated every inch of their being and the heavens entertained them with crashes of thunder and lightning such as Joshua had rarely witnessed before.

When at length they resumed their journey, the conditions had deteriorated still further. The road was now a brown sheet of whirlpools and swirling mud and water that in parts had merged with the river Thames, so that it was almost impossible to see where one began and the other ended. Joshua's morbid fear of the river came once more to the fore and was uppermost in his mind. His predicament was worsened by many of the occupants of the carriage, who began sobbing and wailing and praying to Lord God Almighty to save them from drowning in the deluge. Meanwhile the poor driver sitting up in front, drenched to the skin, could make only the slowest of progress to avoid being washed away into the swirling waters of the Thames. Joshua clutched the edge of his seat, gazing at the rivulets of water coursing the window, wondering if he was about to be drowned and, if not, how long Lancelot Brown would wait.

Two hours late he strode into the parlour at the Roebuck.

Taking off his sopping hat and coat, he shook a small river of water to the floor. He glanced about but saw no sign anywhere of Brown. In his present saturated, over-anxious condition Joshua hadn't much appetite for prattle, yet he needed to discover Brown's whereabouts. He approached a man serving ale behind a counter and introduced himself, adding that he wondered if perhaps there was a message for him from Mr Brown.

'Aye, sir,' returned the barman with a nod of acknowledgement. 'He guessed you were held up by the bad weather, and since he wished to call in at Astley he bade me tell you to follow him there.'

Joshua found himself now in a dreadful dilemma. Brown had proceeded ahead without him, expecting him to follow and knowing nothing of Joshua's banishment or his recent speculation concerning Lizzie Manning. Even if Lizzie was innocent, there was Sabine to consider in the light of her visit to London and the death of Nell Lambton. Not only that, Brown's ignorance might very well lead him into real danger. Joshua firmly believed his unfortunate conversation with Caroline on the terrace had prompted her murder and he dreaded being the unwitting cause of another death. Should Brown let slip something about Joshua's impending arrival and the urgent reason he wanted to speak to him, the murderer might be provoked to take drastic action to silence him.

He had to act. With Herbert's leave or without it, he must warn Brown of the dangers – but how should he proceed? He stood by the fire in the front parlour of the Roebuck Inn. As the steam from his sopping clothing rose all around him, a scheme emerged in his brain. He would approach the house on foot, make contact with Granger, who he knew would be somewhere in the gardens, and, after impressing the need for discretion in this matter, ask him to send word to Brown to meet him in the gardens. In due course Joshua could decide whether or not he should send word via Brown to inform

Herbert of his recent conclusions, or whether he dared request a meeting face to face.

Joshua wasted no time in renting a horse. Then, having donned his coat and hat once more, he ventured out. The whole of Richmond Hill was swathed in mist and cloud; the trees lining the route were bowed down with the weight of the water that had besieged them, and the road was strewn with sticks and leaves and stones washed down by the deluge. Nevertheless the weather was easing. By the time he was a few hundred yards from the gate of Astley, the rain had dwindled to no more than a persistent drizzle.

Joshua dismounted and circumnavigated the boundary wall until he came to a garden gate. To one side stood a small cottage, the sort of dwelling a country yeoman might inhabit, nestling amid an orchard of fruit trees. A boy holding a sickle was sheltering beneath one of them. Ignoring him, Joshua walked past to the cottage door and banged upon it. There was no reply. He knocked several times more and, when there was still no answer, peered in through the windows.

The scene within was unremarkable: a small parlour, comfortably furnished with a couple of upholstered armchairs and a mahogany table, the walls hung with engravings of country houses set in parks, a couple of painted landscapes, half a dozen botanical plates; a portrait of a lady hung above the fireplace. The lady was round-faced, with a determined set to her chin and full mouth. Her hair and eyes were as dark as a gypsy's. She was painted in the act of drinking tea from a porcelain cup. The cup was delicately painted with a coat of arms on its side. Joshua peered at the portrait critically and concluded it was of surprising quality; the pose was original although it lacked animation. He guessed from the style of brushwork it was the work of Thomas Hudson or possibly, depending on its age, of his master, Jonathan Richardson.

Next door was a kitchen hung with a few iron and copper pots. Pieces of printed crockery sat on a dresser rack by a large range and a stone sink was set in an alcove at the back. There was no sign of life in either room.

Joshua strode purposefully back to the lad. 'I would like to tether my horse,' he said rather impatiently. 'I take it neither you nor the occupants of this dwelling would have any objection?'

'No, sir,' said the lad, screwing up his eyes to keep the rain from his face, as he looked up at him. 'There's no one here for the time being but me, and I'll keep an eye on him for you.'

'Here's a penny for your trouble,' Joshua said, handing him a coin. 'Is this your father's cottage?'

'No, sir,' said the boy. 'I'm Joe Carlton. The cottage belongs to Mr Granger, the head gardener at Astley.'

It occurred to Joshua that he could send the boy in search of Granger and wait here by his cottage, where there was no danger of him meeting any member of the household. In the end, though, he decided against it. He was too impatient to wait.

He tied his horse to the fence and entered, through an arched wooden gate, the grounds of Astley. He found himself in a grass walk bordered on either side by lilac, cherry and walnut trees. The entrance to the kitchen garden was via a small gate set into another slightly lower wall a short distance to his left. Joshua walked through the gate and headed towards the head gardener's office, where, owing to the inclement weather, he hoped to find Granger sheltering.

The wind had picked up, but the rain had ceased for the time being and a swathe of purple clouds had parted to reveal a thin melon-slice of sun. The only sounds were the patter of water dripping from the leaves to the ground and the faint rustle of wet leaves buffeted in the wind. There was no evidence of activity, no sound of voices. Presumably the workers had gone home when the storm broke.

Joshua shivered as the wind pressed his damp clothing against his warm flesh. By his estimation it was only about six o'clock, but the murky weather made the day seem

354

prematurely dark. Despite his eagerness to resolve matters and find Brown, the gloom invaded his senses. His nerves felt unstrung and he sensed the sinister throb of a headache coming on.

A few minutes later found him at the entrance to the small brick-built shed that Granger called his office. Granger was not inside, although there was evidence that he had not gone far and would return shortly. His clay pipe, which Joshua had rarely seen him without, was lying on the desk atop a neatly ordered pile of papers, alongside a half-eaten crust of bread and mutton. Joshua sat down on the only chair in the room to wait for his return.

# Chapter Forty-three

It had begun to drizzle with soft persistence again when, some minutes later, the door swung open. Granger stood there, a look of bewilderment upon his face. His outer clothes were as drenched as Joshua's and, despite his hat, which he now removed, his hair was whipped wild by the wind and rain. He had evidently sprinted back to the shelter of his office and his face glowed with his exertion. Once he had overcome his surprise at Joshua's sudden appearance, he looked far from pleased to see him sitting in his hut, in his chair, dripping water all over his tidy floor.

'Mr Pope,' Granger said. 'I thought you had gone away.' Clearly he must have heard Herbert's last bellowing command that Joshua leave his property immediately, yet he was much too circumspect to mention it.

Joshua decided his wisest course was to be equally politic. 'You are correct in that respect, Granger. I have returned only briefly to speak to Mr Brown. He left a message for me that he would see me here. I believe he is visiting Astley this afternoon?'

'If that is so, then I haven't been informed of it.'

He looked wary now that he had recovered his breath a little and Joshua saw that he would have to speak frankly if he were to get anywhere. 'Mr Granger, I have a favour to ask of you. No doubt you heard Mr Bentnick's parting words. He sent me away in a temper and warned me against returning to

Astley. I cannot show my face at the house just like that, for I fear his reaction may be unreasonable. Yet Mr Lancelot Brown has something of importance to tell me, and I also have something I would communicate to him. I should be grateful, therefore, if you would go to the house and let him know of my arrival here. Please do not, whatever you do, let anyone else know of my presence here.'

Granger's delicate fingers flicked nervously on a packet of seeds. A sheaf of worried channels appeared between his brows. 'Don't think me disobliging, Mr Pope, but I would not wish to anger Mr Bentnick on account of your presence in my office, particularly since I didn't invite you here. I have my position to consider – it might be jeopardized . . .'

The strain of the past hours, and his anxiety to get the message to Brown, raised a surge of annoyance in Joshua's breast. Was the gardener to present yet another obstacle? After all he had already endured? Nevertheless he quashed his self-pity and his temper and managed to respond evenly to this objection. 'Quite so, quite so, Mr Granger. Getting you into his disfavour is the last thing I would wish to do. I will wait for Mr Brown in the pinery, if that is more convenient for you.'

Granger mulled this over, brushing his chin with the hairy back of his hand as he weighed up Joshua's suggestion. Perhaps he sensed the tension in the air, for at length, with obvious reluctance, he agreed to comply. He gave a curt nod, then wordlessly donned his hat and coat and trudged towards the kitchen entrance to the house. The rain was once again becoming heavier.

Joshua headed directly for the pinery. He was still bubbling inwardly with anxiety for Brown, irritation towards Granger, and the injustices of his fate in general, mainly because his heart was still shattered by the shock of Bridget's duplicity. It was she he longed to berate, she who owed him some explanation for treating him so shabbily.

Once inside the pinery, the heat hit him like a wall. Steam began to rise from his sodden coat like moisture from a sunlit manure heap. An unpleasant pungent smell of rotting bark and dung infiltrated his nostrils. Seething with frustration, Joshua ripped off the garment, flung it at the wall and began to pace the path, staring blankly at the ranks of pineapples growing on each side. Suddenly he sympathized with Hoare, who in his final death throes had wrought havoc in this orderly place. Joshua was usually a man of impeccable control, yet now he too felt an overwhelming desire to kick the pots, hurl one on top of another, see the white roots snap and break and the young fruits smash on the stone walls. If Sabine had spent just half the money she had lavished here she might have saved poor Nell Lambton's life. What, he asked himself, was the point of pretending a Surrey garden could emulate one in Barbados? Pineapples were not destined to belong in the soil of Richmond, any more than he belonged here. Whether or not Sabine and Granger succeeded in bringing these unfriendly plants to fruit, nothing altered the fact that they were as bogus as Bridget Quick's affection.

At some point during Joshua's agitated pacing, his temper reached a plateau. He became aware of how weary he was, how his head hurt and his heart ached. He sat down on the wall and fell into a reverie in which he ran through all the adversities he had weathered and what he would have liked to say to Bridget and Lizzie and Sabine were they here.

He was roused by a slight cough at the doorway. 'Mr Pope,' said Granger, 'I have tried to pass your message to Mr Brown, but I couldn't find him at the house. Apparently he is gone to the grotto. It seems Mr Bentnick has called him in to resume the scheme.'

'Is he alone?'

'I believe so.'

'Then I must go there immediately.'

'You must allow me to accompany you. I have already explained the dangers. The place is more treacherous than ever in such bad weather. As I explained to you, there is a channel that links the tunnels to the octagon and the cascade. If the water rises too high, the whole place might flood.'

Joshua remembered clearly Lizzie Manning telling him that Herbert had taken measures to make the place safe by installing the metal door in the octagon house, but he had little appetite to argue. Anyway, he reasoned, it might prove useful to have Granger with him.

Joshua put on his steaming coat and hat once more and, with Granger by his side, sprinted towards the grotto, avoiding the pot-holes and puddles that peppered the path like pox. A vague sense of impending misfortune began to trouble him. He felt twinges of alarm at the thought of what might happen if Herbert or Sabine caught sight of him. Then he began to feel nervous at the thought that Arthur Manning might still be lurking somewhere in the vicinity. But he reminded himself that the chances of anyone venturing out in the rain were slim. Once he had found Brown and warned him, and heard what he had to say, both of them could leave. Afterwards, he would write an explanatory letter to Herbert; under the circumstances, it would be far more prudent.

Joshua was panting loudly with exertion by the time they arrived at the cavern mouth. The metal door was ajar. There was no sign of Lancelot Brown or any indication that he had been there. Joshua shouted out Brown's name loudly; it took all his efforts to make himself heard above the thunderous rain outside. There was no response. He shouted again. Still no reply.

Granger was as perplexed as he. 'I was certain we would find him here, sir. The footman was quite convinced of it. And the door is open, which suggests someone has been here.'

'Might he have ventured into one of the tunnels?'

'I doubt it, sir. Miss Manning said nothing of that.'

'Miss Manning?' Joshua's voice rose an octave. He was stupefied at what he had just heard. 'Did *she* hear you ask for Brown on my behalf?' He raised his eyes to heaven. 'Granger,' he said sternly, 'did I not tell you *expressly* to avoid any mention of my name?'

'Yes, sir.' Granger's response was sharp, as if offended by the unjustness of Joshua's accusation. 'I did my utmost to observe the instruction. It was only that when I went to the servants' hall to ask about Mr Brown she happened to enter while I was in mid-conversation with the footman. She must have guessed our discussion concerned you, for she said something like, "I might have known Pope would not let the matter drop." '

'And nor have you,' cut in a familiar voice behind.

Joshua spun round, unable to believe his ears, unable to trust his judgement. Blocking the threshold of the cavern, silhouetted against falling rain, stood Lizzie Manning. At first Joshua could not make out her expression; the light was behind her and the cloak of her hood was raised. She was no more than a rather ominous shape to him. However, she moved quickly towards him, and though his first reaction was to back away he managed to steel himself and hold his ground. As she approached, he could see her cheeks unusually flushed and her eyes ablaze with emotion; what that emotion was he dared not hazard. Another rustle caused him to look behind her. To his even greater amazement, he now saw that Lizzie had been joined by Bridget Quick, who bade him good day as normally as if she and he had crossed paths in the middle of St Martin's Lane. They had been escorted to the grotto by Francis Bentnick, who stood, arms crossed, Herculean and expressionless as ever, and said nothing.

Not knowing what to say or do, Joshua took a step towards the ladies. For one rash minute he had it in his head to take the pair by the shoulders and shake them and tell them how furious he felt at their deception. But then he thought again. He remembered that one might well be a brutal murderess and the other was certainly the most duplicitous female conceivable. Francis Bentnick had doubtless come as their protector and at the slightest show of aggression would defend them. Joshua had no wish to test the puissance of a man ten years his junior, and six inches taller, with thigh muscles the size of gammons of ham. Circumspection got the better of him. 'Miss Manning!' he exclaimed, 'I had not expected to find you here. Do you come in search of your errant brother or does some other quest now preoccupy you?'

She pushed down her hood and gave Joshua a mysterious smile. 'I came to see *you*, Mr Pope,' she said in a low voice.

'Then I should be flattered indeed.'

'Flattery has naught to do with it. I came to tell you to leave this place at once: you are not safe here. The rainwater has put twice the usual volume of water in the cascade. I told you about the tunnel joining this grotto with the lake; if the water seeps in, it might flood this cave.'

'You also told me that safety measures had been taken. And in any case, what of your brother? I told you before, I strongly suspect he might be hiding in one of the tunnels. Indeed, in view of the dangers posed by the weather I will speak frankly, for I would rather not see another corpse. There is more to my warning than mere suspicion: I know for a fact he has been here.'

She shrugged her shoulders. 'I don't know what makes you so adamant. But you may rest assured you are mistaken, sir. My brother returned to Barlow Court yesterday evening. We are quite reconciled. And since the necklace is now returned to its lawful owner, his name is no longer under a cloud and I have no further need to interfere in these investigations. I confess that was the sole reason I persuaded you to let me help you.'

'How good of you to speak so candidly, Miss Manning,' Joshua said curtly. 'You omit to mention the small matter of the fortune he lost to Mr Cobb, which was contained in Cobb's bag. I believe that had something to do with your concern.'

'Of course it did,' said Lizzie evenly, 'but, as I said, Arthur and I are reconciled. We will manage somehow without it.'

'But have you forgotten that two people have lost their lives here? And one of those was your closest friend – Caroline Bentnick. Can you so readily turn your back on such heinous crimes, or do you ignore them because you already know the culprit?'

She drew back, gasping in disbelief at his accusing tone. 'I have already confessed, Mr Pope, that I led you along because I wanted to find out Arthur's whereabouts and, I admit, to recover the money he lost. It was that, more than anything else, that troubled me. Caroline's death has come as such a shock I scarcely know what I should think or do. But staying here and risking our lives won't help her.'

Joshua scrutinized her face. Was the sorrow and confusion she expressed genuine? Anger welled up in him once again. He had intended to inform Herbert Bentnick of his suspicions regarding her, rather than confront her himself. He had meant to wait for Brown's evidence before drawing his conclusions, yet his emotion got the better of him.

'You play the concerned sister and friend to perfection, Miss Manning. What an accomplished actress you are. But Mr Cobb has told me that ever since the ill-fated night he relieved your brother of his fortune there have been several attempts upon his life. He lives in terror, unable to show his face for fear of further reprisal. It strikes me that bearing in mind your eagerness to restore your family's fortune, *you* might well have poisoned Hoare in the belief he was Cobb.'

Lizzie's face became a pale mask; her lips blanched, her eyes grew dull and grey as pewter. She shook her head dumbly, as if the accusation he had just made was so outrageous she hardly knew how to begin to refute it. But after she pondered a minute or two longer this expression altered. She fixed Joshua with a piercing stare, as if wordlessly challenging him to speak further.

After several minutes the atmosphere became so strained that even Francis was unable to support it. He interrupted the hostile hush, stepping forward and whispering something in Lizzie's ear. Then he took her arm and tried to lead her away. She hung back, turning her head over her shoulder to issue a challenge to Joshua.

'If that is what you honestly believe, why don't you have me apprehended?' she said.

362

'First, because although you had plenty of reasons to wish Cobb dead, and you have acted scandalously and led me a merry dance, I still have my doubts that you would stoop to killing Caroline. Second, because it is not my place to do so,' he replied promptly. 'Nevertheless, I would ask Mr Granger to escort you, together with the rest of your party, back indoors while I wait here for the arrival of Mr Brown. When we have finished we will return to the house, where, if Mr Bentnick so desires, I will inform him in person of my findings. What he does as a result of them is entirely his affair.'

Now, suddenly, she seemed to feel the import of Joshua's words. She coloured deeply. 'Do you honestly think Herbert will give more credence to your testimony than to mine? Do you believe I was responsible for Hoare's death and that of my dear friend Caroline? Why, I wasn't even here at Astley when Hoare's murder took place.'

As she spoke, her gestures grew increasingly animated; she broke free of Francis's grip, flinging her hands and arms about with unrestraint. At last here was some evidence he had riled her as she had riled him. He felt a small but unmistakable thrill of vengeful satisfaction and gave her an inscrutable smile.

'In that case, you have nothing to fear. As I said, my mind is still unresolved. Nonetheless, you must comprehend why your conduct places you under suspicion. It would have been easy enough for you to come covertly and kill Hoare. After all, you live no distance from here and if you were bent on murder you would hardly wish to advertise your presence. And as for your credibility over mine, we will put it to the test very soon. In the meantime, if you truly wish to prove your innocence I can think of no better way to do it than by co-operating with my request.'

Lizzie seemed to see the reason in this remark, for as suddenly as she had grown agitated she now grew calm and rational. Joshua observed her dispassionately. Her ability to alter and change at whim was an intrinsic part of her character, but was this the behaviour of a vicious murderer?

Swivelling towards Granger, who was hovering nearby, Joshua said, 'If you please, Mr Granger, escort Miss Manning and the others back to the house. Send word to Mr Bentnick that I beg leave to address him one final time. I will arrive as soon as I am able.'

Before they left, Joshua couldn't help singling out Bridget, who all this while had waited in fidgety silence with a look of agitation on her face. 'As for you, Miss Quick, I cannot think why you have come here, unless it is to make further mischief regarding the necklace, now you have learned it has been restored. I now know you deceived me over Crackman's death, although I am baffled at the reason for your deception. What is your interest in all of this? Did *you* hope to get your hands on the jewel? I wish you would tell me, for I have no notion.'

Bridget reddened; her eyes seemed larger than usual. 'Then you are less perspicacious than I thought, Joshua. My interest has nothing to do with the necklace. My interest, and regard, lies with you.'

Joshua swallowed. He still smarted within. 'Then your regard manifests itself most strangely.'

'Don't dismiss me without at least hearing me out, Joshua. I came here now precisely because I wanted to straighten matters between us. I acted foolishly, I regret what I did, but I had your wellbeing at heart when I led you astray.'

'How did you know I had found you out?'

'This morning Crackman sent word demanding an explanation for my telling you he was dead and for keeping the truth about Nell Lambton from you.'

'Then perhaps you would be good enough to share that explanation with me. You cannot be surprised I feel irked by your underhandedness. Had I not called on Crackman myself, I would still be stumbling about in the dark thinking Nell Lambton had something to do with all this, when all the time she's been dead.'

Bridget blanched. 'I repeat, I know now I was mistaken in

my actions, but my motives weren't malicious. I merely wanted to keep you in London. You have narrowly escaped one attempt on your life. Coming here again you expose yourself to further danger. When Crackman told me Nell was dead I meant to write to you directly with that information. But the more I thought about you and the recent assault on your life, the greater was my conviction that your life was in grave peril at Astley. If you learned Nell's fate you would know that the answers to the matter could have nothing to do with her, but must lie at Astley. And thus you would stay there longer and remain a target for the assailant. So I kept the news to myself. When my mother told me you had returned from Astley and as far as she knew had no plans to go back you will well imagine that I was delighted. I thought then that you must somehow have resolved the matter, but at the same time my fears for your safety were not entirely allayed. I worried that if I told you Nell Lambton was dead it might change your view of things, and you would want to return here to pursue your investigations. And so I wrote the letter in which I concocted the story of my visit to Crackman's and how I learned of his demise. It seemed easier to write rather than face you with such deception, but I justified it by telling myself it was in your best interests.'

Joshua hesitated. He wanted to believe her, but having been so completely taken in his trust was not entirely restored. 'I am touched by your concerns for my safety, Miss Quick,' he said with feigned levity, 'but I have no alternative now but to face the dangers, whatever they are. I suggest that you return with Mr Granger and the others to the house, so that you at least will be protected from the perils that lurk here.'

Bridget hesitated, her mouth pursed and anxious. 'Let me stay with you, Joshua, while you wait for Mr Brown. Then you can say all you like to me and I will have a chance to further explain.'

'That's out of the question . . .'

'Are you certain *you* won't come with us, Mr Pope?' said

365

Granger, stepping forward and cutting in as if his patience was wearing thin.

'One moment, Granger, if you please,' said Joshua, closing his eyes and holding up his palms as if to show the mental battering he was weathering. What should he do? Misgivings threatened to engulf him. He held them at bay, telling himself that what he had begun he couldn't give up now. A cowardly part of him wished he were anywhere but in the grotto at Astley, with no easy means of escape, rain pouring outside and a handful of hostile faces surrounding him. But his bolder side stood firm and remained confident that the final answers he sought lay just around the corner in what Brown would tell him.

Maintaining an air of detachment, Joshua managed to make light of Granger's offer. 'Come with you – why? Are you afraid Miss Manning may assault you? If that is the case, fear not, Mr Granger. Francis Bentnick will ensure she restrains herself.'

Granger shook his head. 'My concerns have nothing to do with Miss Manning, whom I have always held in the highest regard. I am only uncertain of *your* purpose, sir. What would you have me say to Mr Bentnick?'

'Say what I have told you to say. No more or less. I request Mr Bentnick's presence to explain all presently. Surely that can't be too much to ask!'

Colour flooded Granger's cheeks. He flashed a glance towards Joshua that made his feelings quite plain. 'Very well, sir, if that is your wish. May I remind you before I leave of the dangers of entering the tunnels in this weather. I told you of the accident in which two people—'

'You have warned me several times.'

Joshua was immovable and Granger at last acknowledged that fact. He nodded curtly, doffed his hat and turned to lead Lizzie and Francis away.

Joshua watched them slide and clamber down the sloping track. Despite his request that she leave, Bridget had remained obstinately in the cave. He knew he should insist she follow the others. Until today he had never doubted her, but the discovery that she had lied hurt him more profoundly than Lizzie Manning's obvious manipulations and Meg's abandonment. She had given a plausible explanation but he remained sceptical. He wanted to tell her so, and tell her to go, but bruised pride hampered his ability to speak.

He was still in this state of tongue-tied suspension when, unexpectedly, Bridget spoke. 'Joshua,' she said excitedly, 'come here. I think I heard something.'

Joshua turned back and walked into the grotto. At first he couldn't see her anywhere in the chamber. Then he heard a rustle of skirts that seemed to come from the very back of the cave, at the junction with the tunnel. He walked towards this spot and found her a few steps into the tunnel. She stood sideways on, her head at a slight incline, holding a finger to her lips as if to bid him be quiet.

'What is it?' Joshua said loudly, aware as he spoke of the sudden race in his pulse. 'Whatever it is, you shouldn't enter the tunnels. Everyone says they are most dangerous, particularly in bad weather.'

'Yes, yes, I know,' she said, waving her hand impatiently. 'But listen. Don't you hear it? That noise . . .'

Half wondering if this was just a distracting ploy – it wouldn't be her first – Joshua stopped talking and listened. The only thing he could hear was rain. Rain drumming overhead; rods of rain pouring down outside the entrance to the grotto as straight as the bars of a prison; rain trickling off every blessed leaf and branch and rock in the vicinity.

'There's nothing,' he said tetchily. 'It's only this infernal deluge you heard. Will it never cease! In any case, we shouldn't stand so far in; you heard Granger.'

'Listen! There it is again.'

This time Joshua heard it too – a scratchy thumping sound, as if something hard and heavy were being drummed on the rock not far from where they stood. Joshua cursed the dingy day, which made it even more gloomy than usual inside the cave, and the fact he hadn't had enough presence of mind to bring a lantern or a torch.

'Who's there?' he shouted into the dense black void ahead. He heard his voice echo mockingly, but then, quite unexpectedly, the sound seemed to respond to his call. It became more rapid and, if anything, a little louder. He took a couple of steps further towards the darkness.

'Is that wise?' said Bridget, making no attempt to stop him.

'Probably not,' he said, faltering on another few steps, hands groping in front of him to determine which way the channel went. 'You stay here,' he said, turning to issue the order over his shoulder. 'Then at least if I get lost I can call out to you and your voice will help me to find my way out.'

'Very well,' she replied.

Joshua stumbled on in the black oblivion, arms outstretched, feeling his way around stalactites and stalagmites, which threatened to trip or crown him, and dips and crannies in the floor. He could easily break his ankle if he didn't take care. In this manner he progressed a distance of no more than twenty yards, though to him it seemed infinitely further. All this while, he had the strange impression that he was not alone, that close by in the tunnel there was someone who shadowed him. Several times he thought he heard a sigh or a rustle and turned to look back over his shoulder, but since there was not the smallest ray of light in either direction he could see nothing but darkness.

Nevertheless, the notion that someone else was in the tunnel made Joshua uneasier than ever. He did not know whether his secret observer was friendly or hostile or what his or her intentions might be. Was he about to be ambushed in the dark by some unknown assailant? Lizzie had said Arthur Manning was safely ensconced at Barlow Court, but horrid memories of his recent assault in the barn returned to trouble him. He swallowed and passed his tongue over his cracked lips and tried not to dwell on such thoughts. To make matters worse, the sound that had spurred his rash journey now ceased. He was surrounded by nothing but deep silence.

To rally his courage Joshua shouted loud details of his journey back to Bridget, triumphantly detailing each obstacle that he successfully circumnavigated as if he were an explorer on some epic voyage. All too soon, however, even this distraction ceased. Bridget's echoing responses to his reports became gradually fainter, and eventually they ceased altogether. Joshua didn't want to ponder the implications of this, though it crossed his mind that if he couldn't hear her and she couldn't hear him, his contingency plan was foiled. He would have no way of navigating his way back to the entrance.

As soon as Joshua had fallen silent the blackness in the tunnel seemed to press in on him with redoubled force. He felt as if he were interred alive in a coffin of rock. Fear clenched his innards, his temples throbbed, his lungs rasped with the cold dank air. Instinct told him that he should turn back; determination ordered him to advance. Someone or something was challenging his wits. He would not let them win. Moreover, if he did retreat and then failed to find his way out, he would have to confront the hopelessness of his position. His progress slowed almost to nothing and he was on the brink of halting altogether, when a spark of hope returned. The silence was broken. He heard the sound again.

Now he didn't have to strain to hear it. Moreover, the scuffling and thumping was accompanied by a deep groaning and sounded quite close, as if it were only yards from where he stood. Joshua called out again, not to Bridget this time, but to the source of the sound. 'Who's there?' he cried, as firmly as he was able. 'Where are you?'

He had arrived at a sharp bend in the tunnel. Feeling his way through the blanket of black, placing palm over palm on the tunnel wall, he inched forward, not daring to imagine what might lie ahead.

He rounded the corner and found that the tunnel

unexpectedly widened to a cavernous chamber, only slightly smaller than the one at the entrance. Best of all, he was no longer in total darkness. Light dimly filtered down through a hole that punctured the apex of the cavern's domed roof. The hole appeared to be roughly two foot in diameter; if he looked through it he could just make out the sky fringed with grass and bracken like the lashes of a celestial eye. The light given off by this aperture was little more effective than a solitary candle illuminating a cathedral, but there was enough for him easily to make out the shadowy forms of the rocks around him.

'Bridget,' he yelled, too excited to realize she would never hear, 'I have found something!'

No sooner had he uttered these words than two things happened simultaneously. First, he realized that the groaning and thumping noise emanated from a far corner of the cave. There, bound up like a sirloin of beef, was none other than Mr Lancelot Brown. The thumping sound issued from his boots, which he was crashing on the rock in front of him. The groans flowed from his gagged mouth. Second, the instant Joshua rushed over to begin to loosen his bonds, a noise of gushing filled the cavern. He had scarcely time to register the sound before a torrent of water flooded in.

# Chapter Forty-four

Joshua had managed to remove no more than the gag binding Brown's mouth, when he felt the first wave of icy water lap at the sole of his boots.

'Thank God you are here, Pope! What took you so long? Hurry, man!' Brown urged Joshua, who was now fumbling with the bindings on his hands and feet.

'I came as fast as I was able, given the circumstances. I am doing all I can, sir. If you would just lie still, it would be easier for me.'

A few minutes more of frantic pulling and pushing and the bonds were loose. Already the water had formed a pool some six feet in diameter in the centre of the cavern where the ground dipped down. The ledge on which Brown was perched jutted up a good three feet higher than the cavern floor; even so, oily black waves were soon rippling over Joshua's feet. His fear at the sight of water made him tremble. He noted with alarm that Brown's ruddy complexion had grown pale in the dim light and he appeared to have an unhealthy greyish tinge. There was a large bruise on his temple. Joshua wanted to ask him how he had come by these injuries but for the time being the influx of water distracted him.

'We must make haste. The way out is over there,' Joshua stuttered, pointing over his shoulder to the entrance on the opposite side of the lake, whence he had arrived.

'We will have to wade through the water to reach it.'

'No, Pope. That way is useless. Look – don't you see?'

Joshua turned uncomprehendingly towards the tunnel he had walked through no more than five minutes earlier. It had transformed to a conduit of grey swirling water that spewed into the pool in the centre of the cavern. The level rose even as he watched.

'I don't understand,' he cried. 'I have just entered this chamber from that passage. It led here directly from the outer cavern. There was no water then. How can the water possibly be entering here from that way?'

'I am afraid I understand all too well,' replied Brown quietly. 'I made surveys of every nook of this terrain prior to designing the grotto. The hill above the lake is a natural labyrinth of caves and tunnels. One particular fissure, a mere few feet wide, leads all the way from the tunnel you have just entered to the lower chamber of the octagon house bordering the lake. It enters in the ceiling through an aperture not more than two feet across. You would not have noticed it unless you had raised your hand at that exact spot or the water had begun to enter as you passed it.'

'But I understood there was a door installed to prevent such occurrences,' Joshua said, remembering Lizzie's assurances.

'There was,' replied Brown evenly. 'Which is why, if torrents are entering here now, it is because the water has breached that door or someone has opened it.'

'Someone who knows we are here and wishes us dead,' said Joshua, as the terrible realization dawned upon him. 'But surely it cannot be Lizzie Manning. I have just had her escorted to the house and placed in the custody of Herbert.'

'Perhaps, though I doubt it,' said Brown, shaking his head. 'It required considerable strength to get me here. A man's strength, I hazard. And to think I would not have come at all had I known the necklace was recovered. I sent word to you because I recalled something relating to that, not the murder. But your murderer must have feared I knew something to

372

endanger him. And now both our lives are unnecessarily jeopardized.'

Joshua was confused. 'You must explain properly. What did you want to tell me concerning the necklace? Who did this to you?'

Brown was poised to answer, but at that moment came a strident cry. 'Help! Help me, please! Joshua ... where are you?' The voice was female and sounded half hysterical with terror.

'What!' Joshua said, looking round. 'Is someone else here? Did someone speak?'

'Yes!' came the wavering reply, 'I did. I intended to keep myself hidden, but the water is grown too deep; I can't go back to the entrance, because the water is even deeper in that direction and I will drown if I do.'

With this, the strapping but now saturated figure of Bridget Quick rounded the corner of the tunnel. The water in that part of the cave was now a good three feet deep and swirled around her skirt and cloak with such force that, despite her sturdy build, she waved about like a water lily in a stiff breeze. Fearing she was in danger of being swept away at any moment, Joshua launched himself off the ledge and waded manfully towards her, forgetting in the rush of the moment his own horror of water.

'Bridget,' he said, holding out his hand, 'come here this instant. Take hold of me.'

She grasped his fist with petrified fervour. Joshua planted his feet wide apart to give himself better traction, and thus, with difficulty, managed to steer her to the ledge where Brown was now squatting like a worried toad.

'Get up on there,' Joshua commanded, as Brown took hold of her and hauled her to safety. 'What on earth were you doing following me?'

'I thought it would be safe. Herbert assured me there was a door that prevented the tunnels flooding. I kept some distance behind you all the way and stopped replying to your calls so

373

you didn't suspect I was following you. But when the water came in I had no way of retreating.' She regarded him with half-terrified, half-rebellious eyes, as if daring him to scold her. Although she was an unusually robust girl Joshua saw from her pallor and shallow breathing how gravely she had been shaken and felt unable to do so. He was surprised to find he felt no sense of his earlier outrage towards her. Rather, he was sorry that she should have got herself into this terrible place.

'Fear not,' he said, taking command in what he hoped would seem a masterful manner that would inspire confidence in both Bridget and Brown, and prevent panic setting in. 'I sent Granger to escort the others to the house. I have no doubt that as soon as he has done so he will return here. He is obsessed by the dangers of this place and detested the thought of leaving Miss Quick and me alone here. It will take him no more than twenty minutes there and back. By my estimation, that time must nearly have passed.'

'But even if Granger returns and sees the water gushing out of the grotto, how will he be able to save us?' cried Bridget, her voice rising in pitch with every word she spoke. 'It is impossible to return the way we have come and impossible for him to reach us.'

'Look up,' Joshua said calmly. 'There is an opening above us. Granger will surely know of its existence. If not, we will draw his attention to it by calling out when we hear him come.'

Bridget and Brown looked doubtfully upwards. Brown, however, seemed a little heartened by what he saw. 'Compose yourself, Miss Quick. Pope has reason. Granger hasn't been here long but there is very little he doesn't know about the terrain in this garden. I recall that when he learned of the accident that happened last year, he took it most gravely.'

Joshua pointed to another ledge, a little above the one on which they were presently perched. 'If we all move up there, we will be safe for some time from the rising water.'

Brown and Joshua helped Bridget up onto the ledge – no easy feat, owing to the weight of her saturated skirts – then did likewise. Bridget had begun to shiver and tremble un-controllably with the cold and shock of her ordeal. Joshua took off his coat and wrapped it about her shoulders.

They stood there listening intently for the sound of voices or footsteps overhead. Minutes dragged by. The water began to lap over the ledge on which they stood. Bridget found the waiting unbearable; her breathing was fast and audible, her eyes unnaturally wide open. Brown, meanwhile, had crouched at the farthest corner of the ledge. Now, with the advancing waters, he too showed signs of perturbation. He stood up and pressed himself against the back wall of the cave, raising his coat-tails in one hand while he kicked futilely at the waters advancing on his boots.

It struck Joshua then that waiting was pointless. There was no indication their disappearance had been marked or that anyone was aware of the peril they were in.

The pool in the centre of the cavern floor had become a subterranean lake. The floor of the cave was now entirely covered in swirling water as blackly iridescent as a raven's wing. Light entering through the hole in the roof reflected on the surface, a small stain of silver grey in a sea of hopelessness. Looking up, Joshua saw that beyond the lattice of bracken and grass the sky had begun to darken. If they didn't do something soon, not only would the waters rise and wash them away, but dusk would fall and they would die in total darkness. For some reason the thought of death in blackness seemed infinitely more terrifying. The only glimmer of hope lay above their heads.

Joshua guessed the opening to be some twelve feet above. How deep the water was beneath it he didn't like to hazard. Quivering with apprehension he decided now was the time to find out. 'Miss Quick, Mr Brown,' he announced, 'Granger has not returned. Unless we do something immediately we are likely to drown.'

Bridget turned her terrified eyes on him. 'What do you suggest?'

'Our only hope is to try to get out through that hole in the roof.'

'And how do you propose we do that without benefit of a ladder or wings, Mr Pope?' asked Brown.

Joshua ignored the edge of bitterness in his response. 'We must try to reach it by some other means. I believe that if I held you on my shoulders, and Miss Quick sat on yours, we might just be able to reach it.'

'We are not a circus act, sir!'

Joshua looked at him sharply. 'Can you think of a better alternative?'

Brown considered for a moment; then he rubbed his temple and scratched his cheek and a sheepish expression came over his face. 'Forgive me, Pope. I am not myself since the knock on the head. Of course you are right. There is nothing for it: we must make an attempt.'

Joshua turned then to Bridget, who stood with her hands clasped in front of her, fingers locked as if in prayer, looking up at the hole in the roof. 'What about you, Miss Quick? Are you willing to try?'

For some time she did not answer. Her eyes were fixed on that small circle of light, as if she were weighing their likelihood of success. Joshua noticed that there were tear stains on her cheeks but that she had stopped trembling. She gave a bleak smile. 'I am willing to try, Mr Pope. What other alternative do we have?'

'Very well,' Joshua said, with greater certainty than he felt. 'Then this is what I propose. First, I will descend from this ledge and make my way on my own to the point directly beneath the hole to test the level of the water. There is no point in all three of us drowning if it's too deep. All being well, I will return, you will take up your positions, and the three of us as one will make our attempt. Agreed?'

The pair murmured their muted assent. Neither of them expressed any concern about what might happen if the water should prove too deep and Joshua were washed away. Neither of them offered to hold his hand as he jumped and, while Joshua put this nonchalance down to the fact they were both confused by fear, it bothered him for all that. Nonetheless he was obliged to follow the course he had set. Banishing all thoughts of being swept away and his morbid terror of drowning, he turned to face the murky flood.

For a second or two he stood on the very brink of the ledge, poised to jump, staring at the water wherein his fate lay. He fancied in that instant he felt no different from those poor unfortunates who, from time to time, in desperation, threw themselves off the piers of London Bridge. Only he was jumping to save himself, not drown himself. And so, terror thrust to one side, he plunged from the ledge.

He gasped as he felt the water penetrate his clothes and strike his skin. Almost instantly he felt himself pulled and pushed this way and that by the churning currents. Thus with one leap he had become a piece of flotsam of no more consequence than a broken branch or an empty bottle jettisoned by a drunkard. His feet slipped on the rocky floor; the water was too deep and his head went under. His legs shot upwards, he gulped icy black water and in his panic he lost all sense of bearings; surely, he thought, he would die.

Then, from what seemed a long way off, Brown's voice roared out to him. 'Put down your feet, Pope! Did you hear me? *Put down your feet!*' Joshua registered the voice; after a second or two he comprehended its meaning; he followed the instruction. By some miracle, his feet now discovered firm ground beneath them. He was not out of his depth as he supposed. He recovered his senses sufficiently to cough and splutter his way to a standing position – the water reached only halfway between his chest and waist. Shallow enough to walk, deep enough to drown, should the current carry him off and prevent him regaining a foothold.

Still quivering at his close brush with mortality, Joshua began to wade his way towards the point directly beneath the hole, a distance of some five yards. The journey there was easy enough, though he was aware all the while that he edged his way closer and closer to the hole that the water was growing deeper. By the time he reached the disc of light, it had reached his armpits. He turned back towards the ledge where Brown and Bridget waited. 'It's all right, just,' he shouted back to their blankly expectant faces. 'It will not be too deep, but we must hurry: the level is still rising.' He began to make his way back towards them, but as soon as she saw him do so Bridget called out. 'No, wait, Mr Pope! Do not risk yourself further by returning. We will come to you and climb up once we're there.'

'No!' he replied adamantly. 'The current is too strong. You saw what happened to me. And your skirts will only add to the problem. You might easily be washed away.'

'Very well, then,' said Bridget, 'if that is your only objection, I shall remove them.' To Joshua's utter astonishment, she threw off his coat, undid the clasps of her skirt, and let it drop, then untied her petticoat hoop and removed this with similar speed and dexterity. There was now covering her lower half no more than shoes, stockings and a flimsy under petticoat that barely reached her knees. Joshua would have averted his eyes, but Bridget showed not one glimmer of shame or modesty.

'Do not, I beg of you, discuss the seemliness of this conduct,' she said, before turning abruptly to Brown, who was as astonished as Joshua by her sudden disrobing. 'Come, sir, did you not hear Mr Pope? There is no time to waste,' she said sharply. Then, without warning, she took Brown's hand and pulled him into the water.

'No, wait,' Joshua shouted again as he realized her intentions. Too late. Before he knew it the pair had been washed over by the current just as he had been. And in the same state of spluttering confusion they came to their feet.

'Come slowly,' he directed them, once they had begun to make their way towards him. 'Mr Brown, I think it would be prudent if you held onto Miss Quick until I can reach her. The current is particularly strong in parts.'

'Don't trouble yourself on my account,' protested Bridget, who, having overcome her earlier fears, now appeared more robust than either of them.

When they were all assembled at the requisite spot, Brown lowered himself to allow Bridget to climb onto his back, and Joshua did likewise for him. Brown held onto Joshua's shoulders with a talon-like grip that seemed to bite into his flesh even through the linen of his shirt. His knees clenched at Joshua's jaw and neck as if Joshua were an unreliable mount and Brown feared being thrown at any minute. Joshua held onto his calves in the hope it might steady him and encourage him to release his grip a little, but no such effect was forthcoming.

With the current eddying about, and the combined weight of Brown and Bridget on his back, Joshua's stance seemed almost insupportable. His legs buckled and several times he thought he was on the brink of collapsing, but on each occasion he found the strength to lock his knees, brace himself as best he could and hold upright under the teetering burden.

'Can you reach?' Joshua shouted up to Bridget.

'Yes,' she shouted back, 'but you will have to hold still, and I will have to stand up on Mr Brown's shoulders or I won't get out.'

For several minutes after that, silence fell. Joshua heard the groanings and puffings of Bridget's exertions, but he dared neither look up nor shout for fear of interrupting some delicate manoeuvre and causing her to fall. Then, suddenly, miraculously, the burden on his shoulders lessened.

'Brown,' Joshua gasped, 'is she up? Has she succeeded?'

'Yes,' he answered, 'I believe she has.'

With this they tipped back their heads. Framed in the bracken window they saw the round, fair, bedraggled face of Bridget Quick smiling triumphantly down on them.

'Thank God it's your turn now, Brown. At least then you will desist from clawing my shoulder and crushing my skull.

You have ruined a perfectly good shirt, not to mention the damage to my senses!' said Joshua wryly.

'Pardon me, I hadn't realized!' Brown replied with the same *faux* light-heartedness. 'I promise to buy you a new shirt, but as for the damage to your brain, I fear it was far from perfect in the first place.'

'Go, Brown,' Joshua urged, serious once more. 'No time to lose.'

'Tell me first, how will you manage after I've gone?'

'You will have to lower something for me. I am confident that the price of a new shirt won't deter you from effecting my rescue.'

'You may rest assured on it,' Brown said, patting Joshua on the head, rather as one pats a horse that has run a good race. 'I suppose now I shall have to stand on your shoulders.'

'Then if you hadn't already ruined my shirt you will do so now. You realize it cost twenty shillings?'

'I never paid more than ten for any of mine,' Brown declared, kneeling and then crouching. He clutched at Joshua's hair as he raised himself up to stand. Joshua winced at the searing pain in his skull, but just then Brown grabbed at the rim of the opening. Then Bridget leaned down and grasped his arms, and with her vigorous assistance Brown hauled himself out.

From overhead Joshua heard distant shouts, two echoing voices congratulating themselves on escaping death. He looked up, trying to quell a surge of envy and mounting panic. Two faces now looked down from above. How far away they seemed – a distance of twelve feet might have been a hundred times more. All this while, the floodwater had been rising. It was now up to Joshua's neck, creeping inexorably higher with every passing minute.

In truth this was where his plan became even more perilous. To avoid futile argument and wasting precious time he had deliberately neglected to explain to the others that his own escape relied upon them. Once they were safe they had to find a means to rescue him. He had resigned himself to this uncertain fate. If the good Lord intended him to live another day something would present itself to Brown and Bridget. If not, at least two lives had been saved.

Now, turning away from the light, facing the sinister waters about him, his optimism seeped away. Reality and his terror of water settled upon him. In a few minutes the water would have risen to his chin; then it would reach his mouth, and his nostrils. At some point during its deadly progress he would no longer be able to remain standing and since he had never learned to swim, his lungs would fill with horrid blackness, he would be unable to breathe, he would be washed away . . .

# Chapter Forty-five

So engrossed was Joshua in his proximity to death, he ignored the possibility that any activity to assist him might be taking place above his head. Having prepared himself to drown, he found the prospect less terrifying than he supposed. After all, he told himself, once he was dead there would be no more fear, no more uncertainty, only blessed oblivion.

He was rudely roused from these melancholic thoughts by the sound of Bridget's voice trumpeting down from overhead. 'Mr Pope,' she bellowed. 'Pay attention, I beg you. Look up; catch it.' By now he was stupefied to the extent that his eyes were scarcely capable of registering anything. Nevertheless, he looked up and saw that a rope of jute, with a noose at one end, was dangling towards him, like some great tar-scented serpent of deliverance. 'Catch hold of it,' Bridget said again, 'tie it round you and we will pull you out.'

Joshua came slowly to his senses. He grabbed the rope; its prickly roughness and bitumen smell helped penetrate his stupefaction. He secured it under his armpits and raised his hand to indicate he was ready. Then, almost before he knew it, he felt himself being hauled up from the black cavern, into the air, towards the light.

He grabbed at the turf surrounding the opening. Aided by Bridget – Brown could not let go of the rope, which was turned once round the trunk of a tree – he heaved himself out of the opening like a cork pulled from a bottle. He felt the rain, which was still falling, drum down on his face. He wanted to express his joy at surviving, his gratitude for being able to feel as wet and cold and miserable as he did. The very fact that he felt anything at all meant he was alive. But exhaustion took hold of him and before he could open his mouth to utter a word he collapsed on the ground into unconsciousness.

Some time later, he became dimly aware of a glass being thrust between his lips and the powerful taste of brandy in his mouth.

'Drink this, Mr Pope. It will revive you,' someone said. 'Should we summon the physician?' another voice said. 'No,' answered the first. 'Nothing ails him other than cold and nervous shock. Rest is the only remedy.'

Soon after that he opened his eyes. He found himself laid out in bed, in the same room at Astley he had formerly occupied when he was engaged to paint the Bentnick portrait. It was dark outside; a fire had been lit and his wet clothes removed. He was now clad in what he guessed, from its capacious size, was one of Herbert's nightshirts and a nightcap. Despite the fact that the bed was piled high with blankets and coverlets, he was trembling violently.

Seated in an armchair in the place where his easel had once stood was Lancelot Brown. He too was dressed in a large nightgown. He too nursed a large glass of brandy. There was also a blanket about his shoulders and a nightcap set upon his head.

'Brown,' Joshua said urgently, half raising himself up as if he intended to hop out of bed and leave as quickly as possible, 'where is Miss Quick? How long have I been unconscious? Has Herbert been? Does he know I am here?'

'Calm yourself, Mr Pope,' said Brown smoothly. 'Miss Quick is quite well; she has been spirited off to be properly tended. I cannot tell you how long you were insensible, for I have no idea. I myself lapsed into unconsciousness for some time. And, yes, Herbert does know you are here. I regret to tell you that, despite everything, he was enraged to discover your reappearance. He still hasn't forgiven you for delving among his private papers and says he holds you to blame for the death of his daughter. I believe it was only my presence and Miss Quick's that persuaded him to allow you to be carried here and cared for at all. He is adamant that, no matter your condition, you must leave first thing in the morning. I thought it best that I should deliver this message in person. I am sorry, my friend, there was nothing I could say to move him.'

Brown stood to leave as Joshua sank back morosely into a pile of goose-down pillows. 'I cannot say I am surprised. I myself feel culpable for Caroline's death. But, that being so, we must speak tonight. I beg you to stay a minute or two longer, Brown. Tell me what happened to you before I found you. Did you mean it when you said someone deliberately tried to drown us?'

Brown lowered himself back into the chair. 'It was that very matter I have just been considering,' he replied, as ponderously as if they had been sipping brandy all day in a clubhouse. 'I cannot see any other explanation. But if you are well enough to take in what I have to tell you, I will leave you to decide.'

'Of course I am well enough,' Joshua protested indignantly. 'I have suffered an ordeal, but it hasn't entirely deprived me of my senses. Tell me what happened to you. How did you come to be in that chamber?'

'I didn't see who it was, but I hazard it was a man. I was struck from behind as I entered the grotto and lost consciousness; when I came to, I found myself transported to the ledge where you discovered me. No woman would have had the strength to drag me there, nor to open the gate to let the flood waters in.'

'Then it wasn't Lizzie Manning after all.'

'I told you before, she would not have had the strength.'

Joshua nodded. Lizzie would have known how to open the gate, but he had to admit it was unlikely a woman of her diminutive frame could have hauled Brown into the cavern. 'And now, what was it you wanted to tell me – the subject you mentioned in your letter?'

Brown shook his head. 'I didn't know when I wrote to you that the necklace had been recovered. What I had to say has little relevance now. It concerned the history of the jewel.'

'Nevertheless, Brown, I would like to hear it and judge for myself.'

'Very well. Let me test you a little. What do you know of the origins of the necklace?'

Joshua responded swiftly. 'It was won by Charles Mercier, who left it to his illegitimate daughter in his will . . .'

'Before that? Have you learned the earlier history?'

Joshua racked his memory. 'Violet Mercier and John Cobb described a little of its past. As I recall, it was made in medieval times in Nuremberg for a princeling of the region. Charles Mercier won it from a countess, who gave it to her maid to—'

'Quite,' said Brown, holding up a hand to show he wanted to know nothing further about the maid Miss Baynes and her torrid love affair. 'Mercier won the necklace from a countess. And, ignoring maids and their offspring, what do you know about that countess?'

Joshua raised himself onto his pillows, his mind suddenly alert to a wealth of new possibilities. 'Never mind what I know. Tell me then, Brown, what it is *you* know; I can see from your face you are bursting with it.'

'The history of the necklace you related when you came to visit me reminded me of a story I was told about an estate I was engaged upon. I should add I never knew any of the names of the participants involved. In any case, as I said, perhaps you are no longer interested, since the necklace has already been restored . . . ?'

'Stop toying, Brown. Of course I'm devilishly interested.'

Brown grinned; there was a mischievous gleam in his nut-brown eyes. 'Very well, I shall tell you the tale. Some years ago, I designed a garden at Beechwood House, a mansion in the vicinity of Luton, belonging to the Seebright family. The history of the house and estate was most unusual, and for that reason I suppose it has remained in my mind.'

'Did you say Beechwood?' uttered Joshua, his nostrils flaring and his lips tight with interest.

'Yes, Beechwood. The house was acquired by the present owner, Lord Seebright, after the previous incumbent, another titled lady, was forced to sell following a most tragic sequence of events. And this is what struck me as oddly similar to your tale: she owned a necklace that was no ordinary jewel: it was fashioned in emeralds and shaped as a serpent.'

He paused as if uncertain whether to proceed. He had been distracted by Joshua, who, apparently engrossed in thoughts of his own, was busily muttering, 'Beechwood? Beechwood?' to himself as if it were a question. At length Joshua broke off, remarking his silence. A snort and impatient wave was enough to urge Brown to continue.

'Family history recorded that the jewel had been presented to one of the lady's forebears by Charles I, as a royal token of gratitude. The lady concerned was doubtless a royal mistress. There was a peculiar superstition attached to the jewel: that it would bring ill luck if it ever changed hands for money.'

Joshua nodded impatiently. History was all very well; he recalled Violet relating part of this tale, but that was not what interested him. 'I can scarcely credit you take this so seriously, Brown. In these days, men of enlightenment and science give little credence to such fanciful histories.'

Brown looked a trifle chagrined. 'Of course I concur with you. And no doubt it was mere coincidence that the lady's misfortunes began immediately after the loss of her necklace at cards. She had two children, the elder of whom, a boy, within six months of the necklace being lost died from a bout of typhus, which also killed her husband. Stricken by grief, the lady continued to play without restraint. A year later, having been forced by mounting debt to sell Beechwood House and the estate to Mr Seebright, she took her own life.'

'What became of the other child? Was it a boy or a girl?' said Joshua, suddenly sitting bolt upright.

Brown shrugged his shoulders as if the question had never occurred to him. 'I regret I cannot tell you. I don't believe I ever knew.'

Joshua sank back into his pillows, half closing his eyes in contemplation. 'That is a pity, for it is that fact which interests me most, my friend, not the legend. No matter, with what you have told me I will soon discover it.'

Brown gave a hefty yawn and came slowly to his feet. 'I have no doubt you will, sir,' he said, amiable as ever, 'but now, however pressing it seems, I recommend you let it wait. After our recent ordeal, what we both need is a good night's sleep.'

Left alone, Joshua's eyes remained resolutely open. He stared fixedly at the ceiling, pondering the implications of what he had learned. He had grasped the significance of Brown's statement the moment the words left his lips. Now he was mentally stringing these new pieces together with what he already knew like a jeweller assembling a necklace. Brown's account was the clasp that connected the chain. The countess had come from Beechwood, an estate that was linked in several ways with Astley. Having been cheated of an inheritance by a profligate mother, the countess's only surviving child would have a strong motive to wish to regain possession of the necklace. There were only two questions he had now to ask himself: who was that child and was he or she the murderer?

As Joshua thrashed this about in his mind, he entered a reverie in which faces and images seemed to flash upon his mind's eye like exploding pyrotechnics. The name Beechwood reverberated in his mind with peculiar resonance. He had heard it mentioned by Mrs Bowles in connection with Jane Bentnick, and by Lancelot Brown in connection with the Seebrights; but where else? He envisaged Caroline Bentnick's terrorized expression the night Sabine had insisted she wore the necklace. He remembered her calmness when she tended his wounds, her lack of concern at Herbert's threats regarding the necklace, and her dreadful death. He relived the terrible moment that his own role in this first struck him and Herbert's accusation and his banishment.

It was not until the clock chimed eight that he came to his senses again. Two theories had emerged in his mind with diamond clarity: the reason for the necklace's disappearance and the identity of the countess's child.

But theory was not enough. By allowing his mind to run on and speaking injudiciously, he had made too many false accusations. Until he was certain, until no glimmer of doubt remained, he would keep his thoughts to himself and remain silent.

Joshua rang the bell on his side table and summoned Peters. He asked for a writing box and, when this was delivered, sent Peters to the library in search of a historical gazetteer for the county of Bedford. In no time Peters returned bearing a large red morocco-bound tome tooled in gold with the Bentnick family crest emblazoned on the front.

'Is that all, sir?' enquired the footman, putting the book down carefully on the side table.

'Pass it to me, if you please,' said Joshua urgently. No sooner had the door closed behind Peters than Joshua opened the book and began to search its pages. It took him ten minutes or so to find what he was looking for, whereupon he nodded sagely to himself. This was just as he expected. Then he put the book to one side and began composing a letter to Herbert Bentnick.

# Chapter Forty-six

*Astley House, Richmond*

Sir,
I cannot blame you for holding me partly accountable for your
daughter's murder. I too feel burdened by guilt, and it is that
sentiment which spurs me to write this to you now. Unless I
explain my conclusions her death, as well as that of Mr Hoare,
will have been in vain. Thus, despite your misgivings, I would
implore you to read this communication and consider its contents
most seriously.

During my enquiries several members of your circle, including
you, sir, have fallen under the shadow of suspicion. There was
never any doubt in my mind that your poor daughter Caroline
was strangled because the murderer believed she could identify him
or her. I also think that the murderer may have concluded this as
a result of an ill-considered remark Caroline made to me on the
terrace. Far more complex was the first killing. Bartholomew
Hoare was at first identified as John Cobb. Neither man was a
member of your household. Thus the key questions were these:
how was Hoare murdered? What was he doing on your property?
Was Hoare or Cobb the intended victim?

I believe (though I cannot prove it conclusively) that Hoare
was poisoned by unripe pineapple, probably mixed with wine and
honey to make it palatable. Unripe pineapple is a powerful

*purgative, though it is not usually lethal. In poor Hoare's case it
was certainly strong enough to cause him to lose consciousness,
although the actual cause of his death <u>may</u> have been accidental.
Granger confessed that, as misfortune would have it, the boy
whose duty it was to regulate the temperature of the pinery at
night fell asleep on the night Hoare died. The heat within the
building grew so intense that, coupled with the poison, it was
enough to kill him.*

*Having learned how Hoare died, let us next consider what he
was doing there in the first place. Cobb told me he received an
invitation, purporting to be from Violet, asking him to a nocturnal
rendezvous in the gardens at Astley. He was prevented from
keeping the appointment by Hoare, who, worried that Cobb might
persuade Violet to run away with him, plied Cobb with brandy on
the pretext that it would be good for his ailing health. When Cobb
drank so much he fell to the floor in a stupor, Hoare went in his
place.*

*Although I hesitated to believe you capable of killing your own
daughter, I confess I fleetingly considered the likelihood that you
were in some manner involved in the first death. Your fondness
for Mrs Mercier might have led you to murder Hoare because he
was acting for the claimant for her necklace and thus threatened
to remove from her a jewel that she held exceptionally dear. Violet
reported seeing you in a clandestine rendezvous with Mrs Bowles.
Was Mrs Bowles Charles Mercier's daughter? I pursued this
theory for some time, only to discover she was nothing of the
kind. Your meeting was merely a means of arranging a secret gift
for your future bride.*

*I turned then to the source of this malicious rumour, Violet
Mercier. Hoare was an obstacle between herself and Cobb, with
whom, despite her denials and letters to the contrary, she was
engaged in a clandestine affair. Hoare discovered the truth and
threatened to reveal it to Sabine. It would have been easy for
Violet, with Cobb's connivance, to write the letter luring Hoare to
the pinery, and leave Cobb to poison him with a substance whose
effects she well knew from her mother, while she went to London*

for a few days. Perhaps, too, Violet stole the necklace, intending
that the money raised from its sale would finance her life with
Cobb. She might subsequently have returned it when she
discovered that Cobb's financial circumstances had changed (I will
explain this presently) and that the theft was no longer necessary.

Sabine Mercier had two equally compelling motives. First, she
was troubled by the possibility she would lose the necklace she
treasured so dearly; second, she was worried that her daughter
was poised to elope with a penniless attorney from Bridgetown –
Cobb. If she <u>had</u> sent the message to the inn asking Cobb to meet
her late at night in the gardens at Astley, she could not have
foreseen that Hoare would arrive in his place; nor, since she had
never met either man, would she have recognized that it was
Hoare not Cobb whom she poisoned.

A further possibility only struck me more recently: Lizzie
Manning, whose family misfortunes, it transpires, have been
largely brought about by Cobb. Arthur Manning and he met at a
gaming house in Richmond and after two or three evenings' play
Cobb relieved his opponent of two thousand pounds drawn upon
Barlow Court. Lizzie kept her brother's circumstances concealed
from me; furthermore, from the very beginning she insisted on
involving herself in my investigations into Hoare's death. She
inveigled her way into my bedchamber after she learned I had
acquired Cobb's bag, in which the banknotes drawn upon the
family account were hidden. Thus I asked myself did she kill
Hoare, believing him to be Cobb, in a desperate attempt to recoup
her brother's losses?

And so, my dear sir, we come to the inevitable questions. Who
among this wretched cast of players was the guilty culprit who
killed Hoare and then to preserve this evil secret killed poor
Caroline? Which of them stole the necklace, and for what motive?
The answer to the first question is that I now believe it was none
of them.

My final revelation has come only tonight, after a conversation
with our mutual acquaintance Mr Lancelot 'Capability' Brown.
As you know, the necklace came into the possession of Charles

Mercier after it was lost some decades ago by the Countess of Burghley, who wagered it on a hand of cards. If you ask Brown he will tell you the sad history of the countess. Once you have heard it I advise you to consult the historical gazetteer of Bedfordshire, which I borrowed from your library and have left by my bed. The answer to this mystery is to be found within the entry for Beechwood House, near Luton, on page 414. The truth lay before us all in details we all saw without comprehending.

As to why the necklace was taken and then returned, thus far I know only part of the story. It had nothing to do with the claimant, a certain Nell Lambton, who died, apparently from poverty, shortly after she received a visit from Sabine Mercier. It was your own daughter who took it, in her dread that Mrs Mercier would force her to wear the jewel at the forthcoming ball. Caroline detested Mrs Mercier, for she believed her responsible for the death of her mother – whether this was so is impossible for me to ascertain – and for this she developed a morbid dread of the jewel and Mrs Mercier herself.

Before I follow your wish and leave Astley, I intend to verify all of this by approaching the culprit. I am aware that in doing so my own life may be jeopardized, but I view it as recompense for my foolhardy conversation that cost your daughter her life. I set these facts down here so that, no matter what fate holds for me, you will know what happened and decide what should be done.

I am, sir, your humble servant,
Joshua Pope

# Chapter Forty-seven

Next day the clouds had lifted and the deluge was spent. At five minutes before nine Joshua closed the side door to Astley House and walked, in blazing sunshine, through the kitchen gardens towards the gate where he had left his horse tethered the previous day. As he passed by the pinery he remarked how magnificent the building looked, freshly washed by rain. Its glass panels sparkled in the morning light; the verdure of the plants within seemed more lush and bountiful than he remembered; truly, he thought, there were occasions when plants could seem as imposing and worthy of an artist's attentions as people.

Joshua caught sight of Granger busy inside the pinery. He looked as he always did, easy, complacent, rugged of hair and regular of feature, apart from the disfiguring scar on his cheek. Hearing the crunch of Joshua's boots on the gravel path outside, Granger glanced up, but then, seeing who it was, he gave Joshua a brisk nod and continued with his work. Joshua progressed towards the atrium beneath the cupola, trying to ignore a lurching sensation in his stomach. His chin was held high. His letter was written and despatched; whatever happened now, the truth would be known.

As Joshua opened the door leading from the atrium to the pinery he saw that Granger was removing dead leaves from the larger pineapple plants with a small pair of shears. 'Good day to you, Mr Pope. Are you quite recovered?' said Granger, pausing between plants after Joshua bowed and bade him good morning. 'I am astonished to see you so soon out of bed after yesterday . . .'

'I am perfectly well, Mr Granger. In fact I am returning directly to London. I felt I should exchange a few words with you before leaving.'

Granger moved to the next plant and began to examine it closely for any imperfections of foliage, stroking each leaf with his long, delicate fingers. Even though it was stiflingly hot within the pinery, for some reason this gesture made Joshua shiver.

'Thank God we found you when we did, or you might not be so well recovered,' said Granger.

Joshua could not allow this remark to pass unchallenged. 'Forgive me, Mr Granger, but were it not for a certain amount of good fortune and my own presence of mind, three people would have drowned. I believe I have you to thank for that dreadful event rather than for saving me. Indeed, that is why I have come.'

'What do you mean? I warned you not to enter there, did I not?' His voice was calm yet laden with perplexity.

'You warned me, but you left a baited trap that you knew I would not ignore.'

Granger's affectation of bewilderment continued. He shook his head, half smiling. 'I fear I do not comprehend, sir.'

'I mean that, when Mr Brown arrived earlier yesterday at Astley and mentioned he was waiting for my arrival, you must have feared that he had connected recent events here with the history of Beechwood. You knew Brown had been commissioned to work at Beechwood some years ago, and told me as much yourself. You crept up on him while he was alone in the grotto, struck him on the head, trussed him up and dragged him to the inner chamber. You probably knew he wasn't dead, but instead of despatching him forthwith you decided to lure me to the grotto when I arrived, and then put an end to two troublesome birds with a single murderous flood, which you could easily pass off as an accident.'

Still shaking his head and half smiling, as if what had been said was too ludicrous to warrant denying, Granger turned his head to Joshua. 'I'm sorry, sir, but what has my time at Beechwood to do with any of this? I have made no secret of it.'

'Beechwood is your motive, Granger. You should have been its heir. Your mother was the ill-fated Countess of Burghley, chatelaine of Beechwood and once the owner of the serpent necklace. Her tragic losses at cards set in motion this entire sequence of events. Brown told me little I had not discovered except for two crucial pieces of information: the countess lived at Beechwood and she had a child who survived her. Brown didn't know her name or that of her child, but it was an easy matter for me to consult a historical gazetteer of Bedfordshire. I soon found the relevant entry, which names the previous incumbent as Sybil Granger, Countess of Burghley, mother of two sons, one deceased.'

With this Granger raised himself up and gave Joshua a look of curious superiority, as if Joshua were a strange beetle that he had spied upon a leaf and it was a dozen halfpennies to sixpence whether he would squash him beneath his boot or place him in his hand. The air between them was taut with tension. 'How do you know this orphaned child and I are one and the same?'

'You were recognized by Mrs Bowles, who was raised in the same village. That was why you were deep in conversation with her the other day. There is a very fine portrait hanging in your parlour of a lady who I hazard is your mother. The arms on the cup in her hand are doubtless those of the Burghley family.'

'Is that all?'

'Mrs Mercier found Hoare, but of course it should have been you, for it is your practice, I have remarked, to go there first thing every morning, and you later told me that earlier that morning on discovering the boy had fallen asleep, you took steps to regulate the heat. To open the windows you must have stepped over the body. At the very least you would have seen the damaged pots lying about, yet you said nothing.'

Joshua was watching Granger's profile as he spoke and he saw it undergo a most remarkable transformation. The muscles in his jaw twitched, a vein in his neck bulged and his entire expression seemed to bunch up with unpredictable, unmistakable hostility. He paused, waiting for Granger's response, but Granger said nothing. After a while Joshua saw he didn't need to hear his answer, for there was guilt written in every fibre of him.

'You also said you were too busy with your work to see Caroline or her assailant go into the pinery. You lied in Caroline's case, but you told the truth regarding the assailant – you saw no one because the assailant was you.'

Again there was a long silence, during which Granger continued steadily shearing off leaves. The only signs of his inner agitation were the speed with which he cut and snipped at those sharp blade-like leaves and the droplets of sweat that rose on his forehead and ran in conspicuous rivulets down his face. Eventually sweat poured at such a rate he was forced to stop snipping and wipe his face with the back of his hand. As he did so the violence in his manner seemed to ebb a little. He looked about him with the resigned manner of a man of substance surveying his domain before relinquishing it. 'You speak as if you know everything, but what can you know of my sufferings? My life has been ruined by my mother's folly, by the turn of a card in the hand of a frivolous woman. Is that just?'

'The same thing, give or take a little, has happened to Miss Manning. You told me so yourself. Yet she has managed to restrain herself from resorting to murder.'

'She tried other unconventional methods to retrieve her property, though, did she not?'

The knowing smile that accompanied this retort made

Joshua's cheeks burn. Surely he couldn't know of Lizzie's nocturnal visit to his chamber? Joshua had no chance to probe him on this matter before Granger continued.

'The necklace *does* belong to me. It has virtually jumped into my hand. When Mr Bentnick picked his new bride from thousands of miles away and she arrived wearing the necklace, I read that as a sign of destiny: a sign my situation was about to be redressed. The cruel fate that had deprived me of my inheritance had returned it within my orbit. I was destined to pursue it.'

'It was a great coincidence, was it not, to find yourself working at the very place where the woman who had your mother's necklace in her possession resided?'

Granger shook his head and smiled. 'It was no coincidence. I followed it, as I have followed other possessions of hers, although I will allow that fate helped. The portrait you mentioned was the first thing I recovered. I took it from a place where I was employed last year. The necklace was to be the second. The fact my mother lost it in Barbados to Charles Mercier was no secret. When Mr Bentnick's betrothal was announced, and along with that he put out word he wanted a gardener with knowledge of rearing pineapples, I could hardly resist applying. I read up on the subject and convinced him I knew more than anyone else.'

Joshua nodded his head knowingly. 'I am not without sympathy for your case. But, as I said, the evil acts you committed allow no justification.'

'Why should I justify anything to you, when a higher force has propelled my actions? Hoare died as a result of an opportunity that presented itself. Caroline Bentnick died as a result of injudicious talk. None of this happened by *my* instigation. Fate decreed it.'

Granger seemed to be growing agitated once more. His mind had been unhinged as a result of the terrible reversals of fortune he had suffered. Even now, there was no telling how he might react. But Joshua would never rest easy unless he discovered the truth, and Granger was the only person alive who knew it.

'Why did you kill Hoare?'

'To protect the necklace. Because he threatened to remove it from Astley and hand it to the bastard daughter of the man who robbed my mother. It had only just come within my grasp and he wanted to take it away. I might never have regained possession of it if that had happened.'

'And so you lured him to the pinery?'

'No. As I said, it was all done for me. Sabine Mercier did it.'

'How so?'

'She wrote to Cobb, disguising her hand as her daughter's, asking him to a nocturnal meeting. She wanted to try to dissuade him from eloping with her daughter. For some reason Hoare arrived in Cobb's place. I knew who he was because I had watched him at the Star and Garter. But Sabine had never met either man and so she took it for granted he was Cobb. Anyway, the pair of them sat down in the atrium. She, pretending to be friendly, offered him a drink she had specially prepared and then took him for a stroll round the pinery. I shadowed them, an easy enough task in the dark. As he felt the first cramps in his belly, Sabine told him the drink she had given him contained a preparation made from unripe pineapple that would kill him unless she gave him another draft to counter it. She added that he should know, however, that unless he promised to stop pursuing the affair with Violet, she wouldn't save him.'

Joshua nodded. 'What happened next?'

'Hoare doubled over with cramps, cried out that he wasn't the man she believed him to be, he was Bartholomew Hoare. She ignored him until he cried out he knew something that might help her: the name of the claimant. She listened then and, after Hoare had told her, he begged for the second draught, but she laughed, saying none was necessary. He would be ill but he wouldn't die. He lost consciousness soon after. After she had gone I went to the hut where Joe, the night boy, sits. I told him he looked tired and suggested he sleep for a while. I would keep watch and wake him when I left. Then I went back to the pinery to check on Hoare.'

Joshua shook his head in an agony of realization. Of course now he comprehended. Hoare's death from overheating wasn't accidental: Granger had engineered it.

'At that moment Cobb came in, but he must have heard me and taken fright, for he took one look at Hoare and ran off. I followed him a short distance, but in the end I decided I had no need to chase him. He was too afraid to cause any further trouble.'

Granger furrowed his brow and raised his eyes heavenwards, as if picturing the scene as he spoke. 'What a vile spectacle Hoare made, lying on the ground, surrounded by a pool of his own vomit. He was quite comatose, but breathing steadily. Standing there, I felt overwhelmed by fury at the sight of the man whose actions might keep me in my subservient position for ever. I threw a few pots about, and though that didn't make me feel any better it helped me determine how to proceed. I would leave him to cook. I closed all the windows. Within an hour or two the temperature in the pinery was quite sufficient. Next morning, when I arrived I opened the windows and roused Joe, telling him he must have dreamed me saying he could sleep. I fined him two days' wages and made it clear he was lucky to keep his position. When Mrs Mercier came, I didn't accompany her as usual, I let her go in first and find him. It entertained me to see her try to rouse him. She was dumbfounded to find him dead and her precious plants all in disarray.'

Joshua shuddered at his cold-hearted tone. 'And having brought about Hoare's death so callously, do you still feel nothing for him – no remorse whatsoever?'

Granger blinked slowly and began to walk towards Joshua, opening and shutting the shears as he did so. 'No more than he or anyone felt for me, Mr Pope. On the death of my mother, I was treated no better than some urchin destined for the workhouse. Not a soul showed any concern for me. I was treated as a servant, forced to work as an under gardener, to shovel dung and scythe grass till my hands bled and I could scarcely stand. Can you blame me?'

Joshua backed away, acutely aware of the danger he was in. 'I do not wish to apportion blame, Mr Granger, only to discover what happened. Was it you who attacked me at the barn?'

'It was. I had to take measures to put you off. You kept interfering in matters that didn't concern you.'

'What about the necklace? When did you steal it?'

'I didn't. I intended to take it. I knew where it was, but I was going to bide my time. Once Hoare was dead there was no hurry. I was sure it would remain in Mrs Mercier's possession. And then, to my horror, I learned it was gone. It was many days before I discovered what had happened. That was why she had to die.'

'Caroline Bentnick?' Joshua had convinced himself he had provoked Caroline's death. He could barely bring himself to raise the subject and hear Granger affirm his conviction.

'She said something that gave me no choice but to kill her.'

This was what he had feared. 'What did she say?' Joshua asked morosely.

'The morning of her death, just after you had returned the keys to me, Caroline met her brother in the sunken garden. I was passing on the other side of the hedge and heard her talking to him quite clearly.'

This wasn't what Joshua had expected. The conversation that he thought accountable had taken place the day before, on the terrace.

'What did she say?' he managed to mumble.

'Francis Bentnick asked her what she was doing. She told him *she* had taken the necklace from Mrs Mercier's room, to avoid having to wear it at the ball, and that it was hidden in one of the pots containing an orange tree in the atrium of the pinery. Caroline said she had taken the necklace with the intention of returning it afterwards, but she had since considered the matter further and decided that she detested the necklace so much it would be more prudent to dispose of it. She was about to go and dig it up, after which, she said, she would throw it in the lake.'

'And what did Francis say?'

'He said, "What about Pope? Our father was threatening him with arrest." But she said that was no more than a threat. He knew perfectly well that you had not taken it and would drop the whole matter in due course.'

'And what did you do after the conversation?'

'I had no alternative. I followed her, I watched her retrieve it, then I killed her. I had to do so or my property would certainly have been lost.'

A stillness hung in the air. Joshua's relief at not having been the cause of Caroline's death was tempered partly by the knowledge that she had deliberately placed him in his dreadful predicament and partly by the chilling tone of Granger's confession.

'At any rate, her death brought results in my favour. I didn't expect Mr Bentnick to banish you, but you will well imagine I wasn't sorry when he did.'

'And when I returned you decided to commit triple murder?'

Granger hesitated, as if he were weighing up whether to tell the truth or dissemble. 'Again, I would not have chosen to do so, but you drove me to it. Miss Quick insisted on staying with you. I had no need to kill her. Brown had to be silenced because he knew something about my past. You made it so easy for me to accomplish. Instead of returning to the house with Lizzie Manning and Francis, I told them I had matters that needed my urgent attention. I returned to the octagon house, opened the trap door and let the flood waters in. I knew that within a few hours at the most the entire cavern would be full of water.'

'It must have come as a disappointment to find us drenched but alive on the slope,' Joshua said wryly.

'I didn't find you. It was Joe Carlton, the boy you left looking after your horse. He grew worried when you didn't return and happened upon Brown and Miss Quick. He ran to get a rope and then fetch me. Unfortunately I was within earshot of the house when he arrived, which is why Francis came too.'

'Otherwise you might have made another attempt?'

'Possibly.' Once again he began to walk towards Joshua. His eyes were blinking in a most disconcerting manner, yet there was a blank, unseeing expression on his face. 'But that's neither here nor there now, is it? Indeed, as I see it, Mr Pope, there's only one question remaining.'

'What's that?'

As he spoke, Granger was still advancing. His face seemed empty, devoid of emotion, bereft of soul. Joshua backed along the path away from him. He had reached the threshold of the pinery now. He reversed to the atrium and paused beneath the glittering cupola, uncertain whether to run like the devil or face Granger. In the event he stood his ground, more from indecision than bravado. Granger reached forward and clutched his arm with an overpowering grip; his face came to within an inch of Joshua's, so that Granger's hot, sour breath brushed his cheek.

'What do you intend to do about it?' said Granger between gritted teeth.

Joshua looked at him hard and long. Logic told him Granger's mind was unbalanced and that he might attack most viciously at any minute. The realization made his heart race and his stomach feel as heavy as a stone. And yet, despite all this, Joshua still felt a small flicker of sympathy for Granger. He was an outsider like his hapless victim Hoare and Joshua himself. Who was Joshua to say what might have happened had he found himself in such sorry circumstances? Joshua shook his head and gave him a brief, thoughtful smile. 'That is not for me to decide. I have written my findings down for Mr Bentnick to judge. Whatever happens to me, he will

402

know what you did. And now, Mr Granger, it remains only for me to bid you good day.'

No doubt it was the knowledge that even if he killed Joshua on the spot he would be discovered that stayed his hand. No doubt it was fanciful of Joshua to believe that Granger saw the flash of sympathy in his face and reciprocated. In any event, Granger released his grip on Joshua's shoulder and Joshua turned away and walked to the gate. Granger made no attempt to prevent him.

# Chapter Forty-eight

December 1786, St Peter's Court, St Martin's Lane, London

On the day that Joshua Pope expected his nocturnal visitor to return, a month after she had called, he did not set foot out of St Peter's Court. He had written his account and bound it, ready for her perusal. He listened for a knock at the door or a footstep on the stair, but although he waited up past midnight there was no sign of the visitor.

A fortnight more came and went; winter chills relieved the gales of November, ice crystals lined the inside of his windows and Joshua's manuscript lay bound with a vermilion ribbon in a corner of his rooms. On occasion he looked at it fretfully as it gathered dust. Suppose she never returned? Would he ever discover her purpose or who she was? Sometimes his consternation ran deeper. Writing the account had stirred strange memories, reawakened sentiments he had thought long forgotten. Was this the purpose of her coming so long after the entire business was forgotten? Did she intend simply to ruffle the tranquil waters of his middle-aged, family-oriented existence and leave him always to listen for a creak of the stair? If so, he resolved, she would not succeed. He would concentrate on the day-to-day and banish all thoughts of the terrible episode he had endured at Astley and his peculiar visitor.

One gloomy afternoon in mid December he was busy in his painting room. His two daughters were seated before him, grumbling at having to hold the pose he had set them. He was answering their complaints good-naturedly, but without giving way, for he was sure the painting would be one of his best, and although he was a devoted father he was as energetic and avid an artist as ever. Just then his wife opened the door and announced he had a lady caller.

'Who is it?' demanded Joshua, instantly alerted.

'She won't give me her name. She says you have something for her and asked me to give you this.'

Joshua looked at the object his wife held out towards him. It was the same shagreen box his nocturnal visitor had shown him – the one in which the emerald serpent was contained. He was so astounded to see it in his wife's hand that he felt the blood drain from his face. He had told her of the woman's previous visit, but for reasons of his own he had failed to mention the box and its contents.

'What is it?' said his wife. 'You are grown very pale.'

'It is she,' Joshua whispered. 'And I told her I won't take this wretched thing in payment. Nor will I give her what she has come for unless she tells me what I want to know: her name and her purpose.'

'In that case,' said Joshua's wife unflinchingly, 'I will descend and tell her so.'

She departed, leaving the door ajar. Joshua sent his daughters away, stoked up the fire and drew back the curtain a little. The sky was overburdened with clouds as grey as his spirits, but there was light nonetheless. He paced the room, his thoughts to racing. What would he say? How should he address her? From below he could hear the sound of faint echoing conversation. He distinguished his wife's voice from that of the other woman, although he couldn't make out what they were saying. The exchange lasted some minutes and then silence, the sound of the door slamming, followed by footsteps approaching on the stair.

A few minutes later his wife returned with the visitor at her side. The woman was dressed as before, all in black, only this time instead of shielding her face with the hood of her cloak she appeared intent upon drawing attention to it. Set upon her head was a hat, trimmed with a crimson ostrich feather, which curled over the brim like the frond of a fern and caressed a pencilled brow.

'Come in,' Joshua said to her calmly. 'Allow me to take your cloak and hat. I have been expecting you for some time now.'

'I won't stay. I came only to collect what you promised me.' She glanced about the room. With astonishing speed her eyes settled upon his manuscript. 'Is this it?' she said, hurrying to the place where he had left it.

Joshua swiftly intercepted her before she could pick up the bundle. 'That was not our agreement,' he pointed out. 'I said I would give you my account provided you identified yourself and your purpose.'

She regarded him levelly. 'Have you still no idea who I am?'

'Madam, I have racked my brains, for I feel I do know you, yet I have not the faintest notion who you are.'

'Then look again.'

She came towards him, removing her plumed hat to reveal an elaborate coiffure in all its glory. She looked him straight in the eye and then turned slowly towards the window, holding up her chin as though she were a model presenting herself for his perusal. He saw a well-formed face, a full mouth, straight nose and blue-grey eyes that were almond-shaped and set slightly tilted in her face in a manner that reminded him curiously of a cat. On her previous visit he had judged her to be aged about fifty, yet now, in the light of day, lines around the corners of her eyes and the furrows between her brows seemed incised less deeply than he recalled. She wasn't as old as he had first believed, but she had led a life that had marked her. He found himself returning to her eyes, the shape of which now seemed uncannily familiar. Yet though he searched his memory, for the life of him he could not remember where he had seen them before.

Joshua shook his head and sighed, a deep almost theatrical sigh redolent of frustration. He felt more than a little absurd to be standing there in his own room, in the presence of his wife, with a strange woman who claimed to know him. 'I regret, madam, I am no wiser than before.'

'Then let me save your blushes and tell you. I am Violet Cobb.'

'Violet, Sabine Mercier's daughter?'

'The very same.'

Joshua looked again with renewed interest. When he had been acquainted with her at Astley, Violet had been a startling but chilly beauty. This lady gave herself airs, she held herself as if she knew her attractions, she had the cool demeanour that he remembered, yet the remarkable radiance was gone. Time had mellowed her loveliness but had failed to warm her.

'Tell me, Mrs Cobb, what has brought you here?'

'Before I do that I should tell you a little of what has passed in the last two decades. Perhaps you already know that my mother never married Herbert Bentnick?'

Joshua nodded his assent. 'I had heard something of the sort, though I never knew the details.'

'Herbert broke off the engagement on receiving your letter and learning of her involvement in the death of Bartholomew Hoare. He said he couldn't rid himself of the suspicion that if she was willing to poison Hoare – albeit not fatally – she might have poisoned his first wife Jane and possibly her two previous husbands as well. My mother vehemently denied this, but Herbert wouldn't be swayed and said the trust between them was broken. She had no alternative but to return with me to Bridgetown, where we took up residence in the house Charles Mercier had left her. A year later I married John Cobb with her blessing. The next two decades passed uneventfully, but my mother never married again and became preoccupied by the notion that the necklace was cursed, and that since her refusal to give it up to Charles Mercier's daughter ill fortune had dogged her life. Six months ago, after a short illness, my mother died.'

'I am sorry to hear it, but that still does not explain your coming here and offering me the necklace,' Joshua said, in a tone that bespoke his sympathetic detachment.

Violet swallowed, dabbing her eyes with her handkerchief. 'I am coming to that very point. My mother left her house and all her possessions to me. But there was a codicil stating that although the necklace was mine to do as I pleased with, she strongly advised that I shouldn't keep it. It had brought her nothing but misfortune and she would not wish the same upon me. I considered her wishes most carefully. I determined to follow her advice and give the necklace away, but the question was: to whom should I give it?'

'And what made you settle upon me?' said Joshua without prevarication.

Violet looked at Joshua. 'Did I say it was you I had settled on?'

'I believe you did, at our last meeting.'

'And you, I believe, turned me down. You said you wanted no more than to know who I was and why I had come. Both those demands I have now met. Which is why, Mr Pope, I intend to offer the necklace to your wife. You are married, I take it, to this lady?' Here she waved her hand to the window at the far side of the room where Joshua's wife was presently seated.

Joshua nodded, shivering inwardly. Now he understood. Although he was not usually given to superstition, he had never doubted the jewel's evil associations and thus he recognized Violet's offer for what it was. Violet held him culpable for the part he had played in preventing her mother's marriage to Herbert. She too believed the necklace was a talisman of woe and was using it to exact vengeance. If she could not attack him directly she would do it through the person he held most dear.

But despite his fears, now that he understood what drove her, Joshua felt strangely sympathetic towards Violet. Clearly she was distraught at the loss of her mother, but her eagerness to hear his version of events, her willingness to give away such a valuable possession, revealed she was not as unfeeling or mercenary as Sabine had been. Had Violet recognized his wife? Was the offer of the necklace partly prompted by the fact that she too had been involved in the sorry tale and had helped him unravel it? It was with trepidation that Joshua thus turned towards the window, 'Bridget, do you hear that? Violet wants you to have Charles Mercier's necklace.'

Bridget rose abruptly to her feet. She looked flushed and uncharacteristically nervous as she took the box Violet tendered and slowly opened it. As the lid fell back and revealed the necklace, she gasped. The jewel was more dazzling than ever; brilliant green stones set in a strand of heavy gold links glittered as radiantly as the day they were made.

'No,' said she, gently but firmly closing the box and thrusting it back into Violet's hand. 'I want nothing to do with it. I need no further proof that the jewel brings little joy and much sorrow.'

Joshua met his wife's level gaze. He felt his heart pounding with relief in his chest and the same flood of affection for her he had two decades earlier, when he had seen her, in her sprigged muslin gown, coming along the road in Richmond seated on the dog cart. 'Are you certain, Bridget? The jewel is worth a fortune,' he said.

'I have no desire to be blighted by the unhappiness it brings,' said Bridget firmly.

'Then what would you have me do with it? I don't want it either,' said Violet.

'You might take it to Astley and leave it at the cottage where Granger once lived. Bury it in the pinery; throw it in the lake; keep it yourself; do whatever you will; 'tis no concern of mine,' said Bridget, crossing her arms across her capacious bosom as if defying Violet to contradict her.

But Violet did not contradict her. Her eyes glistened like wet pebbles caught in sunlight and her upper lip wavered. She looked away. In that moment Joshua thought he glimpsed, beneath Violet's desire for vengeance, a core of sorrow now softened by resignation. She had tried to execute her mother's wish, but she had not succeeded.

Violet curtsied to Joshua and Bridget, then she left, taking the necklace and Joshua's manuscript with her. A week or so later a liveried messenger returned with the enclosed letter.

*Cavendish Square*
*20th December 1786*

*Sir,*
*Your account is all very well but it doesn't say clearly whether or not my mother was guilty of murder, nor does it state what became of the portrait you painted of her and Herbert Bentnick. I only ask because knowing would settle matters in my mind. I have always been haunted by the same doubts that caused Herbert to break off with her. It would bring me peace of a kind to know the truth. As to the portrait, if it is still in your possession, as I believe it must be, I would like to purchase it. My mother's striking looks inspired many artists to paint her, but in her opinion no other portrait so accurately captured the essence of her spirit.*

*You may tell your wife I took her at her word. I buried the necklace beneath the ruins of Granger's cottage. No one has lived there since he was hanged for the murder of Caroline Bentnick. While I was there I chanced to look in at the gardens of Astley. The head gardener, a man by the name of Joseph Carlton, remembered me and let me look around. I found the place well tended as I remembered, although the pinery was greatly dilapidated. He tells me Herbert lost his interest in gardens after the death of his daughter and my mother's departure. The pineapple plants were all torn up and burned; not a single fruit*

410

*was ever consumed. Lizzie Manning, or Lizzie Bentnick as she is*
*now, has overseen the garden ever since her marriage to Francis.*
*But even she cannot abide entering the pinery.*
   *I am, sir, your humble servant,*
   *Violet Cobb*


Joshua went upstairs to the garret where he kept his store of
new and old canvasses, stretchers and the occasional work
that for one reason or another he had never sold. The paintings
were stacked according to size and subject. There were half a
dozen clumsy head-and-shoulders portraits dating from early in
his career; eight or ten unfinished landscapes. Most of these were
executed immediately after he left Astley, when his appetite for
faces was so dampened that he took to painting country scenes.
Reason had only prevailed when penury threatened and Bridget
accepted his proposal. Since then he had returned to earning a
comfortable and enjoyable living from his craft.

Near the door a single full-length canvas was propped
against an oak roof joist. The canvas was covered with a dust-
sheet. It had rested there so long that the cloth was infused
with a thick sediment of grey and festooned with cobwebs.

Joshua pulled away the sheet and threw it to the ground. A
cloud of dust rose, like mist on a summer morning. He looked
through the haze at Herbert Bentnick smiling proprietorially
as he surveyed the reclining Sabine. Despite the distance of time
and the yellowing of the varnish, she reminded him as vividly
as ever of an odalisque in a sultan's seraglio, or Venus watched
over by Vulcan; her beauty was unchanged – ripe, sweet,
exotic and as dangerous as the pineapple she held out to him.

For two decades Joshua had kept her sequestered here
against her will. Herbert had refused to accept or pay for his
portrait, but Sabine had written several times enquiring after
it and he had never replied. Now she was dead. Although
Violet had sought him out and tried to perpetuate her
mother's malignant influence, she had been easily deterred.
Sabine need trouble him no longer.

411

Joshua took up the canvas and carried it down to his painting room. He sat at his writing table and wrote the following short note.

Madam,
*You ask about your mother's guilt. I don't believe she wanted to kill Hoare (who she thought was Cobb); she merely wished to dissuade him from eloping with you. That he died was undoubtedly Granger's fault.*

*I trust the enclosed painting will remind you of your mother's beauty and bring you the peace for which you search.*

Joshua looked at the page thoughtfully. Should he raise the subject of the death of poor Nell Lambton, Charles Mercier's unfortunate daughter, with whom Sabine had arranged a rendezvous? Nell's death had troubled his conscience for many years. Crackman believed she had died from want but he hadn't known about Sabine's visit.

Joshua dipped his quill into the inkpot and prepared to write, but then he halted. He didn't know for certain Sabine had visited Nell. What would be the purpose in resurrecting further doubt? Sabine was dead. It was time for the whole matter to be buried like the necklace.

He signed the note with an exuberant flourish, sanded and sealed it with a wafer, then summoned his manservant, Thomas. He ordered him to wrap the painting and send it, together with his message, to an address in Cavendish Square where Mrs Violet Cobb was presently residing. Then, with renewed vigour, he stepped back to his painting room, picked up his brush and returned to the portrait of his daughters. It would certainly be the best thing he had ever painted.

THE END

THE THIEF-TAKER
by Janet Gleeson

Agnes Meadowes is cook to the Blanchards of Foster Lane, the renowned silversmiths. Her quiet world of culinary activity, preparing jugged hare, oyster loaves, almond soup and other delicacies for the family, is a happy refuge from the hustle and bustle of 1750s London. But in a single night everything is to change.

When the Blanchards' most pretigious and expensive commission, a giant silver wine cooler destined for the house of Sir Bartholomew Grey, is stolen, a sinister chain of events is set in motion. That same night a young apprentice is murdered and a young maid, Rose, disappears. Are these portentous happenings connected?

Called upon by her master, Theodore Blanchard, to investigate 'below stairs', Agnes now enters a dark world of hidden secrets, jealousy and murderous intent. Before the game is played out she will be forced to act as mouse to the infamous Thief Taker's cat as she is slowly drawn into a seamy underworld of London crime. But the truth, like the expensive tea leaves that Agnes keeps under lock and key, comes at a high price and she must decide how big a sacrifice she is prepared to make to bring the villains to justice.

Once again Janet Gleeson has produced a gripping historical murder mystery, and in Agnes Meadowes has created a heroine whom readers will love. *The Thief Taker* is an evocative and spell-binding novel of crime, chicanery and cooking

0 593 05260 9

NOW AVAILABLE FROM BANTAM PRESS

# THE GRENADILLO BOX
by Janet Gleeson

'Mystery and intrigue set in 18th century London . . . colourful and wildly entertaining, the novel spins enigma after enigma, all based on fact. A wonderful read'  *Guardian*

It is New Year's Day 1755 and young Nathaniel Hopson, journeyman to celebrated cabinetmaker Thomas Chippendale, is installing a magnificent library at the country seat of Lord Montfort. During dinner a shot rings out and in the new library Montford is discovered dead, a pistol at his side and leeches on his face. The immediate conclusion is that he must have taken his own life. Nathaniel, however, is not convinced. The gun suggests suicide, but what of the blood on the windowsill and the confusion of footprints on the library floor? And there is another strange detail: the small, elaborately carved box of rare grenadillo wood clutched in the aristocrat's lifeless hand.

When another body is found in a pond, frozen and missing four of his fingers, Nathaniel's detachment is shattered. For this man was a friend. Now Hopson finds himself on the trail of a killer who will stop at nothing to keep a dark and chilling secret from being revealed . . .

As intricately crafted as a Chippendale cabinet and set in a vibrantly recreated Georgian England, *The Grenadillo Box* – the first novel by the bestselling author of *The Arcanum* – is a hugely enjoyable historical murder mystery.

'A delicious five-course banquet . . . a richly flavoured, full-bodied, 18th-century whodunnit . . . You'll be kept guessing right up until the last page in this splendid novel'  *Harpers & Queen*

'A compulsive page-turner . . . will appeal to anyone who was spellbound by Charles Palliser's *The Quincunx*'  *Daily Mail*

'Masterful . . . the sheer weight of events carries you on . . . a cheerful whodunnit'  *The Times*

'An auspicious fiction début . . . engaging and enjoyable'
*Observer*

A Bantam Paperback
0 553 81389 7

# THE BLIGHTED CLIFFS
By Edwin Thomas

Book One of the Reluctant Adventures of Lieutenant Martin Jerrold

Not many men emerged from Trafalgar without an ounce of credit, but Lieutenant Martin Jerrold R.N. managed it. In February 1806, he is given one last chance to redeem his reputation and dispatched to Dover.

Things don't augur well when, walking off the effects of a night in the tavern, he stumbles across a corpse lying on the beach. And they take a distinct turn for the worse when he is suspected of murder. With the local magistrate determined to see him hang, Jerrold knows clearing his name will require an improbable reversal of his miserable fortunes. Somewhere in Dover's twisted streets, someone must know something. But he soon discovers that nothing is as it seems in a town where smuggling is a way of life . . .

Distrusted by his superiors, set upon by suspiciously well-informed thugs, attacked by the French at sea but finding sympathy in the less-than-respectable arms of Isobel, Martin Jerrold has two weeks to save his skin – or perish in the attempt.

*The Blighted Cliffs* marks the beginning of a rich, swashbuckling adventure series, featuring a reluctant hero for whom life rarely turns out as he intends.

'At last, the nautical Flashman! Martin Jerrold looks set to become one of the great British anti-heroes, boozing and lusting his way through Regency England' Andrew Roberts

'Will fill the gaping hole stoved in the timbers of the sea-saga genre by the sad death of Patrick O'Brian . . . Jerrold swashes his buckles and splices his mainbraces to good effect' *Scotland on Sunday*

'Rip-roaring . . . a rollicking yarn with razor-sharp dialogue, introducing a hilarious protagonist' *Good Book Guide*

A Bantam Paperback
0 553 81514 8

# A SELECTED LIST OF FINE WRITING
## AVAILABLE FROM BANTAM BOOKS

| | | | |
|---|---|---|---|
| 81343 9 | WITHOUT FAIL | *Lee Child* | £6.99 |
| 81344 7 | PERSUADER | *Lee Child* | £6.99 |
| 81416 8 | THE CRUSADER | *Michael Eisner* | £6.99 |
| 815520 | FULL DARK HOUSE | *Christopher Fowler* | £6.99 |
| 81429 X | THE SURGEON | *Tess Gerritsen* | £6.99 |
| 81432 X | THE APPRENTICE | *Tess Gerritsen* | £6.99 |
| 81389 7 | THE GRENADILLO BOX | *Janet Gleeson* | £6.99 |
| 50692 7 | THE ARCANUM | *Janet Gleeson* | £6.99 |
| 81247 5 | THE MONEYMAKER | *Janet Gleeson* | £6.99 |
| 81261 0 | DANNY BOY | *Jo-Ann Goodwin* | £6.99 |
| 81383 8 | A KISS OF SHADOWS | *Laurell K. Hamilton* | £6.99 |
| 81384 6 | A CARESS OF TWILIGHT | *Laurell K. Hamilton* | £6.99 |
| 81265 3 | BIRDMAN | *Mo Hayder* | £6.99 |
| 81272 6 | THE TREATMENT | *Mo Hayder* | £5.99 |
| 81485 0 | THE AIR LOOM GANG | *Mike Jay* | £7.99 |
| 81221 1 | PRAYERS FOR RAIN | *Dennis Lehane* | £6.99 |
| 81222 X | MYSTIC RIVER | *Dennis Lehane* | £6.99 |
| 81351 X | THE SABRE'S EDGE | *Allan Mallinson* | £6.99 |
| 50713 3 | A CLOSE RUN THING | *Allan Mallinson* | £6.99 |
| 50694 3 | GARNETHILL | *Denise Mina* | £6.99 |
| 81327 7 | EXILE | *Denise Mina* | £6.99 |
| 81258 0 | WALKING ON WATER | *Gemma O'Connor* | £5.99 |
| 81259 9 | FOLLOWING THE WAKE | *Gemma O'Connor* | £6.99 |
| 81332 3 | TIDES OF WAR | *Steven Pressfield* | £6.99 |
| 81386 2 | LAST OF THE AMAZONS | *Steven Pressfield* | £6.99 |
| 81406 0 | BOUDICA: DREAMING THE EAGLE | *Manda Scott* | £6.99 |
| 50542 4 | THE POISON TREE | *Tony Strong* | £5.99 |
| 81520 2 | TELL ME LIES | *Tony Strong* | £6.99 |
| 81404 4 | THE LOST ARMY OF CAMBYSES | *Paul Sussman* | £6.99 |
| 81514 8 | THE BLIGHTED CLIFFS | *Edwin Thomas* | £6.99 |